The Twyning

TERENCE BLACKER is the author of four
novels and many stories for children.
Visit www.terenceblacker.com

The Twyning

'This novel deserves praise and prizes. This is powerful stuff, a *Watership Down* for our times. Bravo!' *The Times*

'There is rat gore and rat lore in abundance here, nicely seasoned with the grime and crime of a great Victorian city. Skilful plotting, brisk narrative and sharply drawn characters put us firmly on the side of the ratpack and its gripping tale of apocalypse and triumph.'
Daily Mail

'Four unlikely outsiders overcome the odds, with last-minute escapes and near-fatal encounters deftly handled. An exciting story for all ages.' *Independent*

'Inspired.' *Sunday Herald*

'This tale of the war between humans and rodents is a pacey adventure with a knack for conveying a rat's-eye-view.' *SFX*

"A truly brilliant and moving book that pulls you in and won't let you go until you have finished." *Geek Syndicate*

'Split between the viewpoints of the urchin Peter and the rat Efren, *The Twyning* tells of the war between the rat and human populations. A delight.'
Interzone

'A classic for our age.' *Morning Star*

'Brilliant worldbuilding, potent prose, tortuously tense, a darn charming yarn.' *Speculative Scotsman*

'I implore you to cast rat prejudice aside. Reminiscent of John Boyne, this is a story attracting a readership from the ages of 10 to 100 and up.'
The Bookbag

"There is little as charming as talking animals, especially ones that have complex inner lives and political struggles. Blacker's writing brings his unnamed city to life."
Strange Horizons

"This story of two rats and two young humans, equally marginal, equally fragile, set against a world that suggests Dickensian London seems to elude classification. ButMr Blacker's book reduced me at times to anger, to horror, even to tears, and, in its climax, to elation." *The Dabbler*

"Subtle, wonderful, a novel that really makes you think."
Falcata Times

'Stunning. A *Watership Down* (with rats) for today which deserves the same recognition. Astoundingly good.'
Bookseller

The Twyning

Terence Blacker

HEAD
of ZEUS

First published in the UK in 2013 by Head of Zeus, Ltd.

This paperback edition published in the UK in 2013
by Head of Zeus, Ltd.

9 7 5 3 1 2 4 6 8

A CIP catalogue record for this book is available from
the British Library.

Paperback ISBN 9781781850725
eBook ISBN 9781781851296

Printed and bound by CPI Group (UK) Ltd,
Croydon, CR0 4YY.

Head of Zeus, Ltd
Clerkenwell House
45-47 Clerkenwell Green
London EC1R 0HT

www.headofzeus.com

To Angela

I

But O! 'Tis human vanity
That will bewray Mankinde.
Our fate and that of humble Beastes
Will ever be entwin'd.

Sir Edmund Gower, 1558

1 There was a smell of hope in the Great Hollow that night…

… and loyalty, and sadness, of course. Somewhere in the cold, damp air, was the sharp tang of fear.

But overpowering them all, singing through the brain of every rat, buck and doe, wild and fragile, twyning and ratling, was the scent that made us dizzy with pleasure.

Love.

In a harsh and dangerous world, where loss and death awaited round every corner, it was the smell of love which gave each of us strength and hope to survive, even when a king was facing death.

Without strength, the sadness of loss would make citizens weak.

Without hope, the act of acclaiming his successor would be without meaning.

Without love, the kingdom itself would die.

The multitude waited in silence.

On each side of the river which ran through the Great Hollow, there was a carpet of rich brown pelt, pulsing with life.

Dark eyes glittered from every crevice and ledge on the brick walls.

The high timbers that supported the vaulted roof writhed with expectation.

Only a series of steps on the far wall of the chamber, leading upwards from the watercourse, was visible, unattended by those who waited. No rat, unless he were part of the Court of Governance, would lay a foot upon the Rock of State.

There was an order to our assembly. Each of the courts who conducted the work of the kingdom had taken its place according to rank and status.

Against a far wall, members of some of the junior courts had gathered. The Court of Entertainers was there, the Tasting Court, the Court of Translation, the Court of Historians.

Beyond the river could be seen the Courts of Spies, of Correction and of Prophecy, and behind them, taking up an unnecessary amount of space, were members of the Court of Warriors.

Then, in front of the Rock of State, were two groups whose place had not been gained through strength and power but through weakness.

A mottling of white, grey and brown betrayed the presence of those known as 'fragiles'. Although every court in the kingdom brings some kind of skill or strength, it is for some citizens difficult to understand quite what the Court of Fragiles provides.

These lightly coloured, slack-muscled rats have been raised among the enemy, bred in captivity for some kind of strange human sport. Quite how they return to the world below remains a mystery to us, but what is certain is that they are weaker and less able to fend for themselves than any rat should be.

Although some help in the Courts of Spies or of Translation, where their knowledge of the ways of humans is occasionally of some use, most fragiles do little real work. The rest of us accept that they are what they are. It is not really their fault that they have been infected by the most deadly disease that a human can bring: that of doubt.

The problem with the fragiles, it is generally agreed, is that, like the enemy, they think too much. As a result, they soon become in the kingdom what they have been in the human world: amusements for those who are more powerful than they are.

They make the bigger, stronger rats of the kingdom aware of just how fortunate they are. Life may be tough but it could be worse. At least they are not a fragile.

Standing in front of the Rock of State, given a respectful

amount of space by all other citizens, was a group of thirty rats, none of whom had a name but who, together, were owners of a strange kind of power within the kingdom.

They were The Twyning. They tugged against one another, forever in motion, forever going nowhere. For almost all their lives, they had been united by an accident of nature that had occurred while they were still in the nest.

Their tails had become inextricably entangled. As they had grown, the knot of living tissue that was at their centre melded and fused together so that, with adulthood, each of them was less an individual rat than a limb on a greater shared body, a spoke on a wheel of flesh.

We know that to have a twyning within the kingdom is a rare blessing. As it grows, it is fed and kept alive by citizens, and is respected by all, even by the Court of Governance and by the ultimate source of power among rats, the king.

No great decision is made in the kingdom without the involvement of The Twyning. Many beings in one being, it stands for unity in the kingdom. It is a force of spirit, embodying the past, the future, the strong, the weak, life, death.

Each member of a twyning will have the gift of hearing. At times of great peril, it is they who will sense the glow before any other citizen.

This day, as on every occasion when we gather for great occasions, The Twyning was at the centre of all things. Already, we could hear the sound of plaining which only members of The Twyning can make. It starts, as it was starting now, with a throbbing pulse of rhythm created by the chattering of teeth. Soon, a clear, single note will be heard, then another and another, until every rat in that sacred circle is part of the plaining. The sound they make can thrill or chill the youngest or oldest heart.

Rats who are part of a twyning are nameless. They would never be asked to fight nor to forage, nor to father or to mother, but in times of peace and war it is to them, to it, that courtiers, warriors and even spies and historians will turn for wisdom and guidance.

The Twyning expresses life's mystery. Unable to move in any one direction except at an awkward, complicated shuffle, it has its own kind of strength, for nothing terrifies a human more than the sight of rats, helpless, bound together, yet powerful.

Above all, it shows the power of the kingdom.

For it is love which keeps The Twyning alive.

In a corner at the back of the hollow on that fateful night, Alpa, captain of the Tasting Court, glanced about her. Although she had been at two gatherings in the past, there was always a new worry.

This time it was a young apprentice whose past was a mystery, whose future was uncertain but whose present was always trouble. He was too undisciplined to be a taster, too small to be a warrior, too restless to work in the dustier Courts of History, Translation, Strategy or Prophecy. He was something of an outsider even among the other rats of his age.

It was said that his father had escaped from a prison in the world above. Certainly the dash of white between his ears, like the crest of a bird, suggested that some rogue blood, a hint of fragility, ran through his veins.

Yet there was nothing fearful or weak about this apprentice. He had the oddity of a fragile but none of its dependence on other rats.

Alpa, who had mothered many ratlings, had learnt that there was no fighting a wild spirit. Her bones aching, she sat up on her hind legs and peered over the multitude. Raising her eyes, she caught sight of a smudge of white on a ledge high above her head.

—Efren! Efren!

She revealed with all her strength, but it was too late.

*

From my perch on high, I looked down on her without moving a muscle.

There was no going back.

I, Efren of the kingdom, was not born to obey.

I wanted to find out more.

2 River, path, doctor, moon…

… shining over the rooftops.

Home.

Autumn night.

Sound of water.

Horse and cart on the road above.

Home. Always home.

Ahead, the doctor has seen something. He lays down the hazel thumb-stick he is carrying. He crouches on his knees, like a man in church.

'Rats.'

He looks around and sees me on the path.

'Rats have been here, Dogboy. We are in luck.'

He walks on, his stick tapping the path.

The cage is heavy in my hand.

He waits on the path, until I am near to him.

He shakes his head and sighs.

'Is there anything happening in that head of yours, Dogboy Smith?' he says.

Then, continuing his walk, he murmurs to himself, 'I fear not.'

3 Gazing down at the hollow ...

... I crouched, my young heart thumping fast within my breast. My captain, I knew, would prefer me to be with the other ratlings but I avoided her stare.

The feelings of duty within me – respect for my elders, loyalty to my court, obedience to Alpa – were at that moment little more than a distant niggle at the base of my spine. I knew of course that all good ratlings should be with their court when the kingdom gathered. And I was obviously aware that it was right and natural that we young rats should be quiet and respectful, catching only glimpses of the ceremony beyond the adult rats that were in front of us.

By this time in my life, though, I had already discovered that, as far as other rats were concerned, I was not good, nor right, nor perhaps even natural. There was a stronger urge within me than that of obeying my elders.

Curiosity. A hunger to know, to understand.

I wanted to see the shape of the ceremony through my own eyes, hear through my own ears. I wanted to feel for myself, not as part of a crowd.

Many times Alpa had told me that I was too selfish for my own good. Old and wise rats of the Tasting Court saw the way I was and said that I suffered from a weakness of character that almost certainly would lead me to an early death.

But I had no choice. It was just life. The life that I, Efren, wanted to live.

Below me, the sharp smell of excitement rose up from the restless bodies of the congregation, pricking my nostrils. From an entrance behind the Rock of State, members of the Court of Governance filed out, one after another, forming an arc at the top of the steps. Moments later, from beneath the brick arch under which the river ran into the Great Hollow, there was a movement. At first I thought it was some great fish, making its way beneath the murky waters, leaving a trail of silvery ripples behind it. Then I saw that each ripple was a rat from the Court of Warriors, swimming slowly and in perfect time.

As the procession glided into the Great Hollow, the gathering grew still and silent so that only the rhythmic chatter of the teeth of The Twyning could be heard. Then a stout branch of oak, with a warrior on each side and one behind it, came into view. Upon the wood there lay the still presence of a single mighty rat.

There was a note, high and heartfelt, from a member of The Twyning. Another replied, followed by a third. It was the first time in my young life that I had heard the sound of a plaining, and it seemed to reach into me, making every muscle tremble. The congregation replied. At first it was like a general whisper, caressing the senses, but soon it grew in volume until it echoed off the high ceiling and around the glistening walls of the Great Hollow.

King Tzuriel, upon his royal raft, was being acclaimed for the last time by his subjects.

The king, old and dying, stirred, raising his grey head, which seemed bonier and older than the rest of his body, so that his subjects could see him.

The acclamation grew until it seemed that the earth itself was breathing its loyalty and love for the king.

From my ledge, I felt the sound enter my being, making me stronger. My blood felt hot and thick in my veins. Now, involuntarily, my teeth began to chatter, like those of the thousands of rats below me.

It was my first acclamation and, for all I knew, my last. Most rats, I had been told, rarely experience an occasion like this more than once or twice in their lives.

Soon the hammering of my teeth had set my whole body a-jangle. In that moment I knew that nothing in my life would ever be the same again.

4 The doctor stops, cocks his head…

… like a blackbird listening for a worm.

'What was that?'

He speaks in a whisper.

'I heard something. In the sewerage.'

We stand.

At that moment, a sound comes from the earth beneath our feet. It is like a ghostly, distant scream.

'It's them! The rats!'

He kneels on the ground, his frock coat spreading on the path around him.

'They must be in the main sewage chamber. The flushers who work in the drains told me I would find them here. Rats love underground waterways.'

He stands, takes a white handkerchief from his pocket, and wipes the dirt off each hand.

'Let us continue our search.'

I stay, and he looks back.

'What is it, Dogboy? You think it would be better to wait here?'

I nod.

'You'd better be right,' he says.

5 Pain shone white…

… and bright as it led the king towards us.

I imagined the dazzling ache within him. King Tzuriel seemed aware of the presence of his people all around him. It was as if we were a single being, staring at him with its two eyes, acclaiming him with one set of chattering teeth. Watching him, I felt a surge of sympathy. He looked alone. He looked cold.

The three warrior rats who had been propelling the oak branch forward were slowing now as they approached a step which was a few lengths from the Rock of State.

King Tzuriel looked around him. Once he had become used to the smell of respect, of awe. Now, even I could smell it; there was something else in the air.

Anticipation?

The king sniffed, his nose nodding upwards. It was more than mere expectation.

Excitement?

That, of course. But also a scent which he would not have smelt for years.

Impatience.

Without knowing it, his subjects were eager for newness. He was the past. They had drawn belief and strength from him until now, when there was nothing left within him except death, growing in his stomach like a baby, like life.

By the time the branch was being held fast against the dark brick step, the plaining and the acclamation had slackened, and silence was returning to the Great Hollow.

The king gazed upwards for the last time at the place of his greatest glories. At the top of the four steps stood two of his most devoted friends: Quell, slender, elegant and smoothly powerful; and Grizzlard, the greatest warrior in the kingdom, his pelt marked by the scars of ancient battles. Behind them, ranged in a respectful arc beyond the Rock of State were members of the Court of Governance.

Painfully, he made his way to the edge of the raft where he was helped ashore by two warriors. Breathing heavily, he ascended the first step, two, three, four to reach the stone of state.

He turned to face the mighty congregation, gazing first at the citizens who waited beyond the rippling water, looking up at him, then raising his eyes to those who were perching bird-like from bricks and timbers around the wall. For just a second, he gazed at me. I could swear it. Perhaps every rat in that Great Hollow felt the same thing.

Tzuriel had never been handsome but I could see that, in his prime, there must have been about him a magnificent ugliness that spoke of strength and honesty. Tonight, alone on the Rock of State, he seemed to be looking back at his people from the gates of death, reminding even those courtiers who stood in a respectful group behind him of the skeleton beneath skin, of the fate that awaits us all.

Rats do not like to think of death. It is too personal, too intimate. It reminds us that, beyond the family, the court, the kingdom, there is the beating heart of one individual. Most rats (here I am something of an exception) dislike the idea of being alone.

Go: that was what those thousands of eyes, gazing in silence, were now saying to Tzuriel. Do the kingly thing. Do what you have always done so well. Make us feel better about our world. Your last great duty is to disappear.

The king looked into the searing whiteness within, and then beyond it. With a final surge of strength, he gave the last revelation of his life. The lapping of the river against its banks was the only sound to be heard as the kingdom prepared to receive its dying ruler's silent words.

—My subjects.

It was like a shock coursing through my body. Nothing I had been told had prepared me for the power with which the king's words entered my brain.

Revelation, you should know, is one of life's highest skills. It is something humans (most humans) have never managed: communication through thought. As a young rat, I had the strength to reveal to two or three of my fellows at most. A captain (Alpa, for example) is able to address a group of a hundred or so rats. A king, and a courtier who dreams of being king, can address thousands. His power lies in revelation.

—I am here to bid you a last farewell.

It was as if the king stood before each of his subjects and spoke to him or her alone.

—We live in a time of tumult. The victories of the past, that of the great invasion, our mighty journey across the world above, still course through our veins.

A few of the rats closest to the platform began to chatter in acclamation but a sharp, silent reproof from the king, like a whip-crack in the brain, silenced them.

—They are as nothing. They are as dust.

For an instant, King Tzuriel seemed to lose track of what he was saying. Then he raised his weary eyes to the stone ceiling over his head.

—Above us, there is change. We have information from the Court of Spies that those who have the power to harm us will not hesitate to do so. It is important that we understand that power, that we stare it in the face.

The king paused now for so long that Quell, the most senior courtier, moved closer, ready to remind his friend and monarch what should be said.

—I shall name it now, as my last act as king. It is… humankind.

The sharp scent of fear filled the hollow. Had the approach of death turned the king's mind? It was accepted that the greatest danger that faced the kingdom should be known but never ever named. Giving it a name gave the enemy strength.

—Humankind— Tzuriel looked around him —Let us not cower from the word. Too often we think in fear of the evil that struts and stalks the world above. It is, we tell ourselves, the enemy. That is all we think we need to know. It is not. The enemy is… human. They fear us. We fear them. Yet, in many ways, we depend upon one another. They provide us with our food. Their habitations and burial grounds give us shelter. We need them, citizens. Perhaps they need us. If we live our lives, they will one day learn to live theirs.

The king twitched, as if the pain within him had twisted like a torturer's blade.

—Please— The revelation was growing stronger now —I address you as a warrior who has seen too much fighting. Live your lives in peace.

The king paused. Even breathing, it seemed, was difficult these days. He moved forward towards the steps. His legs weak, he almost fell upon the oak raft. No one moved to help him now. Kingship was falling from his shoulders. Old and alone, he faced death.

In the water around the raft, the young warrior rats looked towards Quell. The old courtier, the king's most faithful friend, cast one final look at Tzuriel, then turned and limped away. Those who had been holding the raft retreated, letting it go. Gently, bearing the king, it drifted away from the steps.

Tzuriel slipped from the raft into the water. Proud to the last, he swam rather than drifted towards the archway where the river disappeared into the darkness beyond.

The white pain was everywhere now. For a few strokes, all that Tzuriel would have heard was the ripple of water, the rasp of his own breath but then, through the whiteness, came the sound which he had last heard on the day he had become king and his predecessor Calix had departed. The kingdom was keening.

He closed his eyes and swam, allowing the dark water to direct him. It was almost over. He was going home.

6 The scream from the earth...

... goes on and on.

For a moment, the doctor looks scared.

Then, recovering himself, he murmurs, 'Interesting,' and scrambles down the bank.

By the time he has reached the water, the sound has faded into the night.

I hear a noise coming from the place where the river emerges from under the ground. A movement in the dark water.

I click my teeth and point.

A ripple. It is a creature, swimming slowly.

I hear the doctor whisper, 'What the deuce ...?'

It might have been an otter or a dog, but it is a rat. I have come across many rats around the town, but this is the largest I have seen.

The rat swims towards the doctor. For a moment, it seems to rest its chin on the bank, heaving itself out of the water.

On land, it lies down. Its flanks are heaving from the effort.

The rat is dying.

It stands unsteadily. Walking stiffly, more like a hedgehog than a rat, it crosses the towpath.

There is loose earth by the path. It begins to burrow feebly.

The doctor grips his cleft stick more tightly in his right hand.

Slowly, he approaches the rat.

7 Sadness comes with the end of a reign...

... and I had been warned of that.

There would be a sense of loneliness, Alpa had told me, of having been abandoned by someone dearer than a parent. But then, I had also heard, there would be celebration and hope for the future as a new king was proclaimed.

Here is the truth: I felt not the slightest stirring of joy. It seemed wrong to me, the way the kingdom had deserted our king, left Tzuriel alone to face death. Even now, after all that has passed, I think it was unnecessarily cruel and heartless.

In the Great Hollow, attention had returned to the Rock of State. Quell, the revered courtier whose coat was now almost white with age, was explaining how the Court of Governance had debated as to who should succeed Tzuriel, weighing several issues. The candidates. The moment in history. The kingdom and its needs.

There was silence in the hollow. It was as if King Tzuriel had never existed, as if only the future mattered. I felt, not for the last time in my life, out of step with other rats.

What did tradition matter at this moment when a great king was dying alone? How could citizens behave as if Tzuriel had been but a name in the past?

Across the Great Hollow, there was movement behind the Rock of State. Quell was welcoming forward the kingdom's most famous warrior to a surge of acclamation. Grizzlard. As he stepped past Quell and on to the Rock of State, I realised that there was to be a revelation.

Another revelation.

I was restless. There had been enough revealing. More than enough. What did the court, the Great Hollow, the mighty process of government matter when my king was facing death?

I wondered where Tzuriel would be now. Would he have found a place to die, pawed a small cradle of earth in which to await the end? It seemed a cold and lonely way to depart the world.

As I thought, I noticed something. Along the ledge, above where a small stream issued into the river, a small crack in the brickwork was visible.

I glanced in the direction of Alpa. My captain's eyes were fixed on Grizzlard as he started his revelation to the kingdom. I moved backwards, slowly down the ledge until the dock of my tail touched the gap in the wall.

From where I was, I could now see that light from the world above seemed to stab the dark earth beyond the Great Hollow.

Light is danger, as every rat knows, but something drove me on, backwards along the narrow ledge. Afraid that turning would draw attention to me from the rats below, I edged towards the opening, pressing my body against it, feeling the cold brickwork scraping my skin. I pushed harder. Then, when only the front half of my body can have been visible in the hollow, something unexpected happened.

The earth beneath my hind legs crumbled. Suddenly I was falling downwards, my legs scrabbling for purchase on the sides of the narrow gap until, with a splash that would have been heard by many in the Great Hollow, I plunged into the water.

Surfacing moments later, I found myself gazing back through the low arch under which, not long before, Tzuriel had swum. I saw the river's course through the hollow, citizens flanking it on each side, so caught up in the occasion that many of them had let their tails hang in the cold water.

There was no going back. For a ratling to be in the river at any time is forbidden; to be there on a day such as this could only mean a one-way visit to the Court of Correction. I felt the tug of the current beneath my belly as it pulled me away from the throng.

I turned and swam slowly, not knowing where the water would lead.

I had been swimming for only a minute or two when I saw light ahead. The river was taking me towards the dangers of the world above.

I emerged under the brightly shining moon, the mist of my breath skimming the water before me as I swam. There was a ditch close to where the river issued from its underground course. I scrambled on to the dry land.

Immediately I felt the trem, stronger than that of a dog or fox. The enemy. Looking upwards, I saw two humans, an adult and a younger one, standing on the bank.

The larger human was carrying a stick in his hand. As I watched, he raised the stick and stood, motionless, for just long enough for me to see a sight that has remained scarred in my memory to this day.

The stick fell, stabbing downwards.

I heard the scream. I was some fifty lengths from the scene but where I stood in horror an acrid whiff of terror reached my nostrils.

The small human moved closer and I saw now that he was holding a small cage. He reached for the shape held under the cleft stick of the larger man, then lifted a writhing body.

The adult human gave a shout of cruel laughter, said something to the child, and stared into the prison for a while. Then, whistling softly, he began walking away from me, down the path.

The child followed, with the cage containing my king and the ruler of all the rats in the kingdom swinging from his left hand.

At moments of extreme danger, a deep calm descends upon us. We can move quickly as we escape, or we can attack, or we can still in order to survive, but within each of us (even within a young rat) the process of thought, even reaction, will have slowed.

We see what is happening to us as if from afar, yet allow our instincts, the blood memory of thousands of years, to guide us to safety. A rat is never calmer than when alone and facing death.

So I can remember little of the moments which followed. It was my body, my history, that sent me hurtling into the darkness of a crack in the bridge wall behind me. I plunged downwards away from the dangerous light, along the touch-path which, worn by the pelts, teeth and feet of countless generations of citizens, requires no sight or even smell.

Pausing briefly in a rest, I caught my breath. I seemed to be in the ruins of an old human burial place. Amid the rubble before me, the white of a long leg-bone glowed in the darkness.

To be truthful, the remains of a dead human have no more importance to me than a piece of flint. Alive, you are dangerous. Dead, you are food. When only your bones and teeth remain, your corpse is merely part of the earth. Please don't take it personally.

I looked beyond the crypt and wondered, without too much alarm, which direction would lead me back to the Great Hollow. As I waited, I became aware of a distant sensation, not more than a tickle, in the base of my skull.

Revelation.

I listened. There was no doubting it; the tones of Grizzlard, low, droning, solemn and dull, could be heard within my brain. I moved out of the rest, down a passage, and with every length Grizzlard's revealing became clearer.

Following a track along the base of the wall, I reached a crevice through which the smell of life indicated that I had reached an entrance to the Great Hollow. I pushed. The wall was soft. I was pressing against flesh.

I pushed harder. The body blocking my passage moved slightly to reveal the dark, irritated eyes of a young warrior rat, looking over his muscular shoulder. I knew I had to be brave.

—I have urgent news.

The warrior's response was to turn his back and fart in my face.

21

I tried again.

—It is important that I am let through.

The warrior revealed to another large rat that was beside him. I noticed that their backs were shaking with amusement.

No ratling in its right mind will press a point when dealing with young warriors. The Court of Warriors is second only to the Court of Correction when it comes to cruelty. Its members pride themselves on neither asking nor responding to questions. They communicate one way to those that annoy them. With their teeth.

But then I was not born to be sensible. I nudged the rump once more, and revealed.

—King Tzuriel has been captured.

At first it seemed as if even this revelation would not penetrate the warriors' brains but, after a few seconds, they glanced at one another and shuffled apart, allowing me to move between them.

—What was that?— one of them asked.

I stood on my hind legs, peering towards the Rock of State.

—It's the king… in the world above—

But, at that moment, attention within the hollow shifted to what was happening before them.

Grizzlard's bold, honest, tedious revelation had seemed to be drawing to a close.

—I shall say again what I have said before. In the event of my winning the noble prize of kingship through the support of you, the inhabitants of this great kingdom, I shall be proud, pleased and honoured to continue down the path of peace trodden with such dignity by our great and beloved ruler Tzuriel.

—To this end— Grizzlard actually raised his right paw towards the congregation —I humbly place my person at the disposal of the kingdom.

—No.

There were gasps from several of the rats around me. What was happening? Another revelation, louder and clearer than that of Grizzlard's, was reaching them.

It was a female revelation.

Even I, a ratling unversed in the ways of the kingdom, knew that this was very strange indeed. At any one time, there are never more than two or three does within the inner court. Mothers and sisters enjoy a certain power within the kingdom as captains of some of the courts. Yet they are rarely, if ever, admitted to the Court of Governance. In matters of war and death, it is a basic rat belief that those who have brought life into the world will see less clearly than bucks who are their husbands or brothers.

Ahead of me, the crowd pressed closer to the platform where Grizzlard stood, caught in a rare moment of indecision and bewilderment.

Behind him, there was a movement among the courtiers. Pushing forward, past the bulky figures of those who were in the front row, there emerged a figure who was so small that at first I thought a ratling had found its way into the court.

It made its way forward with a busy scuttle, as if impatient with the slow, dignified gait with which, traditionally, courtiers would move on a state occasion.

Slender, tense, female, the rat reached the Rock of State. Then, to a rustle of astonished disapproval, she stepped to the front lip of the platform, in front of Grizzlard, standing between the king-elect and his citizens.

Attempting to exert his authority, the senior courtier Quell advanced towards the newcomer, towering over her with a glowering revelation.

—Courtiers are required by convention to introduce themselves before addressing the gathering.

The newcomer did not offer, nor even humble before the might of Quell. Ignoring him, she gazed towards the back of the Great Hollow.

—I am Jeniel. But then many of my friends know that.

She showed her teeth, and those near the front of the crowd pressed closer to catch her revelation. There was something unusual about this Jeniel which drew them in. Even the most distinguished members of the court were uneasy when communicating to the kingdom; it was as if kingship could only be expressed by a cold and clumsy awkwardness.

Jeniel was different. She addressed them like someone telling secrets. Although her revelation was as clear as that of Quell or Grizzlard, it was also confiding, gentle.

—I speak to the friends I know and to those I have yet to meet, to those who know me from the Court of Translation and those who may have heard of me.

She glanced briefly towards Quell and Grizzlard.

—I am suggesting that there is a new way forward. My old friend Grizzlard, with all his many words, is unable to understand it. He is sharper with his teeth than with his revelations.

A rustle of amusement spread through the hollow like the wind in the trees. One or two of the members of the Court of Governance, standing beyond the Rock of State, looked at one another in surprise. Citizens were actually laughing at the rat who would be king.

Jeniel waited. Then her revelation continued.

—It has always been a good thing in times of certainty to have experience and strength in a position of power. But now the world is different. There are new perils. It is the moment for change.

Quell had heard enough. He moved towards her, his bony old body dwarfing hers. For a moment he seemed to be about to attack her, but instead he revealed.

—It is for the court to deliberate these matters.

Jeniel inclined her head slightly to one side.

—The court? And what of the people? Many rats, ordinary rats who will fight and work and mother for the kingdom, believe that it is not right to be told from on high who is to be king, who is to live and to die in the kingdom. We are all rats together. We should listen and love one another. We can create a kingdom of the pulse in which every citizen can share. Power is good, friend Quell, but there is something that is better. Respect for one another will make the kingdom strong. Has Grizzlard truly earned this respect?

Grizzlard, looking uneasy, remained silent.

—Perhaps he has— Jeniel pondered for a moment —He has fought many battles. But it is we who should decide.

I had heard enough. For me, the strange quarrel that was taking place on the Rock of State seemed meaningless and trivial beside the enormity of what I had just seen.

King Tzuriel, the stick falling, the scream, the wire door to the cage slamming shut.

I nudged the warrior rat to my right.

—We must do something. The king has been captured.

Something then happened which even now I find truly astonishing. The two young warrior rats glanced at one another, and then began to move forward through the crowd. One, then both of them, repeated my revelation.

—King Tzuriel. He has been captured.

—The king is in danger.

Rats in front of them seemed to melt away, at first slowly but then accelerating, as if the importance of their message was spreading through the hollow. The three of us moved through the Courts of History, of Prophecy, of Spies, until a single obstacle remained between us and the Rock of State.

The Twyning.

—Yes?

One of the many bodies of The Twyning loomed out of the mass. As it shifted its position, I noticed that the fur between it and its neighbours had been rubbed away, leaving the skin shiny and dark. Its eyes were wide, like that of the most innocent ratling.

I revealed.

—King Tzuriel has been captured.

Several other heads on The Twyning turned towards me. Out of nervous politeness, I addressed them all.

—I… I saw it with my own eyes.

For a few seconds, The Twyning was still, as if absorbing this information into all thirty of its brains and bodies. Then it set up a shimmering motion, spreading across its backs like a breeze rippling over the water of a pond.

Seeing it, Grizzlard, Quell and Jeniel looked down. No rat, not even a courtier on the brink of kingship, would ignore The Twyning.

The head that was closest to the Rock of State delivered a revelation which reached all of the Court of Governance and many rats in the congregation.

—There is news from the world above. It concerns our king.

8 I was not born with the name Dogboy…

… and I did not always live on the streets. I had a house, a mother, a father.

Once I was Peter Simeon.

Sometimes, even now, the memories catch me before I can stop them.

I remember warmth, a bed with heavy blankets, the sounds of the house – Mary, the maid, singing as she worked, the ticking of the grandfather clock in the hall, my mother and father talking.

We were happy. We were the Simeon family.

My father went to work every morning, in his suit, the worried look of a busy man already on his face.

And my mother? She was beautiful. She still is, probably. She talked to me, she played with me. Sometimes when my father was not there, I sat upon her lap, warm and safe.

Home, school, food, walls, servants. How could all that have been a dream?

It was soon after my ninth birthday when late one night, I was awoken by the sound of voices. My father and mother were having an argument.

All parents argue but, lying there in the darkness, as he shouted and she cried, I knew that this was different.

The next day, I was told to take my breakfast in the servants' quarters.

My father had left for work by the time I came upstairs from the kitchen.

My mother, as pale as death, her eyes red, avoided me. She cast not so much as a single look in my direction. Mary took me to school.

Soon I became used to looking for her large uniformed figure at the end of the school day.

A few times I asked her what I had done wrong. She would frown and say, 'They're grown-ups. Sometimes grown-ups are like that, Peter.'

From that moment onwards, I ate all my meals with the servants. Now and then I would catch them glancing at one another as if they were in possession of some important, terrible secret.

Fights between my father and mother continued. Every night, after we had all gone to bed, the voices would start, rising and falling in the darkness. Often I heard them mention my name.

What had I done? What awful deed?

Soon I no longer asked myself the question. A feeling of cold dread entered my heart. Something bad, beyond my understanding, was happening.

I slept lightly, like a cat. The slightest sound awoke me. Even when my father and mother were not arguing, I was waiting for the next fight to begin.

I would sit on the landing in the dark, listening to the voices below. I wanted to understand.

One word, shouted by my father every time he argued with my mother, confused me.

Bastard.

What was a bastard?

I asked the children at school. None of them seemed to know. When I asked a teacher, she made me stand in the corner.

I asked Mary and she looked away, as if I had said something sinful.

'What is it, Mary?' I asked again. 'Please tell me. What is a bastard?'

Mary's face was as big and pale as the full moon. She was kind and sometimes would sing to me when my parents were not in the house.

Now, though, she frowned and pursed her lips.

'Bad blood, Master Peter,' she said. 'It means bad blood. Better not to talk of it.'

There came a night when there was no argument. The silence was even more frightening than the angry words. The next night was the same.

One evening, during this time of quiet, something unusual happened. When my mother said goodnight to me, she cried. She held on to me, squeezing the breath out of me. Then, quite suddenly, she pushed me away from her.

'Goodnight, Peter,' she said. It was as if she had suddenly been reminded of the terrible thing I had done, of my bad blood.

At dead of night, I was awoken by a sound.

This time, it was not an argument. Someone stood at the door to the bedroom. It was Frank, the footman.

'Put some clothes in this,' he said, holding out a laundry bag.

'Clothes?' I sat up in bed.

'And get dressed. Quietly. We are going for a ride.'

I put on some clothes, and looked in my chest of drawers for a shirt, some flannel britches. Was this some kind of test?

'Warm clothes. You'll be needing a coat.' Frank spoke gruffly, irritated by my slowness.

I opened the wardrobe and took out my only tweed coat. When I turned, Frank was on his way down the stairs. I followed him, past the door of my parents' room, down into the hall, out of the front door.

Waiting there, in the dark, was a carriage with a coachman slumped at the front. Frank held my arm, as if afraid I would run away, then pushed me, in a way that was not polite, into the carriage.

The carriage jolted forward.

'Where are we going?' I asked.

'You'll see.' Frank looked out of the window.

Plucking up my courage, I asked the question which now worried me night and day.

'Is it because of my bad blood?'

It was as if I had not spoken.

Only when the carriage slowed did Frank speak. 'This will do,' he said, and tapped on the back of the driver's seat. When the carriage came to a halt, he stepped down and looked around him.

'Out you get,' he said. 'Take your bag.'

I stood beside him on the pavement. It was dark and we were in a part of town I had never seen before.

'You wait here, lad,' he said, almost kindly.

He stepped back into the carriage and immediately it moved off.

I watched it go, listened to the horse's hooves until I was standing there in the quiet of the night.

Minutes. Hours. I looked down the street, waiting for the carriage to return, but it never did.

Light began to break. I was cold. I was hungry. I was alone.

I began walking. As day broke the streets came to life, strangers hurried by. One or two glanced at me, then quickly looked away.

Bad blood. They could smell it in my veins.

So began my new life. Where does a boy find food and warmth on the street of a great town? Not among humans, that was for sure. I learned soon that, to survive, I had to stay close to the dogs who lived wild.

Something strange. They were as hungry as I was but I soon learned that, while they would fight each other for scraps, they would become quiet when I spoke to them. The moment we looked into each others' eyes, dog and human, we understood that we were stronger together. I could help them find food. They could protect me and keep me warm as I huddled close to their bony, scabby bodies at night.

People began to say that I had a gift, that I could tame wild curs and make them do what I wished, but the truth was simpler. Dogs and I were close because together we could survive.

There is work of a kind for those who can understand animals. Men who hunted the fields and rivers would use me for pegging out rabbits for their ferrets or simple skinning work. Sometimes I would go ratting or netting hares. Once I was put down a fox's earth to retrieve a terrier that had found a vixen and cubs. At the end of the day, I'd be given food or a couple of pennies for my labour.

I soon discovered that it was not only my bad blood which brought trouble. When I spoke, men and women seemed alarmed, children stared open-mouthed.

My tones were too gentle for the ragamuffin way I looked. They asked questions. Who was I? Why was I there?

Soon I kept my talk for the animals. With humans, I said little or nothing. I was a silent shadow in their company.

'Dogboy', they called me.

I became used to the streets. I lost all sense of time passing. I found a home of sorts.

It must have been soon after my thirteenth birthday and by now I was working for a rat-catcher called Bill Grubstaff. A tall, whiskered gentleman in a frock coat would pass the compound, watching Bill and me as we worked.

One evening, as I returned home, he talked to me in the park. He told me his name was Dr Ross-Gibbon. He was a scientist and was working with rats.

He asked me if I wanted to earn some pennies, helping him catch 'specimens', as he called them.

I nodded my agreement. That evening, he showed me where he lived and asked me to call by the following day.

'And what do they call you, my boy?' he asked.

'Dogboy, sir.'

He laughed. 'Do they, bigod? Well, I shall call you Mr Smith. You shall be Mr Smith while you work for me.'

That was how I met the doctor.

9 It had been a mistake…

… to speak to the Court of Governance.

Within moments of The Twyning's announcement, as I stood before the thousands of rats of the kingdom, I knew that this time my curiosity had taken me too far. I was that most outrageous, most unthinkable thing, a ratling on the Rock of State on the day a new king would be announced.

What was I doing there? That was the thought in my mind, and it was shared by every citizen of the kingdom who saw me.

But there was no going back.

Quell stared at me for a moment, his old face grey and sorrowful. I humbled, then, realising it was not enough, rolled on my back, offering to him and to the kingdom. He darted clumsily towards me and I smelt the rot of his ancient teeth as he buried them briefly into my cheek.

I screamed, as I was expected to, and lay still.

Quell looked down at me, breathing heavily. He was old but his revelation, when it came, was powerful.

—Your name, ratling?

—Efren.

—And the information you claim to have?

The court had moved threateningly close to me. Even if I revealed with all my force, I could only hope to reach some of them. I stood, still crouching, ready to humble if threatened.

—I have visited the world above.

—Today? While the kingdom was gathering?

I closed my eyes, and trembled respectfully.

It was Jeniel, the doe rat who had spoken earlier, who rescued me.

32

—Surely, Quell, why he was in the world above matters less than what he saw.

His eyes still resting on me, Quell nodded.

—Go on then.

I thought of Alpa. What would she be feeling now as she watched her young taster after he had interrupted great matters of state? Fury? Shame? Fear, perhaps, for her own future.

I, of course, now had no future.

I crouched low. It was for my captain that I now revealed. I confessed to the members of the court that, yes, I had followed the king down the river into the world above. I told them the terrible things I had seen. The river, the two humans, the stick, the prison. I finished my account as quickly as I could.

—I returned to the Great Hollow. I believed I should do my duty as a citizen and tell the court— I looked at the eyes around me —He was... he is... our king.

When I had finished, Grizzlard stepped forward to face the assembly. He told them, in his own slow way, the story I had told. As his revelation reached the brains of those gathered there, an angry chattering sound arose from the throng.

I was finished, I was sure of that now. My life was over.

—The court will decide what to do about the king, ratling.

Grizzlard inclined his head slightly in my direction, and I thought for a moment he was about to show me mercy. I was wrong. The court moved to the back of the Rock of State and revealed quietly amongst themselves.

Grizzlard led the discussion.

—This ratling must obviously be sent to the Court of Correction, never to return.

There were chatterings of agreement from the other courtiers. Grizzlard was about to continue when he was interrupted.

—I have a better idea.

The revelation, languid with disapproval, came from a young courtier who stood beside Jeniel. He was sleek and dark, and the absence of the slightest scar or marking on his pelt suggested that, unusually, he was not originally from the Court of Warriors.

—Swylar?

Grizzlard's revelation was icy cold. The courtier called Swylar moved forward, then continued.

—When Tzuriel left the hollow to find a place to die, he was a citizen. But now he is in the hands of the enemy, he is our king once more. Until we know what has befallen him, there can be no other monarch.

Grizzlard moved towards him, his long teeth chattering dangerously.

—This is just a tactic to delay things, Swylar, so that your friend Jeniel will be Queen. It is ambition speaking.

Swylar smiled dangerously.

—They shall not be pleased, the people, when they are told that their new ruler put his own crowning before the safety of their beloved Tzuriel.

Quell raised his head.

—And what are you suggesting, Swylar?

—We send someone to the world above to discover where King Tzuriel is held.

—This is dangerous rubbish— Grizzlard hunched his back angrily —No courtier can visit the world above at this time and we cannot risk telling the kingdom what has happened. Besides, who will be prepared to lay his life on such a foolish enterprise? It is—

—Almost certain death— Swylar smiled, then turned to me —There is one young citizen who will know where to start the search.

And suddenly the eyes of the most powerful rats in the kingdom turned towards one, young, humble citizen.

Me? *Me?*

I might have revealed. I might just have thought the word. What Swylar was suggesting was madness. I had no experience of the world above. I was not even a warrior.

—Or would our young friend prefer a trip to the Court of Correction?

There was a moment's uncertainty in the court. Grizzlard seemed to have reached a decision.

—Perhaps he should take his companions.

—My companions?

I glanced across the hollow to the Court of Tasting, then noticed that Grizzlard was looking beyond the lip of the Rock of State where the two young warrior rats who had escorted me were looking up at them. The court seemed to be expecting an answer from me.

—Yes. I would like them to come with me.

Grizzlard walked to the lip of the rock.

—What are your names, ratlings?

—Floke.

—Fang.

—Floke and Fang, this is your lucky day— Grizzlard smiled sadly —The three of you are going on a great adventure.

10 'Just live twenty more hours, my old friend...

... and you shall have served your purpose to the great cause of science.'

The doctor is at the long table in his office where he does his experiments. It is the dead of night. When we returned with the giant rat, he said to me, 'We must work just a while.'

Although I am tired, there is no questioning him.

I sit on a stool in the corner of the room, watching. The doctor likes me to be here, ready to help him with the rats who are still awake before the chloroform begins to work on them.

He talks at times like this, sometimes asking questions, never expecting an answer.

'Have you seen the like of this creature, Mr Smith? If we can keep him alive, he will be the most famous rat in history.'

He pokes with his sharp blade at the limp body of the giant rat we found by the river.

My stomach aches with hunger and my eyelids are heavy. Now and then my head nods forward, before I snap awake. All I want now is the sixpence I will be paid, and to be on my way home.

'Give me a rat on a slab and I am a happy man.' The doctor laughs quietly to himself. 'They find it strange, Mr Smith. They say, "That Ross-Gibbon's a bit of an odd one".'

He reaches for his magnifying glass and inspects the rat for a moment.

'You want to know why? Because I am a man of science, Mr Smith. The outside world is suspicious of scientists. Particularly women – watch out for the females, Mr Smith.'

The doctor makes a small cut in the rat's stomach.

'When I came down from Cambridge, I attended a dinner party and happened to mention to my neighbour at the table, a young lady, that I had the pancreas of an interesting water vole in my pocket. When I showed it to her, you should have heard the screams, Mr Smith! It was bedlam! I was actually asked to leave. Such are the trials of the scientist.'

He lays down his knife and looks at me solemnly for a moment.

'Poor boy. You don't have the slightest idea what I am talking about, do you?'

He reaches into his pocket and, just for a moment, I think he is about to pay me, but it is not money that he holds in his hand, but a dirty handkerchief with which he wipes his hands.

'Who needs women, Mr Smith? Give me the inner workings of a small mammal any time.'

He beckons me over.

Almost too tired to stand, I walk over to the table.

The rat is on its side, a small wound glistening red on its fur.

'Show me a rat with its organs intact and I will reveal the mysteries of the world,' he says softly.

Gently, almost like a nanny with her baby, he turns the rat on its back with a pencil. A smell of rotting flesh fills the air. He breathes in, as if it were the scent of spring.

'Is that not the most beautiful case of rodent cancer you have ever seen, Mr Smith?'

He lays down the pencil and reaches for the knife. I watch as he cuts into the flesh in the pit of the rat's stomach.

It stirs, opens its eyes, and at that moment gives a scream which seems to fill my brain.

I give a little gasp and stagger back.

'Squeamish, Mr Smith?' The doctor gives a little laugh.

I shake my head. It was not a loud scream but something about this rat upsets me.

I hear the echo of its pain in my skull.

11 The pulse was my welcome…

… to the world above.

I felt it within me as I lay huddled beneath a small wooden shed surrounded by greenery. Somewhere, a rat was pulsing, and needed help. Nearby, Floke and Fang were scurrying back and forth in search of trails.

Maybe it had not been such a good idea to take company on this mission to the world above. The two young warrior rats were bigger and stronger than I was. They had claimed that the Court of Warriors had trained them in the arts of survival, tracking, attack and defence. But, even before the three of us had emerged into the dangerous half light of the early morning, I sensed that they had yet to learn the lesson which even I, a humble taster, already understood.

It is never wise to attract danger to yourself.

Ignoring me, they had competed noisily with one another as they made their way from the Great Hollow upwards. Without waiting, they had burst out from under the shed and set about trail finding, ignoring the presence of risk in the human-infested land that was around them.

As I crouched, my nose against the damp earth, I could hear the young warriors at work.

—Here's one. Here's a trail.

—That's not a trail. It's a dog's scratchings.

—Dogs! I want to fight a dog!

—Come on, let's show that dog what a warrior is made of!

I felt the pulse within me once more. It was a revelation and yet, I was certain, the rat who had revealed was not nearby. Only the greatest, a king or a courtier, were able to reveal across a distance.

It was time to plan. How to find a captured king? It seemed a hopeless quest. Yet surely Quell and the Court of Governance would never have sent us into danger for no reason. Maybe, I thought, we could hide out for two or three days and then return safely to the kingdom.

No. I had been the last to see King Tzuriel. It was for me to find out what had happened to him.

Approaching the bush where Floke and Fang were engaged in a mock battle was a female human, followed by two of its young. I issued a sharp warning to the others. They ignored me. The humans passed, chattering and laughing.

I shivered, feeling suddenly lonely and young. What was I doing here? The ground beneath my paws was damp and cold.

Again, I heard the pulse of pain, louder this time. It raised the hair along my backbone. As it faded, I heard a heartbeat, throbbing slowly.

Suddenly Floke and Fang were beside me, revealing one after another.

—Did you feel that?

—It was from a rat. He sounded in trouble. Let's go!

—If it could reveal to us here, it must be one of our rulers.

—But which ruler would be up here in the world above?

—Pulsing.

They crouched lower as, slowly, the truth reached their brains. Fang's perfect teeth chattered with alarm.

—It's the King.

Another pulse, fainter this time, reached them.

—So now what? Floke asked.

The two young rats stared at me, awaiting my decision. It was odd how quickly they had accepted the leadership of a rat who was younger and smaller than they were, but then warriors were used to following.

Briefly, in a flash of thought that came and went within an

instant, it occurred to me for the first time that perhaps I was not quite the same as other ratlings; that there was something slightly different about me.

—Well?

Fang huddled closer to Floke.

—Where to?

I moved towards the light, aware for the first time of a throb within me, a mysterious tug from some unseen exterior force.

Beyond a stretch of grass and some tall trees, there were human habitations. It was from there that the pulse was coming.

—Follow me.

I darted across the thirty lengths of short grass to the shadow of the trees, followed by Floke and Fang.

I was breathing heavily as we rested in an old rabbit hole. Floke and Fang, I noticed, were as fresh and at ease as when they had first emerged from the world below.

—Where are we going? Floke asked.

I glanced at the two warriors whose lives had been changed when I had appeared behind them in the Great Hollow.

—You hear the pulse, then the heartbeat? It is Tzuriel's. We follow the heartbeat.

Floke and Fang glanced at one another, puzzled. It was Floke who revealed first.

—Heartbeat? What are you talking about?

—There! Listen.

Floke and Fang looked at one another again. They heard nothing. It was Fang who revealed what they were both thinking.

—You're a hearer.

I allowed Fang's words to rest in the brain for a moment. Most things are a mystery to warriors but few are quite as mysterious to them as the gift of hearing. Those born with this talent – hearers – are able to hear information in the very air around them; not by sound or smell or sight but through a higher instinct that no rat will ever question.

When a young rat is found to be a hearer, he – it is always a he, for reasons no rat quite understands – would be sent to one of the courts where his gift will be of most use to the kingdom. The Courts of Spies and Prophecy are among the most favoured.

But being a hearer involves sacrifice. When they reach adulthood, hearers will lose their precious gift upon their first act of carrying with a doe rat. For that reason, it has become accepted that they are not required to do their family duty – in fact, they are forbidden from fathering.

As a result, they hold a privileged, but slightly sad, position within the kingdom. They can hear but they can never love, never know the pleasures of being a father.

I was a hearer. A heartbeat, the pulse of a king, was calling me.

It throbbed in the air around me, growing stronger as I moved towards it.

12 I walk, talking, through the empty streets…

… of the town. My head is fuzzy from working all night.

It is not just tiredness that has me talking to myself.

When no one is around, I like to hear my voice. It reminds me of the Peter Simeon that still lives deep within the grimy guttersnipe who is known as Dogboy.

I hear the chattering of starlings, sparrows and blackbirds as they greet the day. Turning a corner, I see a milkman's dray making its way towards me. The piebald horse considers me with its wall eye, and I know in that moment that it has a contented life. The milkman, whistling, does not see me.

It is how I like it. As I reach a road which leads to the centre of town, some young swells, their suits dishevelled, pass by unsteadily after a night of revelry. A whiff of rotting vegetables from a nearby market reaches me. At other times, I would harvest the gutter for food.

Now I only have thoughts of home and sleep.

As I walk, a small dog, a terrier bitch of some kind, falls into step with me, as if she knows that I will lead her to food.

I take a path off the road, quickening my steps as I head eastwards, now and then talking quietly to the dog trotting beside me. By the time I reach Mrs Bailey's bakery, there are two men being served at the counter.

I wait outside until they have gone. She is a kind woman, Mrs Bailey, but I know that she would not welcome my presence while she is serving respectable folk.

As I enter, she gives me a smile like sunshine. It makes me uneasy with its brightness, and I look down at my feet.

'Oh hello, it's our little ratter,' she says. 'Been out working, have you?'

I nod.

She is slicing a big steak and kidney pie. 'Your usual?'

'Two pies, please.'

Mrs Bailey glances at me curiously, as adults always do when I speak. I could say 'poy' and no one would notice me, but I will not. I say 'pie'. I am who I am.

She reaches into the oven and with a cloth takes out two chicken pies.

'Got a bag, love?'

I shake my head, then untuck the front of my shirt and hold it like an apron before me.

Mrs Bailey lays the two pies on the shirt. Then, to my surprise, she cuts a small extra slice of the steak and kidney pie, wraps it in some paper, and puts it with the other pies, winking at me as she does.

I smile quickly, politely, and give her a penny for the pies.

As I leave the shop, I hear her say to herself, 'Poor little thing. What's going to become of you?'

Outside, the dog is waiting. She puts her head on one side as I come out of the bakery.

When I have rounded the corner and am out of the sight of Mrs Bailey, I break off a piece of the steak pie. It's hot. I blow on it. The dog whines, longingly.

Once it is cold, I give it to her. She follows me for a few paces but when I tell her to stay, she stands, watching me go.

The pies are warm against my aching stomach as I walk, more quickly now.

Home. Friend. Sleep.

There are fewer people now and the houses are smaller, made of rotting timber and crumbling bricks. There are no carriages, only the occasional cart.

A smell, the scent of belonging, reaches me as I turn into the lane.

Old food. Dirty clothes. Waste. The rich smell of the maggoty flesh of a dead dog or cat.

An enormous pile of rubbish, as high as a house, is in front of me. Here is the place where respectable people bring what they do not want in their lives to be dumped out of sight.

The tip. Its smell is with me, on my hair and clothes, wherever I go, yet it still surprises me when I return home.

It has a life of its own, the tip – not just in the darting rustle of the creatures within it, but its shape, too.

Like a boil on the skin of the city, it changes every day, yet is always teeming and throbbing and alive.

I glance over my shoulder. Few people bring their rubbish at this early hour, but no one must know I am here.

Around the side of the tip, past a blackberry bush still glowing with fruit, there is an old door, its paint peeling, which lies against a tangle of brambles and wire.

Taking care not to crush the pies in my shirt, I pull the door back.

Beyond it is a burrow, a dark passage into the centre of the tip.

I enter, pulling the door shut behind me. It is dark but I know my way. I crawl forwards for several yards, until I reach a home-made room, a little cave, supported by branches, which I have made in the heart of the tip.

Home. I stand, happy, for this moment.

I lay the pies upon a board on the ground near to me. As their lovely smell fills the air, the stench of the tip fades to nothing.

I give a long, low whistle.

From the tangle of rubbish which surrounds me, there is the sound of movement, so quiet at first that it might be a beast.

But it is not a beast.

13 I followed the heartbeat until the sun…

… was high in the sky.

We were far from the kingdom now, Floke, Fang and I. Now and then I wondered how we would find our way home.

For the two warriors, it was an adventure.

—Where now, Efren?

—Just follow me, Fang.

—Are we close yet?

—Not yet, Floke.

The heartbeat was growing weaker, and yet I felt it more powerfully within me.

We reached an area of wood and bushes. Young humans were playing nearby. Perhaps it was weariness, or maybe my thoughts were with the desperate pulse of my king that was summoning me. Whatever the reason, I was not ready.

There was a sudden movement from the direction of the humans, a trem that could only be caused by one kind of enemy.

—Dog!

It was Fang who revealed the warning. We scattered, a citizen's first instinct when under attack. I raced across the clearing. My body, not I, found refuge by dropping down a deep hole beneath the root of a tree.

I heard the terrifying trem of the dog as it raced past my hiding place, its deafening bark rattling my bones.

Like any rat, I knew what I had to do. I stilled, turning myself from a living creature into something so without movement, sound or even scent that I might have been a clod of earth or a stone.

There was a silence as the dog sniffed the air, then a roaring, crashing noise above me.

It had found me. I smelt the hunger on the dog's hot breath close to my head, its desperation for blood and flesh, yet nothing, no terror on earth, would move me. Still, still, still. Even my heartbeat seemed to slow.

Beyond the barking, I heard the sounds of humans. They were calling the dog. It whined its frustration and rage. The ground shook as it attacked the earth with its paws and teeth. A heavy drop of warm liquid from its mouth fell on to my head. Still, still, still.

I felt the trem of a human, smelt the enemy. They were there for a few moments. Then, silence.

We stayed, the three of us, each in our hiding place, cold, terrified but alive, until the light began to fade.

14 'We are about to change the world, Mr Smith…

… and we should be proud.'

The doctor is talking to me as we walk down a street of great buildings. He is wearing a suit smarter than I have ever seen him wear. His housekeeper has given me a clean white shirt.

It is a great occasion. The doctor is to talk to the institute about rats. Hanging from my hand, and weighing heavily, is the giant rat we captured by the river. It is still just alive.

'By tomorrow, I shall be famous.' The doctor continues to talk without looking in my direction as he climbs the steps of a large house. 'And the rat, of course.'

He pushes open a double door. We are in a large entrance hall and, for a moment, the doctor seems uncertain as to where to go.

He mutters to me, 'You'll probably have to wait in the servants' quarters with our friend, Mr Smith.' He nods in the direction of the cage I am carrying. 'The institute likes to think of itself as a gentlemen's club for scientists.'

A man of great age, stooped and with long silver locks, is sitting behind a desk in the far corner. He does not yet seem to have noticed our presence.

'Not that one will find many gentlemen here.' The doctor raises his voice. 'Deliver one disappointing lecture at the institute and you are quickly forgotten. Wallace, the bird migration man, has never recovered from the mauling he received here.' He clears his throat loudly. 'At the institute.'

The old man behind the desk looks up from his papers.

'Can I help you?' he asks.

The doctor crosses the hall, and I follow. As I approach, the man behind the desk casts a look of distaste in my direction. He stares first at me, then at the rat I am carrying, and shudders.

'Dr Henry Ross-Gibbon at your service.' The doctor is speaking in the clipped accent of an army officer. His voice is different when he is in company, I have noticed. 'I am to deliver the lecture tonight.'

'Ah yes.' The old man is not thrilled by the news. 'That will be Dr Ross-Gibbon, the rat man.'

The doctor squares his shoulders. 'Understand the rat, sir, and you understand the world. There are five billion of them on earth, and they are breeding more quickly than even science can imagine. In many ways, they are similar to ourselves. They mate all the year round, for example.'

The man behind the desk raises his eyebrows.

'I would ask you to remember that you are in the institute,' he murmurs, glancing in my direction. 'We do not welcome that sort of language.'

'I was being... scientific.' The doctor seems embarrassed. It is unusual for him.

'Your animal and the boy will not be allowed to enter the institute for the lecture, of course.'

'I need my assistant,' says the doctor. 'I am a scientist. I do not handle my specimens.'

The man from the institute stands up and, without looking at me, mutters, 'Follow me.'

He opens a small door at the side of the hall and stands aside to let me pass.

There are steps, leading to a dark cellar. Before I have even found somewhere to sit, the door behind me has closed, leaving me in darkness.

15 From the shadow of a giant tree, we gazed…

… across a wide expanse of ground where the human traffic of horses, dogs and mighty, clattering carriages were passing to and fro.

I was watching the road where the buildings met the ground. It was no time for discussion with Floke and Fang. I waited for my moment, then dashed forward. During the seconds when I crossed the open ground, I was aware of the sharp scent of danger, the sound of horses' hooves, an enemy voice, as, belly to the ground and ignoring the searing pain in my paws, I took the road, then the pavement, and crammed my body below a stone by the house.

I waited, knowing too well what was about to happen. Fang, then Floke arrived, seconds later, bundling on to me so violently that they knocked the wind out of me. It took several moments for the two warriors to extricate themselves from one another.

—Did you see that, Efren? Did you see me?

—You? It was me that made that human scream.

The throb within me shook my whole body. We were close. Emerging from the bolt hole, I galloped along the pavement until I reached stone steps which led down towards a basement. I took them, half running and half falling, coming to rest in the damp and musty shadows beside a wooden door. The other two blundered down seconds later.

I sniffed at the base of the door. The wood was rotten. I turned to the others.

—How long would it take you to get through that?

Fang looked at Floke. They gnashed their teeth noisily, then set to work.

I listened to the pulse within me. I could tell now that it was different from my own. Older, slower, weaker.

Floke and Fang made short work of the door, stepping back moments later. A hole, small but good enough, was in the ancient timber.

When I revealed, it was in a tone which I hardly recognised as my own. I sounded like a leader.

—Wait here, I can do this alone. If I am not back by sundown, find your way back to the kingdom and report what has happened.

—Can we…?

—Why shouldn't we…?

I heard them, but already I was through the hole, into the house and on my way.

16 I sit to the side of the stage…

… just out of sight of most of the audience in the large lecture hall on the third floor of the institute.

Through a crack in the screen in front of me I can see the audience – men in frock coats, some of them smoking cigarettes.

The scientists. The doctor has spoken much of them in the past. 'The so-called men of science,' he calls them.

They seem more amused than interested as, from the other side of the stage, the doctor appears and takes his place behind a lectern.

There is something unusual about him as he stands there. He has a smile stuck on his face like some sort of mask. It doesn't seem to be convincing the so-called men of science.

'They call me "the Rat Man", I am told.' The doctor speaks up, and the buzz of conversation in the hall slowly dies down. 'It is for you to judge.'

He looks around the lecture theatre and I notice now that his hands, resting on the lectern in front of him, are trembling.

'It is true that I have studied our friend *rattus norvegicus* – the brown rat, of course – more than any other scientist in the world. From this knowledge, I have reached the conclusion that, when it comes to the future of our species mankind, it is the rat that holds the key.'

One of the gentlemen at the back of the hall says something at this point which causes those around him to laugh, but the doctor seems not to notice.

'In many ways, the rat is, of all the mammals in the world, that which is most similar to us,' he says. 'Like us, it is omnivorous and can eat a huge variety of food. Like us, it has been known to eat its own kind. Like us, it is able to reproduce throughout the year. Like us, it has had its own wars. The black rat, or ship rat – *rattus rattus* – was present in Europe from, we believe, a time after the Crusades, playing its part in the plagues and epidemics. Then, in the early eighteenth century, the great brown rat invasion from Asia occurred – caused, we think, by a powerful earthquake. They swam in their millions across the River Volga and advanced towards Europe. There followed a bitter war between the brown and the black rat. It was *rattus norvegicus* who proved the stronger and more ruthless.'

The scientists listen, half interested. I have heard every part of this story many times before in the form of mutters at the laboratory as the doctor does his work, or at night as we are out searching for beasts.

'Like us, the brown rat covers the globe – it has the widest range of any mammal in the world.' The doctor raises a finger. 'Like us, it never has quite enough. Gentlemen, we should beware of its savagery and ambition.'

The hall is quiet now. One or two of the men have produced notebooks into which they scribble occasionally.

'The rat is a magnificent example of God's work,' the doctor is saying. 'He can mate five hundred times a day. He can fall sixty feet and survive. He can swim proficiently. He can tell which food is poison. There are stories of rats foretelling the future – moving before an earthquake, leaving a market days before it is moved to another place. This, gentlemen, is a superb species.'

He looks around the hall, now all solemnity, making the most of his dramatic pause.

'So superb, in fact, that it is our mortal enemy. It could destroy us.'

As if someone in the audience has protested against what he is saying, the doctor raises a hand.

'The rat is ruthless. It has become the undisputed ruler of the animal kingdom. Already it eats our crops. It destroys the fabric of our lives – books, clothes, houses, pipes. It has caused floods by gnawing through dams. But it wants more. There is only one species that stands in its way.'

'Us.' A member of the audience says it out loud.

'Yes.' The doctor allows a chilly smile to flicker briefly across his face. 'Us. I believe that we are already under attack. From Sweden to Spain, there are stories of packs of rats behaving in an entirely new way. Infants have been killed in their cots. A beggar on the streets of Amsterdam was found with his throat torn out. In France, couples have been attacked in their beds.'

He has the audience now. There is silence as he delivers his warning.

'We are entering the Rat Age. They are beginning to attack us, their greatest enemy. They are multiplying in number. For centuries, they have eaten our food. Now they are killing our children.'

He glances towards me. My moment is approaching.

'I believe that it is no longer enough for us, as scientists, to study the rat. To survive, we need to defend ourselves. We have a brilliant and dangerous enemy who is even more ruthless and deadly than mankind. We must destroy him before he destroys us. Above all, we must show no fear before the rat. Gentlemen, I believe it can actually smell the terror of other creatures.'

The doctor reaches under the lectern for a pair of heavy leather gloves which he puts on his hands, watched in silence by his audience. He nods in my direction.

I carry the cage on to the stage. There is a stirring and a muttering around the lecture hall.

I lay the cage before the doctor. I release the latch.

The doctor pauses, glances with a little smile. 'No fear, please, gentlemen.'

He half opens the top of the cage. When he withdraws his hand, he holds the giant rat dangling by its tail.

Over its screams, the doctor cries, 'Behold the enemy!'

17 I was climbing, making my way upwards...

... through the timbers, along the pipes, behind the panels of the old building, when a terrible sound caused me to stop and stay still.

It was the scream of death, a sound that has no meaning beyond itself. With it, a last desperate pulse racked my body.

My king needed me.

It was close, just beyond a thin wall of timber. The disgusting smell of humans, of the smoke they sometimes breathe, was almost overpowering.

I paused for a few seconds. Another scream reached me, weaker this time. Every instinct in my body told me to flee, but I knew that I had no choice. I moved towards the sound. A small light shone through a crack in the wood to my left.

Closing my ears to the sound of the enemy, my nostrils to the scent of them, I began to gnaw at the wood. It was soft, half rotten. Soon I was able to squeeze through it into the dazzling, dangerous light.

The enemy was all around. It loomed above me as I crouched in the corner of the room, ready to disappear back into the safe darkness of the house.

Then I saw him.

King Tzuriel was swinging, only half alive now, from the hand of the enemy.

I attempted to reveal to him but King Tzuriel was too weak to see or to hear anything.

The human laid him on a surface, then reached for a long, gleaming line of metal that was on the table nearby.

I knew, for all my terror, that I had no choice.

18 The doctor seems disappointed…

… that the rat is only just alive as he lays it on a table that is at the front of the stage. He looks at that moment like a magician in a circus. He wants to scare his audience a little.

He is holding in his hand a long syringe.

'This rat weighs fully three pounds in weight – rats are growing larger with every generation. But it is not merely his size I wish to show to you this evening. I will show how *rattus norvegicus* is a perfect disease-carrying organism.'

He smooths the fur of the rat around its heart. It is hardly breathing now.

'Alive, a rat is dangerous, a perfect walking mechanism for spreading disease. Even when it is dead, its war against humanity continues.'

He glances up at his audience, and smiles. He is enjoying this moment.

He aims the syringe at the heart of the rat, then plunges it into the flesh.

19 When I saw the flash of metal, heard the dying cry…

… of King Tzuriel, I lost all sense of safety. His pulse was within me, summoning me. He needed the help of citizens, and only one citizen was there.

A loud scream bubbled up from within me, shaking and racking my body as it emerged from my throat.

The sound of the enemy was all around me. I ignored it. With all my strength, I ran towards my king.

20 Someone swears loudly and stands up...

... pointing at the floor. Others around him, on one side of the hall and near the front, move quickly from their seats.

Soon that part of the hall is in tumult.

Then I see it. A rat, quite small and with a dash of white on its head, is scurrying down one side of the lecture room towards the stage.

The scientists near the beast stand up. Some of them try to stamp on it as it runs by. Yet still it continues towards us.

'Get it, someone! Get it!' A voice, squeaky with panic, can be heard above the confusion. It is the doctor. Eyes wide, hands clutched together in front of him, he is backing away as if, at any moment, he might run out of the room.

The rat reaches the base of the stage and seems to look up. Unable to get any further, it scurries along the skirting before vanishing into another hole.

'Oh. Oh. Oh.'

Slowly all eyes return to the doctor. When he realises that the beast has gone, he gives a nervous little laugh. 'Oh... what a surprise that was,' he says.

'You'll be all right now, Ross-Gibbon,' a stout, bewhiskered man in the front row calls out. 'Return to your talk. You were just telling us how important it was not to show any fear.'

And the moment of alarm is suddenly broken. The room rocks with laughter.

The doctor's face has turned an angry red. He walks slowly back to the table and the big rat which is now motionless.

'I shall dissect our friend,' he says, his voice still shaky. He runs a scalpel along the rat's stomach. Dark blood oozes on to the table, a smell of putrid flesh fills the air.

The man with whiskers, sitting in the front row, takes a handkerchief from his pocket and covers his nose and mouth.

'Yes, gentlemen, the smell is not good,' says the doctor irritably. 'That is the very argument I am making.'

He points with his scalpel to the purple and red innards of the rat. 'There are in my opinion no fewer than fifty-five infectious diseases, many of them fatal, that can be carried and passed on, in one way or another, by the rat. Typhus, plague, leptospirosis, infectious jaundice, trench fever, influenza, trichinella spiralis...'

He starts to list beast-related sicknesses, but it is clear now that the so-called scientists have heard, seen and smelt enough of rats for the evening.

One or two leave their seats, and others sidle out of the room with obvious relief. By the time the doctor has finished his list of diseases, the lecture hall is half empty.

He finishes hurriedly. When he asks for questions, there is an embarrassed silence. The man in the front row makes a show of looking at his timepiece.

It is done. The moment which the doctor has been talking about for so long is over.

'Where did that blinking rat come from?' His question is directed to me as I lift the corpse of our specimen back into the cage. 'Did someone release it as a joke?'

Saying nothing, I lay a cloth over the table. It is soon dark with blood.

'I wasn't afraid of it, you know.' The doctor sniffs and squares his shoulders. 'I was just a bit taken aback.'

I nod. Of course you were, doctor.

'No more rats in public, Mr Smith.' He glances at me as if I have somehow been responsible for what has happened, then makes briskly for the door. 'From now on we change our tactics.'

21 In the park, the noise of the enemy...

... grew quieter. Now and then the sound of a voice or the bark of a dog would make the heart quicken but, as night closed in, the danger from the enemy faded.

We crouched in silence beneath a pile of logs. Our paws bled from the distance we had travelled. We ached with hunger.

We were completely lost.

In the darkness, I sensed the eyes of Floke and Fang upon me. Without a word of revelation, I had become their leader. The thought made me feel stronger.

—I shall search the wood. You rest. I shall be back.

Ignoring my aching muscles, I moved through the towering trees. I looked about me, noting that we were now on the frontier where the green met the expanse of hard earth where humans travelled. If we moved along that border, there was just a chance that we might find the scent which would lead us home.

I was returning to the others, still sniffing for some kind of scent which would tell me where I was. At any other time, I would have been more alert. By the time I had smelt danger, it was too late.

Out of nowhere, something hard struck me on the back, followed quickly by a sharp, tearing pain across my shoulder blades. I was lifted, sharpness holding me gently on each side, then released. I was falling, tumbling downwards.

As I hit the ground, the universe around me had turned dark. It had also grown claws and teeth. It held me so fast that, even squirming with all my might, I was helpless.

Cat.

I had never seen one but in the world below they spoke of cats. Cruel, cowardly creatures with a love of causing pain.

It could only be a cat.

Writhing in panic, I caught a glimpse of yellow, gleaming eyes.

I smelt my own panic but then, just as quickly, a sort of calm was within me. Cat, human, fox, dog. There was no difference right now. I would escape. I knew I would escape.

I let myself go limp, and ceased to struggle. The cat's grip on me eased. It walked away, leaving my body, wet and cold from its mouth, lying in the grass, gasping in the evening dew.

Strength slowly returned to my muscles. I tried to make a dash towards the log pile. At the very instant when it seemed as if, by some miracle, I might be free, the cat hit me again. There was no sharpness this time, no claws or teeth, just the suffocation of being held against the ground.

I felt the soft weight of one paw rolling me over. I lay still again, then, foolishly thinking that the cat was distracted, I made another bolt for it, staggering a few steps until the heaviness caught me once more.

Three times, four. Exhausted, I felt my legs buckle. I would not die. I will not die. The cat's broad face filled the sky above me. It seemed to be smiling. I closed my eyes.

An ear-splitting scream made them start open. I got to my feet. The cat seemed to be having some kind of fit, falling backwards, shaking its head, attacking itself in fury and terror. Then I saw why.

Floke had bitten hard into the cat's cheek. Fang was on its back, like some human on a horse, but holding on by his teeth which were clamped to the back of the cat's left ear. For a moment, the cat trapped Floke against the ground. The warrior seemed to relax. Then, when his attacker was least expecting it, Floke brought his hind legs up beneath the cat and kicked his way free, only to attack again from the other side.

It was a rout. Cats, believe me, are no heroes. Like all bullies, they hate experiencing the pain and punishment which they love to inflict on others. After a few seconds of yowling confusion, our attacker managed to shake Fang off his back. He galloped away, with Floke still clinging to his neck. Assured of victory, Floke let himself fall to the ground.

There were a few seconds of exhausted silence. Then the two warrior rats who had saved my life approached me, their mouths flecked with blood. Fang, who had been limping slightly, prodded me with his nose.

—Are you all right, little one?

I was shaking too much to be able to reveal. I was only distantly aware of the revelations of Floke and Fang, something about a cat, about the need to get some food, before I drifted off into the sleep of shock and fear.

When I awoke, I was wedged between the heavy bodies of my two friends. Somehow, the three of us were back under the log pile. I turned, becoming aware as I did so that my paws were raw from the previous day. The cat had left me sore and bruised. I was desperately, mortally, hungry.

I was about to awaken Fang and Floke when I smelt a powerful scent in the air. There was food nearby. I turned and gazed back across the park from where the first glow of dawn could be seen over the distant trees. Some instinct caused me to look to my right.

There beyond a clump of trees was a small lodge.

I nudged Fang.

—We've got to go.

Neither Floke nor Fang stirred.

—Find our way back to the kingdom.

Floke stretched his hind legs, keeping his eyes closed.

—I know where we can get some food.

And, suddenly, they were awake.

Too weary now even to conceal ourselves, we made our way across the open ground. There was a high wooden door barring the entrance to the area from where the smell of food was coming.

Fang attempted to scale the wood in the way he had seen some of the older warriors doing but the cat had inflicted a deep wound upon one of his front legs and he fell back, with a sharp squeal of pain. With Floke, I explored the length of the fence for some way in.

The only opening was in one corner, a crack between the timbers more suitable for a field mouse than for a rat. Maddened by hunger, Floke hurled himself against it, cutting the skin above his eye in the process.

I approached. I gazed at the opening, thinking myself into smallness.

I pushed my nose forward in a gentle, snuffling movement. I felt my bones soften and bend, my aching muscles grow tighter, squeezed by the wood.

I was through.

There was a small yard behind the cottage and, against a wall only a few lengths from where I stood, was a large bowl of cooked scraps. I climbed into the bowl. With some difficulty, I rolled out half a roast potato, then a scrap of bacon. My mouth drooled as I took them to the gap in the fence and allowed Floke to pull them through.

I turned back to fetch some food for myself and at that moment I became aware of something else. At first, it felt like a pulse. Then I sensed it was something different, a sort of murmur within me. Not one pulse, but many.

Somewhere very near to where I stood there were other rats, and they were in trouble. With all my strength, I sent out the message.

—Who is there?

I waited. The only sound that I could hear was my own heartbeat. I tried again.

—I am a stranger. I need help.

A prickle of fear raised the fur on my back. There were rats nearby and we were on their territory. Even if they belonged to another kingdom, they would normally be quick to reply, if only with threats.

What explained the silence?

Then I saw, beyond the food bowl, a square of wood on the ground.

I moved towards it, sniffing. Definitely, there were rats nearby. But why were they silent?

I heard a sound from beneath the wood. I tore a couple of strips from it with my teeth. Then, after a moment's hesitation, I squeezed my head into the tiny hole that I had gnawed.

I looked down, then quickly drew back, fearful.

I looked again. Below me were hundreds of rats, pressed together in a pit in the dark. They were strangely silent, asleep I suppose, but, as I watched, the light from the hole I had made caught two dark eyes.

I revealed with all my strength.

—Who are you?

Silence. I could see more clearly now. The walls of the prison were bricks and impossible to climb. From the dark mass of bodies, one struggled clear.

It was a fragile, a doe, light in colour and smaller than the rest. I tried again.

—Tell me who you are. What is this place?

The eyes looked up at me.

—Go!

Her revelation was weak.

—I am Efren. I come from the world below. I have seen my king...

I thought in that moment I could smell the doe's impatience.

—Leave this place.

She sniffed the air. Her eyes seemed to understand everything that was happening to me, that I was lost, that I needed to return to my kingdom to bring news from the world above, that I felt more alone than ever in my life.

—Cross the highway of humans. There is an entrance to the world below, half hidden beside where the water gathers. You will find the touch-path there.

But it felt wrong to leave these rats. My instinct was to help. Even a fragile in the world above deserved help.

—Go.

She seemed to reveal with her last remaining strength.

—What is your name?— I asked.

—Malaika.

—I shall see you again, Malaika.

A scent of sadness reached me as I drew back.

There was silence from the pit. I breathed deep of the early morning air.

Never look back. It is a rule of the kingdom.

I crossed the yard, squeezed my way through the hole I had made in the fence. Floke and Fang had left some of the potato for me.

I ate, but strangely was feeling less hungry now.

—Follow me.

They did, Floke staying close to me, Fang limping after us.

We crossed the human highway.

We searched around and soon found the tells of rats from the kingdom, leading to the touch-path which had been mentioned by the fragile.

Her name echoed in my mind as I led Floke and Fang downwards into the welcome damp and darkness of the earth.

Malaika.

22 There are days when I wonder...

... about all that has happened to me while I have been on this earth.

I see children playing on the street, or walking with their mothers or nannies. I pass a school playground.

The memories return and, just for a few moments, I wonder.

So it is, the day after the doctor's speech to the institute.

I am walking to the rat-catcher, Bill Grubstaff. I need money for food, and today is a pit day.

I like my work with Bill, especially on days like this. It is not just the noise and warmth at the tavern on pit days, and the money. It is watching Bill, his shyness falling away from him as dogs and rats are about to do battle in the bar of the Cock Inn.

Let me tell you about Bill Grubstaff.

It was some time after I was left alone on the street by Frank the footman that I met him.

It was the worst time for me. I thought I would starve in those early days, or die of cold.

Like the dogs who had become my friends, I would linger around the taverns of the town, waiting for scraps of food.

A group of men, some of them with dogs, were drinking outside a public house. They were, I later discovered, part of the ratting community – men whose sport was around the rat pits of the town.

Suddenly that night, there was an uproar. Two fighting dogs had set upon one another. Their owners laughed to see the two animals scrapping, but I could see from the dogs' eyes that the fight would be to the death. Each believed he was doing his duty to his master.

I made my way through the men and laid my hands on the scruff of each dog's neck. They paused in their growling, more out of surprise than anything else.

Stop. Leave it. Now.

My words were soft, but the dogs understood. They had permission not to fight.

They separated, eyed each other for a moment.

Stop. Leave it now.

Each looked at me. I could tell that they were grateful that I had rescued them from killing or death. After a few moments, one wandered back to his owner, his hackles raised but with peace in his eyes.

The crowd was silent as I turned to walk back to the alley where I had been waiting.

It was several minutes later that a man stood before me.

He was of middle age with something of a hunched back, but with powerful shoulders and arms. His face had the hard, wary look of a man to whom life has never been kind. In one hand he held a slice of bread with a lump of meat on it.

He held it out to me.

'Here you – dog-boy.' His voice was gruff but gentle. 'You deserve this.'

I took it.

'I'm Bill,' he said. 'Bill Grubstaff.'

I had seen him among the men, with them but standing slightly away from the group, rarely talking.

He talked now, though. He asked me where I learned to work with dogs, where I lived, who I was.

I said nothing. Talk was dangerous. Grown-ups, even when they seemed friendly, are never to be trusted.

He was about to leave me when he said, 'Would you be man enough to earn a few pennies now and then? Do a bit of rat catching? Could you do that?'

I nodded.

'What do they call you, boy?'

I said nothing. When you are on the street, it is best to be nameless..

The man called Bill shrugged. 'Suit yourself,' he said. 'Dogboy.'

He pointed to a stretch of green and some woods.

'You'll see a shed in them trees behind some wire. Call by tomorrow if you're interested.'

I looked towards the wood, then back at Bill Grubstaff.

He smiled and winked. It had been a long time since anyone had smiled at me.

I have become better acquainted with Bill Grubstaff since then, and I know that he is never happier than on days like this – pit days. When I arrive for work, Bill is there in his moleskin waistcoat, a bucket of scraps in his hand. Unlike other rat catchers, he likes to feed beasts on the day of their death.

He nods in the direction of the fence nearby.

'Visitors last night,' he says.

I walk over to the fence. There is a spot of blood on the wire where it has been gnawed.

'Rats,' I say. 'One was hurt.'

'He'll be more than hurt if I catch him.' Bill gives a little laugh. 'They even tried to get into the well, bloomin' varmints.'

He walks over to the trapdoor over a disused well where he likes to keep the beasts, and puts a finger over the wood where toothmarks can be seen. 'They were curious, I suppose.'

He lifts the wood, and throws in some scraps from his bucket. The rats squeal as they fight for food.

'Must be a fair few in there,' he says. 'It's going to be a good day for us, Dogboy.'

He looks at the beasts, and a little smile is on his big, weather-beaten face. He could be a farmer looking at his prize pigs.

He passes me a sack. 'In you go then, boy.'

I take the ladder that is leaning against the fence, and slowly lower it into the well.

Carefully, I descend. On the last step, I feel the warmth of scurrying feet and tiny claws around my ankles.

I reach down and my fingers close around a tail. In a quick movement, I pick it up and drop it into the sack.

One after the other, I take them, counting them aloud as I go. Bill is not good at figures.

I have been counting for several minutes when I lift a beast who is smaller and lighter than the rest.

To my surprise, I see it is a pet rat, of the type which has become all the rage among the gentry.

'A fancy,' I say to Bill.

Bill glances at it. 'That'll be from Barnaby Smiles,' he says. 'He gives me the beasts he can't sell in the market.'

'Bit small for the pit,' I say, feeling a touch sorry for the little thing.

He laughs. 'You're going soft, Dogboy,' he says. 'A rat's a rat. She'll do.'

I lower the fancy rat into the sack.

23 Above us, we heard the thunder of…

… hooves. Now and then, light shone through a drain from the street. The tread of the enemy, the sound of their feet.

It was a long and frightening journey back to the kingdom. The touch-path led below a place where humans travelled, in all their noise and smells.

There were moments when all I wanted was to rest my poor bloodied feet. Behind me, though, I smelt the pain of Fang, who was now limping badly.

His brother Floke, beside him, revealed every stride or so.

—Onward. Onward. We shall soon be there.

The path reached a turn, and then descended rapidly. The earth beneath our feet was wet now. We were not far from the kingdom.

It was Floke who first sensed we were not alone.

—Danger!

His revelation was so urgent that it could almost be heard out loud as he bundled past me.

There was a bank in front of us. Fang and I waited as Floke carefully lowered himself.

The sound of alarmed squeals filled the darkness. The rats ahead of us were certainly not warriors.

Then we smelt it. The kingdom. We were among citizens.

I eased myself down the drop. Behind me, Fang fell and a scent of pain briefly filled the air.

We were on a flat, damp stone. Ahead of us, under some

rotting wood, was a gouge. There, watching us, was a group of five rats, citizens of the kingdom.

I stood beside Floke, and revealed to them.

—We came from the world above. I am Efren.

I noticed that the strength of my revelation stirred the rats into life. They advanced towards us.

—Are you from the Court of Governance?— one of them asked.

I hesitated and in that moment Fang replied.

—He is. And we are warriors.

The rats, who I now saw were quite old, turned to one another and seemed to be having a nervous debate about what to do.

Floke moved towards them.

—Who are you, citizens?

One of them faced us, crouching. His revelation, when it came, was so feeble that it was little more than an irritation in the head.

—Hrrrrhhh.

Floke glanced in my direction. It seemed an odd sort of name.

—What is your court?

—I am Hurh.

Another of the rats stood beside him. Their revelations came tumbling out one after another.

—My friend is named after Hurh, the king of many generations back.

—Although there is some doubt whether Hurh was actually king in this kingdom.

—But he was certainly a king somewhere.

—Not that the Court of Governance has seen fit to recognise him.

—The name of Hurh should be a lot more famous in the kingdom than it is.

—These days all citizens think about is today and tomorrow.

—What about yesterday? That's what we say.

—Exactly. We believe yesterday is the most important time of all. Without yesterday, there would be no today.

—Or tomorrow.

—We tell this to the kingdom all the time.

—But no one listens.

—Ever.

—Ever at all.

Floke had heard enough. He seemed to breathe in deeply, becoming twice his normal size. The rats shrank back. The one called Hurh revealed nervously.

—We're historians, you see. We're part of the Court of History.

I had never really known what the Court of History did. By the look of them, Fang and Floke had never heard of it. Hurh was gaining in confidence.

—We believe historians are important because—

—No!

I interrupted the old historian as sharply as I could manage. I was tired, my feet were bleeding. One of my comrades was badly wounded. History could wait.

—Hurh, we need you to take us to the Great Hollow.

Hurh was taking a closer interest in me.

—Are you a fragile?— He was looking at the white streak on my head —There has not been a citizen with fragile blood on the Court of Governance since—

—Now!

As I revealed, Floke bared his teeth.

Another historian, lighter in colour, emerged from the back of the group.

—Are you with the changers or the keepers?— he asked.

—Changers? Keepers? What is this? We have been in the world above.

Historians, we discovered, like to tell a story. They gathered around us and, taking turns, told us what had happened since we had left the world below.

The news which I had brought about the capture of King Tzuriel had changed the succession.

In every court, sorrow had turned to anger. King Tzuriel's

words of peace had been forgotten. If humankind was prepared to do such terrible things to an old king, citizens were asking, what else would it do? Where would the violence end?

The certainty about who would succeed Tzuriel had disappeared. Grizzlard was a figure from the past. He was too old, too peace-loving to rule the kingdom at a time of peril.

Some citizens believed the doe Jeniel should become Queen. They were the changers. Behind Grizzlard were the keepers.

I had been told enough. It was time for the kingdom to hear the truth of what had happened to Tzuriel in the world above.

—Two of you, please take us to the Court of Governance.

It was Hurh and the light-coloured rat, who name was Divnit, who led us away from the Court of History on the winding touch-paths and passages to the Great Hollow.

When Hurh reached the entrance to the area behind the Rock of State where the Court of Governance stayed, two warriors blocked his path.

As bravely as he could manage, he revealed.

—I am Hurh from the Court of History.

—And I am Divnit.

The revelation from Divnit was like a small sneeze in the brain.

One of the warriors snickered, and went back to nibbling at a root. Historians, I was discovering, were not widely respected.

I pushed forward.

—I am Efren. Let me through.

The warriors ignored me. I felt Floke tense beside me, ready for a fight. I tried again.

—I have seen the king in the world above.

There was movement in the hollow behind the warriors. The ancient form of Quell appeared.

—Efren? Is it you?

The warriors moved back. I led Floke and Fang, followed by the two historians, on to the Rock of State.

—Tzuriel is dead. Stabbed to death by the enemy. I saw it.

Quell lowered his old head in sadness.

Fang held up his injured paw.

—We fought a cat.

But Quell was uninterested in tales of heroism. In fact, he seemed almost displeased that the three of us had returned from our mission. Eventually, he appeared to have reached a decision.

—You will be fed and given water. When your strength has returned, you will tell the court what you have seen in the world above.

Hurh pushed forward, his eyes glistening with the excitement of the moment.

—It would be a useful item for future historians if one of our court could attend this… this occasion.

His revelation tapered off as, ignoring him, Quell turned away. As we followed, the two historians were approached by the warrior gatekeepers.

—Thank you, historians— I revealed, as they were led off the Rock of State.

Quell moved slowly. He seemed to have aged by another lifetime since we had been away.

As we reached the Court of Governance, I noticed for the first time a smell of fear and anger in the dark air.

—The ratling is back.

Quell's revelation caused all eyes to turn in our direction. They were not welcoming.

A guard led me into a small chamber to the side of the main court, where a cache of food, some grain, cooked potatoes and apples taken from a human cellar, had been left. There was a disturbance behind me. As I turned, I saw Floke and Fang being nipped and bustled away from me by four guards.

—Where are you taking them? They must eat with me.

Desperation added strength to my revelation.

A dark figure filled the entrance to the chamber. It was Swylar, the sleek young deputy to Jeniel.

—They are injured. Do not worry, young Efren. They shall be taken good care of.

He moved closer to me and nudged me with his nose. Normally the gesture would have been to judge my mood by the scent of my breath – whiffling, as it is called – but Swylar, I could tell, had no interest in how I was feeling. He simply wanted to make me afraid.

I turned to the food and began to eat.

—They didn't want you back, you know— Swylar's revelation was easily conversational —They assumed you would all die in the world above and that the kingdom could continue as it always has. I fear that you are now in rather serious danger.

I stopped eating.

—Danger? Why?

—Some members of the court, the keepers as they are known, were hoping that, if nothing was known of the end of Tzuriel, the succession would be as normal. Grizzlard, the foolish old warrior, would become king. Now that we know the enemy stabbed our old king to death, it changes everything. For some, a subject who caused all this to happen is a traitor and must suffer a traitor's fate.

—I saw what I saw. What can I do about that?

Swylar prodded me once more.

—You have to do nothing, little Efren. Fortunately, I have it in my power to help you. The guards listen to me these days. You will be safe if you do the right thing.

—And what is that?

—Tell the truth— Swylar glanced towards the entrance of the chamber from where there were sounds of courtiers approaching —Tell the truth and, above all else, do not disagree with me. Remember that we are in this together.

He scuttled away into the darkness at the back of the room.

The old courtier Quell stood at the entrance to the chamber.

—Are you strong enough to address the courtiers?

When I emerged from the chamber, I was aware that the area outside the door was thronging with members of the court.

Courtiers climbed over one another in their attempts to get closer. Some of them had scratches around their faces, suggesting that scuffles and skirmishes had even broken out within the Court of Governance.

—Is this ratling to be trusted?— One of the courtiers revealed as if I were not standing before him —We have had too many plots recently. This could be another one.

Quell stepped in front of me.

—We need to close this business. Let us hear what this young rat claims to have seen.

I have never been good at lying. My revelation was slow and, in spite of my tiredness, it reached all the courtiers who were listening. I told of the events which had happened to the three of us in the world above, from the first time we had first sensed the pulse of the king to the meeting with Malaika which had brought us home.

As I finished my revelation, a figure pushed to the front of the crowd. It was Grizzlard, the rat who would be king. He seemed less in control, more dishevelled and ordinary, than he had been until recently. As he addressed the courtiers, a whiff of disrespect was in the air.

—If what we have heard is indeed the truth and not some story invented by a ratling, it is a tragedy for the kingdom. What our subjects need now is their new king to bring back stability. As the courtier nominated by the great martyr Tzuriel, I—

—Your moment is past.

The revelation came out of the darkness of the chamber behind me from where, after a few moments, Swylar stepped forward.

—This brave young rat from the Court of Tasting has shown us that courage does not have to involve the noise and fighting and aggression of the Court of Warriors. It is not the time for a warrior to lead us. Efren has borne witness to an act of open war by the enemy. The planned capture of our king and his execution before cheering crowds.

Quell looked up sharply.

—That is not what the ratling said. There was no talk of war or execution.

Swylar moved forward to stand closer to Quell than was deemed respectable at court. Beside the creaking, ancient figure, he seemed lithe and young. I was crouching low, hoping not to be seen, but to my horror he turned to me.

—It was no accidental death, the end of our king, was it? More like a declaration of war, surely.

I gazed into the eyes of Swylar. They narrowed with the merest hint of a threat. I remembered the courtier's words, *We are in this together.* I revealed quietly.

—It was no accident.

—See?— Ignoring Quell, Swylar turned to the court —We are in a state of war. Grizzlard belongs to yesterday. The kingdom calls out for a new leader.

Grizzlard attempted to interrupt.

—It is for this court, not for subjects—

Before he could finish, Swylar scurried forward and delivered a contemptuous nip on the side of the neck. In spite of his superior strength and his famed courage in battle, the courtier did nothing to retaliate.

—We have discussed enough. The court must unite for the future. It is time to choose a new ruler. The kingdom awaits.

As if some silent but powerful command had been given, the citizens who had been pressed together in the centre of the court began to move back, allowing a passage through their midst. A small figure, gazing ahead as if into the eyes of destiny, moved through their ranks. It was Jeniel.

—I request the nomination of this court. Let us end this uncertainty and go to the Great Hollow now for the final ceremony.

The heads of several courtiers turned to Grizzlard and then to the senior courtier Quell. One after the other, they lowered their heads in agreement. In response, relieved that the uncertainty was over, the courtiers acclaimed their new Queen.

Swylar had moved closer to me.

—Stay near to me— The revelation was low and urgent —You have just become part of the court.

He nudged me in the direction of Jeniel.

Part of the court? What was he talking about? I was gripped by panic.

—Can I return to the Tasting Court? I want to see Alpa and all my friends.

Smiling coldly, Swylar replied.

—Too late for that, little one. Step out of my protection now and you will quickly be dead. You are with me and the Queen now.

—What of Floke? What about Fang? Are they part of the court, too?

—I hope you are not serious. I had always assumed that you were reasonably bright for a ratling. Efren, your dear, simple friends have, unfortunately for them, seen things which will require them to make the small sacrifice of their insignificant lives.

—You told me that they were being taken care of.

Swylar kept walking.

—And so they are. In a sense.

24 Seeing a rat-catcher on the streets brings bad luck…

… or so many people believe anyway.

I sit in the back of Bill Grubstaff's cart, a cage full of rats at my feet. His old black horse Jim, hairy heeled and with a tragic look in his eye, takes us through the town.

Some of the townspeople recognise Bill and his cart. Others catch sight of the sign painted on each side. It reads, *BILL GRUBSTAFF, Rat-Catcher*, and has a rough drawing of a big rat beneath the letters. I have never thought that was a very good idea.

Children stare at us now and then. Their mothers or nannies hurry them along. Men joke to one another as we go by, but I can tell that they are uneasy.

Nobody wants bad luck, do they?

You would think people would welcome Bill. Stories are told about giant rats being found in cellars, under the floorboards, in pillar boxes. I have never understood why someone who catches them should be seen as a person to avoid.

Bill cares nothing for all this. He is slumped on the seat, his old cloth cap over his eyes. Now and then he shakes the reins against Jim's neck. The horse ignores him.

It is a grey November morning when we reach the Cock Inn, an old tavern that has the look of a place hemmed in by the houses on each side.

As we pass, I see faces peering out of the window. There is movement behind the glass as we approach.

Bill looks in their direction, and smiles.

'Well, they're pleased to see us anyway,' he murmurs.

We continue down the road until we reach a yard behind an ironmongers' shop. It is here that Bill tethers Jim, by a stone water trough.

I once made the mistake of asking Bill why we had to hide the cart away from the Cock Inn.

He became unusually angry.

'Anybody would think we was animals,' he said. 'Ducking and diving, hiding ourselves away from the rozzers. All because we provide a few rats for sport.'

The pit was against the law now, he told me. He talked of the days when the Cock Inn was famous for its bouts – cockerels, bears, dogs, monkeys and even humans had fought in the pit which was to be found in the big back room away from the street.

Now, Bill told me, they had to be careful. Coppers needed to be paid off. News of the next pit day was passed on, quietly, from sportsman to sportsman, pub to pub.

On days like this, though, the Cock Inn is full of life and noise and sport, just as it was in the times gone past.

We carry the rat cage, covered in hessian sackcloth, down a narrow alleyway which leads to the backyard of the Cock Inn.

There's something different about Bill now. His cheeks are flushed, his eyes alert. He knocks on the door, winking at me as if I know the reason for his cheeriness.

And I do. It is called Molly Wall.

The landlady of the Cock Inn is a round, smiling woman whose dark curly hair makes her easy to spot in the pub – that and her loud laughter which can often be heard above the buzz of conversation at the bar.

'Molly was a beauty in her day,' one of the regulars once told Bill while I was standing nearby.

He looked over to where she was talking to her husband Jack.

'Still is,' he murmured.

There's certainly a kindness to Molly. When she smiles, it is as if she really means it. She asks me questions about my life and, although I am careful not to tell her too much, I am pleased that she is interested.

'And here are our rats,' she says, opening the door wide to us. 'How many have you got, Bill?'

'Some four hundred, Molly.'

'We'll need all of them.' Molly Wall ruffles my hair as I walk past her. 'We've got six dogs in tonight.'

'Not so easy to get the beasts as it used to be, Molly.' I have noticed that there is something about the landlady's name which brings a smile to Bill's lips. He likes to say it as often as he can.

'It's you that's getting slower, Bill.' She winks at me. 'Eh, Dogboy?'

I nod. Bill blushes.

I walk ahead of her down a narrow corridor. As Molly reaches forward to open the door at the end of the passage, the noise, smoke and laughter from the public bar seem to burst over us.

We enter, and some of the punters call out Bill's name. There are dogs in every corner of the room, barking and tugging at their harnesses as they sense the approach of rats.

25 I think of Malaika...

... and the terror of a fragile surrounded by noise and rage and the bodies of other stronger rats.

She could hardly breathe for the writhing movement all around her.

But when the dogs began to bark, and the smell of the enemy was thick in the throat, she sensed there was greater danger than she had ever known.

—Fight!

—Fight!

—Fight!

The revelations were all around her. She felt a stirring within her.

—Fight!

—Fight!

26 Molly leaves us at the corner of the bar...

... where Bill likes to stand on pit days. Behind the bar, Jack Wall, Molly's husband, brings him a beer and is about to hurry off when Bill says, 'And a ginger pop for the lad, please, Jack.'

I have noticed this about Bill. Pit days give him courage. They bring him alive. He is less shy, more talkative.

Standing by the bar, watching the setters and ratters with their dogs, Bill talks in a way he would never do at any other place or time.

For the Cock Inn brings back the past to him. He tells me about the Bull and Bear, a pit on the other side of town.

'There was quality in them days.' He shakes his head and drinks deep of his beer. 'Excitement. Sport. Money changing hands. Beasts in play. Fighting dogs...' He looks around the bar. 'Better than this lot, anyway.'

The warmth, the ginger pop, the noise: they make me feel good. This afternoon, I begin to feel, will be a happy time.

'Tell you what, boy.' Bill drops his voice. 'I've heard talk of the sports out in the country – coursing hares, hunting foxes and the like. I'll lay you money they wouldn't compare to the sport you get in that pit.'

He nods in the direction of the centre of the room where a low wooden barrier seals off a hole in the ground. When dogs and rats are in sport, the setters and trainers, punters and drinkers will gather round and look down into the square pit where animals have fought and died down the centuries. Their blood

– rats, cockerels, monkeys, dogs, even badgers – has coloured the zinc walls of the pit, giving them a dull coppery look.

I let Bill talk. In my heart I know that he will never persuade me that dogs killing rats is sport, however loudly men roar, however much money is made.

Bill speaks, as if sensing my doubts.

'You got courage here, boy. You got the power of nature, the skill of man. And tricky as a bagful of monkeys! People think that betting on which of two dogs can kill rats quicker would be easy, but it's not. I've seen a Manchester terrier, in its prime and bred for the job, lose to a wispy little mutt that had never been in a pit before. In this job, no one – not the best setter in the world – knows exactly what's going to happen when a dog gets dropped in that pit.'

I nod. There's no reaching Bill Grubstaff on a day like this.

'Got some good 'uns with you today, Bill?' a voice calls out from the direction of the throng at the bar.

Bill laughs. 'Beauties,' he says.

At that moment, from behind the bar, Molly Wall rings a bell. Conversation dies down.

'Come on, boy.' Bill drains his glass. 'We're on.'

Between us, we carry the cage to the centre of the room where Jack Wall is seated at a table. At moments like this, it's difficult to understand how Molly and Jack are together. He is small, about a quarter of his wife's size, with the nervous, nippy look of a weasel.

'Ah, the merchandise.' Wall glances down at the cage, which is now seething and boiling with rat life.

'There's more than four hundred,' says Bill. 'Mostly streets but with a few fancies thrown in.'

'We'll have two contests between now and mid-afternoon.' Jack runs his fingers nervously over the pitted surface of the table. 'First up, it's Bermondsey Bob against Drum, the bitch from Edmonton that did so well last time. Then Charlie Buckingham's Kentish Lad is taking on a young Manchester of Wilf Barstow.'

As Jack sets off to tell the setters the order of the afternoon, Bill wanders over to the pit. Leaving the cage of rats under the table, I join him.

Elbows on the ledge surrounding the pit, he gazes downwards.

'Some of them were circular,' he says, almost to himself. 'I prefer them square like this one. If there's no corners, the beasts get confused and the kill's too easy.'

He turns and leans against the edge of the pit, watching the setters as they prepare their dogs.

'There was a dog called Billy,' he says suddenly. 'You'll have heard of him...'

I hadn't.

'The most famous ratter of all time. He once killed a hundred beasts in nine minutes and fifteen seconds. That was a circular pit. The beasts didn't have a chance against Billy. Folk don't like it when dogs are too good at their job. It was a sport they come to see, not a massacre.'

Jack is back at the table. It is time to work.

'Put 'em in, boy,' Bill mutters.

I fetch the cage and lug it to the side of the pit. From the watching crowd on the other side, two men emerge. They are two setters whose dogs will be in the first bout, Jem Dashwood and Charlie Buckingham.

According to Bill, Jem and Charlie have been rivals for over ten years, and in all that time not a friendly word has passed between them.

'Gentlemen.' Jack Wall raises his voice above the din. He sounds a bit strangled, like someone trying to be more important than he is. 'Our old friend Bill Grubstaff has provided us with some fine sport, as usual. The two setters will scrutinise the filling of the pit.'

Bill lifts a ladder into the pit. I descend and take the cage of rats from him. Opening the small trap in the roof of the cage, I put my right hand in and take out a rat, holding it by its tail.

Carefully, I put it on the ground. The first thing Bill told me was to take my time while releasing beasts for a bout. A rat with a broken leg or stunned by a fall can cause disagreements and delays.

With the onlookers staring down at me, I count out the rats until exactly one hundred of them are scurrying around the edge of the pit, falling over one another as they search in vain for an escape.

Dashwood, a former prizefighter who has a hard, bony face and piercing blue eyes, watches the rats with the stare of a hungry hawk. As usual on pit nights, he is wearing a pair of tan and white gaiters, made from the skin of his most famous dog, a champion rat killer called Blackjack.

His opponent's dog has been drawn to fight first. When money and pride are at stake, he knows how important it is that every rat in that pit is a healthy, strong specimen.

In the past, Dashwood has asked Bill to remove a couple of beasts. There was nothing wrong with the animals, Bill says, but Dashwood wanted to show his opponent that he had an eye for the way a rat should be.

Today, though, he is against his old enemy, Charlie Buckingham. The little tricks which have worked on less experienced setters are a waste of time with Charlie.

Hands in pockets, Dashwood walks back to where a boy not much older than me, but a lot bigger and broader, is holding on with both hands to the lead of a snarling, scarred Manchester terrier, who is shivering with excitement, his red eyes dilated and lips drawn back over his teeth in a slavering smile of anticipation.

Bermondsey Bob. The dog is tugging so hard in the direction of the pit that there's danger of him throttling himself before fighting a single rat.

Jem Dashwood lays a strong, long-fingered hand over his dog's muzzle, resting it there for a moment before beginning to squeeze. Bermondsey Bob whimpers, then snarls angrily, shaking his head free as if already a rat is in his jaws.

'He's ready.' Dashwood stands up and wipes the dog's drool from his hand. 'It'll be a good time we're looking at today.'

Around the pit, the gamblers and drinkers are inspecting the wild-eyed, dazzled rats before laying their bets. Even when a ratter as reliable as Bill Grubstaff has provided them, the punters like to assess the beasts for strength, health and savagery.

In the past, I have heard it said at the Cock Inn that it is as important to know your rats as to know the dogs who are about to kill them. No two pitfuls of beasts are quite the same, they say.

'How's your dog, Jem?' an old man standing nearby calls out.

'He's well enough.' Dashwood glances in the direction of Buckingham. 'Honest as the day is long, too.'

'Betting's even today.' As I step out of the pit, Bill talks to me as if I really cared who was to make money from this game of killing. 'Buckingham's dog Drum is a game bitch – she killed her hundred beasts in under ten minutes a couple of days ago, but Bermondsey Bob's stronger, fitter, more experienced.'

Bill points to where Jack Wall is sitting. I had heard that Dashwood was careful with his money. Today he seems to be feeling lucky. He lays a £100 wager on the gaming table.

At that moment, the noise in the room – men shouting encouragement, dogs barking – grows louder. Charlie Buckingham is bringing Drum towards the pit.

Winking to his son, Dashwood ambles forward to see how his opponent will fare. The spectators stand back, allowing him a prime spot near where Bill and I are standing.

Having taken the last bet, Jack Wall places a chair beside the pit and stands on it. Silence descends, broken only by the yapping of dogs and the scratching of rats' claws and teeth as they try to gnaw their way through the zinc walls that surround them.

'Gentlemen, we have a one-hundred-rat contest between' – he pauses, like a man in a music-hall act – 'Mr Charles Buckingham's fine Staffordshire bull terrier bitch. All the way from Edmonton, it's Drum!'

There are cheers from Drum's supporters.

'And from the stable of our own Jem Dashwood, one of the finest dogs ever to grace the pit at the Cock Inn, the one and only Bermondsey Bob!'

'Come on, Bob, my son.' A voice, hoarse with excitement, calls out from the far side of the pit. There are more cheers.

Buckingham, a small man with the shifty look of someone who is never far from trouble, lifts Drum, a strong, white bitch with scars from previous bouts on her face and neck, over the pit. Hanging by the scruff of her neck, she whimpers, pitching and writhing at the sight of the rats below her.

Jack Wall watches carefully. At the pit of the Cock Inn, no setter is allowed to drop his dog into a crowd of rats, giving them an advantage when it came to killing. It will be Jack who holds the watch and decides where each dog can be released.

He holds his left hand high, watching as Buckingham holds Drum over the centre of the pit. As he brings it down, with a brisk cry of 'Go!', a mighty roar rocks the room.

'Here we go,' says Bill happily.

Drum falls, snarling and snapping, into the pit.

She quickly goes to work.

27 Now there was just the sound of screams…

… around Malaika. Screams of rage, terror, defiance.

The sound of rats fighting for their lives, facing their deaths.

In the cage, those that awaited their fate pressed in, clambering over her in fear.

Malaika cowered beneath the weight of the other rats.

Waiting.

28 Jem Dashwood has a look of grim concern…

… on his face as he watches Drum working, but it is largely for show.

After ten minutes and thirty-five seconds, Drum is lifted out of the pit, her white coat now drenched dark red.

'Good bitch.' Bill turns his back and speaks to me out of the side of his mouth. 'Brave, strong. But she's too slow. See the way she shook every rat to kill it? That's not how champions work.'

When I climb into the pit to clear it of corpses, I find that Bill's right. I have seen enough contests to know that the best dogs kill their victims cleanly, leaving their bodies so unmarked that, by the end of the contest, it would be as if the pit was full of slumbering rats. One nip of the neck or backbone was all it took.

The bodies left by Drum are broken and bloodied, in some cases beyond recognition. As the punters chat above and fetch drinks from the bar, I collect every trace of dead rat in the pit, dropping them in my sack, wiping my blood-covered hands on the sides of my trousers before passing the bag up to Bill.

'Jem's dog'll win it,' he mutters, passing the cage full of live rats to me. 'You mark my words, boy.'

I try not to think of what happens to the beasts. The Cock Inn is a place of warmth and friendship. I feel safe here, with Molly and Jack Wall in charge.

'Sport.' I say the word to myself as I open the cage. I have to keep it in my mind. This is sport.

As I begin to count out the next one hundred rats, something odd happens. I feel within my head a sort of jolt. It is as if I am sickening for something, a sudden pulse within me.

Shaking my head, I continue to count out the rats. When all the beasts are dashing, panic-stricken, around the pit, Jem Dashwood moves forward, his dog Bermondsey Bob tugging and choking on his lead, eager to be about his business.

As man and dog approach the pit, the setter lifts the dog and unhooks the harness from his shoulders in one easy movement. With both hands on the scruff of the dog's neck, he holds him over the pit. Bermondsey Bob looks down at the rats like some monstrous bird of prey.

Jack Wall directs Dashwood to the right position for the drop.

When Jem is on the far side of the pit from where Bill and I are standing, Jack calls out, 'That'll do you. Get ready, Jem.'

The hubbub of talking and laughter dies down once more in the bar. Jem takes his right hand from his dog's neck and, with a smile in the direction of the punters, he strokes its shiny coat. Then, slowly, he brings his hand down and between its hind legs until he seems to find what he is looking for.

There is a smattering of applause from around the pit. Pit goers like this trick of Jem Dashwood's.

'Give 'em a squeeze,' someone shouts.

As Jack Wall says 'Go!', Dashwood clenches his mighty fist tight around the dog's balls. Bermondsey Bob gives a roar of outraged pain and in that instant, Jem lets him drop into the pit. Even as he touches the ground, his head is whipping furiously left and right, his death-dealing jaws snapping all the while.

Other ratting dogs like to corner the beasts, then pick them off one by one. Bob is different. Like a hound of hell, he bursts upon the largest group of rats, scattering them left and right, seeming to cast the merest glance in the direction of each as he passes.

But it is not a glance. It is a bite, executed so swiftly that the human eye cannot see it.

Within three minutes of the drop, half of the rats lie dead, some of them twitching their last breaths. There is no danger of rats fighting back now, so Bob moves into his second phase, galloping around the perimeter of the pit like a greyhound on the track, dealing death as he goes.

After six and a half minutes, the dog is drenched with blood, his flanks heaving and flecked with saliva. There are no more than twenty or so beasts still alive but we can all see that Bob is exhausted now. The rats find it easier to avoid his snapping jaws.

'He's too honest for his own good, that one.' Beside me, Bill murmurs. 'If he could finish just half as fast as he started, he'd be a champion.'

Even tired, though, Bob is deadly. Moments later, Dashwood steps into the pit. As he lifts his dog, panting and drooling, the setter has a grim, victorious smile on his face.

'The time of Bermondsey Bob' – Jack Wall looks at his timepiece for a few seconds – 'was ten minutes and five seconds. I declare the winner to be—'

'The bout ain't finished yet.' The voice is that of Charlie Buckingham. He stands, arms crossed, on the far side of the pit. Slowly, he leans forward and points to where the bodies of ten or so rats are lying. 'The beast down there – he's no more dead than I am.'

Jem Dashwood passes Bermondsey Bob to his son, then dries the blood from his hands with a large red handkerchief. Punters step back as he walks around the rim of the pit, his face pale and expressionless.

There is no doubting it. We can all see now. The twitchings of a large male rat, its back or pelvis broken, are not the nerves of death. He is still alive.

Jack Wall gives an unhappy wince. 'It's moving, Jem,' he says nervously. 'We'll have to chalk it.'

Dashwood gives the publican a hard, unforgiving look. 'What you talkin' about? It's dead – good as, anyway.'

'If it's dead, then let's chalk it anyway,' one of the spectators calls out.

I notice Molly has approached the pit from the bar. Like her husband Jack, she knows that when bouts end like this, trouble is never far away.

Jack glances across to me. 'Fetch him out, Dogboy,' he says.

Once more, I climb into the pit. A silence has descended on the room. Making my way carefully between the bodies, I pick up the rat by the tail. It screams, its eyes wide with fear, and there is a murmur of concern from those who have backed Bermondsey Bob.

Jack Wall, followed by Jem Dashwood and Charlie Buckingham, makes his way back to the judge's table, and takes a lump of chalk from a drawer. Then, on one knee, he draws a circle the size of a dinner plate on the timber floor.

He looks up at Dashwood and Buckingham. They both nod their agreement.

Holding the rat in front of me, I climb out of the pit and walk through the anxious punters who have gathered around the chalk circle. As I lay the beast on its side within the circle, the rat twitches energetically.

'Waste of time,' Jem Dashwood mutters.

Jack stands up and reaches for a gnarled hazel clout, two foot long, that is lying beside the gaming table. He kneels before the rat, raises the stick, then brings it down hard across the beast's tail.

With a scream of pain, the rat makes a desperate galloping movement, edging its way slowly out of the circle. After a few seconds, it rests short of the line but, as if suddenly remembering the pain, it starts to move again until, beyond any doubt, its body is outside the circle. It may be dying but, as far as the contest is concerned, it has moved enough to be judged to be alive.

'No!' With a bellow of rage, Dashwood picks the rat up and hurls it with all his force back into the pit.

'The bout was uncompleted.' There is a tremble in Jack Wall's voice. 'So I declare Charlie Buckingham's bitch Drum the winner of the contest.'

Dashwood's face darkens as if all the unspoken words within him are massing like cavalry beneath the pores of his skin.

He walks slowly to where Buckingham and Wall are standing. Since the bout finished, the atmosphere and good humour has drained from the room and now, as the three men face one another, even the dogs are still.

'You know the rule, Jem.' Avoiding Dashwood's glowering eyes, Jack Wall points to the clout. 'The rat left the circle.'

Molly touches Jem Dashwood's arm.

'We'll give you a return bout next month, Jem.' Her tone of voice is husky, caressing. 'You can choose your opponent, eh?'

Dashwood's eyes remain fixed on Jack Wall. 'Today,' he says. 'Now.'

'Your dog's not fit for another bout.' Jack Wall speaks quietly. 'You know that.'

Dashwood shrugs, defiant. 'I've got a second dog. A young Yorkshire. Today's his day.'

Another setter, Wilf Barstow, steps forward and whispers something in the publican's ear.

Jack smiles with relief. 'Wilf is prepared to stand his dog down for the good of the sport,' he announces. 'Will you set your Yorkshire against Kentish Lad?'

'Steady, Jem.' One of the punters speaks up. 'Your dog has never been in the pit. One bad experience could sour him for life.'

'And Kentish Lad's a twelve-minuter,' someone standing beyond Jem calls out.

Jem Dashwood looks up, his eyes blazing. Pride is pushing him towards a bad decision. 'What you talkin' about? I know when a dog's fit for the pit. Scrapper's more than ready. He's young but he's a champion in the making. He could be another Blackjack.'

He turns to Charlie Buckingham. 'Same purse as last time?' he asks.

Buckingham's reply is lost in the cheers.

29 Weak with hunger and fear...

... Malaika felt her prison move.

There was light above her, the giant face of a human looking down.

Second by second, the wall of flesh that protected her was being removed as, with screams of terror, rats were lifted upwards and out of sight.

Malaika felt a tightness around her own tail. Before she could shrink away from it, she was swinging face down through the air, the dancing lights and smoke and the faces of the enemy swirling before her eyes.

Her journey seemed to last for ever. Then, suddenly, her tail was released and she was falling.

For the briefest of moments, she felt the welcome earth beneath her feet and looked about her for the nearest way of escape. Then she smelt the blood, the terror and death.

She began to run.

30 There are no ordinary pit days…

… Bill Grubstaff likes to say. Each one of them has a story to tell.

Today the memories are not going to be good.

I stand beside Bill, looking down on the pit.

'I think there might be a little bit of bother tonight,' he mutters with an unhappy smile.

It is true. The good humour of a few minutes ago has gone as if it were never there. Instead, there is an edginess, an anger, in the smoky air of the bar.

Jem Dashwood's pride and joy has been disqualified for an uncompleted kill. A dog with a lot of punters' money riding on it had won and had then been robbed by a rat which refused to die.

'If it was anybody else but Jem, I'd say he'd lost his reason,' Bill is telling me. 'Setting a virgin ratter against an experienced dog like Kentish Lad.' He shakes his head. 'Still, Jem knows his dogs.'

Nearby, Dashwood speaks to a punter. The man walks a few yards to where Charlie Buckingham is preparing Kentish Lad and says something to him.

Charlie nods.

'Mr Dashwood has asked if I am prepared to let my dog go first. Since the Lad's been ready for a week, I'm happy with that.'

The men near him laughed nervously.

'Let's be doing this thing and have done,' Buckingham says more loudly.

Dashwood has been inspecting his dog Scrapper's teeth. Now he straightens up, wiping the saliva off his hands. He walks to the pit and watches the beasts scuttling desperately around the metal wall.

His colour is still high in his cheeks.

'Not happy with all these beasts,' he says to Jack Wall. He points to a rat cowering in the corner. 'It looks sick. Out.'

Jack nodded to me. I climb into the pit with a sack, grab the rat and drop it out of sight.

'The lame one over there.' Dashwood points to another. 'Where did Bill get these beasts? They're half dead already.'

'They're good fighting rats, Jem,' Bill growls.

'And that's not a beast – it's a bloomin' mouse.' Dashwood jabs his finger in the direction of a small grey and white rat.

As I reach for it, I feel that strange lurch within my head once more. Lifting it, I see that it is the fancy rat I had noticed. She's quaking with terror as I lift her.

'The rest will have to do.' Dashwood turns away from the pit.

I climb the ladder, the sack in my hand. The first two rats I return to the cage but, when I hold the grey and white doe in my hand, it is still, almost trusting, as it looks at me.

Glancing around me to check that no one is watching, I slip her inside my shirt. As I reach into the cage for three new rats for the pit, I feel her scrabbling frantically against my skin and, for a moment, I wonder if she is going to bite me.

She reaches my armpit. I feel the small body trembling.

One rat at least will survive tonight.

31 The human body has a strong and truly disgusting smell…

… for a rat but, quelling her shame and her helpless terror, Malaika surrendered to warmth and closeness.

… I walk over to where Jem Dashwood is preparing his young dog Scrapper.

The dog, I can see, has the right breeding in him. He needs a bit more muscle around the shoulders, but the way he is put together, low slung and powerful, suggests that when he has grown into his strength he could be among the best on the circuit. He has the manner of a ratter, too – his face is one of the ugliest I have ever seen.

But when I look into his eyes, another story is being told. The sounds of other dogs, the smell of rats and blood, have not excited him as they should. He looks up at me, as if sensing that only I can understand his fear, and whines softly.

When Dashwood's son Ernie approaches, Scrapper actually wags his tail.

'Dad.' Eddie Dashwood is looking concerned. 'He's a bit young, isn't he? He's only just turned two.'

Jem is gazing towards the pit. Kentish Lad's supporters are growing quieter, and Dashwood smiles.

'The Buckingham dog's tiring,' he says.

Without looking at a timepiece, Dashwood can tell that Kentish Lad is already worrying those who have backed him.

'Old dog, see.' Dashwood nods in the direction of the pit. 'Old dogs get bored of the game. They kill sixty or so beasts and lose interest.' He winks at his son as he runs a hand down Scrapper's flank. 'Stick with youth, son. That's the secret.'

It is still a while before Buckingham's dog is taken from the ring. The time announced by Jack Wall, thirteen minutes and forty-five seconds, gets jeers and boos from the discontented crowd.

'Your dog's home and hosed, Jem,' an almost perfectly round man with a neat moustache calls out to Dashwood as he inspects the blood-soaked pit to ensure that all of Kentish Lad's rats are truly dead. A glance is enough. The old dog may have been slow, but he was thorough.

I go to release the final batch of rats, leaving fewer than twenty in the cage. Buckingham looks them over, but finds no weaklings.

And now Jem Dashwood advances, the young dog Scrapper in his arms. There is a cheer from his supporters.

'Good old Jem,' someone shouts. It is as if his dog has already won. The animal glances at me, terrified.

I notice that Bill looks worried. Too many men want this dog to win. Too many men will be disappointed if it does not.

Dashwood smiles with a hard-eyed confidence as he raises Scrapper above the pit in preparation for setting the dog on its first bout.

'Set him ready, Jem,' Jack Wall calls out once more.

Dashwood releases his right hand. He strokes Scrapper's pelt, down his spine, then his muscular haunch until he reaches between the dog's hind legs. With a wink at Eddie, he squeezes.

The dog yelps with pain, then whimpers, looking not at the rats below him but over his shoulder towards his owner.

'You've got a lady's lapdog there, Jem,' someone shouts.

'Go!' shouts Jack.

Dashwood hesitates slightly longer than usual before releasing his charge. The rats have gathered at one end of the pit and are watching, motionless.

'Trouble.'

I say the word out loud. The rats, I can see, are not as afraid as they should be.

Bill sees it too. 'What's up with them beasts?' he murmurs.

'They smell the dog's fear,' I murmur.

Bill looks down at me and frowns. 'You could be right, boy,' he says.

One of the spectators bangs the metal wall behind the rats impatiently with the palm of his hand, but the noise merely makes the rats press more closely together.

The dog has still not been dropped into the pit. The time has not yet started.

'Look lively.' The voice was Buckingham's. 'We ain't got all night.'

Dashwood moves round the edge of the pit to the right-hand wall, giving Scrapper a run at the beasts with his left side protected.

He drops him. There is a cheer from the crowd around the pit.

'Go on, my son,' one of the punters shouts. 'Finish 'em off.'

Then, quite quickly, the noise dies down. Something is going wrong. Scrapper is looking up at his master, wagging his tail uncertainly, as if asking what to do next. The dog moves away from the protecting wall, then glances, fearfully, towards the far corner where a hundred pairs of dark, glittering eyes are staring at him.

Scrapper sniffs the air, then lifts a paw like a pointer who has seen pheasant. There is nervous laughter around the pit.

And it is in that instant, when the dog looks up, surprised by the noise of the spectators, that the unexpected happens.

As if at a given signal, the rats move forward, no longer fearful. For a second, it seems as if their idea is to break past their would-be attacker to the other end of the pit.

Then the reality becomes clear. The rats are not retreating at all. They are attacking.

The first beast to reach Scrapper leaps upwards, seizing the soft base of his ear and holding on, swinging against it. The dog yelps in pain but, by the time it starts to shake its head, a writhing hairpiece of rats hangs from it.

Jem Dashwood bellows encouragement at his dog but it is too

late. Scrapper's long legs and thick fur provide an easy target for the rats. The dog screams as every part of his body seems now to be covered by attacking beasts.

He staggers forward, unable to see for the creatures that swarm over his face and eyes. He falls against a wall but the rats' teeth are too firmly sunk in his skin for them to be shaken off.

Nothing of what was once Scrapper can now be seen, under the writhing cloak of rats. Like a giant rat himself, he totters forward, across the pit towards where Jem and Eddie Dashwood are standing. In the centre of the pit, he stumbles and falls under the weight of the beasts he is carrying.

It is as if the rats are angry, too. They keep up their attack, tearing into Scrapper's flesh until it quivers no more.

There is an astounded silence in the room as the beasts, their mouths and teeth bloodied, scuttle over the corpse, all terror forgotten in that moment.

Jem Dashwood gazes in disbelief at what had once been Scrapper. He takes out his timepiece and glances at it as if any moment his dog will come to life and complete the bout.

One minute fifty seconds. Scrapper's career in the pit has lasted under two minutes.

Jack Wall clears his throat and, when he speaks, it is in an embarrassed murmur. 'I – I declare that, er—'

A mighty bellow cuts through the room. Dashwood walks quickly to the edge of the pit and vaults into it. Grabbing the bloodied corpse of his dog, he lifts it over his head and hurls it in the direction of the rats that are now trapped in the far corner.

Growling like a dog himself, Dashwood kicks out at a passing rat, catching it with a heavy boot. A cheer echoes around the room. A grin of determination on his face, he corners another group, then begins to kick and stamp on them. Soon his famous dog-skin gaiters are splashed with blood.

Something about the crunch of small bones, the sight of the big man taking revenge for his dog, brings the room to life. One of the punters, a man in his fifties, shouts, 'Let's 'ave 'em then,

Jem!' and clambers into the ring himself. Laughing, he brings down the heel of his foot on a nearby beast.

Soon others are clambering into the pit.

'Gentlemen!' There is a hint of panic in Jack Wall's voice. 'Please do not enter the pit. The pit is for dogs and beasts only.'

But the smell of revenge is in the air. It is as if each of the men feel ashamed by the way Jem's dog has been killed and gnawed before their very eyes. It is strange, unnatural.

The men stamp and shout. They are angry about the money they have lost, angry that pit day has ended in shame, angry about the entertainment they have been cheated of, angry perhaps with themselves and their lives.

Soon there are more men inside the pit, whooping and laughing and killing, than there are looking on.

Jack and Molly Wall stand by, grim-faced. Beside them, Bill mutters again and again, 'This is wrong. No, Molly, this is wrong.'

One of the men, drunker than the others, notices that a few rats are still in the cage. He lifts it, carries it to the pit and, to cheers, opens the latch.

More stamping, more cheering, more blood.

The massacre lasts five minutes, maybe longer, before the men begin to lose interest. All the rats are dead now. For a moment, the men stand in the crimson pit, looking at the blood that is now all over their boots and trousers. Then, one by one, they climb out of the pit, reddening the floor of the pub with their footprints.

'Collect your winnings and be off with you.' The voice is that of Molly Wall. 'There'll be no more bouts in this pub.'

Swearing, Jem Dashwood shoulders his way towards the door followed by his son with Bermondsey Bob tugging at his harness.

Jack Wall seats himself at the judge's table as Charlie Buckingham, who has watched the slaughter with distaste, steps forward to collect his purse. The few gamblers who had laid money on Kentish Lad formed a queue behind him.

'Did you mean that, Molly?' Bill is frowning. 'About there being no more bouts?'

'Sorry, Bill.' The landlady lays a hand on his arm. 'There's no place for that sort of thing at the Cock Inn. We'll be a pub and nothing else from now on.'

She looks down at me. 'Poor lad.' She speaks softly. 'You should never have seen that.'

She walks off, through the door at the back of the bar.

'This is bad, boy.' Bill walks to the rim of the pit. We both stare down at the gore-covered floor.

I am feeling sick, and weary at the thought of clearing up the remains of the rats.

Bill lays a hand briefly on my shoulder. 'You'll be needing a shovel, lad. I'll get one from Molly.'

I watch as he walks away. Just for a moment, I am tempted to tell him that there is one rat who survived the massacre at the Cock Inn, and she is resting in the arm of my shirt.

No. Bill would probably think me soft in the head. I take the shovel and get to work.

33 There had been a time when citizens would be silent…

… and respectful when Quell appeared on the Rock of State. Now as he shuffled forward, all grey and important, the bustle of activity in the Great Hollow continued. A couple of ratlings scrapped over food. A captain was calling her courtiers. Near the front of the crowd, warriors were jostling one another as a doe turned away from them, invitingly.

It was not as large as the throng that had attended the farewell of King Tzuriel, and the mood in the Great Hollow was utterly different.

I stood behind a wall of courtiers, hoping to be invisible on the Rock of State. Since my return from the world above, I had heard rumours that the kingdom's new monarch was to be Jeniel. She was, it was said, the way of the future.

Jeniel would inspire loyalty. Jeniel understood the rats of the kingdom. She would lead us all, with love in our hearts, to war and victory over the enemy. At least that was what was said.

As for me, I was already tired of the power games, the fights which would break out within the court, the half-heard revelations, the rumours. I was a taster. I wanted to go home.

On the Rock of State, Quell looked about him, quested the air with his grey, scarred snout. It was several seconds before eyes turned to him and he was able to start his revelation.

Even then, the audience was only half listening until he mentioned the word for which, I now realised, every citizen had been waiting.

—Jeniel...

The noise of chattering teeth started quietly but grew louder, so that Quell had to wait before he continued.

—Jeniel...

He tried again. As the acclamation echoed off the walls of the Great Hollow, Quell seemed to lose his thread, as if what he had been about to reveal no longer made any sense.

It was at that moment that there was movement among the courtiers not far from me. A small figure emerged from the shadows of the Rock of State.

The noise was deafening. Jeniel walked forward, not with the strut of warrior and courtier but with a sort of scuttle, her head lowered, her eyes fixed to the ground before her. She passed Quell as if he were not there.

When she reached the front of the rock, the acclamation grew louder. Slowly, she raised her eyes until she was staring out at her audience, returning their adoration with a loving gaze. The warmth in that look seem to say to every rat that the future of the kingdom, the future heritage of rats, was safe with her.

She was Queen, without it even being announced on the Rock of State. She was the Queen of our hearts.

Some of the warrior rats, forgetting duty in their excitement, dived into the river in front of the Rock of State, in order to be closer to her. I noticed one or two of the courtiers glanced in the direction of Quell, expecting a command to be issued to the court guards, but the old rat seemed no longer to care what was happening in the hollow.

The closing words of his revelation were weak, but the two words for which the kingdom was waiting were clear enough.

—Queen Jeniel.

At the back of the Rock of State, I peered past the courtiers as the new Queen delivered her first royal revelation.

There was nothing new in the speech. Destiny, duty, faith, loyalty – citizens had heard it all before. But Jeniel's manner was not like that of a courtier or a queen. She was easy, relaxed almost, like a mother revealing to her ratlings.

And yet I found it difficult to concentrate. Her words skittered off the surface of my brain. Matters of state were all very well but at that moment I had other worries. Where had Floke and Fang been taken? As the Queen revealed, I scanned the ranks of her audience for any sign of my friends.

—Efren!

I was so deep in thought that when I heard my own name it took a moment for me to realise that it was part of Jeniel's revelation.

That's right. The Queen, addressing her subjects, had just mentioned my name.

—Efren!

The revelation was as strong as a pulse of pain flashing across my skull. I looked towards Jeniel, who had turned and was questing the air, as if searching for me.

—Step forward, ratling. They need to see you.

Fearfully, I moved forward, holding myself low and humble against the stone beneath me. There was polite, confused acclamation. Turning to me, Jeniel continued.

—What this young rat from the Tasting Court has done shall act as an example of bravery and intelligence to other young rats in the kingdom. Without his bravery, we never would have known the evil and deadly plans of our greatest enemy. The name of Efren shall be remembered in generations to come.

I squeezed my eyes shut, praying that the moment would end.

—For this reason, I am appointing him to the Court of Governance.

At that moment, I glanced at the Queen in astonishment. Her face showed nothing. It was as if I were not there. I shuffled backwards to stand beside Swylar once more.

Now I knew it.

Now it was certain.

There was no escape.

34 Beside the lane which leads to the tip, there lies a blood-soaked sack...

... and in it are the bodies of hundreds of dead rats, killed by the teeth of dogs and the boots of humans.

Tomorrow I shall find a place away from here where I shall leave them. Food for my friends, the dogs of the town.

Now I have something more important to do.

I crouch by the tip, pull back the door. I scramble down the passageway that I have made through the rubbish.

In my shirt, spattered with blood, are presents.

Two pies.

A rat.

I whistle, a low, long note. From the heart of the tip, there is a shorter whistle in reply.

She is there. When I reach the room, the small stove is open, its burning logs lighting the face of a girl, her eyes dark and wary, her face a pale, dirty smudge of light in the gloom.

'Caz.'

'Hullo, Peter,' she says quietly.

I hand her one of the pies. She eats ravenously.

'Good?'

She nods, smiles. With her mouth full, she says, 'God bless Mrs Bailey and her pies.'

Watching Caz eat, I remember the moment when I first saw her, sleeping in a doorway, a pair of pink dancing shoes in her hand. She looked even younger than her eleven years.

Caz. What would I do without Caz? She makes me feel normal.

There are no more words until we have both finished our pies.

'It was a strange night,' I say.

Sometimes, when I come home, it takes time for the habit of speaking to come back to me, but tonight there is so much to tell Caz that the words come spilling out.

She listens as I tell her of the terrible things that happened at the Cock Inn.

When I describe the men shouting and stamping, she looks away. She has never liked my work with Bill Grubstaff.

'Poor creatures,' she murmurs, running a finger over her left hand to collect the few remaining crumbs.

'They say there will be no more bouts.'

'Good.'

'Fewer pennies for us.'

Caz is looking around at the tangle of wood, metal, paper and rags which we have turned into a home.

'There aren't many places that have rats like we have here,' she says. 'And what harm do they do to us? They eat up the food which people have no use for.'

'Maybe.' It is true, over the months we have lived in the tip, that the rats who live here have become a sort of company for us. When they stop moving at night, I am alert for danger. They are our guard-rats.

It is now I remember the other present.

I reach into my shirt. 'I saved one,' I said.

Carefully, I take out the brown and white fancy rat. She rests in my hand, making no attempt to escape.

Caz laughs, a happy sound. 'It's so small.'

'She. She's a fancy rat. They reckoned she would not be much of a fighter.'

'I think they reckoned right.' She takes the beast from me and holds it to her chest. 'Why is she that colour?'

'Bill says that it was Jack Black, the queen's rat-catcher, who started collecting strange-coloured rats that he found. He bred them as pets.'

'Rats as pets.' Caz shakes her head. 'Who would have thought it?'

'Fancy rats are all the rage among the gentry, Bill says. I thought she could join her friends in the tip.'

'No.' Caz strokes the rat's head with a finger. 'Let us be fashionable, too. We'll keep her as a pet.'

'We'll need a box. Food and water.'

'Now?'

'After we've slept.'

Caz puts the fancy rat into the front of her dress, then lies on the ground.

Soon all three of us are asleep.

35 It was soon after sunrise, when rats are going to sleep...

... that I discovered more of the secret life of the Court of Governance.

I was lying in a hollow to which I had been sent by Swylar after the ceremony, when, in the quiet, I sensed that a stranger was nearby.

I sniffed the air and at that moment I saw, sidling between two stones, an adult buck.

—You have been played for a fool, Efren.

The stranger remained in the shadows. His revelation was low and intimate.

—Who are you? I asked.

—My name is not important. Follow me.

Ignoring my aching body, I followed the rat, keeping him a few lengths in front of me all the time. He took me through a network of tunnels behind the court until, eventually, we came to a clearing where two paths intersected. A slab of ancient brickwork lay almost blocking the path.

The stranger scuttled over the brick, marking it with his scent.

—This is where the court sends its undesirables.

And then he was gone, disappearing into the shadows.

I was alone. There was no noise except the distant sounds of humans going about their business in the world above.

I looked around me. Was this some kind of a trap? Then I heard the faintest sound. It seemed to come from below my feet.

I approached the slab. Sniffing, I noticed a crevice beside the brick. I put my nose to it and knew in that instant what, who, it was that I was smelling.

—Floke! Fang! Are you there?

A faint sound, somewhere between a groan and a gasp, came in reply. I pressed with my nose, pausing occasionally to look downwards. There seemed to be some kind of pipe, at the end of which I could see the faint outline of rat shapes.

Desperate now, I pushed harder. Taking a step back, I hurled myself at the slab. It shifted and, nose first, I found himself slithering downwards. My fall seemed to be in slow motion but was broken by the softness of a body. It was Floke.

His eyes were open but flecked with dust, his coat matted and dull from lack of food. The flesh around his mouth was stiff with dried foam. A faint smell of approaching death clung to him. When he revealed, it was weak, hardly a thought at all.

—They got you too.

I saw now that we were in a hollow, a few lengths square. Our only escape was up the sheer clay pipe above our heads. Only the strongest warrior rat would find purchase with his claws on the smooth surface. From the darkness across the cell, there came a low moan.

—Fang?

I moved closer. It was a horrible sight. The poison in Fang's injured right leg was bloated and swollen. It had reached the top of the thigh and was about to spread through his body.

—We have to do something about him, Floke.

But even as I revealed, I knew that Floke was too weak to do anything for his brother. I crouched down, placing my head close to Fang's.

—There's only one way to save you. Push yourself into the corner.

With a feeble scrabbling of his hind legs, Fang wedged himself against the wall. He closed his eyes, delivering a brief revelation.

—Do what you must.

I stood over the infected leg. I moved closer until the stench of poison made me dizzy. There was no question, only action. I knew what I had to do.

I tested the flesh briefly, pressing my teeth against the spongy thigh until yellow poison oozed through the hard skin. I bit gently nearer Fang's body. The poison was there, too.

At last, above the elbow, where leg met body, the flesh was firm and uninfected.

I closed my eyes, willing myself to be strong. Then I bit hard. Ignoring the violent start of pain that racked Fang's body, forcing it against the wall behind him, I gnawed through the muscle, then into gristle and bone.

In no time at all, my teeth had done their work. Fang's leg lay on the floor of the cell. Head pounding, I picked it up in my aching jaws and flicked it away. Then, licking like a doe cleaning her newborn ratlings, I began to work on the bleeding wound on Fang's body.

Floke staggered across the cell and, perhaps out of thirst as much as through any sense of comradeship, also licked at the wound. Soon the saliva of the two of us had helped the flesh congeal before Fang's lifeblood had flowed away.

He lay, semi-conscious, his body twitching occasionally. Floke and I, our tongues raw, our faces and necks covered in the blood of our friend, rested at last.

It seemed as if I had hardly closed my eyes before I was woken by the sound of movement. I looked up. The stone above our heads was slowly moving. There was the unmistakeable scent of adult rat in the air.

I knew that smell.

I nudged Floke with my nose.

—It's Swylar. He's come for us.

Floke half opened his eyes. He looked close to death. Rescue, if this was rescue, may have come too late for him and his brother.

There was a chattering of teeth above my head. It was not friendly. There, his face framed by the circular pipe, was the figure of Swylar. For a moment he stared at the three of us with a cold eye. Then he sniffed contemptuously in my direction.

—You stupid young thing. What more did you want? You were born a nobody, sent to the Tasting Court. Yet you are now a courtier, praised by the queen of the people, applauded as a hero. Some hero! Your first night in court and you try to run away.

I tried to sound brave and strong as I revealed in reply.

—Why did you leave my friends to die?

Swylar snickered.

—They are warriors! The whole point of warriors is that they die. They had served their purpose to the kingdom. And now you shall join them— he yawned —Starvation. Not a great death, I imagine.

He stepped back from the opening and glanced in the direction of unseen attendants. Slowly, the slab moved forward. When Swylar revealed again, all but his mouth was concealed. It was as if we were being addressed by two yellowing teeth.

—Leave them, you little fool. They have played their part. We shall give their names to the Court of History so that they will be honoured in an appropriate way. For an intelligent ratling with a future to die with a couple of stupid warriors is futile. Life or death, being of use to the kingdom, or making a pointless sacrifice. How odd it is that you should find these choices so difficult. Perhaps, in the end, you are no brighter than your dying warrior friends.

And suddenly I knew. As Swylar wheedled, mocked and cajoled, I was aware of another voice from deep within me. As clearly as I had once sensed the heartbeat of my dying king across the rooftops of the world above, the voice of Jeniel reached me from another place and another time.

—The ratling cannot die. The kingdom will not accept his disappearance so soon into my reign. We need Efren at court. Do it, Swylar!

I was hearing.

I wondered, just for a moment, whether I should reveal to

Swylar that I had the gift of hearing, that I was able to sense revelations across time and space.

No. That would remain my secret for the moment.

—Swylar.

A nasty chattering of teeth could be heard from beyond the brick slab.

—Changed your mind, ratling?

—I shall return with you to court.

—Good, then—

—But only if you save my friends. Treat their wounds. Save their lives and give them work at court, and I shall serve you and the Queen like a loyal subject.

—Making terms, are we? From a dungeon. What a peculiar little thing you are, Efren.

I remained still.

Silence. Then, at last, an angry revelation.

—There is another entrance— Swylar tried to disguise his defeat by a show of impatience —I shall send some guards to fetch you.

—Only if you agree.

Swylar's nose, then his teeth and then his entire mouth appeared at what was left of the opening.

—You have your way this time. But one day you will find that I am not always so giving.

From behind me I heard the sound of distant gnawing. The rescuers were on their way

36 It is time to tell you the story of Caz…

… as she has told it to me; of how she had come to be lying in a doorway, her only possession in the world – a pair of dancing shoes – in her hands.

Late at night, in our house of rubbish, she talks sometimes about her past. Her eyes are distant, her voice quiet.

She tells me of when she was not Caz, but Catherine Lewis, and of her mother, Mary Lewis. Mary was young, beautiful, lost in her life. She taught her only daughter one lesson – how to make herself invisible when voices are raised and punches are being thrown. Caz says it was the most important lesson of her life.

Just now and then she speaks of her father. Her eyes grow hard when her memories are of Bob Lewis.

When Bob came home – and that was not often – life for Catherine became louder and more dangerous. He was angry at the world, and took out his anger on Mary and Catherine. The merest look in his direction would set him off.

Bob drank. Bob stole. Bob shouted. Bob hit.

And then, one happy day, Bob left.

After that, Mary would go out most nights, leaving Catherine in the room at the top of a house where they lived. When she returned, it was usually with a man.

The days were all right. Caz remembers the good things – the sun shining through the grimy window, her mother talking of the future when, she promised, the two of them would leave the town to live in a place of fields, with chickens and pigs in the yard outside.

The nights were different. Catherine tried to sleep or, when she could not, pretend she was sleeping.

A gentleman of middle age, smartly dressed and with a neat grey beard, took to visiting her mother. Mr Knightley. He would pace the room, filling it with the exotic perfumes which he liked to wear, talking and talking, trying to get Catherine, lying in her bed eyes tight shut, to join the conversation.

Other men would stay in the shadows of her mother's side of the room. Mr Knightley liked the light. He would strut around, sometimes singing songs from the opera in a surprisingly deep voice. He wanted to be noticed.

When Catherine called him 'Mr Knightley', he laughed.

'I am Ralph,' he said, pronouncing the name as if to rhyme with 'safe'. He smiled. 'We are going to be friends, Catherine.'

One night he asked her to dance for him.

She was sleepy but, when her mother insisted, she climbed out of bed. As Mr Knightley sang one of his songs, tapping his knees with his hands in time with the beat, she skipped across the candlelit floor in her flannel nightdress.

He was delighted. Dancing became part of the evenings he spent there. Sensing that the better the show she put on for Mr Knightley, the happier her mother would be, she spun and twirled about the room, a fixed smile on her face.

'She has a talent,' Mr Knightley said. 'She has a real talent, Mary.'

One night, returning home with Mr Knightley, Catherine's mother seemed strangely happy.

'Ralph has a surprise for you,' she said.

Mr Knightley sat on the edge of Catherine's bed and took her hand.

'You are to be a dancer, Catherine,' he said. 'You might be famous one day.'

'Famous? How?'

'You're a very lucky girl, Catherine.' Her mother's eyes shone in the candlelight. 'You are to go to a dancing school.'

Mr Knightley said he had a friend who ran a school near the centre of town. Her name was Madame Irina Blavitsky, and she had once been a very great dancer. She had agreed to take Catherine on a dancing scholarship.

'What do you say to your Uncle Ralph?' her mother said.

'Thank you.'

Mr Knightley squeezed her hand.

'Will I go every day?'

'Scholarship girls stay with Madame Irina.' Mr Knightley spoke quickly, as if he would quite like to change the subject. 'That's how they learn to dance and become famous.'

'Stay? And then I come home?'

Catherine remembers that she looked at her mother and noticed that her lower lip was trembling.

'Not for a while,' said Mr Knightley.

'Mother?'

Mary Lewis looked at her now. There were tears in her eyes.

'Do you want to help your mother, Catherine?' she asked softly.

Catherine nodded.

'Well then.'

'That's settled.' Mr Knightley stood up, and glanced at the gold timepiece that he kept in his waistcoat. 'It's all very, very good.'

The following week Catherine took her first, and only, trip in a carriage. With her mother and Mr Knightley, she crossed town. At her feet was a small suitcase containing the few possessions she had in the world.

They reached a large house. Mr Knightley stepped out of the carriage. Catherine's mother held her close, both of them crying, then pushed her away.

As Catherine stepped out, the door to the great house opened and there stood a tiny woman, dressed in black, her dark hair tied back in a bun.

'Ah *mes enfants*!' By her front door, Madame Irina flung out her arms, as if greeting her oldest friends. 'You are 'eeere at last!'

It was the strangest accent Catherine had ever heard.

They ascended the steps. As she drew closer, Catherine saw that the ballet mistress, who at first glance seemed as delicate and graceful as a small bird, was more frightening when you stood close to her. Her face was covered in white powder, like a clown's. Her thin lips were painted red, like a fresh scar. Her nose was unusually sharp and beak-like.

Madame Irina's dark eyes glittered as Catherine curtsied before her as Mr Knightley had instructed her.

'Bonjour, Madame,' Mr Knightley said. 'This is Catherine.'

'Ah, she is so *jolie*!' It was as if Madame Irina had only just noticed Catherine. She looked down and held Catherine's chin between two bony fingers. 'She 'as the face of a dunce air.'

While Knightley spoke to Madame Irina, Catherine glanced back to the carriage. Her mother was still sitting there, her face in the shadow.

Noticing the direction of her eyes, Madame Irina said, 'Go, Monsieur Knightley. Leave 'er to me.'

Mr Knightley smiled at Catherine and then did something which seemed a little unlike him. He winked. 'I'll see you very soon, Catherine,' he said softly.

He turned and walked briskly down the steps and into the carriage. Just before they moved off, he passed something to Mrs Lewis. Only when her mother pushed it quickly down the front of her dress did Catherine understand what it was.

Money.

She watched the carriage go, hoping that her mother would look back through the small window. She never did.

These days, when Caz talks of her mother, she pulls her blanket around her. Her eyes have the look of someone staring into the far distance.

Remembering her months with Madame Irina, she is different. She sits up as straight as a heron, her eyes empty of any expression. It is as if she is about to dance, but without pleasure, obeying orders as she did at the school.

The smile left the painted lips of Madame Irina as soon as the carriage was out of sight.

'*Alors*,' she said, picking up Catherine's suitcase and walking through the front door.

Catherine remembers that there was a butler in the dark hall – a crumbly old retainer who smelt of yesterday's food.

Madame Irina passed him the suitcase.

'The usual,' she said.

The words were spoken quietly but Catherine heard them clearly enough to tell that the accent was as English as any that could be heard in the street outside.

'So, Catherine.' Madame Irina turned back. 'Let me find one of ze gairls to show you where you will be sleeping.'

That day was the end of Catherine's old life, but the lessons she had already learned stood her in good stead.

Don't ask questions. Never let your guard down. Keep smiling.

Soon she learned the way things went at her new home. The girls danced and did exercises from early in the morning until late afternoon. Teaching them, Madame Irina would scream her orders, prodding and slapping them with the cane she called *le Maître*, the master. She only became slightly calmer when one of the girls hurt herself, with a torn muscle, bleeding feet or a bruise caused by a crashing fall. Looking down at a girl who was sobbing in pain on the floor, Madame Irina would smile and seem almost happy for a moment.

'It hurts to be a *grande* ballerina, doesn't it?' she would murmur quietly.

When their aching bodies needed rest, the girls would learn French from Monsieur Henri, a neatly dressed man in his twenties who rarely smiled but would mock the girls' accents.

'*Quoi? Pardon?*' he would shout, his face so close to theirs that they could smell the sickly scent of the pomade on his hair. '*Je n'y comprends rien!* I understand nuzzing of what you say.'

The girls ate once a day, and there was never much to the meal that they were given. Sometimes it was a watery soup with a slice of bread, now and then some boiled fish. Hunger became part of their lives. A great dancer must be *maigre* – thin – Madame Irina would tell them.

Although she spoke to them and to any visitors in a strangled French accent, Madame Irina was no more French than they were, Catherine discovered. There was a rumour among the girls that she had once been a dancer, that, when she was young she had caught the eye of a rich Frenchman and had run away to France with him. Now, it was said, all that remained of that life was a memory of how to speak French. After dark in the dormitories, the girls would joke about Madame, but in the hours of daylight, their teacher's double life was never mentioned.

She had the power, each of them knew, to change their lives, one way or another. If a girl fell out of favour with Madame, they would soon disappear from the school, never to be heard of again. Sometimes a girl had answered back. Or, in spite of the meals, one might have put on weight. One girl was sent away because her skin was slightly spotty.

'My gairls must be pairfect,' Madame Irina would say.

Petits rats, she called them. Catherine had at first thought it odd that children doing something as beautiful as dancing should be described as little rats but soon, like the other girls, she took the name for granted.

She was a *petit rat* and that was all there was to it.

Most of the pupils at the Blavitsky School of Dance were older than Catherine. Sometimes, when there were no adults around, they would talk of the homes they had left. Among the girls who had been there for some time, there was a sort of hopelessness in these conversations – they seemed to Catherine like someone starving who dreamed of food. Pupils who were serious about becoming dancers, she discovered, were not expected to return home, even at Christmas.

'*Chez vous? Ça n'existe plus!*' Madame said in class on her first day. '*Votre maison est la danse. C'est tout!*'

Later, Catherine asked one of the other *petits rats* what those words had meant.

The answer haunted her. Your home no longer exists. Your house is dancing. That is all there is for you.

What had Mr Knightley and Madame Irina agreed about her future? Catherine never discovered. All she knew was that dancing became her life and her hope for the future, that the pupils were now her family.

Mr Knightley had been right about one thing. Catherine was a natural dancer. She loved music and, when it played, it seemed to enter her muscles and bones, her hands, her feet and her head. When she was dancing, she could say all the things that she was feeling without speaking a word. She soon became a star pupil of the Blavitsky School of Dance.

One day, Madame told Catherine's class that the school had been asked to provide a troupe of children to play the part of dancing dolls in an opera in Paris. Catherine was among the *petits rats* who were chosen.

Soon afterwards, almost a year after Catherine had last seen her mother, Mr Ralph Knightley re-entered her life, appearing at a student production.

As she danced, Catherine sensed him watching her but later, when she hurried from the dressing room eager for news of home, Mr Knightley had gone.

She asked Madame whether the gentleman would be returning.

'Gentleman?' Madame Irina had actually laughed. ''e is more zan a gentleman. *C'est ton oncle.*'

With those words Catherine felt a chill of fear. *Ton oncle.* Her uncle? An uncle to take care of a *petit rat*? Uncle Ralph.

Madame Irina seemed to think that Catherine was disappointed that her new uncle had left without a word. She laid a tiny hand on Catherine's arm. 'Don't worry, *chérie*,' she said. 'You will see him in Paris. Your uncle will be staying there.'

There was jealousy in class. For some of the other girls, it seemed unfair that Catherine was not only going to Paris but had already found an uncle to look after her. It was not just to dance that they had been sent to the school. With an uncle, the lowliest *petit rat* had the chance to become a famous, great ballerina.

Lying awake that night, Catherine thought of her mother – of how she believed that nothing good could happen to her unless it was with the help of a gentleman.

No. Anything was better than that. Catherine felt within her the strength that she had on the dance floor.

She slipped out of her bed, dressed in her warmest clothes, put her ballet shoes into the pocket of her coat, then went downstairs, opened a window and slipped into the dark autumn night, leaving the Blavitsky School of Dance for ever.

Her plan was simple. She would go home, find her mother and tell her what had happened. Maybe they would face poverty and need, but at least they would be together and free.

With the help of the driver of a brewer's dray who had taken pity on her, Catherine found her way back to the street where she lived.

But when she knocked on the door of the flat, there was no reply. An old man who lived downstairs told her that, some months back, Mrs Lewis had moved away. She had come into some money, he said, had become quite the little lady. He had no idea where she lived now.

As alone as anyone could be, she was a child of the street. She learnt to steal. She scavenged for rags on the waste tips. She discovered where to find scraps of food in the rubbish barrels behind the houses of rich people. The elegant, beautiful dancer who had dreamed of being a ballerina became a darting shadow of the streets and alleys.

Then, one evening, after falling asleep near to Mrs Bailey's pie shop, where she sometimes waited out of sight in the hope of gathering scraps and presents from the shop's customers, something very unusual happened to her.

Luck.

She met me. I saw her, asleep in a doorway, pink shoes held tightly in her hand.

I sat down beside her. We talked. I told her I knew a place where we could shelter.

She smiles now, and I smile back.

'And that was how I became Caz.'

'That was how you became Caz.'

37 The time a taster is most likely to die…

… is when he is learning about poison. At every court ratlings are set to work as soon as they leave their mothers' teat. If they can find food for themselves in the world above, then they are ready to work for the kingdom.

And, very often, die for it.

There is a moment when a taster knows that death is upon them. A strange burning in the throat, the first throb of pain in the stomach. I have seen it in the eyes of my friend and, with an aching heart, have turned away.

A dying rat is a dead rat: there is no real difference in the kingdom. The first lesson that our captains teach us is that, once our life is ending, we are no longer part of the kingdom. It is as true for kings as it is for the humblest citizen.

As captain of the Tasting Court, Alpa has seen many young deaths. More tasters die learning their work than any other citizens, except, of course, for warriors.

Trapped in the Court of Governance, I longed for my old life. I thought of Alpa, and my first lessons with her in the world above.

As night descended on a wood next to the river, we would roam the world above in search of food. A taster's job is simple. We find food left by the enemy in obvious places, by the water's edge, near a path, covered by stones. We smell. We use our tongues, our instinct as tasters, above all our training.

It is said that tasters are brave. The truth is, the possibility of dying does not occur to us.

Yet we do die. I had seen four of my friends go by the time Alpa offered me my first chance to work.

It was a small pile of grain within a pipe. When Alpa sent me in, she must have known that she was giving me my first test.

I approached slowly. Ratlings at the Tasting Court are kept hungry, and the smell of grain was almost irresistible. Then I sensed something else, a sweet smell which might have been in the air or on the pipe.

I ran my nostrils across the grains in the way Alpa had taught me, and in that instant I knew.

I turned, a touch regretfully because I had been hungry, and sprayed the grain.

The scent of a taster on food tells citizens all they need to know.

Nothing which I had done since, even discovering what had happened to King Tzuriel in the world above, made me feel as proud as when I returned to the kingdom that night with my captain.

—You might be good at this.

Her revelation had been so faint that it hardly entered my brain, but it has stayed with me.

I was to serve the kingdom. I was to be a taster.

All that had changed. I was in the Court of Governance, yet none of the courtiers revealed to me. I was at the centre of power in the kingdom, but was powerless to escape. Even before I was fully grown, I was lost.

Soon after I had found Floke and Fang, something strange and frightening happened.

I had been making my way to the chamber where food was left for courtiers when three rats crossed my path. Two of them worked for Swylar. The third, a hesitant older figure walking between them, I thought I recognised. As they approached me, I heard a revelation from the past in my head.

—My name is not important.

Now I knew where I had seen this old rat. It had been he who had awoken me in the early hours and led me to where Floke and Fang were imprisoned. I looked at him, and asked:

—Where are you going?

One of his escorts replied.

—Steadfye is returning to the Court of Warriors.

—Warriors?— I moved closer to them, mystified by what I had been told —Surely he is too old for fighting.

Steadfye sniffed the air.

—I am in need of re-education, it seems.

The second escort nudged him onwards.

—I'm sure we'll be seeing him back here soon enough.

I followed them, revealing as I went.

—This is wrong. Wait!

Without warning, my nostrils were filled with the scent of danger.

—It is essential, ratling Efren.

The revelation was powerful and unmistakeable.

Swylar.

I turned quickly. It was never sensible to have one's back turned to Swylar.

He stood in the shadows nearby. Now he moved closer.

—It is the price of these dangerous times. Security must come before everything. Steadfye was a good enough citizen in his way, but he was unvigilant. He represented a danger to the kingdom. He needs to be re-educated.

—Danger? What did he do?

Swylar turned away and expressed contemptuously, sniffing at what he had done. Glancing in my direction, he revealed.

—Certain incidents showed that he lacked race loyalty. He may look innocent but in his own hopeless way he was as big a danger to the kingdom as a human might be. Oh yes, he definitely needs to be re-educated.

Swylar looked more closely at me, as if something had just occurred to him.

—You didn't know him, did you?

Danger. I smelt it.

—We met once. He did me an act of kindness. It was nothing important.

—In times like these, even kindness can be dangerous.

He lifted a nose imperiously towards the guards. They continued on their way with Steadfye. When I turned back to where Swylar had been standing, he had vanished.

Was I being given a warning? Steadfye had helped me. Now he was being punished, yet another victim of the changes that were taking place at court.

At first they had seemed harmless. They were what happened after one ruler has died and is being replaced by another. The old courtiers, with their traditions of independence, were replaced by younger citizens, often from the Courts of Spying or Translation, who were more loyal to Jeniel and Swylar.

Even the language of revelation seemed to have shifted. Certain words had entered everyday discussions, having first been heard in the speeches of Queen Jeniel. When spoken by the Queen, they had seemed casual. Then those who were close to her at court began to use them. After a while they had become a useful way of displaying loyalty to the new regime, of showing that you were acceptable in the new kingdom.

'Unvigilant', 'security', 'emergency', 'modern', 'safety from fear', 're-education', 'race loyalty': I knew what these phrases meant – or rather what they should mean. Now, though, I saw they had another meaning. They were a secret code among those who belonged at court.

Those who used them possessed race loyalty.

Those who did not were being unvigilant.

The few who were foolish enough to ask questions were almost certainly in urgent need of re-education.

Few of the old guard had survived at court. Quell was still there, using the new language but with a look of distaste on his old face. Grizzlard, now a scuttling bundle of resentment, preferred to remain silent. He was, he knew, too famous within the kingdom to be expelled. Even among subjects, newly fearful of the future, the idea that the great Grizzlard required re-education would cause alarm, perhaps even anger.

I was no hero myself. I learnt to use the new words when appropriate. It was true that I was in the unusual position of being neither a follower of Jeniel nor part of the old court. My reputation, so far, had served to protect me: I was Efren, the ratling who had followed King Tzuriel into the camp of the enemy and had brought back news of his fate. I could not be removed from the court without questions being asked. In fact, my release of Floke and Fang suggested that I had a small sort of power in the kingdom.

But what was I meant to be doing at court? Where was my duty? I was spending too much of my time thinking of what had been, longing to be somewhere else. All I wanted was to be a citizen working for the kingdom once more.

The evening after I had seen Steadfye being taken to the Court of Warriors, I decided that it was time to pay a visit on Swylar.

In our empire, movement is power. The restlessness which you might have seen in rodents as they quest for food is part of our lives. Nothing that is alive remains still for long. Day by day, every court is expanding and contracting, changing and moving.

Since the beginning of this story, the kingdom had moved along the underground river which divides it. The runs and touch-paths connecting to the Great Hollow had changed shape and direction like a snake in the sun.

So the chamber I visited that night, now occupied by Swylar and his followers, had never been home to rats before. It was beneath an old culvert, a dark and rank place through which there ran a thin and regular trickle of human waste leaking from a nearby pipe. It was typical of Swylar to have found a good spot and to have taken it for himself.

Every courtier now knew that, while Queen Jeniel was a busy and powerful ruler, it was Swylar who enforced her wishes. At court he had no title, but then he had little need for one. His power transcended titles.

I was no stranger to fear but, for reasons I had never questioned, I was not afraid of Swylar in the way that other courtiers were. Perhaps it was that if you had been to the world above, had seen the savagery of humankind at close quarters, had survived the claws and teeth of a cat, then the power of a sleek and soft-skinned rat, even one favoured by a queen, was less impressive than it might have been.

I was surprised to find, early in the evening, that the courtiers in Swylar's chambers were still slumbering, their bodies tangled comfortably together in the dry part of the room.

For a moment, I stood before them, aware for the first time that there was a scent in the room I was unable to identify.

—Is Swylar here?

My revelation, when it came, expressed more confidence than I felt.

The bodies stirred. Several pairs of eyes shone from the hill of pelts. Those who ran with Swylar, I had noticed, had begun also to look like him, with the same sleek, dark grey skin, the same way of looking at you through narrowed eyes as if they had sensed something untrustworthy which no other rat could see.

Slowly the bodies were peeling away from a central rat who had been all but obscured by them.

Swylar.

—Efren, the brave little ratling. What a pleasure.

—Can we be alone?— I asked.

As if in reply, Swylar raised his snout.

—These are senior colleagues of mine, Loyter, Clonin, Slathe. I hope you are not telling me that you have secrets from them. This is no time for secrets— Swylar gave a silky smile —An emergency in the kingdom is a moment for sharing.

—I want to return to my court.

Swylar closed his eyes briefly, but did not respond.

—I shall take Floke and Fang. Fang is no good as a warrior

now and Floke has seen too much to be trusted by you. Alpa, my captain at the Tasting Court, will find a use for both of them.

—The Tasting Court. What are you talking about, ratling?

—I need to be of use in the kingdom. At least as a taster I can do my duty. Here at court, I am useless.

Swylar's eyes remained closed and, for a moment, he seemed to have drifted off to sleep once more. His revelation, when it came, was gentle, almost caressing in its tone.

—Oh, you have your uses, Efren, and it is not for citizens to decide where their duty lies. But, as it happens, I would like you to return to the Tasting Court…

My stomach lurched in excitement.

—… but only as a messenger— Swylar continued —There is to be a great event in the kingdom and it is important that all citizens are present. You shall instruct Alpa to attend. You may even order her as courtier. Would you like to give an order to your own captain, ratling?

Around me, Swylar's followers snickered in appreciation.

—And, after that, may I stay there?

—Please attend to what I say. There is a great event. You must be there. After that, the Queen may agree to let you make your decision. Or she may not.

—And what is it, this meeting?

Swylar seemed bored with the conversation. He yawned then curled his body around that of his neighbour, Slathe. It was in that moment that I recognised the unfamiliar scent that was hanging in the air. It was power.

—Leave us now— Swylar's revelation came from the mass of bodies— We have matters of state to discuss.

38 Every day I spend working for the doctor brings a surprise…

… and it is usually a nasty one. With Bill Grubstaff, the pennies may be few and the work hard, but I know they have been earned doing honest work, catching beasts or lugging them to a pit night.

With the doctor, it is different. When I arrive at his house, I never know what he wants from me. His hatred of beasts is strange.

War on rats. It just seems mad to me.

It is late one morning, a few days after the massacre at the Cock Inn, when Caz and I walk together towards the centre of town.

These days she wears ragged flannel shorts and an old coat we found on some waste ground. With a pair of old scissors, I have cut her hair short. It is safer being a boy than a girl when she is out in the town.

Most days we wait near the taverns where the townspeople eat – scraps are always to be had there.

Then she makes her way to the part of the town where there are restaurants and halls and theatres. If people are waiting for their entertainment, she dances for them until her legs ache and her feet are sore.

Sometimes there is as much as eight pence in her pocket by the time she returns to the tip where her pet rat Malaika awaits her in the cage I found for her.

Today my afternoon is to be spent with the doctor. He has been in a strange humour since the night of his disaster at the institute.

We have looked for rats once or twice but have found none.

He is more silent than he used to be, but now and then says something to me which makes me worry about what is going on in his head.

The enemy is on the attack. War has been declared.

The interruption to his lecture was no accident, he believes. It was the enemy's work.

I have said nothing as usual, but I begin to wonder where this madness is leading.

'Ah, Mr Smith. You're here.'

The doctor opens the front door and turns back into the darkness of his house.

When I follow, he leads me not to his laboratory as he usually does, but to a small office next door to it.

The desk by the window can hardly be seen for the papers and scientific books that are upon it.

There is a simple wooden chair in front of the desk. A small pair of trousers and a grey coat are hanging over the back of it.

'Change of clothes for you, Mr Smith.' The doctor speaks briskly. 'The gentlemen at the institute – those important men of science – seemed to think you were some kind of street urchin. Didn't, er, exactly help my case, did it?'

Not expecting an answer, he holds the clothes out, then shakes them impatiently.

'Come on, boy. You may be a simpleton but at least you'll look the part of an office boy from now on.'

I turn my back, take off my rough and dirty clothing. I'm about to put on the jacket and trousers when the doctor looks up from the desk where he now sits.

'Oh, for pity's sake, go and wash yourself in the bathroom,' he says. 'And use the soap.'

Five minutes later, and I am back in the doctor's office, my skin scrubbed, my hair brushed, and wearing clothes which feel oddly cool and smooth against my skin.

He looks me up and down. 'A haircut and you will almost look respectable,' he says coldly.

He stands up, placing some papers in a Gladstone bag.

'We are to make an official visit this afternoon to a Mr Valentine Petheridge MP. You know what MP means, Mr Smith?'

I shake my head.

'Member of Parliament. He is what we call a politician. Not a very bright or successful politician, it is true, but a very ambitious one.'

He walks to the door. I follow.

'Other politicians fight great campaigns about factories or slaves or war or even women, but Mr Petheridge has never found one which suits him. That's our job, Mr Smith.'

He turns as he opens the front door to lead us out, and looks down at me. 'You don't understand any of this, do you?'

I look at him with as blank an expression as I can manage. He closes the door behind us.

'Still, you have your uses.'

39 I had never heard of the Justice Room...

... but it was to that place that I was summoned soon after my return from the Tasting Court.

It was in the ruins of some small human habitation that had been buried deep in the earth. The remains of three of its walls were still standing, giving it a prison-like look. When I arrived, most of the courtiers were already there, waiting in place around the edge of the gouge.

There was something different about this place. It had none of the bustling and business of everyday life at court. It seemed to me, as I entered, keeping as low and invisible as was possible, that there was a scent of cruelty in the air.

I stood near to Loyter, the friend of Swylar.

—What is happening?

Loyter expressed casually, and then turned to me.

—In the Justice Room, there tends to be justice.

—Will the Queen be here?

Loyter looked at me for a moment, as if surprised that such a question could be asked.

—The Queen likes to see justice being done. It is one of her special interests.

I moved away. I had learned that it was unwise for a courtier to ask too many questions. Queen Jeniel and Swylar discouraged curiosity.

I crouched at the back of the throng and waited. I had been away less than a day, but something had changed in the court.

My visit to the Tasting Court had not gone well. When I had first appeared at the warren of runs that I knew so well, I had been mobbed and bundled over by my old friends. But Alpa, who arrived some moments later drawn by the noise the young rats were making, had seemed somehow colder than I remembered.

She was not pleased to see me. When she approached, her hackles rose. She whiffled, sniffing at my breath, almost as if I were a stranger to her court.

—What does the Court of Governance want of us, Efren?

I crouched, less a courtier now than a ratling.

—I wanted to see you all. I want to return.

Slowly, Alpa's hackles settled on her back.

—You have left us, Efren. Your future is at court. You have other friends now.

I had been about to reveal again, when Alpa interrupted.

—And I know that is not why you are here.

How had she known? What is it about a doe rat that makes each of them able to tell what we are about to reveal before we have even thought it? As I hesitated, she revealed once more.

—You are here about the court's business, aren't you?

I stood. Somehow, crouching now seemed wrong. Whether I liked it or not, I was now a courtier. With an odd sense of shame, I began to reveal. I passed on the message Swylar had given me about the great event, how it was the duty of all citizens to attend such occasions, particularly at a time of emergency and when war had been declared on fear.

As I revealed, I was aware that even my old friends, who knew me so well, were looking at me differently. Everything I said and did now set me apart from them. The way I addressed them. The strength of my revelation. Perhaps even the way I stood and walked. These things all reminded them that I was now a member of the ruling court. I may have felt equal to the tasters, but they no longer felt equal to me.

There was nothing left for me to do. More coolly now, I bade them farewell, then approached Alpa. I nudged her with my nose, just as I used to.

—Will we meet after the gathering?

To my surprise, her eyes softened. She rubbed against me, reminding me of a time when I was younger and life was easier.

—We shall see what happens, Efren— She looked at me sadly, almost as if she were saying goodbye —We shall see what happens.

Back in the Justice Room, the rats in front of me stirred, their teeth chattering. I stood on my hind legs to see what was going on.

At the end of the chamber stood three rats: Swylar, Slathe and another new courtier whom I had never seen before. Beyond them, on a ledge looking down on the scene with an expression of stern dignity, was Queen Jeniel.

Each side of the chamber heaved with courtiers who pressed against each other, chattering with excitement. Now and then, a high angry scream could be heard above the noise as a fight broke out.

Something else. I now realised that on my side of the Justice Room were gathered the followers of Jeniel and Swylar, young rats who had been introduced to the court under the new regime, the so-called 'loyalists'. Facing us across the room were those who had been at court during the days of Tzuriel, those now known as 'traditionalists'. They looked wide-eyed and afraid.

Swylar began his revelation to the gathering.

—Your Majesty— He turned to the Queen and lowered his head —Members of the Court of Governance. We have entered a time of peril for the kingdom. The enemy has declared war upon us by cruelly assassinating our king. We face hidden danger from the world above. We also face betrayal from within.

There was angry chattering from the loyalists. Some of the traditionalists shrank back in fear, pressing themselves against the wall.

—It is subtle, this betrayal— Swylar continued —Sometimes it goes under the name of 'traditional values', or 'the right of rats to question' or even 'freedom'. But it is a poison which will weaken us as we go to war.

The smell of anger was in the air now. The rats around me jostled and nipped one another impatiently. My eyes were drawn to Jeniel. She gazed over the head of her subjects as if none of this had anything to do with her.

Swylar moved forward as his revelation became so piercing that it seemed to hammer within my brain.

—Courtiers, I am ashamed to have to tell you that the poison is in every part of the kingdom. Loyalty tribunals are being set up in each court. They shall show that peace can only come through strength. As the greatest court in the land, we must set an example to our citizens. When it comes to the betrayal of the uncommitted, we shall prove that no one is above our law.

He nodded to Slathe, who raised his snout self-importantly and announced:

—Bring out the prisoner!

There was a movement to my left. Two figures were standing in front of a row of guards at the entrance to the chamber. The senior courtier Quell was one and, at first, I failed to recognise the other rat who, if such a thing were possible, actually seemed older than Quell. His brown coat was dull, and his flesh hung loosely from his bones which protruded from the skin. There was a fresh scar across the rat's shoulder. Only when it raised its eyes from the ground and levelled them defiantly at Swylar did I realise who it was.

Grizzlard.

Slowly, and with painful dignity, the two of them advanced between the ranks of courtiers in a silence only broken by the sound of Quell's wheezing breath. When they reached the end of the chamber, Quell looked beyond the three judges to where Queen Jeniel was sitting.

—I have come to speak for a great warrior and courtier who has been treated disrespectfully and who should not be in this place, Your Majesty.

The Queen stared ahead in silence. As if the words had been directed to him, Swylar replied.

—You are here, Quell, to defend the traitor?

The old rat's eyes remained on the Queen.

—Your Majesty, Grizzlard is not a traitor and he needs no defence beyond the history of his life. He has brought honour and sacrifice to the kingdom. What is in question here is whether there is now a place for those who express any kind of disagreement with those who are in power.

For the first time, the Queen looked down at Quell.

—We can discuss philosophical matters later, old friend— She showed her teeth, her favourite gesture of friendship —But first it is time for matters of the law.

She inclined her head in the direction of Swylar, but Quell was not finished.

—Where is The Twyning?

I sensed an unease in the Justice Room. Loyalists and traditionalists looked about them, sniffing the air, as if somehow the presence of thirty rats, their tails grown together, had been overlooked.

Quell revealed more strongly.

—When great decisions are made in the kingdom, The Twyning must be present to give its verdict. It is a matter of freedom. Where is—

Swylar darted forward and, with a squeal, bit Quell on the shoulder. At any other time, the warrior would have fought back and soon Swylar would have retreated. Now he merely shifted away.

—There is only one freedom that matters in a time of war— Swylar's eyes were on Queen Jeniel —And that is the freedom from fear. I have discussed the fate of the traitors with The Twyning. It is in agreement with the court and our queen, and has graciously allowed us to deliver its verdict.

Moving more closely to Quell, Swylar continued. Now his revelation was low and dangerous.

—You talk of rights, Quell. What of the right of the kingdom not to be conquered by the enemy? Those who are not prepared to go to war for the kingdom, the uncommitted, can play no part in it. There is no room for the questioning, the doubting, the morally feeble, no matter how distinguished they might have been before they grew— he hesitated, then delivered the final word like the crack of a whip —old.

As Quell seemed to sag in defeat, Grizzlard stepped forward. When he revealed, his words had none of the fire or strength that they once had when he had been a great warrior and claimant to the throne.

—Leave Quell, Swylar. Your dispute is with me.

—There is no dispute, only a case of treason, you miserable old traitor!

Swylar turned to Slathe who announced:

—The court summons its first witness. Efren!

For a moment, I thought there must be another Efren present in the Justice Room. Then Loyter pushed me forward through the crowd and into the centre of the room.

I looked around. Staring eyes. Curious. Suspicious. Surprised. Hostile. What was this ratling doing at the centre of the Justice Room in a great trial? I made my way to stand beside Grizzlard, in front of the tribunal.

Swylar gazed coldly at me and began to reveal.

—Young Efren. You see the accused standing beside you? Is he the courtier Grizzlard?

—He is.

—When you returned from the world above, having witnessed the torture and assassination of our great king Tzuriel, did you go to see Grizzlard?

—I saw Queen Jeniel and then Grizzlard.

—Saw and revealed?

—Yes.

—You told of the cruelty, the humiliation and the death of our great king.

—Yes.

—And did Grizzlard grow angry? Did he talk of war?

—He was sad. He said Tzuriel had been his closest friend in all the kingdom.

—No word of revenge, then?

—It was not the moment. He—

—Or surprise that humankind had done this terrible thing?

—Not at that time.

—Thank you, Efren. You are young but already you have served the kingdom well.

That was it. The conversation has remained with me every day since it took place. I wanted to say more, to explain how the great warrior was innocent. I looked at Grizzlard, hoping to convey my regret, but he was staring at the ground.

I returned to my place. Swylar summoned the next witness.

So the case continued. One courtier testified that Grizzlard had expressed fears as to where Jeniel would take the kingdom. Another said that Grizzlard opposed war. A third had been told that Grizzlard distrusted Swylar. Listening, even I began to believe that perhaps it was true. By expressing doubt at a time when war approached, Grizzlard and those like him, the uncommitted, had put the kingdom in danger of the enemy.

Eventually, with obvious impatience, Swylar addressed the accused.

—Grizzlard, speak.

The old warrior gazed hard at Swylar, fire in his eyes, exposing his yellow teeth, still strong in spite of his age. For a moment it seemed as if what remained of his fighting spirit might launch him at the neck of his enemy. When he revealed, there was an icy contempt in his words.

—All my life, I have been loyal to the kingdom. I have risked my life for it many times. Anyone who knows me will know that I would never do anything to harm or to weaken it. I shall take the accusations made against me one by one.

But, as Grizzlard continued, Swylar turned to his fellow

judges and casually began to click his teeth together, an impatient snickering sound.

For a moment, Grizzlard persisted, addressing the back of Swylar's head, but then he faltered and fell silent.

Swylar continued making the noise for several moments. Then he seemed to become aware that the accused had stopped revealing.

—Was that it?

The question was sharp, as insulting as a tail lashed across Grizzlard's face.

—You were not listening, Swylar.

—So that was it then?

—If I may now continue—

—The accused has completed his defence. We shall now consider our verdict.

Before Grizzlard could say anything else, the three judges had turned in upon themselves and were in low discussion. The moment of consultation lasted no more than a few seconds. Then, with an air of boredom that suggested that the court had many more important matters to consider, Swylar delivered the verdict.

—This court finds the accused guilty. The usual sentence will be applied. The Court of Correction will be summoned to the Great Hollow. Citizens of the new kingdom should see that justice is for all.

Quell attempted to move forward to address the courtiers, but three young warrior rats barred his way.

Swylar was about to continue, when another revelation rent the air.

—No! This is wrong.

There was a moment of astonished silence in the Justice Room. The voice was not of an old courtier, but of a ratling. He was not among the traditionalists but standing at the back of the loyalists.

Me.

I heard only the thumping of my own heartbeat.

I revealed again, more quietly now.

—This is wrong.

Before I could say any more, the warrior rats were upon me.

40 The trousers and coat the doctor has given me…

… are made for summer. I sit upon the dicky of the carriage, shivering, as we make our way across town to see the politician, Mr Valentine Petheridge MP.

We travel to a part of the town which I have never seen, with large houses, each like a palace, overlooking a great park. Nervously I walk behind the doctor as he climbs the wide steps to the front door.

A maid in a uniform opens the door and shows us in. We are led through a hallway with pictures of great men from history looking down at us. The maid opens a heavy door at the end of a corridor.

We walk into a large room with leather-bound books on every wall. There is a smell of cigar smoke in the air.

'Sir.' The maid speaks nervously in the direction of the leather armchair with a newspaper covering it. 'Your guest is here.'

There is a movement beneath the paper, a pair of hands, then a head of thinning hair. Finally, a pale face, with watering eyes blinking behind heavy spectacles, appears over the top of it.

As Mr Petheridge looks at us, like a man who has just been awakened and is not sure whether he is dreaming or not, the doctor directs me to a nearby corner with a little shooing movement of his left hand.

'Val, it has been too long.'

He advances, his hand outstretched.

The politician looks confused.

'Remind me again.'

'Ross-Gibbon,' said the doctor, shaking the politician's hand.

'Doesn't mean a thing, I'm afraid.' The politician's voice is thin and impatient, like someone who has had a toothache for several days.

'We were up at Trinity together.' The doctor's smile is looking a little uncertain now. 'You dined in my rooms. We went beagling.'

Mr Petheridge seems to notice me for the first time. Blinking from behind his glasses, he asks, 'What's the child doing here?'

'Mr Smith is my assistant,' says the doctor. 'We shall need him later.'

'Later?' Mr Petheridge makes no attempt to conceal his alarm. 'There's going to be a later?'

The doctor moves towards a leather armchair.

'May I take a seat?' he asks.

The politician gives a bored wave of his hand. When the doctor lowers himself into the armchair, it is so deep that he almost disappears from my sight.

'I believe,' he says, 'that I have a plan which will help you with the next election.'

'A mouse!' Mr Petheridge sits up suddenly in his chair, awake at last. He gives a little reedy laugh. 'You were the mouse man.'

'Well, actually—'

'I distinctly remember you now. The Gibbon, we called you. We had a dinner one night and the girl sitting next to you asked you what subject you were reading. You pulled a mouse out of your pocket. There was quite a scene. Old Gibbon. Well I never.'

'It was a pygmy shrew, actually.'

The MP continues to chuckle to himself. 'The mouse man, goodness me. Rummest thing I ever saw while I was up at Cambridge.'

The doctor purses his lips. He is looking pale now.

'Mouse at dinner, never seen such a thing.' Mr Petheridge shakes his head. After a few moments, he pulls himself together. 'Still, we were young then. No time for mice these days, eh, Ross-Gibbon? What are you up to now?'

The doctor clears his throat. 'Rats, actually.'

That sets the MP off again. 'Oh, very good,' he laughs loudly, slapping the arm of his chair. 'You've become quite a joker since we left Cambridge. But seriously…'

There is an awkward pause. When the doctor speaks, it is in a quiet, dignified voice.

'I wasn't joking, actually. I am a scientist, and my current field of research is *rattus norvegicus*, the brown rat.'

'Oh dear. What a funny thing for a chap to be doing.'

'The rat, Val, is our most deadly enemy. It is all around us. The female is fertile within three weeks of producing a litter. They reproduce at an astonishing rate. When they first arrived in the city of Selkirk last century, there were so many runs and burrows that the townspeople feared that buildings would collapse.'

The MP's interest seems to have shifted to something outside. He gazes out of the window, looking bored.

'Rats kill children, every year, Val. They can live off anything – rotten food, roots, eggs, young birds. They swim rivers and catch fish. D'you know, they can bite through metal? Their jaws are among the strongest in the animal kingdom. And their population—'

'Look, I'm sure this is all terribly interesting but what exactly has it got to do with me, Gibbon?' The MP suddenly sounds rather annoyed. 'I'm a busy man, you know.'

'So I see.'

The doctor speaks coldly.

'I'm a member of parliament,' says Mr Petheridge sulkily. 'It's a jolly important job.'

'And are you likely to remain so?' The doctor's voice is lower now, almost threatening.

'Of course. I... I... I think I'm quite a popular chap.' In his desperation, the MP darts a panicky grin towards me, as if to prove how nice he can be to ordinary people.

'My information is that you will lose next year's election unless something dramatic happens,' says the doctor.

'My enemies might say that but—'

'I can make something dramatic happen.'

'Oh, really, Gibbon? With your rats? Are they going to vote for me?' A nastiness has entered the MP's voice.

The doctor sits forward in his chair.

'What you need is a campaign that will make you loved and famous among voters. At the moment, we are poisoning the rat. And we are making it stronger! My research shows that poisoning these animals merely makes them breed faster, and the next generation stronger and bigger. Eradicate them from your constituency and you will be a hero.'

The MP does not look impressed by the idea.

'Does it really have to be rats?' he asks.

'Did Sir Joseph Bazalgette say, "Does it have to be sewers?" Yet now he is one of the most famous men in the country.'

'I can't see *The Times* writing stories about rats.'

'They are killing babies, Val. You will be saving the lives of little ones.'

The MP shows a flicker of interest.

'Babies are always good, I must admit.' He sighs, still uncertain, then asks moodily, 'What sort of campaign did you have in mind?'

'I shall organise it all. It shall be a war against the rats of your constituency. But you will lead our campaign to victory. You will be a man of the people.'

The MP gives a little smile. 'Man of the people, eh? That would be rather good. How long would this campaign take?'

'I think...' Dr Ross-Gibbon frowns like a man making a complicated calculation in his head. 'I think we could complete the whole operation in time for the next election.'

He beckons to me. 'Mr Smith, bring me my maps and papers.'
I lift the case and walk across the book-lined room.
We have our politician.

41   I have never been more alone…

… than I was that day, imprisoned, in the Justice Room. My company consisted of two old rats facing death and ten warriors, under the captaincy of Slathe, who were guarding the entrance.

I realised that to every one of them I was a traitor.

For the younger warriors, I was the fool who had been given the chance to escape from the Tasting Court and had done nothing with it. Now and then one of them would swagger across to me, say something boneheaded and insulting, then climb on my back contemptuously or turn his back on me and spray in my direction.

Grizzlard and Quell remembered only that I had been one of Swylar's witnesses. In their eyes, I saw that I was just another small disappointment in a bitter, ungrateful world.

Night must have been falling when there were sounds of activity outside the Justice Room. The warriors parted, and Swylar stood in the doorway. He sniffed haughtily in the direction of Grizzlard and Quell.

—The kingdom awaits you, distinguished courtiers.

There was an excited snickering among the guards.

Slowly, painfully, Grizzlard stood. He stared defiantly at Swylar for a moment, then shuffled towards the door. Quell followed him.

As they reached him, Swylar seemed to remember me.

—Oh, and the little loyal subject will come too. For his reward.

Eyes down, I approached, anxious to avoid the painful attentions of the guards.

Swylar looked at me. His revelation was quiet, almost pitiful.

—Fool. The chances I gave you. An insignificant little taster becomes a member of the Court of Governance. And where does he end up? In the Justice Room prison.

I was facing death. There was nothing to lose now. I turned to him, standing as tall as I could. Our noses were almost touching. Behind me I sensed the guards moving closer.

—I did what was right, Swylar.

One of the guards nearby bit me hard on the shoulder. I made no sound.

Grizzlard turned to me. For the first time that day, I scented friendliness.

—Die honourably, ratling— The revelation was low, weak — Your friends will remember you.

With that, he walked into the ranks of the guards, and out of the door.

—I will, Grizzlard.

It was a short procession to the Great Hollow. As we entered, I saw that it was as full as it had been when the kingdom had gathered to bid farewell to King Tzuriel.

But there was no acclamation, no chattering of teeth now. The three of us, the condemned, appeared on the Rock of State to a tense silence.

I looked around. What seemed like a million eyes were fixed on me. I wondered where Alpa was, what she would be thinking of her ratling now. Pride? Shame? Regret that she had ever been my captain?

Queen Jeniel, I noticed, had found herself a ledge to the right of the Rock of State from where she looked down, involved yet above the proceedings in her Court of Governance. She looked only slightly interested.

My eyes searched for The Twyning. It was in its normal place, close to the Rock of State, but there was something strange and lifeless about it. The many heads rested upon the ground. There was no movement or sound from them. They breathed quietly, each gazing emptily into space, none showing the slightest interest in what was happening around them. Something terrible had happened to The Twyning.

—Citizens!

Swylar revealed from the very place where Grizzlard, not so many sunrises ago, had addressed the congregation as a courtier about to become king.

—The Court of Governance has been at work on behalf of the kingdom. It has considered three cases which have struck at the very heart of our safety at a time of peril. I call the traitor Grizzlard!

The guards attempted to move Grizzlard, but he shook himself free, and walked slowly to the centre of the Rock of State. For a few moments, he gazed out sadly at the thousands of citizens before him.

Swylar turned his back and scratched himself, then glanced in the direction of the Queen. She raised her head slowly.

It was time.

Behind me I heard a movement, and suddenly the choking scent of terror was in the air. I heard the revelations all around me, from citizens and courtiers alike.

—The Court of Correction.

—The correctors are here.

Turning, I saw a group of rats slouching their way towards the front of the rock.

Only Grizzlard seemed unafraid. He turned slowly to face those who were here to destroy him.

The correctors, young rats from the Court of Correction, were widely feared throughout the kingdom. Neither as strong nor as brave as warriors, they were chosen because they had a talent and a taste for inflicting pain. Some had been badly treated as ratlings, others had suffered misfortunes and unhappiness which had nurtured within them a useful hatred of the world. A few were just very unpleasant and ill-adjusted. Together, they were ideally suited to do some of the kingdom's nastier tasks.

Grizzlard, a warrior to the last, made the first move. Teeth bared, he hurled his bulky figure in the direction of the passage. Instantly, his body disappeared beneath the bustling fur of the correctors. Squealing with delight, they swarmed over his old body like pups around their mother's teats.

I looked away and found myself looking into the eyes of Swylar. He held my look for a moment, then yawned.

The struggle seemed to last for ever. Unused to open fighting, the correctors made the mistake of turning the old fighter on to his back in the hope of reaching his throat.

It was his teeth that they met. As Grizzlard flipped and squirmed, his razor-sharp incisors slashed the flesh of his tormentors, now and then closing swiftly and decisively upon the jugular of one of his attackers.

But as some fell back, others arrived from the darkness of the passage behind us. One leg was held fast, then another. Soon all four were in the teeth of young rats and the bucking, tugging and writhing became weaker.

They turned him over, holding him face down upon the damp earth. An older corrector, with a withered rear leg, limped forward, then closed his jaws about the base of Grizzlard's skull between his ears, forcing his chin to the ground.

For the briefest instant, the mass was still. Grizzlard ceased struggling. Panting with exhaustion, held on all sides and pinned down from above, he awaited his fate.

There was a movement from the passage. The way cleared for an older, slightly smaller figure.

—Ozorka.

The revelation was from a courtier.

I had heard of Ozorka but had never seen her. It was said that she was the cruellest corrector that there had been for generations, that she willingly entered her own ratlings into the Court of

Correction, mistreating them from the day that they were born to ensure that the family gift of inflicting pain lived on in them.

Could it be true? She looked unremarkable, ordinary, slightly plump. Were it not for the tracery of ancient scars around her mouth and neck, she might have been a stalwart of the Court of Breeders or a minor translator.

She advanced upon the tangle of bodies. In no hurry, she walked round the pinioned figure of Grizzlard, inspecting the handiwork of the members of her court.

Then, casually, she did a terrible thing. She clambered clumsily on to the courtier's back. Enraged, he bucked and squirmed but Ozorka held on. No one had been prepared for this level of humiliation. For any doe to clamber on the back of a buck in an imitation of the act of fathering was the ultimate insult. For a plump, matronly doe to commit the act upon a once-great courtier shocked even those who had seen the House of Correction at work.

She fastened her teeth into Grizzlard's neck in such a way that he seemed paralysed. The correctors released him, moved back, so that for all the world it looked as if Grizzlard had wished this grotesque act of mock carrying to take place.

Ozorka writhed casually for what seemed a lifetime. Satisfied at last that Grizzlard was truly degraded, she slid off his body. He remained motionless. An odd chattering sound could be heard. The correctors were mocking their victim.

Ozorka moved to stand in front of Grizzlard. Nose twitching, she lowered her head and sniffed at the dark eyes that were looking up at her in silent, powerless rage.

From the direction of Swylar there came a small stir of impatience and it was at that moment, when Grizzlard's attention slipped away, that Ozorka made a neat, little darting movement towards his head. She seemed to nod at him, striking him briskly in the forehead.

When she stepped back, a bloody morsel hung dripping from her teeth. Where Grizzlard's left eye had been, there was now a glistening red socket.

Ozorka shook her head and the eye skittered across the floor, to be collected proudly by one of the younger correctors.

It was at that moment when I heard within me, with the searing intensity that only a rat blessed with the gift of a hearer could experience, the sound of a mortal scream. I closed my eyes, as my body was wracked with the pain of a fellow rat.

Loyter nipped me, hard.

—Look and learn, ratling.

Ozorka had returned her attention to Grizzlard. The warrior closed his remaining eye in defeated resignation, awaiting the strike.

Ozorka looked slowly in the direction of Swylar.

Calmly, Swylar seemed to notice a scrap of something or other on his right paw. He nibbled at it as casually as if he had been alone and unwatched.

That was enough for Ozorka. She moved towards Grizzlard. As if to show her younger correctors that there are many different ways to remove an eye, she lowered her teeth slowly towards the warrior's right eye, then stabbed downwards. When she looked about, a gory burden hanging from her teeth, the damage upon Grizzlard's face was messier, with blood pouring from the open wound that had been a socket.

Flicking the eye over her shoulder, Ozorka gave a signal to three of the correctors who stood nearby.

With undisguised pleasure, they pushed forward and, like creatures who had been starved of food for days, they fell upon Grizzlard's right ear, tearing its delicate flesh with their teeth.

Now, for the first time, a scream filled the throat of Grizzlard. The smell of terror was in the air. I thought of the end of Tzuriel in the world above.

When all that was left of both ears were two small, uneven ridges of glistening gristle, the rats who had been holding Grizzlard released him.

Somehow, the courtier managed to stand. A line of correctors was behind him so that there was only one way for him to go. He staggered towards the lip of the stage, then dropped in to the river. The water reddened with his blood and for a moment it seemed as if Grizzlard would drown before the eyes of the kingdom, but his body twitched. Gently, he was carried downstream towards the world above.

After he had disappeared from view, the correctors turned their attention to Quell.

42 I walk the dark streets of the town, ahead of the doctor…

… carrying a heavy metal box. We have returned from our visit to Mr Petheridge, and the doctor is in high spirits. When I make to leave, he tells me we must go out to work this evening.

'There's a shilling in it for you, Mr Dogboy Smith,' he says.

I have no choice. Caz will be expecting me back at the tip, but there is no arguing with the doctor, and there is no arguing with the shilling.

It is hard work. I am carrying a heavy metal case containing three bottles which the doctor has taken out of a locked cold cabinet in the laboratory. I can feel it contains liquid of some sort, and I worry.

We are walking towards the place the river emerges from underground, but the doctor seems anxious not to be too close to the case I am carrying. He follows, twenty yards behind me. Now and then, he shouts out directions. 'Carry it carefully,' he says. 'As if your life depended on it.'

I fear it does.

We reach the path by the river where we found the giant rat.

Still standing a distance away from me, the doctor tells me to place the metal case on the ground.

When I have done so, he approaches slowly, his eyes on the box, as if some fierce creature might jump out of it at any moment.

He points to the road, up a slope from where we are.

'There is a drain up there,' he says. 'Together we shall lift the cover. Then you shall drop the bottles into the cavern below.

When we hear the bottles break, we shall cover the drain post-haste.'

I say nothing, as usual, but the doctor behaves as if I have asked a question.

'There is nothing to worry about, Mr Smith. We're killing rats with a little poison of my own making. Tomorrow, our new friend Mr Petheridge will ask the local sewerage company if he can check the underground sewer for signs of rodents. They will find thousands of corpses.'

He gives a little smile.

'I shall be standing over there.' He nods in the direction of a nearby bridge.

Poison. Now I am truly worried, and the expression on my face shows it.

'You need not be concerned so long as you do what I say.' The doctor rubs his hands together, although it is not particularly cold. 'Tomorrow we shall show the world just how many rats there are down there. It will be the start of our great campaign.'

I say nothing.

'Now, Dogboy.' The doctor points to one of the bottles. When he speaks, it is slowly and deliberately, as if to a fool. 'Poison. When bottles break, they will release fluid. When it reaches the water below, vapour will be released.'

Now I understand why the doctor has been keeping a distance from me. But when he points to the drain, I nod.

Together we lift the heavy wooden cover off the drain. Then he moves away. He smiles at me but looks nervous.

'Open the case,' he calls out.

Carefully I do so, feeling the cold air from the ice on my face.

The bottles packed into the ice are filled with a clear liquid. The glass looks unusually thin.

'Now, be careful, Mr Smith.' The doctor looks around him. 'The bottles break very easily. Pick one up very slowly, then drop it down the drain.'

With two fingers, I lift the bottle out of the ice. The liquid within is heavy. I hold it over the drain, and drop it.

Below us, there is a sound of glass shattering.

'Now the other two – quickly!' The doctor holds a white handkerchief over his mouth.

The second bottle falls and breaks, then the third. With his mouth still covered, he moves forward and, with me, lifts the cover back over the opening in the ground.

For a moment we stand over the drain as if expecting to hear sounds of death from below us.

The town is unusually silent.

'Well done, Dogboy.' The doctor folds his handkerchief and returns it to his pocket. Squaring his shoulders, he sets off down the path in the direction of his house. He is talking to himself, as I pick up the case and follow him.

'The war has begun,' he says.

43 I stood, ready for death on the Rock of State...

... with the citizens of the kingdom before me, waiting.

It was not terror that I felt, nor rage. Pain, yes, but even that felt distant. Death is wisdom. In that cold moment when you know for certain that all is over, you understand the truth.

And it is not fear you feel, but love and pity for those around you.

The citizens, staring up at you on the Rock of State, their eyes wide as if afraid to look away for even the merest moment. The courtiers, uneasy in spite of themselves, about what was going on. The queen, pretending (badly) to be asleep on the ledge overlooking the Rock. Swylar, never entirely present, always scheming the next move.

Even the correctors, those poor lost souls. As they moved towards me, I smelt the sadness on them. Their only language was pain. Hurting others was how they felt alive.

It was as I faced my death that I changed for ever. I loved the kingdom. I loved the citizens. At my most helpless moment, I felt strong.

—Efren.

The revelation of Swylar was a sharp stab to the brain.

—Yours is a sad case. So young, so foolish, so utterly evil.

I turned to face him. Mine had been a short life, but at least it would end with honour.

—I am innocent, Swylar. As you know.

—The Court of Justice has decided. Those who help and

support traitors— He turned and faced the citizens of the kingdom —are traitors themselves. However young, however stupid. Loyalty is such an easy thing, after all. We all understand what loyalty is, don't we?

A rustling of agreement spread across the Great Hollow. Only The Twyning remained still.

—Of course we do— Swylar stood on the edge of the Rock of State —Those who put our kingdom, our families, our little ones and their little ones in danger by their disloyalty must pay the penalty.

—I am innocent.

Swylar ignored me, but my revelation was strong enough to reach every citizen in that hollow.

In front of me, there was movement among the correctors. They fell back as the large, soft figure of Ozark shuffled forward. Her eyes shone bright. It was for these moments that she lived.

—I am innocent.

Ozark moved closer. Her revelation, when it came, was almost tender.

—Innocent? Ratling, you are innocent only of the true meaning of pain. But not for long.

This, I now knew, was how it would be. No battle with the young torturers of the Court of Correction, no noble fight to the death. The punishment of Grizzlard and Quell had allowed them a sort of honour. Mine would be small, humiliating, a nip delivered to a ratling of the Court of Tasting. A nip that would kill me.

Ozark, a doe rat alone, would face me and finish me.

Fight? I was no warrior. Yet, to the watching kingdom, not to fight would be an admission of my guilt. I bared my teeth. Even to me, it was unconvincing, pathetic.

—Crouch, ratling.

—Innocent.

Now Ozark showed her teeth. They were brown, as if stained by the blood of her thousands of victims.

I stood tall. Once she was on my back, it would soon be over.

She looked at me, not angry but amused by my defiance. Unhurried and confident, she circled me.

As I turned, facing her as she went, something I saw among the courtiers caught my eye.

A rat with one leg missing.

Could it be? The next time Ozark reached the same spot, I looked more closely.

It was my friend Fang. Beside him was Floke, and they were both surrounded by warriors. With even a glance, I could tell they were battered and exhausted. Their pelts, scarred and bloody, hung on them as if somehow they had been hollowed out. Their eyes were dull, half closed. My poor friends had been tortured. What a terrible day it had been for them when I had entered their lives in this very hollow.

There was a splash from the water behind me and, for a trice, Ozark was distracted.

Behind her, high on a ledge, the Queen stirred. She yawned and, as if sensing that Her Majesty was tiring of my little dance with Ozark, the correctors moved closer.

Another splash.

My eyes remained fixed on Ozark; I became aware, from deep within me, of a singing in the blood. Something was wrong.

I am a taster and, even as I faced my death, my senses were alerting me to danger in the air.

From a corner of the Great Hollow, I heard squeals of alarm.

—Poison! Poison!

The other members of the Court of Tasters were sensing it, too. There was restlessness among citizens, the scent of fear.

Near me, Ozark bared her teeth and moved towards me.

Beyond her, I saw a movement in the river. The water was bubbling. A thin blanket of steam covered its dark surface.

Citizens near the banks seemed agitated. They tried to move, but appeared only able to twitch their limbs.

—Danger!

The revelations were louder now.

—Danger in the water!

—Flee, citizens!

The warning in my blood was raging now, but Ozark had only thoughts of death, my death, on her mind. I saw the muscles around her hind quarters tense but, before she could pounce on me, I moved in the one direction where she least expected.

I darted forward, skittering past her and, as the correctors broke ranks to catch me, I hurled myself off the ledge of the Rock of State through the steam and into the bubbling water.

Dive. Dive. I swam deeper and deeper through the foaming waters, defying the scream of warning from within me.

Better to drown than be killed by Ozark.

Keep swimming. Dive. My body was bursting, agonised by lack of air but still I forced myself downwards in the water.

I must have lost consciousness because the next thing I remember was floating to the surface. I took a breath of air. It was like drinking fire. I gulped water, but that only made the pain worse.

What was happening? On the shore nearby, I heard the groans and screams of rats, twitching and writhing, their eyes starting from their agonised bodies. Something was killing the kingdom.

I dived again, and was swept downstream by the river.

Deeper. Deeper. Darkness…

I was floating on the water. My insides felt as if they had been scoured by a knife, but I was alive. There was something bright above me. It was the moon.

I was in the world above.

44 The doctor is happier than I have ever seen him…

… when he finds those dead beasts.

It is the following night and I am at home, in the tip, with Caz. I am tired after another day working with the doctor, but there is a warmth in my heart which comes from a full stomach.

It was not happy work I had done today, but I had made another shilling.

'Do his face.'

Caz lies under the coverlet she has sewn together from rags, sacking, feathers and wool she has found around the tip. The pet rat lies asleep near her hand.

'Go on, do his face, Peter.'

I think of the doctor, how his face seems actually to get longer, his eyes widening, his eyebrows heading for his hairline, when he is excited.

I make the face, and Caz laughs and hugs herself.

She likes my stories. Sometimes it is as if the things I tell her have not really happened, but are part of a storyland which has nothing to do with the two of us, alone with a pet rat in a rubbish tip.

But it is no bedtime story, what happened today. I have told her how the doctor and I went to a small building near the drain where we dropped the poison, how we met two men from the council, Mr Woodcock, a man with a moustache and a stomach which tugs against his waistcoat, and Mr Robinson, a tall man with the look of someone who has just been given some really bad news.

I tell Caz about the arrival of Mr Petheridge in his carriage. He was late and made no attempt to disguise his lack of interest.

'The building wasn't really a house at all, Caz. It was the top of some steps which led underground into the sewer.'

'Was it dark?'

'Pitch black. All the men are carrying lanterns. I'm at the back, trying not to fall into a sewer.'

So the story continues. How we reached a narrow path beside the underground river which looked so dark and slow in the lamplight it might have been molasses.

'I used to love molasses,' Caz murmurs sleepily.

'So there we are, walking beside the river. It smells strong now and when I catch a glimpse of Mr Petheridge's face, I almost burst out laughing. He is looking around him as if a ghost is about to jump out at him.'

'Does he say anything?'

'He turned to the doctor and said, "I really hope this is worth it, Gibbon. I shan't be able to wear this suit in decent company for weeks."'

After about five minutes' walking, there was a bend in the path and the river. Mr Robinson, who was leading us, stopped as we entered a large cavern. He lowered his lantern slowly.

'Oh jeepers. Oh my goodness me.'

'That was Mr Petheridge?'

'It was. He looked as if he was going to faint clean away.'

Ahead of us, the path was blocked by the dead bodies of rats. Beneath the walls nearby, they were two or three deep, as if the beasts had scrabbled to escape.

'Poor things.' Caz placed her hand over her pet rat's head. 'Don't listen, Malaika.'

'So the doctor gave this little speech about the diseases carried by rats. He said he had conducted a little experiment to show the gentlemen from the council how serious the problem was. He said these rats were the tip of the iceberg. Then he went on about the need for a war on rats. I began to fill the sack I had brought with me with the bodies.'

Caz squeezes her eyes shut.

'I was doing what the doctor told me to do,' I explain.

'I don't like the sound of your doctor.'

'While I was filling the sack, the MP, Mr Petheridge, began to speak. He told the men from the council that public health was important with an election coming up. He said he expected the council to support his campaign. He was just beginning to explain how he had called a public meeting, when he gave a little scream.'

'What? Why?'

'He thought he saw something large swimming towards him in the water. He pointed down at it and said, "It's a rat! I think it's still alive." One of the men from the council held his lamp up. "That is not a rat, sir," he said. "Thank goodness," said the MP. "What is it?" "A human turd, sir." "Oh God!" said Mr Petheridge.'

And I make my revolted MP's face again.

Caz laughs. 'What of the sack of rats?'

'The doctor wants it for the public meeting outside the town hall tomorrow. In the morning.'

'More work for Mr Smith.'

'It's a long way to carry a sack of rats.'

'Here's what we shall do,' says Caz. 'We shall go together.'

45 Let me tell you something about rats…

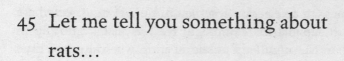

… and why we are strong. No matter what we have been through, however painful a loss, we never look back on sadness. Our duty to the kingdom, to the family, to ourselves is to live, to survive.

It is a simple truth which every citizen understands.

What is, is. What was, lives only in the blood memory. It is now that matters, not then.

I lay within a tangle of dead brambles on the bank of the river. My body ached and I breathed with difficulty. A winter sun was in the sky. The light around me was clear, dangerous. A vision of horror that had been the Great Hollow flashed before me.

And was gone.

Live. Survive. Through me, the kingdom.

I tried to stand but my legs were too weak to move.

Think.

—You are not as other rats.

It was Alpa, still alive, at least in my thoughts.

I am a hearer.

I lay, thinking not of my pain or of my fear, but of my power. A spark within me. A scratch of sound. I listened and it became clearer. I heard the groans and wheezes of a few citizens in the world below, not yet dead.

Other stranger sounds, nearer to me, tried to break through. A small number of rats had lived. Or perhaps they were visitors from another kingdom, alerted by the scent of death.

There was an otter downstream. Two squirrels were squabbling in a tree. The trem of humans on a road nearby.

Breathing hard now, I closed the door on all these things.

Hear. I must hear to save my life.

It is a muscle like any other, the gift of hearing. I felt what little strength I had draining from my body. Noises grew quieter, the noise of the night, the noise of my own breath, of my heartbeat, until I was in a world of perfect silence.

Yet there, deep within me, I heard a distant whisper. I concentrated my whole being upon it.

Malaika.

I knew that sound. I knew it so well. It warmed me. It made me feel stronger.

Tell me. Tell me again.

Malaika.

A face looking up at me. Behind it a mass of rats, trapped, starving, angry.

Malaika.

A fragile. The fragile. I had promised to see her again and now that promise was calling out to me.

Malaika.

And I knew where I had to go.

46 The townspeople stare at us...

... as we carry the sack full of dead rats through the streets the next morning. They look at us in our rags, with our dirty faces, and wonder if our heavy load has been stolen.

If only they knew.

As we approach the Town Hall, there are notices nailed on some of the trees. They read:

ONE O'CLOCK TODAY. YOUR MEMBER OF PARLIAMENT, MR VALENTINE PETHERIDGE MP, WILL SPEAK ON A MATTER OF URGENT CONCERN TO LOCAL PEOPLE.

'They're only animals,' Caz mutters as we continue on our way.

'They're the enemy, the doctor says.'

'How can they be the enemy?'

'You'll see.'

When we reach the Town Hall, a small wooden stage has been put up on a little green across the street. There is no sign of the doctor or the MP or anyone else.

I lug the sack under the stage. We wait, sitting together on the steps leading to the stage. Now and then passers-by glance at us, as if even waiting in a public place on a cold winter's morning is an act of sin.

'Ah, Mr Smith.'

We must have been waiting an hour before I hear the doctor's voice.

I stand up, and so does Caz.

The doctor wears a busy, distracted expression on his face and has a bundle of papers under his arm. I have noticed that, since Mr Petheridge has talked of him as a scientist, he has combed his hair less, and he mutters to himself a little bit more. I think he believes it is how scientists are supposed to behave.

'And where is the sack?'

I point under the stage.

'Excellent.' The doctor suddenly notices Caz and gives a little start, as if she has suddenly appeared out of nowhere. 'You have company, Mr Smith.'

Caz gives a little curtsy. 'Catherine Lewis at your service, sir.'

There's something twinkly and mocking in the way that she says this, and the doctor frowns.

'A friend, Mr Smith? I never knew you had a friend.'

He turns to go, and at that moment Caz surprises me. She stands in front of him, a hard look in her eye.

'We're hungry,' she says.

The doctor reaches into his waistcoat pocket and takes out two penny pieces. He hands the coins to Caz as if the merest touch of her might infect him with a disease.

There is a pie man on one of the side streets and that twopence is well spent.

When we return, a small crowd has gathered a few yards in front of the stage. There are men and women of all ages, and children running around the green. If they have anything in common, it is that they have nothing else to do.

Caz and I sit down with our backs against the stage, facing the crowd. The grass is a bit damp but we don't care. We are earning money today and we're together.

The truth is, I feel stronger when Caz is there. Alone, I will do anything to avoid being noticed. With her, I don't mind. The world can stare. I stare straight back at it the way that she does.

She starts to sing.

> 'I like pickled onions,
> I like piccalilli

> *Pickled cabbage is all right*
> *With a bit of cold meat on a Sunday night.'*

I nudge her.

'Caz!'

'What? My mum used to sing it.'

She sings the song, louder this time.

> *'I can go termatoes*
> *But what I do prefer,*
> *Is a little bit of cu-cum-cu-cum-cu-cum*
> *Little bit of cucumber.'*

An old couple, dressed in their Sunday best, are looking at her as if singing a song in a public place breaks some important law. She smiles at them, and starts the song again.

Just to show I'm not ashamed of my Caz, I start singing along. We're in the middle of a cu-cum-cu-cum when the doors to the Town Hall open, and a group of men wearing dark suits and serious expressions walk down the steps.

I see Mr Woodcock and Mr Robinson from the council in the group. Following them is the doctor and Mr Petheridge.

I nudge Caz and, reluctantly, she stops singing.

As the men approach, one of them sees us and makes an impatient sweeping gesture. We get up and move away.

Mr Woodcock climbs the steps to the stage. As he starts to speak, the doctor edges his way towards us.

'When I need you, Mr Smith, I shall nod my head. You come and do exactly what I say. Understood?'

Without waiting for my reply, he has gone.

'Ladies and gentlemen.' Mr Woodcock looks around as if there were a huge crowd here, rather than a few people who happened to be passing by.

'I am Joseph Woodcock. Many of you will know me. I am the Public Health Officer for this borough council.'

No one seems to be listening. Mr Woodcock puts his hands behind his back which causes his stomach to stick out further. He looks like a cockerel that is just about to crow.

'We face a very serious problem,' he shouts. 'Something which will affect all of us. I have asked our local Member of Parliament, Mr Valentine Petheridge MP, to speak to you about an important public health campaign which your council will launch in the next few days. Pray silence for Mr Petheridge.'

The MP climbs the steps. There is a strange look on his face, which I think is meant to be a smile.

'Oh dear,' says Caz, beside me.

For some reason, her words set me giggling. The elderly couple glance in our direction, frowning fiercely.

Mr Petheridge struts across the stage. When he starts speaking, it is difficult to hear his words above the chatter. There is something about health, I think. He mentions 'a public menace' several times but what little curiosity there was in the crowd seems to have disappeared. At the back, people are drifting away.

'I am talking' – the MP raises his voice – 'about rats!'

A woman standing in front of the stage gives a little scream, and there is laughter. At first, Mr Petheridge seems flustered, but then he realises that at least people are listening now.

'You may laugh but, ladies and gentlemen, what is it that spreads disease throughout this borough? What is it that invades your homes, raids your kitchens, skulks behind the walls, beneath the floors, in the drains and gutters?'

'Rats.' It is the woman who screamed, but no one is laughing now.

'Madam, do you know how much of this city's food is eaten by rats every year?' The MP drops his voice. The chatter in the crowd has died down.

'No, sir,' says the woman.

'One third. For every three loaves of bread you buy for your family, rats will take one.'

'Eh?' The woman looks around her, but all eyes are on the MP now.

'I shall make you all a promise.' He raises his voice and points a finger to the sky. 'If we do nothing, the great rat invasion will grow worse. More of our children will be attacked in their cots. There will be more disease. Rats are on the march, ladies and gentlemen. They are growing bolder by the day. They are among us.'

Beside me, Caz smiles. 'I should have brought Malaika,' she whispers.

'And, ladies and gentlemen, I shall prove it.' Mr Petheridge beckons to the doctor. 'The world expert on rats, Dr Henry Ross-Gibbon, will now reveal the full and terrifying danger which you and your families, especially your little kiddies, now face.'

The doctor looks in my direction. Leaving Caz, I reach under the stage and pull out the sack of dead beasts. With some difficulty, I lug them up the steps on to the stage.

The doctor is there, standing beside Mr Petheridge, as he addresses the silent crowd.

'Ladies and gentlemen. They attack us. They bring disease into our midst. It is my belief that rats now pose the greatest danger to us all. And I can give you proof.' He points to the sack, stained with blood, which is at my feet at the back of the stage.

'Yesterday, the borough chief engineer, Mr Petheridge and myself accompanied Mr Woodcock into the sewers beneath the streets of this borough. There we found millions of rodents, both alive and dying from the very diseases which they can communicate to humans.'

'What's 'e on about?' a man near the back of the crowd asks.

'I shall tell you,' says the doctor. 'The brown rat carries bacteria within its body, and on it there are even greater dangers. Lice. Mites. Fleas. Ticks. All of these things spread diseases among humans, particularly among our little ones. They bring germs from the sewers into our homes, our kitchens, our bedrooms.'

'Speak for yourself, mate,' a joker at the back of the crowd calls out, but nobody laughs.

The doctor turns towards me. 'I shall ask my assistant, Mr Smith, to help me reveal a tiny part of what we found.' He takes a pair of gloves out of his pocket and grips a bottom corner of the sack. I take hold of the other corner.

'If you believe that there is no rat problem in this town, I would ask you to look at this!'

With a sudden movement, he tips the sack. A deluge of rats' bodies – dark, wet, many flecked with blood around their mouths – tumbles on to the stage, causing the MP to jump back in alarm.

There are screams, uproar in the crowd.

'I…' The MP steps forward, looking with disgust at the pile of dead rodents. 'I shall do something about this,' he cries. 'Vote for me and you will be voting for a city free of the rat menace for ever. The great rodent crusade starts here!'

47 The fire within me had spread…

… to my whole being. I could no longer feel my paws, although I could smell the blood on them.

Something had happened to my eyes. They were encrusted, swollen, closed up. I was thirsty beyond longing, but the taster's instinct within me which stopped me drinking from the puddles and gutters as I made my way through the world above was stronger than my need.

I have no idea how long I travelled. Down lanes, over ditches, in the damp shadows of back alleys, along strange walls and through parks and gardens, passing within a few lengths of the enemy, past the barking of dogs, the echo of horses' hooves on cobbles, I followed the only sound which had meaning for me.

Malaika.

There were times that day when I stopped to rest, but the pain grew stronger when my body was no longer moving. I knew that if I slept for even a moment, it would be the end of me.

I shall never know how I reached the end of that journey, sick, exhausted but just alive. For those few hours, I felt invisible, and perhaps I was.

There was a lane. The wet mud on it soothed my burning paws.

I was close now.

Malaika was near.

48 There is a feast in the tip…

… that night. My stomach aches from the sausages, bread and pie we have bought with the day's pay from Mrs Bailey's shop on our way home from the Town Hall. The shopkeeper was suspicious about the money we laid upon her counter.

She asked where the likes of us had come upon two shillings.

'Politics,' Caz said with a laugh.

'That's what they're calling it these days, is it? Thievin', more like.'

Remembering it now, Caz laughs. 'But it was politics,' she says, staring at the flickering candle. Her eyes are bright, and her cheeks are shining, still greasy from the food she has just eaten. 'And rats.'

'Poor beasts.' I think of the bodies we tipped from the sack into the canal on our way home. They had served their purpose.

'How can you declare war on an animal?' Caz asks suddenly. 'I mean it's just stupid.'

'It's as I told you. Rats are the enemy, according to the doctor.'

'Well, he's an idiot.' Caz has an argumentative look in her eye. 'How can we fight this great enemy? With soldiers? With an army and guns?'

'Gas, more like.'

'I don't think so.' She shakes her head. 'Gas is too dangerous. That politician's not going to get elected if people start getting ill from poison.'

My thoughts go to the Cock Inn. 'Dogs, maybe.'

'How will they find the rats? They'll just run away.'

'Not always. Sometimes they fight.'

Caz reaches into her dress and takes out Malaika. She sets the rat down gently between us. The little grey and white beast sniffs the air, her whiskers trembling. Caz strokes her with a single finger between her ears.

It is good to see Caz and Malaika together.

'There's one rat who'll be safe,' I say.

Caz reaches into a paper bag where a last slice of chicken pie remains. She breaks off a corner and lays it on the ground in front of the rat.

'They won't get you,' she murmurs.

Malaika nibbles, but not in the way of a hungry animal. It is almost as if she is being polite to us.

I think of the doctor, the politician and their great campaign. They are not going to give up easily.

'They'll want us to help in the war,' I tell Caz.

She frowns, knowing what I am saying is true.

'We've got no choice,' I say. 'We need to eat.'

'What will they want you to do?' Caz keeps her eye on Malaika. There is sadness in her voice.

'All the dirty stuff. The things they don't want to do themselves. That's how it is. The doctor wants me to be there tomorrow. Mr Petheridge is coming to discuss the campaign.'

'They really do think it's a war, don't they? They think they're generals.' She pushes the morsel of pie closer to her pet rat. 'Eat up, Malaika.'

The rat moves away. Its dark eyes are fixed on the tangled heap of rubbish behind where Caz is sitting.

'He's afraid of rats, the doctor,' I say. 'I saw it when he was making his lecture and a beast appeared in the hall. That's why he likes me to be around. I'm his eyes, ears, nose and hands when it comes to rats.'

Caz is no longer listening. She is watching her pet rat, which stands motionless, staring into the darkness.

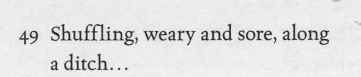

49 Shuffling, weary and sore, along a ditch...

... I reached a mountain made of dead trees, and the broken waste of human homes. Although I could hardly see now, I sensed a light ahead. It was not the moon, but something which seemed to come from within the mountain itself.

I entered the mountain.

I sniffed the air. The enemy was near. Or, at least, the young of the enemy. And something else, a scent which filled me with longing.

The light. Sometimes it disappeared within the mountain. I would tumble forward a length, maybe two lengths, following the sound within me, answering the question. The light would flicker before my half-closed eyes.

The smell of humans was becoming stronger now, the sound of them louder in my ears. I sensed movement.

Then I felt a revelation within me.

—Who is it? Who is there?

With the little strength that was left within me, I revealed.

—Efren. I am Efren.

I was close to Malaika, I knew it, but there was no reply, only the faint smell of fear.

Once more I tried.

—It is Efren. I have come for you.

That is the last I remember.

50 'There's something there,' Caz whispers...

... as Malaika moves away from us, her body alert. She is more like a wild animal than a pet.

Caz follows her eyes. 'Malaika can hear something,' she says.

'Maybe a hedgehog snoring. Or another rat foraging for food.'

'It's moving closer.' Caz is whispering now. 'Malaika's calling out.'

I listen. I have good ears, but I can hear no sound coming from Caz's fancy rat.

'I hear something.' Caz breathes the words. 'Something about offering.'

'I can't hear anything. Caz, this is—'

'She's calling another rat. Look at her, Peter!'

It is true that the fancy rat is behaving strangely now. Her grey and white body is rigid. She is motionless except for the twitching of her nostrils.

'Offering. Offering. Can't you hear that word?'

It has been a long day. We have eaten too much. Maybe Caz is in a dream while still waking.

'It's time for us to go to bed,' I say gently.

There is a stirring, the smallest movement of dry, dead leaves, from the rubbish near where she is sitting.

'Caz, it's a hedgehog.' To tell the truth, I am wondering whether she has suddenly become lunatic. 'Or maybe a mouse.'

Without a word, she points at Malaika. The rat is taking slow, sleepwalking steps away from us.

I reach for her. To my astonishment, her head twitches backwards and she gives my finger a savage nip.

'Ah!' I look at my finger. Blood is seeping from the two holes, the size of pinpricks, made by her teeth. 'What did she do that for?'

Caz ignores me. She is still watching Malaika.

There is another sound of movement from the tip and at that moment Malaika darts forward and disappears from view.

We wait. The scrabbling sounds are more distant now. There is the unmistakeable sound of a rat's squeak.

Caz turns to me slowly.

'Not offering at all,' she says.

'Who wasn't offering?'

'I can hear it in my brain,' she whispers. 'What they're saying to each other.'

'Caz, you're scaring me.'

Her eyes are wide with wonder. She has a strange little smile on her face.

'Not offering, but Efren. What does Efren mean?'

51 Help...

—help...
    —I need help. Malaika, I need help.
    —The kingdom... death... the enemy.
I felt the touch of Malaika, her revelation.
    —Efren, Efren.
Then, beyond her, something which made me believe that I had died.
    Another revelation, different from any I had heard before.
    —We'll help you, Efren. You are among friends now. Sleep, rest.
    Who was revealing to me? In my fever, I believed it was a human.

52 Caz is deathly white...

... as if it is not a pet rat she is looking for in the rubbish which surrounds us, but a ghost.

'Tell me you won't laugh,' she murmurs, her eyes still fixed on the part of the tip where Malaika disappeared.

'Caz? What's going on?'

Now she turns to me. 'Do you remember when we gave Malaika her name?'

'Of course I do.'

'The name didn't come from me.'

'What are you talking about? You just said "She's Malaika".'

'I heard it. Inside my head. She told me.'

'She? Who's she?'

'You promised you wouldn't laugh.' Caz closes her eyes. 'Malaika told me. I heard a voice in my head. I told myself it was the voice of my own imagining, but I knew in my heart that I was being told. She was telling me her name.'

'You're saying a rat spoke to you?'

'Yes. In my head.'

'Caz, this is—'

'And then, just a moment ago, I heard another voice.'

'That offering thing?'

'Efren. It's a name.'

She moves towards the part of the tip where Malaika must be hiding. What else can I do? I follow.

'We've got to find her,' she says. 'She wants our help.'

There are times when it is best to say nothing.

She pulls at a branch, then carefully removes some broken

181

bricks. On her hands and knees, she makes her way into the tangled rubbish.

Moments later, she has found her rat.

'Oh, Malaika.' Her voice is soft. 'What is this?'

She shuffles backwards towards me, slowly. When she turns, she holds something in her hand. At first, I think it is Malaika. Then I realise that the shape is bigger. The only trace of colour on it is a flash of white on its forehead.

'A rat,' I say. My word hangs in the air, like the most stupid and obvious thing that has ever been said. 'A beast.'

'He's alive.' She lays the rat near to the candle. Malaika now emerges from the tip and sniffs at the newcomer.

I notice that each of its paws is raw and pink. Its skin is loose on its body, as if it has not eaten for some time.

'Caz,' I speak quietly. 'This is a wild rat.'

'An animal's an animal. It needs help.'

There is no arguing with Caz Lewis when she is in this mood. I look closer at the rat. I notice that there is blood on its mouth, like those I carried in the sack.

'It's been gassed,' I say. 'Don't give it water.'

Caz picks up the limp body and lays it in her lap. Malaika moves closer to the wild rat. It is as if she knows it.

'That's right, Malaika,' Caz says. 'He needs warmth.'

We are there, not moving, for half an hour. I watch. Caz murmurs softly, all the while stroking the sick rat. We must make a strange sight.

Eventually, the rat stirs and tries to get to its feet. Too weak, it slumps back.

'We'll help you, Efren,' Caz whispers. 'You are among friends now. Sleep, rest.'

'Caz...'

She smiles, looking down at the wild rat. 'This is Efren. He's with us now.'

53 We're together…

… Efren, Malaika, Peter and Caz.
  'Together?'
  —Together.

II

'Let us declare war on rats.'

Dr Léon Calmette, director of the Institut Pasteur

54 Somehow the beast called Efren…

… has survived. Too scared to be in our little room at the heart of the tip, he is now a neighbour, living deep in the rubbish no more than a yard from where Caz and I live and sleep.

There Caz has made it a home, with a plate of water, scraps to eat, rags for a nest – everything a rat could need.

Late at night, we can hear Malaika and her new friend rustling in the rubbish which surround us. There are times when I wonder about what my life has become.

Caz, though, is happy. She still works, dancing for pennies in town, but she hurries back as the light is fading, eager to see her beasts. Caring for something, even a rat, makes her more alive. There is a light in her eyes. She is chatty. She laughs more than she used to.

What do we do next? You don't have to ask. We learn rat, of course.

At first, when Caz tells me she is hearing voices, I keep my thoughts to myself. Yes, Caz, I think to myself, of course you are.

But then it goes on. She tells me what Malaika is saying to the sick rat. Sometimes she goes quiet but her eyes are alive with a conversation she is having.

In her brain.

With a rat.

To tell the truth, it begins to annoy me. She used to talk to me all the time. Now she sits in silence with a crazy smile on her face. Sometimes she laughs at some kind of ratty joke.

Then, after a while, I begin to worry. What if my Caz is going soft in the head? What will I do then? What can I do to bring her back to me?

But it is not only rats' thoughts she can read.

'You don't believe me, do you, Peter?' she says one night.

I'm trying to sleep after another long evening of silent rat conversation.

'They must be really interesting, those rats.' There's a hardness in my voice which takes even me by surprise. 'You've more to say to them than to me.'

'Efren's getting better. He is strong. Sometimes when he reveals, it's so loud that it hurts my head.'

'Reveals what?'

'I've told you. That's how rats talk to one another – by revelation.'

'So why can't I hear his voice?'

'You have to believe. If you believe, you'll hear.'

I really don't like this talk of believing. Caz is beginning to sound like a priest.

'Listen to them, Peter. Just try.'

'Maybe they can tell me where the beasts are hiding.' I laugh. 'So I can help kill them tomorrow.'

Caz is silent. Maybe she's talking to rats, maybe she's just upset.

As I drift off to sleep, I hear her voice.

'You don't understand.'

The fact is, there is so much going on during my daytime life that there is not enough room in my brain for the idea that I should be chatting to beasts.

A few days after the meeting outside the Town Hall, I return there in the company of the doctor.

There is no sack of dead rats this time, no speeches. Instead, we go straight into the big building. With the new, cheerful, loud voice that I have noticed he uses these days, the doctor announces himself to the man behind the desk in the big entrance hall.

Soon afterwards, Mr Robinson, the younger man who had been with us when we visited the sewer, descends the stairs. He shakes hands with the doctor and, without a glance in my direction, leads us upstairs and through some big double-doors.

A group of men in dark suits, there must be almost twenty of them, are seated round a long table. Among them, I notice the MP, Mr Petheridge. At the head of the table is Mr Woodcock, the other man who visited the sewer with us.

'Dr Ross-Gibbon,' he says. 'Very good of you to join us.'

'Gentlemen.' The doctor's smile takes in the whole room. He sits in a chair beside Mr Petheridge.

'Ah.' Mr Woodcock's smile grows a little colder. 'You've brought the boy. Strictly speaking he shouldn't—'

Mr Robinson, seated beside him, murmurs something. I pick up the word 'simple'.

Mr Woodcock nods impatiently and points to a chair in the corner of the room. I take my seat, and listen. Sometimes it can be useful, being an idiot.

'The purpose of this meeting,' Mr Woodcock announces, 'is to put some detail on the plan of Mr Petheridge to rid this borough of a great and growing menace to the health of our citizens – the rodent population. Mr Petheridge, would you like to add anything?'

The politician looks bored. 'I am not the rodent expert here,' he says. 'I am but a humble servant of the people. What voters want – nay, what they demand – is a war on the rat. An end to the killing of their children.'

A man sitting across the table from the MP raises a hand. 'Mr Petheridge, we are a peace-loving borough,' he says. 'Maybe the word "war" is a little strong. May I suggest the phrase "eradication campaign"?'

'It's a war.' The doctor sits forward in his seat. 'And ultimately it is a war for the survival of mankind. A war that we must win.'

'So how would this war be waged?' One of the older councillors asks.

'There are various options,' says the doctor. 'We could introduce a disease, but that would take time. I am confident that, with the manpower, we can use traditional methods – baiting, drowning, dogs and so on – to solve the problem. But rats move from one area to another when attacked. If our campaign could be quick and effective, covering the whole borough, they will be panicked and vulnerable, making our task easier.'

'And how will you find them?' asks Mr Woodcock.

'We have means. There are many rat experts – hunters, official and unofficial – in the borough. We shall use them.'

I am just thinking that matters are not going the way of the doctor and Mr Petheridge when the conversation takes an alarming turn.

'For example,' says the doctor, 'I happen to know that my assistant, Mr Smith, occasionally works for a rat-catcher who supplies beasts for sport in certain public houses.'

Thank you very much, doctor.

'Impossible.' Mr Robinson speaks up. 'Rat pits are illegal these days. If this young man has been a party to them, we should send him to have a word with members of the local constabulary.'

There are murmurings of agreement round the table. Then, to my surprise, Mr Petheridge speaks up. 'In war, sometimes one has to use people who are not at all times on the right side of the law,' he says.

'Out of the question,' someone mutters.

'Mr Smith?' The doctor turns to me, then addresses the meeting. 'Would it be acceptable to question the boy?'

Mr Woodcock looks surprised by the idea that I am able to understand questions. 'Make it brief,' he says.

The doctor beckons. I approach the long table and stand at the end of it, my hands behind my back. My thoughts are of one thing only: policemen. There is danger here for me and for Caz.

'Rat pits, boy.' Mr Woodcock's moustache bristles like the hackles of a dog about to attack. 'Tell us about the rat pits.'

I remain silent.

'The lad has friends – accomplices, shall we say? – who regularly attend pit days at public houses,' says the doctor. 'In those rooms, whether we like it or not, are gathered the men of the borough who know exactly where to find the beasts. They also have the dogs that have been trained to hunt and kill them.'

'A ready-made army,' adds Mr Petheridge.

All eyes are on me.

'Boy?' said Mr Petheridge. 'Are you going to speak up? Or should we call a policeman right now?'

I am so afraid at that moment that my guts feel as if they are turning to water. I think of the pit, the men, the dogs. Anyone betraying the ratting fraternity is likely to meet a sorry end.

'I fear that this meeting is going nowhere,' says Mr Woodcock. 'The council can have nothing to do with law-breaking.'

The doctor is looking as if at any moment he would stand up and throttle me.

There is no choice. I have to speak.

'I know a man,' I say. 'He is a rat man.'

'Come on, lad. Spit it out.' Mr Woodcock opens a timepiece on the table before him, glances at it, then snaps it shut.

'What do you mean by a rat man?' asks the doctor.

'He knows rats,' I say. 'Where to find them. How to catch them. It's his job.'

'Name, boy.' There is a dangerous look in Mr Woodcock's eye.

'Will he get into trouble?'

'Just give us the name. Or you'll be in the hands of the police.'

'Will he get into trouble?' I repeat the words with more determination in my voice.

'If he is on the side of our campaign, no harm will come to

him,' says the doctor. He turns to Mr Woodcock, who seems to think for a moment, then nods.

'No notes will be taken of this part of the meeting,' he says.

I swallow hard, then say the words.

'His name's Bill. Mr Bill Grubstaff.'

55 For me, for any rat, there is no life without…

… movement. It is why the citizens in the kingdom who can never move, those whose tails are forever entangled as part of a twyning, are loved and revered above all else in the kingdom. Fat and helpless, they have their own mystical wisdom, which is beyond any revelation or act. They remind every citizen of the dangers of staying still.

I thought of the world below every day.

My limbs ached to take my Malaika there. I wondered what we would find there, who had died and also had lived on. I thought of Floke and Fang. Where was Queen Jeniel? Did Swylar still live? What of my captain Alpa?

—Sleep, Efren. Rest. You are still too weak. There will be time for this later.

Malaika lay beside me, warming, soothing, feeding me now and then.

Was I revealing without knowing it, or did she sense where my mind was wandering?

The better I knew Malaika, the more I worried about her. At some stage in her life, she had lost the restlessness which drives us forward. She had gone over to the enemy without knowing it. When I revealed stories of the kingdom, she heard but did not understand. I was telling her of a foreign land. Her home was with the humans.

That home, I now discovered, was full of hidden perils. One day, as I was beginning to get stronger, I sensed something strange was happening to me.

It was after sunrise. Patches of daylight had entered the mountain where I found myself. Suddenly above me was the whiteness of danger. The smell, even to me in my weakened state, was overpowering, sickening.

It was a human. The enemy was upon me. It held me in its grip. I was too weak to escape but managed to bite the flesh. The hand released me but then returned.

Strange.

A bite is normally enough to keep a human at bay.

There was human noise all around me. Malaika moved closer to me.

—You are safe, Efren. She is our friend. Listen to her.

Listen? What was Malaika telling me? All I could hear was the human noise. It was as repulsive as the human smell.

—What do you mean, listen?

I turned and writhed, but then rested, panting, in the enemy's grip.

It was then that the strangest, most impossible thing overcame me.

Another voice. Not a noise, not outside, but within the brain. It was calling my name, calming me.

A revelation, like the one I had heard when I had first arrived at this place.

Now, though, I knew it was not a feverish dream.

A human was revealing to me.

I could not answer. I would not answer.

It called again.

—Efren. It's only me. I'm Caz.

56 My betrayal of Bill Grubstaff...

... makes me feel sick to the stomach. As I make my way to work for him the next morning, I am fearful as to what I have done to his life. At the Town Hall, I believed I might be helping him. There would be money to be made in the war against rats. He has worked for the council before.

But in my heart I know that I was most afraid for myself. If the police take me away now, what will happen to Caz?

Entering his compound, I try to forget what I have done. Bill glances up from the seat in the yard where he is hunched over a bucket, skinning moles.

'Word travels fast on these streets,' he says, with an odd little smile on his face.

'Is there any work for me, Bill?'

He nods in the direction of mole pelts. 'You can clean those, and hang 'em out if you like. Then chuck the rest to the rats in the well.'

I take out my knife and sit on the ground. Reaching for one of the skins, I tidy up the remains of the flesh from the inside of the pelts.

'What word on the streets?' I speak as casually as I can manage while I work.

Bill smiles. 'We're back in business, lad. Molly called by last week. They want two hundred beasts for next Wednesday. Pit days are on again.'

My surprise must be obvious, because Bill gives a gruff little laugh.

'There's no stopping sport, boy,' he says. 'The pit's part of life.

Even when' – he pauses to extract the pink corpse of a mole from its covering – 'things happen.'

'What about Jem Dashwood?'

'Molly says he's going to behave. He's kissed and made up with Charlie Buckingham. The pit is bigger than any man.'

'That's good.'

'It is.' He picks up the bloody remains of two skinless moles, wanders over to the well, and lifts the lid. There are screams of hunger as he throws the corpses to the rats below. 'We'll need some more beasts. Tonight?'

'Tonight.'

It is as if nothing has changed. Bill is happy.

'It's going to be the best pit day ever,' he murmurs to himself.

When I say nothing, he glances at me. He knows that seeing the massacre at the Cock Inn has troubled me.

'This time,' he says, 'nothing will go wrong.'

Maybe because he has noticed something different about me today, Bill starts telling me stories of great pit days of the past as if these tales would wipe away my memories of men stamping on beasts.

'Did you ever hear about the time the fighting monkey Jacko Maccacco tore the entrails out of a dog pitched against him at Westminster?'

'I didn't, Bill.'

He tells me the story.

'Of course, the rummest bout I ever did see was when that great setter from Warwickshire, Sam Wedgebury, backed his son Boy Wedgebury, just under twelve years of age at the time, against a thirty-pound dog. I must have told you that one.'

'Never heard that one, Bill,' I lie innocently.

He tells me. The boy won.

'Every pit day tells a story,' he says, opening up another mole.

'I know that.'

'It will be good this time, Dogboy. You'll see.'

But my betrayal is with me, like a dead chicken hung around

the neck of a guilty dog. There is no getting away from the smell of it – not today and not during the nights which follow when we are out hunting rats.

It is a cold, still day when we return to the Cock Inn, bearing two cages full of beasts. The back room of the pub is heaving with life. Every setter and trainer, every gambler and sportsman of the town seems to be there.

There is merriment, laughter, in the room as we enter. Tonight, there will be no rows or fights or stamping upon beasts, just the best of sport.

I try to concentrate on my work but, from the minute I enter that place, I am waiting for the moment when, all because of me, a thirteen-year-old boy, everything changes for the ratting fraternity.

It is just before the first bout that my worst fears come true. Standing at the bar, apart from the main throng of gamblers, are Mr Petheridge and the doctor. They are a little too well-dressed, not quite drunk or loud enough to be your normal sportsman, but there is too much excitement in the smoky atmosphere for that to be noticed.

The doctor catches sight of me and touches his forehead, like a man tipping his hat. I look away quickly.

Soon it is time for the first bout in the pit. It is quickly over, one of Mr Barstow's older dogs easily winning a fifty-rat bout over Nipper, who belongs to a setter from out of town. I am just gathering up the dead beasts when I notice that the doctor and the MP are no longer at the bar.

I breathe more easily. They have gone. I'm saved. Moments later, though, as I am about to count out the beasts for the second bout, a silence descends on the bar, broken only by the whining of dogs.

Molly is walking towards the pit, her face unusually grim. Behind her are Mr Petheridge and Dr Ross-Gibbon.

When they reach the centre of the room, the landlady points to the chair. Mr Petheridge, with a nervous glance in the direction of the blood-stained pit, stands on it. I notice one or two of the setters edging towards the door.

'Gentlemen, I pray you will not be alarmed if I tell you that I am your local MP.'

Bill, standing beside me, swears quietly.

'I have been enjoying the sport.' Mr Petheridge puts on one of his sickly public smiles. 'I have always been a great supporter of gaming, with, er, beasts.'

Something about the way he says the word 'beasts' seems to annoy the men around the pit. They are as good at reading a liar as they are at judging a dog.

'What's 'e doin' 'ere?' someone says, loud enough to be heard by everyone in the room.

'I am not in this tavern to bring problems to sportsmen like your good selves.' Mr Petheridge is more at ease now. 'When I have finished speaking, I shall look forward to the second bout.' He glances down at the piece of paper he holds and clears his throat like a music-hall turn. 'I have it on good authority that Drongo is worthy of a wager.'

There is a rustle of laughter from the corner where the dog Drongo's setter is standing.

'You gentlemen are doing a good and useful thing,' says the MP. 'Yes, I am not joking. You are. It may be not entirely legal as the law now stands but, while you have your sport, you are helping to rid this borough of the great scourge of rats – a growing problem in our city. And here is the reason why I am speaking to you this evening.'

The MP pauses dramatically and, at that moment, one of the dogs starts barking.

'He wants to get on with it,' someone shouts.

'We all do,' says someone else. 'Spit it out, mate.'

Mr Petheridge raises a hand for silence. 'Before the next election, I have promised the good people of this borough that I shall clean our streets, our houses, our gutters, of the great, unhealthy menace of rodents.'

'You'll be lucky,' mutters a man standing on the far side of the pit.

'How shall I do this? With your help, gentlemen. No one knows more about the rat than those gathered in this room. My colleague Dr Ross-Gibbon' – he extends an arm in the direction of the doctor – 'is a world-renowned expert on the creatures' behaviour. But we need practical help. There is someone here, I happen to know, who has better knowledge of where the beasts live than almost anyone else in this town.'

Oh no.

A few people look furtively towards Bill. His head shrinks on to his shoulders like that of a nervous tortoise.

To my utter despair, Mr Petheridge looks over in our direction and smiles. 'That will be Mr Grubstaff.'

Bill growls miserably.

'Then there are setters who know how to hunt them, and dogs with a very special talent for killing them,' says Mr Petheridge.

Now he has the attention of the room. Even the dogs seem to sense that this is no time to whine or bark.

'I'm talking about the greatest rat hunt this city, or any city, has ever seen. Instead of competing with one another, you shall be working together. It will be you and your magnificent dogs against the rat.'

'What's in it for us then?' It is Charlie Buckingham who asks the question which is in everyone's mind.

'Pits will be legal once more.'

There is a murmur of surprise.

'And' – the MP looks again at the piece of paper he holds in his hand – 'Ah, yes, there will be a reward. One pound – yes, one pound – for every fifty rats' tails brought to my friend Dr Ross-Gibbon. Anyone up for the challenge?'

Buckingham shrugs and raises a finger. Others nod and mutter their interest.

'Let us enjoy the final bout then,' says Mr Petheridge, smiling. 'After that, any setters who are interested in this supreme test of their dogs' skill can see me.'

'No.' Bill speaks quietly. 'I don't like it.'

'And that,' says the MP, looking hard in our direction, 'includes Bill Grubstaff.'

It is the end of sport for that night – the end of real sport that is. I count out the rats, the dogs are released, the killing is done, money paid out. But it is as if the news of a greater game, offering money and glory, has made that evening's contests seem small and pointless.

It is towards the end of the evening when what I had most been dreading happens. I am collecting the dead beasts from the second bout when the doctor and Mr Petheridge approach Bill.

Working in the pit, I keep my head down, making much of a business of putting the beasts' corpses in the sack.

The three men talk for a few minutes, the doctor now and then making notes. There are handshakes – hearty from the doctor and the politician, awkward from Bill.

I tie up the sack and make my way to Bill. Even by his standards of misery, he looks unhappy.

'Done?' he asks.

I nod.

'Best be on our way then.'

He picks up the empty cage.

'What I want to know,' he mutters, 'is who told 'em.'

57 There are no good humans…

… and nothing a human does is to be trusted without question. Humans were, are, and always will be the enemy.

The youngest ratling will learn this truth with its mother's milk. In the life of a rat, death is never far away. The hatred of the enemy is a daily reality. There is no understanding why humans are naturally evil. It is enough to know that they are.

And yet here I was, growing stronger by the day. My head was full of something which seemed like a human revelation. The enemy had a name. Caz. The only doe I had ever loved, Malaika, would rest in her hand. I would even see her sleep there sometimes.

From the moment I grew fur, citizens had looked at the white mark on my head and mocked me for the trace of fragile blood it revealed. Now I feared that the fragile in me was allowing me to grow too soft and trusting.

I had to leave that place. I would save Malaika from the enemy and together we would return to the world below. Whatever had happened down there was better than being imprisoned by humans.

And yet…

The sounds and smell of humans nearby were now almost a comfort to me. The revelations of Caz began to seem almost natural. I confess that I was glad to feel them within my head.

—How are you this morning, Efren?

—My legs are stronger. I can drink.

—Stay with us. We are all a family here.

What could I say? How could I explain that I knew of human

trickery, of the deadly danger of them, that all I wanted to do was take Malaika away to the safety of the world below.

When she asked me again and again to stay, I would not reveal in reply. Eventually Caz would go away.

One night, Malaika and I went on a little journey out of the mountain. It was not for ever (I knew that Malaika was strangely tied to these humans), but she needed to see me away from this place. With me, and back in the kingdom, she would begin to understand freedom, the true way of the rat.

I was still weak, and we were unable to travel far. Malaika showed me the eating places where humans left portions of their unfinished food. She took me to a spring where we drank and rested, then to a small wood where, she said, we would find eggs as the year grew warmer.

—But we shall have gone by then, Malaika.

My revelation was gentle, and she had heard it before.

—Perhaps.

She looked into my eyes, and I felt a lurch within me which was so strong that a noise, a small squeak of longing, escaped from me.

—You are tired, Efren. Let us return home.

—I am not tired. It is not home. We are rats, we are free.

—My love.

She moved closer to me in a movement that was more than merely comforting.

I cannot tell what would have happened if, at that moment, I had not become aware of a rustle, a sort of tickle of sound, within me. Something about me must have changed for Malaika looked at me, alarmed.

—What is it, Efren? What is happening?

It grew louder within me, refusing to be ignored.

—I am hearing.

—Hearing what?

I closed my eyes. What was reaching me is difficult to describe. It was worse, in its way, than the scream of agony from King

Tzuriel I had heard all those days ago. It was citizens of the kingdom keening. There had been a great loss, a terrible defeat. The pain of that chorus made me shake. I was hearing death.

I turned to Malaika and, in that moment, I was suddenly lost in a new unhappiness. The gift of hearing involves the greatest sacrifice a rat can give. I looked at Malaika, knowing that what I wanted above all else was impossible.

—I am a hearer.

—A hearer?

—Messages reach me. Only a few rats have the gift. They are important to the kingdom.

—Efren.

She looked at me with wide eyes, as if sensing that being a hearer could only be bad news.

—Does that mean you will have to return to the world below?

—More than that.

I moved away from her, knowing in that moment that the choice facing me was no choice at all.

I was a hearer. The kingdom needed me.

Malaika nudged me with her nose, puzzled by my coldness.

—Tell me.

—If I have a family with you, I shall lose my gift.

—Love, Efren. The kingdom lives on love. We can be happy. We can bring more ratlings into the world. Is that not enough duty for one rat?

I gazed into Malaika's eyes. She made it seem so simple, so easy.

She revealed again, moving closer to me.

—Love, Efren. Your duty is love.

58 At first, Bill Grubstaff and the doctor are like two dogs…

… sniffing at each other, suspicious, stiff-legged, their hackles standing. They are as unlike one another as any two men could be – the doctor with his suit and waistcoat and his booming voice, Bill in his baggy working clothes, with his crooked back, unshaven face and eyes that rarely look at you.

They have only two things in common, and one of them is that I work for both of them.

'How d'you know this character anyway?' Bill asks me when we are on our way to the doctor's house the morning after pit day at the Cock Inn.

'I work for him now and then, Bill.'

'Work?'

'I catch rats with him.'

'What does he want with rats?'

'He cuts them up. He studies them.'

As we turn into the street where the doctor lives, Bill stops walking. He looks at the grand houses which surround us, then at me.

'Ah.'

I walk on. Bill may be quiet, and his work may be catching rats, but he is not a stupid man. Now he knows the answer to what has been troubling him throughout the night.

'It was you.'

I keep walking, head down.

'You were the one who told them.'

Ahead of him, I have reached the front door.

'There's money in it, Bill,' I say. 'This could be an earner for you.'

He walks towards me and for a moment it seems as if he is going to strike me. I wait for the blow, knowing it is what I deserve. But instead he just shakes his head, like a man used to being disappointed by what people do.

It hurts more than any slap.

'Sorry, Bill.'

He lifts the knocker on the door of the doctor's house and raps it twice. 'If this goes wrong, I'll know who to blame,' he says.

The door opens, and they are face to face at last, my two employers. We enter the house.

And here's the second thing they have in common. Rats. I have reason to be grateful for that – soon Bill has forgotten my betrayal.

When we reach the laboratory and the doctor starts talking about his studies of the rat, Bill's body seems to relax.

'My research suggests that a single buck and doe could be responsible for fifteen thousand creatures in the period of one year,' says the doctor.

'They'd be going a bit,' Bill mutters.

'They would, but it is possible. Take a brood of nine young. The doe can conceive within three weeks. Gestation period is—'

'Twelve, more like,' Bill interrupts. 'I've seen several broods of twelve.'

'Really.' The doctor takes out a piece of paper from his jacket pocket and scribbles upon it. 'And where were these broods?'

'There is a granary near the river. The rats in that area always have big families. Strong, too. Great fighters, they are.'

'Fascinating. Would you be able to show me where they are, Mr Grubstaff?'

'Bill's the name.'

'Ah, yes, excellent. Bill.'

Soon they have forgotten my presence altogether. At last, each of them has found someone to share their rat talk. All other differences between them are soon forgotten.

They chat about traps and gas and ferrets and dogs. With the help of a map of the area, they begin to plan their great campaign – 'the battlefield', as the doctor calls it.

Later that morning, the three of us go down to the river near the sewerage run. The doctor shows Bill the manhole where we released the gas. Bill leads the doctor to the places where he has seen and heard rats' nests.

That gloomy November day, we stand by the river. The doctor talks eagerly about the first battle in his war against rats.

'There is a place called Fisher's Field,' he says. 'D'you know it, Bill?'

'I do.'

'Once sheep grazed there but today it is scrap land, a place where stray dogs roam, where beggars sleep in the summer months.'

'Good place for rats, Fisher's Field,' said Bill.

The doctor reaches into his leather bag and takes out a heavy, folded sheet of paper.

'I am no draughtsman,' he says, 'but I have drawn a map of the area.' He unfolds the paper and there, more neatly than I would have believed, is a little drawing of the field and its surroundings.

'The river runs beside it. Here' – he points with a finger – 'is one culvert leading to the gutters. There are two others across the field, there and here. If we could flush the rats from the sewerage channels where they live below the ground, they will escape into Fisher's Field.'

Bill nods, a little smile on his face. 'Put some dogs in the field and you could take a few of the beasts.'

'Or...' Now there is excitement in the doctor's voice. 'Surround the field. Put close-meshed wire on every side. Trap the beasts. Men and dogs all around the boundary.'

'Like a giant pit.'

'Precisely.'

'What about the river? Beasts are good swimmers.'

'We shall have two nets, upstream and downstream. The riverbank is steep brickwork on the far side. They'll be trapped in the water. Boats. Men with clubs. Dogs.'

'And how do you spring them from the sewerage?'

The doctor glances in my direction, as if his secret may not be safe with me. 'Gas.' He speaks in a low murmur. 'The council men don't like it, but it's the way we have to do it. The rats will have only one escape route.'

'Into Fisher's Field?'

'Correct.'

Bill gazes at the map and, just for a moment, it seems to me that a flicker of sadness crosses his face.

'It will be a massacre,' he says.

The doctor laughs happily. 'It will indeed – the most marvellous massacre. Will the setters help us, do you think?'

Bill nods. 'It'll be the best hunt they've ever had.'

It is dark before I am able to go home.

I should feel glad as I trudge the dark streets on my way back to the tip. My betrayal of Bill and the ratters and setters who come to the Cock Inn has been forgotten. My two employers have become unlikely friends. There will be work for me, and money too. Today, the day when I worked with the doctor and Bill, I have been given two shillings.

Maybe Caz will not have to dance on pavements any more. Maybe we can find somewhere to live which is not a rubbish tip.

Yet there is something that tugs at me. Something feels wrong about this great war on rats.

I buy two pies at Mrs Bailey's shop but I'm in no mood to listen to her chat, however friendly.

I have never been happier to return home to the tip. There is a cold mizzle falling as I duck into the passage leading into the mound like the mouth of a fox's earth. I whistle low for Caz.

Normally she whistles back – it's a sound which makes my heart lift – but tonight the tip is silent. Stranger still, I see no candlelight to guide me to our little room within its walls of rubbish.

'Caz?'

I call her name quietly. There is a rustle in the passage ahead of me and I smile, thinking it is my girl.

It is her rat, Malaika.

'Hello, beast,' I say. 'Where's your mistress then?'

I reach our room. It is empty.

'Caz?'

The pile of bedding is neat, the way she leaves it when she goes to work.

I wait. I listen.

Silence.

Malaika emerges from the tangle of rubbish and sniffs about the bedding.

'Caz?'

A feeling of cold dread descends upon me.

She is gone.

59 Rats do not dream as humans do…

… but they can see visions. During the day while I slept, I heard the screams of the kingdom. The pulsing within me of countless citizens facing their death made me tremble. I saw the faces, wide of eye and with blood around their mouths, of those who had died.

And yet somehow I could not recognise the faces of those calling out to me. Now and then I thought I saw the three-legged shape of Floke, the smooth flank of Swylar, the gentle lifeless eyes of Alpa, but I could never be sure.

It was worst at night. The kingdom was drawing me back. As the certainty of what I had to do became stronger, I revealed less to Malaika. I could see in her eyes the hurt I was causing her.

At first, while I was still weak, Malaika had explored with me. As I became well and the urge to return to the world below pressed harder upon me, she found it difficult to travel as far and as fast as I did. She was a fragile, not built for exploration.

One night, she simply stayed in the mountain. It was as if I had been released by her to become myself again.

The journey back to the river was hard, but finding my way was no problem. I followed the voices. The voices of the dead were leading me home.

There were citizens of other kingdoms out on the streets, but none of my own. I reached a wide space that separated a track from the river. Crossing it, I sensed, would be dangerous but, in the end, it would have to be done. The only way to return to the kingdom was through one of the entrances near the waterway.

The voices led me to a human building by the track. The

enemy was not there and wood covered its windows. I found a way in and made my way upwards to the top of the house just beneath the roof.

Under a bright moon, I looked across the space, catching the distant glitter of water which flowed from the world below. There would be touch-paths nearby, the tells of citizens, leading to the gouges, rests and hollows of the kingdom.

The next time I am here, there will be no returning to the mountain and to Malaika. I will tell her that the kingdom needs me. She will be sad. I will promise to return having done my duty, although both of us will know it is as empty a revelation as any could be.

Footsore and with an ache in my heart, I made my way home.

Light was breaking when I arrived back in the place where the love of my life was waiting.

Quietly, I went to where the two humans lived, and where she liked to sleep while I was away.

There was only one human there. He sat, awake, arms around his knees, his eyes wet and gazing into space.

Malaika was nearby. I smelt the sadness and fear on her. She was shivering and seemed hardly interested in my return.

I approached her, in spite of the human's presence. She was cold. I revealed as I moved closer.

—Malaika. I am here.

There was no response from her.

—What has happened?

60 How will I ever find a girl that's lost...

... in this great town of strangers?

I know nobody.

The police are more a danger than a help.

And what can I tell people? The girl I am searching for lives in a rubbish tip.

She is nothing in the world. She hardly exists.

I would have more chance of finding a stray dog.

The day after Caz's disappearance, I walk into the centre of the town. I know the places where she dances for pennies – outside theatres and restaurants, mostly – and visit them one by one.

But when I ask the men and women if they have seen a girl dancing here yesterday, they stare ahead as if my words are no more worthy of attention than the chattering of a sparrow.

'Have you seen...?'

'I'm looking for...'

'She's skinny, small, she dances...'

It is as if I am invisible. Only the thought of Caz keeps me going.

'I know she was here quite often, sir...'

The suited doorman outside a large hotel looks down at me and, for a moment, I have the feeling he might help me.

'I was wondering if you—'

He seems to twitch as if I have uttered some terrible insult. The side of my face is struck by the back of his gloved hand so hard that my body flies through the air before I fall in the gutter.

Someone is crying. I can hear it in the darkness. I open my eyes and suddenly all is pain – in my head, on my scraped knees, in every rattled bone of my body. I stare at the pavement where I am lying. It is wet and, when I touch it, the fingers of my hand are red with blood.

I hear raised voices above me – a man's, a woman's. As my head clears, a hand grabs my arm and lifts me to my feet. I am aware of the strong sweet smell of a woman's perfume.

'You come with me, sonny, before you get yourself into trouble.'

The voice is husky and the hand strong. I try to get away but the woman holds on to me. The left side of my face throbs where the doorman hit me.

'Unless you want the police to get their hands on you, you'll come with me,' the woman says.

I look around me, confused. I am being pulled into a side street by the arm. The woman holding me is tall and is wearing a tight dress which shows more of her than a lady will show. Wild dark curls hide her face but there is something about her that tells me I am safer with her than near the doorman. I sense that she knows the way things work on these streets.

I stop struggling.

'He's a bad lot, that Cribby Barton.' She looks down at me, a woman in her thirties wearing heavy make-up. 'And he's in with the coppers and all.'

Still holding me, she turns down another dark side street, and bangs on a door in the wall so small that it would be easy to miss it. Moments later, it opens. Glancing back down the street, she pushes me into the house before her.

'Welcome to Rose's fun parlour,' she says, following me inside and locking the door behind her.

We are in a room where there is no light from the outside world. Candles are on tables around the walls and, as my eyes grow used to the gloom, I see three other women, lolling on low couches. There is a strange, sweet smell in the air which makes me feel drowsy.

'Now what's she brought home?' A younger woman gazes at me from across the room with half-closed eyes.

'Kid was in trouble with that bastard Cribby. Needs his face cleaned up,' says my rescuer.

'Bloomin' Florence Nightingale.' Another girl, who had seemed to be asleep, gives a little laugh. 'You and your waifs and strays.'

The woman who brought me in pulls up a chair and, without a word, pushes me back on to it.

She leaves the room, and when she returns, she is carrying a basin of water.

'Might as well wash all of the little blighter, Rose,' the sleepy girls calls out. 'It'll only take you a week or two.'

Rose. It is a nice name. Her powdered face looms up in front of me. She winks and smiles at me, then starts to dab at my swollen eye. Something in the water makes the cut on my cheek sting.

'Don't talk to Cribby Barton,' she says. 'That's the number one rule in this part of town.'

There are noises from the dark doorway leading into the house – a man's voice, a woman's laughter.

Rose notices that I am looking curiously into the darkness and, pinching my chin, turns my face so that my one good eye is looking straight at her.

'Don't you worry about what's going on in there,' she says. 'It's grown-up stuff.'

I nod.

'What were you doing talking to Cribby anyway?'

'I'm looking for a girl called Caz,' I say. 'She's my friend. She dances for pennies.'

'Dancing for pennies.' The girl on the sofa murmurs quietly, her eyes still closed. 'The story of my life, darling.'

'She's disappeared,' I say. 'She was meant to come home last night. She's in trouble, I know it.'

'Sounds like she just found someone to look after her,' said Rose. 'That's what I'd do if I was a young girl.'

'I looked after her.'

'Course you did, love.' Rose dabs at my cheek, then rinses the rag in the warm water. 'But a rich bloke can look after a girl in a different way.'

'She used to be at a dancing school, but she ran away.'

'Little fool,' said the girl on the couch. 'What she want to do that for?'

'Maybe she's gone back to the school,' says Rose as she looks closer at my bruised face.

'No.' I shake my head, and wince at the pain. 'I just know Caz wouldn't leave without a reason. And if she did, she'd tell me. Or leave me a note.'

The woman on the sofa laughs quietly to herself. 'You don't know girls, love. We can be ruthless.'

From the darkness of the house, a man gives a drunken shout and a woman giggles loudly.

Rose places a hand on both my shoulders and puts her face close to mine. 'Tell you what,' she says, 'I'll ask around. There's not much that happens round here without us girls knowing about it.'

'Don't get yourself into it, Rose.' The woman on the couch sits up. I see now she is quite a lot younger than Rose. Her face is painted white with black lips.

'Here's the truth, darling.' She gazes at me with big, blank eyes. 'It's the only truth some of us 'ave ever needed to know. If you're a young girl on your own in this part of town, you'll soon be in trouble.'

'But she wasn't on her—'

'Shut up and listen.' She sways and then seems to lose interest in our conversation. 'Trouble is the air we breathe,' she mutters.

I edge towards the door. There's something about the white-faced girl that scares me. Darting an angry look in her direction, Rose follows.

She opens the door for me.

'Give us a few days,' she says. 'I'll ask around. Don't give up on your Caz just yet.'

'Thank you.'

But the girl with the black lips is frowning now, as if something is bothering her. She totters across the room until she stands, swaying, in front of me.

'What dancing school?' she asks.

When I look confused, she says, 'The school what your friend was at. What was its name?'

'It was a dancing school run by a French woman, I think – Madame Irina.'

Rose and Black Lips glance at one another.

'Irina Blavitsky,' says Rose. 'Better known as Eileen Dabbs from Hoxton. She's about as French as I am.'

'How d'you know her?'

Rose laughs, a bitter, rasping sound. 'We know Eileen all right,' she says. 'We know her very well.'

61 The mountain felt empty…

… without the human called Caz. Malaika was eating less without her, and not because she was being fed less. She had been in the world above so long that she had forgotten that she was a rat, that humans were the enemy.

She was sad. She missed her human.

And here is something even stranger. I, Efren, also felt a nagging emptiness within me. I had become used to that pale human face looming over me, uttering its human sounds which, in spite of my every instinct, comforted me.

Sometimes, in the night, I thought I heard her revelation but, when I listened more closely, I knew that it was no more than an echo in my mind.

It was time to return to the kingdom, before it was too late.

—Efren, don't go. Not now.

—I must. You can come with me.

—No. I must wait for my Caz.

What would you have done? Maybe, being human, you would have put an absent enemy before your duty to the kingdom, but I am different from you.

I am a rat. For me, there is no choice.

She knew I would go, and she turned away from me. Even before I had gone, I had lost Malaika.

That night I looked through the tangle of branches into the humans' room. Malaika and the boy human were sitting together, each of them staring, their thoughts full of Caz.

Sadly, I turned to leave. I had known the love of another rat, but it was not my fate to enjoy it.

Goodbye, Malaika. Goodbye, boy human.

I travelled towards the kingdom. Stronger now, I reached the wasteland beside the river while the moon was still high in the sky. I could smell the water but it was distant, and the final part of my journey was the most perilous. Since I had last been here, some kind of fencing had been put around the field. Crossing the open space, I would now have to escape from dogs, cats, foxes.

I made a choice. I would wait in the empty house by the road. I would find food, build up my strength. Tomorrow, as the light faded, I would return to the kingdom.

It was a decision which changed my life.

62 I hear the dogs before I see them...

... as I walk down the towpath the next day with the doctor and Bill Grubstaff. For a moment, the sound of them distracts me from my thoughts of Caz.

I have to keep working. Without pennies I will become hungry. Once hungry, I will steal. I am not made to be a thief – folk can read any thought of wrongdoing in my eyes. I will soon be in trouble. Then I will be of no use to anyone, least of all Caz.

The barking of the dogs echoes in the cold afternoon air. It sounds like something from another world. I have heard a pack of hounds before, when I was working with Bill in a wood outside town, but that was different – low, like the chiming of bells.

These dogs have a hundred different voices – yapping, howling, roaring, some with a bite in the sound, others with a gnaw and a nip.

'Ain't no rat coming out tonight with that din,' Bill mutters.

'They'll be forced out from the sewers.' The doctor's eyes shine with the excitement of the moment. 'The trick with *rattus norvegicus* is to get him to panic.'

'Don't happen often,' Bill mutters.

'You're a prophet of doom, Bill.' The doctor actually gives Bill a playful punch on the arm.

We turn a bend, and there they are. There must be fifty or sixty setters, each with a dog, and some with two. Word of the hunt must have spread because the numbers have been swelled by local people who have come along to have a look and join the fun. I see mothers with their children, old men bearing sticks. It is like being on a fairground.

'They're all here,' says Bill, sounding surprised.

'Of course they are.' The doctor rubs his hands. 'Money and sport. Who could resist that?'

The crowd are gathered near the bridge and, as the three of us approach, the buzz of conversation dies. The doctor pushes through the crowd and stands on the second step of the bridge.

'Welcome, ladies, gentlemen and young folk,' he calls out. 'And welcome, dogs. My name, for those of you who do not know me, is Dr Ross-Gibbon. We are here today to do a great public work – to begin the extermination of the greatest threat to our great town.'

As the doctor makes his usual speech about how beasts are the scourge of all mankind, I look around the crowd. The regulars of the pit are here – Dashwood, Buckingham, the Bristow twins – and there are others too, professional-looking men with dogs I have never seen before. There are some big animals on their leashes and chains, types that would be more suitable for a bear or badger pit than a rodent hunt, and a few scrawny creatures that look as if they would have trouble finishing off a mouse, never mind a rat.

'Your council has been busy,' the doctor is now saying. He extends a hand in the direction of the field to our right. I notice now that, around the edge of the field, a wire-net fence has been erected.

'We shall deploy the dog handlers with their dogs within the fence. When you hear a blast on this whistle, you shall release the hounds to do their work.'

Beside him, Bill murmurs an instruction.

'Ah, yes,' said the doctor. 'I almost forgot. The first instinct of the rat when pursued will be to make for the safety of water. We shall need a line of defence along the path in case any of them break through the netting. Men, use your sticks. Children, use your feet.' There is laughter. 'No rat must escape this afternoon.'

The doctor glances at his timepiece.

'If you would now all like to take your positions, Mr Grubstaff, myself and council sewerage workers will flush the beasts out for your dogs to do their work.'

He steps down, and walks towards me. 'Mr Smith,' he says, smiling. 'Yours will be the most important job of all.' He places an arm around my shoulder and leads me to a drain, just within the fence netting.

'Bill tells me that this is the biggest rat run in the field,' he says. 'When we clear the underground sewers, it is here that the rats will make their escape.' He points to a ditch half concealed by brambles. 'When they bolt, you wait, and then blow this whistle as hard as you can.'

He hands me a small silver whistle.

'How long?' I ask.

A look of irritation crosses the doctor's face. 'What's that, boy?'

'How long should I wait after the rats start coming out?'

He shrugs. 'Say the Lord's Prayer to yourself, lad. When you get to "Amen", blow with all your might.'

The light is growing dim as the setters with their dogs take up positions inside the fence. A row of men, women and children stand on the towpath blocking the way to the river. The field is truly surrounded.

Satisfied that all is in place, the doctor and Bill leave us. There is no more joking now. I am aware of an empty, fearful feeling within me. What if there are no rats, or if I fail to see them, or I blow the whistle too soon or too late?

To take my mind off my fear, I practise saying the Lord's Prayer. Our Father, which art in heaven. Just saying the words takes me back to my home, warmth, food, the smiles of my mother. They are things from another, half-forgotten world, memories I rarely allow into my head these days.

I stand alone, looking down at the hollow, aware that from the path and all round the field, eyes are watching me.

We wait. The dogs, sensing that something is afoot, are impatient, whining, yelping and tugging at their chains.

The noise, the fear fade from my mind. My eyes are trained on the ditch, waiting for the slightest movement.

At some point, I think I can hear a sound from beneath the ground. Is it human? Is it a rat?

Concentrate. Watch.

In the stillness, there is a rustle in the bramble. I see a dash of movement. The black eyes of a rat catch the light. I start praying.

By the time I get to 'hallowed be Thy name,' there is no mistaking the scurried procession of beasts from the ground.

Soon there is a torrent of brown pelts pouring from the drain.

'... on earth as it is in heaven.'

The rats hear the barking of the dogs and tumble over one another in panic. In spite of my best efforts to concentrate, I find myself thinking of Efren, back at the tip.

'The power and the glory...'

The beasts, hundreds of them, are now dashing pell-mell into the field. The barking of excited dogs is deafening.

'For ever and ever...'

Still they scramble from the drain, more and more of them. I raise the whistle to my lips.

'... Amen.'

63 The smell of danger had reached me across the field...

... before I heard the barking of dogs or the sound of the enemy. It had awoken me as I slept in the roof of the abandoned house. Now the sound of a high note, so loud that it hurt my ears, reached me. It was not a human sound, nor did it come from a cat or a bird.

I hurried to a gap in the wall from where I could see the open space between where I was and the river.

Another long, painful note.

I crouched low. As I lay there, it was as if my whole body were being filled with noise. It was not from dogs and the humans outside, but from the world below.

Fear, rage, confusion. Something terrible was happening to the kingdom.

Outside, there was movement in the gloom. Dogs were now in the field below me, darting here and there. At first, I didn't understand what they were doing.

Then I heard the screams. Inside my head, and outside in the world above, it was impossible to tell where revelations ended and noise began.

A terrible fight was happening out there. Rats are used to death, but this was different. It was not the few that were laying down their lives, the weak, the unlucky, the braver warriors. It was all of them. There was no escape.

It was roaring in my ears. It was the sound of death.

There has never been a hunt like…

… the hunt of Fisher's Field. Wherever people talk of the great deeds of foxhounds, deerhounds or otterhounds, the work of the rat-catchers and their dogs in Fisher's Field will be mentioned.

It is a massacre. As hundreds of beasts pour first from one drain, then the second, the dogs go to work.

Some of them, when let off the leash, are confused. A couple of them fight each other. Then they see their prey and forget about anything beyond killing.

Some rats make for the water, as Bill said they would. It is a bad mistake. The old men, women and children gathered there, many of them bearing sticks, set up a mighty din. Almost all of the terrified beasts turn back into the field and into the jaws of one of the dogs. Several become tangled in the netting and are quickly dispatched by stick or boot.

A few – a very few – find a gap in the fencing and, ignoring the roars of those on the towpath, dash past them and plunge into the river.

Most of the killing takes place in the enclosed waste-ground. The dogs, cheered on by their setters and supporters, dart from one scuttling beast to the next. Those I recognise from the pit – Drongo, Kentish Lad, Drum – are quickest at killing, but others work cleverly in twos. Only a few of the dogs, confused and more excited than is good for them, chase the other dogs and bark at nothing in particular.

In the confusion, I see the doctor, pacing up and down behind the fence, his face red with excitement. Near to me, Bill watches in silence. I catch his eye and he looks away, almost guiltily.

Near the centre of the field a group of rats has been surrounded by dogs, and faces them. As if at a given signal, the beasts move together, so that they seem to become one big creature with eyes looking in every direction, still and strong.

For a moment, the dogs are confused by these rats which seem so fearless. They bark, but keep their distance.

Then a young Cairn terrier, unable to hold back, lunges towards the group. At that moment, the beasts – there must have been well over a hundred of them – move towards the terrier. They are not afraid, and there is no panic in their movements. They are attacking. It is such a strange sight that the dogs hesitate, falling silent.

Enraged, the men roar at them. Some of the dogs hurry off in search of easier prey. Others look at their owners, as if asking how to deal with a group of beasts which will not be separated.

The rats are heading for a corner of the field. Too late, the men realise that there is a gap in the line of defence.

The rat battalion moves faster. Men are running to head them off but as the beasts reach the netting, something beyond wonder happens.

The lead rat, like some wingless bird, leaves the ground and soars over the fence. The others follow, almost every one of them. It is as if, for those few seconds, the beasts have borrowed the gift of flying.

The dogs finish off the few rats who have been unable to jump the fence, then bark helplessly in the direction of those who have escaped beyond the wire.

I turn to Bill. He is actually smiling to see a few beasts get away.

'They're good leapers, them beasts,' he mutters.

65 It was a terrible battle and was over...

... quickly. The shouts of humans were there, the barking of dogs, the screams as citizens fought and warriors and does and ratlings were caught, shaken and crushed in the jaws of death.

There was a louder noise, one that filled every part of my body.

I heard the terror and confusion of the kingdom.

I heard revelations from the captains as they tried to gather their courts and lead them to safety.

I heard the pulsing of the dying and the wounded.

I heard the roar of the warriors as they gathered to attack.

I heard that roar fade, voice by voice, hero by hero.

There was nothing I could do. No revelation, no gift of hearing could help the kingdom now.

Where was Jeniel? And Swylar? Had none of the Court of Governance survived the poison that had been released into the world below? At times like these, it is leaders whose revelations reach citizens before all else. No king or queen could save them in that terrible massacre but, all the same, the silence was strange.

One group of warriors at least made a fight of it; I heard them reveal on that field of death.

—Gather!

—Gather!

—Gather!

In the twilight, I could just see the dogs circling what might have been a bear but was, I knew, a group of warriors.

—Wait!

—Hold firm!

—No breaking!

The dogs were confused, and the warriors sensed that moment of weakness. One, braver than the rest, began to approach.

—Attack!

At that single order, the seething mass of life advanced. As it came closer to the dogs, it seemed to move faster.

—Attack!

The dogs retreated just far enough for the group to press through.

The fence faced them. If they had been any other kind of citizen, it would have been the end for them. But they were warriors and had learned the art of flyting. In battle, few obstacles can contain a flyting warrior.

One after the other, they took the jump in one mighty, soaring leap. Only a few failed and were quickly at the mercy of the dogs.

Slowly, the noise of barking faded. The humans moved into the space, collected their dogs, inspected the terrible work which had been done. Now and then there was a brief scuffle of activity as a dog or human found some poor citizen who had survived.

Lamps were lit. Men, women and children roamed the place of carnage. They laughed and made merry as night fell.

I have never hated humans as much, before or since, as I did that night.

66 We decide not to cut the tails...

... because it is too dark to find the corpses. After the dogs have reached the field and have dispatched any surviving beasts, the doctor gathers the setters and their dogs at the bridge.

As he stands on the first step, a few of the folk begin to clap.

Dr Ross-Gibbon raises both hands.

'Gentlemen,' he says. 'This borough is a safer place tonight after what you and your brave dogs have done.'

'Good sport and all,' says Charlie Buckingham. I notice that he is standing near to Jem Dashwood. Suddenly, it seems, they are friends.

'When's the next hunt then?' a voice calls from the back.

'There will be other' – the doctor smiles – 'extermination exercises. The brown rat is a cunning creature. It moves from one area to another. The next part of our campaign is to find more rats, and repeat the very efficient culling process you managed so well tonight.'

'What about the tails, doctor?' Charlie Buckingham looks around for support.

'Tails?'

'The reward.' Jem Dashwood speaks up.

'Ah yes, almost forgot.' The doctor reaches into his pocket and takes out the biggest roll of money I have ever seen. 'It's too dark for cutting tails tonight. I suggest that we ask Mr Grubstaff and young Mr Smith to look over the field and give us a rough sense of how many beasts have been eliminated today.' He holds up the money. 'We shall divide the reward between you all at the agreed rate of one pound per fifty tails.'

Even in this light, Bill and I can see the dogs have done a good job. I hear Bill counting, but I know it is for the benefit of the men who are watching us. Even if he can get beyond ten, which I doubt, a careful count of those bodies would take hours, even in the daylight.

I catch a glimpse of his face. He will be earning good money tonight, but you would not know it from the way he looks.

'A lot of beasts,' he says to no one in particular. 'A lot of beasts.'

By the time we return, we have decided on a figure.

Three thousand.

67 The battlefield was silent…

… by the time I descended from my hiding place. The enemy and the dogs had gone. All that remained of the terrible events of that day was the heavy smell of death in the air.

I walked around on the outside of the fence. In some places, the bodies were in tangled heaps where they had been trapped.

There was nothing I could do but I needed to bear witness to what had happened.

The netting was easy to gnaw. After a few moments I squeezed through and was on the battlefield.

The smell of death never lies, nor does the silence within a hearer. Many citizens had died and those who had escaped would be scattered and disorganised.

I walked around the bodies. Most had been torn apart but I could see that even in death, the courts had largely remained together. In one part of the field were strewn the translators, in another the spies. There was a sad little heap of historians not far from where they had emerged from the world below.

I looked for my court and, deep into the night, I found them in one corner of the field.

In this pile of corpses, I knew their names. Phillus. Gjarg. Bravar. Spyke. I pulled them from the mass of bodies, and laid them side by side.

Alpa was the last I found. She was beneath the bodies of the tasters who had fought to defend her.

With the taste of blood in my mouth, I moved away from the river. There was no returning to the world below tonight. As far as I knew, there was no world below.

I would return to the mountain, to Malaika and her human, and plan my next move.

I made my way down the fencing. It was at the point where the warrior rats had used the gift of flyting to leap to freedom that the last of so many terrible sights awaited me.

There, hunched in death against a large stone, was a shape I thought I knew. Its head was crushed beyond recognition but, when I pulled the body into the open, all doubts disappeared.

Three legs. A warrior with three legs could never leap to escape.

Even a warrior who had once saved the life of a friend and defeated a cat.

Even a warrior called Fang.

68 I earn five shillings for my work in Fisher's Field…

… and, if Caz was waiting for me, I would be returning to the tip with pies in my hand and stories to tell her.

But there is no Caz and, without her, there is no life. The tip can be burned to the ground, with me in it, for all I care.

Her rat Malaika is waiting. She is hungry. I give her a slice of bread and fill her water bowl.

I am deadly tired but, when I close my eyes to sleep, I can still see the dogs – their lolling tongues, their sharp white teeth, their red eyes.

Now they are hunting through the streets of the city, sniffing the gutters and scrabbling at doors.

I am there, and so is the doctor, and Bill, and the dog men and setters.

Somehow I realise in my heart that the baying hounds and the eager men who are following them are not searching for rats at all.

I know these streets. I have been there. As I follow the hunt, a feeling of dread is heavy within me.

We turn a corner. The barking of the dogs echoes around the dark street. There is a door in the wall. I know that door. The pack of dogs hurl themselves at it. They have found their prey.

No, not there. I try to scream a warning but the words are trapped in my throat.

It is Rose's house, the place I visited. I know what they are going to find there.

The rats are not there! Please, they are not there! I scream but all I can hear is a silent roar where my voice should be.

The doctor looks at me, and laughs.

'Thank you, Dogboy,' he says. 'I don't know what we would do without you.'

I am sick with a feeling of guilt.

He pushes through the dogs and opens the door for them.

There is a terrible snarling from the darkness within.

I fight my way through the crowd into the darkness of that room.

Rose is there and the lady with the pale face and black lips. They are looking down as the dogs attack their prey, tearing its flesh.

Seeing me, Rose looks up and gives a sort of sorrowful shrug, as if to say, 'What could I have done? What could any of us have done to save her?'

Now I scream. Again and again.

I awake with a start, shivering, my body wet with sweat although it is cold in the tip.

I hear my own despairing voice in the nightmare. It echoes in the darkness around me.

Caz.

It's Caz.

69 I stayed away from the mountain…

… that night. I had seen too many humans, and what they do, to want to be close to one.

There was a clod-cave under a hedge where I rested.

It was from there at the darkest hour that I revealed to Malaika, calling her to me.

At first, there was no answer. I was afraid that, on this night of death, something might have happened to her, too.

Then, as I crouched low in the hedgerow, I heard her.

—I am here, Efren. I am safe.

—Come out to me. I have news.

There was no reply. After some time, I tried again.

—Malaika? Are you there?

Her revelation, when it came, was more powerful than I expected. It was as if it was not a fragile revealing at all, but a rat born to be a citizen of the kingdom.

—Tonight I stay here. He needs me here.

—He?

—Caz's human. I am staying.

—Malaika, I need you here. Terrible things have happened.

But there was no more revelation. I knew Malaika well enough to understand that, when she had decided something, there was no moving her.

Although it was still dark, I slept.

It was light and a bird was singing in a branch above my head when I opened my eyes.

But it was not song which awoke me. It was a revelation.

—Malaika!

My body tensed. I was hearing. It was a revelation from far away.

—Help me, Malaika.

It took me a moment to understand why this kind of hearing was different and strange.

Then I understood.

What I was hearing was the revelation of a human, far from this place. I knew the person who was calling out. I replied.

—Caz?

—Oh, Efren.

The revelation was faint, and fading.

—Help me.

—Caz, where are you?

There was no reply for a long time. Then, a distant whisper in my brain, I heard her.

—Little dancer... little dancer... little... dancer.

Then she was gone.

I made my way slowly to the mountain and found Malaika, sleeping near to the human.

I told her of what I had heard.

We must have made some kind of noise because the human stirred, turned in his half sleep. With that movement, everything changed. A stench of anger, fear, blood and pain seemed to choke me. I was back on the battlefield of yesterday.

For a moment, I was confused. How could the smell of death be upon the boy, Caz's human?

Then I knew the answer.

He had been there.

70 The empty feeling within me is like a sickness...

... which makes it impossible to eat, or to sleep for very long. It is as if all that was alive in me has left, leaving only a walking, breathing corpse.

The last thing I need is to be bothering with rats.

Yet, when I awake that morning, I catch a glimpse of the beast that has been lurking in the undergrowth of the tip with Caz's pet. After it scuttles away, Malaika moves closer to where I am lying.

She sits in front of my face. We are at the same level and, strangely, it almost feels as if we are equals.

I have seen enough of rats over the past day. I close my eyes. Soon afterwards, I feel the animal climbing on to my arm. She settles there while I doze.

When I open my eyes, she is still there. I move my other hand gently and stroke the grey and white fur. It turns to face me, staring in that strange, direct way that rats have.

'Poor Malaika.'

I say the words out loud because saying them reminds me of Caz. She would spend hours, her face close to the rat's. Revealing, she said. It was the kind of tender fancy that made her special to me. I murmur again.

'How can we find her, Malaika?'

The rat moves up my arm until she is standing in front of my face.

On any other morning, I would get up and start my day, but

the thought of the great hunt by the river is still with me. I remembered Bill's face as we picked our way through the bodies.

'A lot of beasts,' he said.

Yes, there were a lot of beasts. I have no wish to see the doctor on this, the day after his great triumph. I have had enough of killing for the moment.

I lie in my blankets, staring into the eyes of a rat. It is better than going to work. I think of Caz.

The rat noses the air in a peculiar fashion. She does it again. Then again. If I didn't know better, I would think that she is trying to tell me something.

The doctor will soon be wondering where I have gone. He is not a man to rest on his victories. Already, he will be planning the next hunt.

A world without rats. His great dream. All the people he speaks to – the politician, the important men in the council – seem to find it a marvellous idea. I wonder about that. They can be brave and clever creatures sometimes. If they fought yesterday, it was because they were being attacked.

My mind is suddenly filled with the sight of the dogs at work. I groan quietly to myself.

—Do not be sad.

What? Those words enter my head, unbidden. It is as if I am still asleep, in a dream.

—Do not be sad.

I sit up, slightly scared. I am hearing voices now. Being alone is making me lunatic.

—It is not you. It is me.

I look down, and find myself gazing into the dark eyes of Malaika.

—Me.

She is a charming little thing, so delicate. She moves on to my hand. I raise it slowly. She makes no attempt to escape. She rests on my palm in front of my face.

She stares at me, and makes that odd upward movement of her nose once more.

No. It can't be. That doesn't happen.

—It does.

Now I am beginning to feel scared. I move my hand even closer to my face. Most creatures would show at least a flicker of fear, but this rat actually rests on its haunches, its whiskers quivering.

—Believe it. I can reveal to you and you can reveal to me.

I laugh softly. Revelation! This is true madness. For the game of it, I let my imagination talk to the rat.

—Is this how you talk to each other?

There is a tickling deep within my head, almost like silent laughter.

—Some can reveal strongly, others more weakly. Yours is so feeble I have to stand close to you.

'No.' I say the word out loud. 'I mustn't go mad. Not now.'

—It is no dream. Reveal to me. You will see.

Enough. I must awake. It is time to bring myself back to the world. I look at the rat and think these words.

—Tell me something which my own brain could not bring me.

There is a moment when my head is empty of noise. Then she is back.

—We have heard from Caz.

I start, closing my fingers around the rat. She makes no effort to escape.

—It is true. We have heard from Caz.

The voice in my head is stronger. I have no choice but to answer.

—How? Where is she?

—Efren has heard two words.

—Efren?

—He can hear revelations from far away.

—The two words. What were they?

—Little dancer.

It is at that moment that I begin to believe it. Perhaps Caz was right. We can talk to rats, but only if we listen to them.

There is some bread left from the night before. I scoff it down, leaving a corner for Malaika, and make my way out of the tip.

I walk fast across the city. The world is going to work but I have no eyes for it.

Little dancer. What does it mean?

I reach the centre of the city, turn into the narrow street I last saw in my dream. I knock hard on the door.

Nothing. I bang again.

Two men, passing at the end of the street, stand to watch me for a moment. At any other time I would return to the shadows which are my natural home but, somewhere in the night, I have lost my fear.

Let them beat me. Let them kill me. My little life counts for nothing now that Caz has gone.

One of the men says something to his friend. They both laugh and go on their way.

I crouch beside the keyhole of the door and put my mouth to it.

'Rose!' My voice echoes in the empty street. 'Rose! It's me.'

Silence.

I turn and rest my back and head against the door. I slide downwards until I feel the cold pavement beneath me.

After a few moments, the door moves behind me.

I look up. It is the white-faced girl who was there before. Her face, then so sharp and tidy and severe, is now smudged and disordered. Her hair, which was straight and brushed when I last saw her, is like a madwoman's. Now that she has no make-up, I see that she is barely more than a girl.

Looking down at me, she groans.

'Not you again.'

'I need to see Rose.'

She swears to herself, steps back into the darkness of the house and makes to close the door. I am too quick for her and push my leg so that, short of breaking it, she is unable to lock me out.

Muttering another oath, she goes inside.

I stand up, push the half-closed door and walk in.

The room is in utter darkness, with the same heavy smell of scented smoke in the air which for a moment makes my head swim.

Something moves at my feet. It is a man, youngish but with so much hair about him that his face is like a moon on a cloudy night. His eyes are wide and dark but he seems to be seeing nothing.

With a great effort, he reaches towards the door behind me, and slams it shut.

The weak flame of a small candle lights the middle of the room. I see now that there is a sort of big glass pipe there. Sleeping figures are all around me on the floor. The girl who opened the door is sitting on the sofa, her arms around her knees, shivering.

'Rose?' I call out, peering through the gloom.

From a far corner of the room, a figure untangles itself from a heap of bodies. It looks like an older, more wrecked version of Rose.

'Who's that?'

The voice is hers.

'It's me. Dogboy.'

She utters a long moan. 'You? What are you doing here?'

'I need to ask you something.'

She lies back against a man who is lying beside her. He is so deep in sleep that he could be dead for all I know.

'You picked your time.'

I walk further into the room. 'It's about Caz – the girl who's disappeared.'

'I told you, love. I can't help you. Lots of girls disappear.'

'Does…?' I hesitate, suddenly feeling stupid. 'Do the words "little dancer" mean anything to you?'

'Little dancer.' She closes her eyes. 'Little… dancer.'

From the floor, an old man sings in a croaky voice. He sounds like a sickly jackdaw.

> *'She was just a little dancer,*
> *A sapling in the green*
> *The prettiest this romancer*
> *Has ever ever seen.*
> *She twirled and she…'*

The song peters out in wheezy coughs. The man farts noisily, then turns over.

'What a lovely old song,' another male voice murmurs.

One of the girls laughs.

'Little dancer,' I repeat. 'Could that mean something?'

Rose appears to have fallen asleep.

I look in despair around the room. There must be seven people here, and none of them is in any fit state to help me.

I turn towards the door, picking my way carefully over the bodies on the floor.

My hand is on the door handle, when someone speaks.

'Champagne Charlie.'

It is the white-faced girl. She is in the same crouched pose as she has been in since she let me in. She gazes ahead of her as if she is in a trance.

'Knightley.' Her voice is hushed. 'Champagne Charlie, they call him.'

The man on the floor begins to sing again.

> *'Champagne Charlie is my name,*
> *Champagne Charlie is my name…'*

He sings the whole song. It is a long time before he is finished.

'Knightley.' Slowly, the girl's eyes find mine. She frowns, as if an unwelcome thought has entered her head. 'Lots of people know Champagne Charlie, but the girls know what he's like. He's' – she gives the matter deep thought – 'a nasty piece of work.'

'What's that got to do with Caz?' I ask.

'It's what he collects,' she says. 'Little dancers. That's what Champagne Charlie really really likes. Little dancers. They're his hobby.'

'I don't understand.'

'Course you don't.' The girl gives a light, wheezy laugh. 'Good thing too.'

'What happens to the little dancers?'

'Stow it, kid.' Rose speaks up, her eyes still closed. 'You've lost her, love. If your friend's with Champagne Charlie, she's finished.'

'Champagne Charlie is my name…' The man on the floor starts singing again.

'Where does he live, this Mr Knightley?'

The white-faced girl shrugs. 'Search me, love. Somewhere posh. Forget her, that's my advice.'

The man with all the hair looks up at me. Narrowing his eyes as if trying to remember something of great importance, he opens and closes his mouth silently as if he is dreaming. Eventually, he manages to speak.

'Plenty of other fish in the sea.' He laughs, as if he has said the funniest joke ever heard. 'Plenty of other fish in the sea.'

71 The day after I smelt the death of my friends…

… on the body of the boy human, the kingdom was calling me back more strongly than ever. I knew now that to stay with Malaika, I would have to betray the citizens who had died.

I loved her, but I could not do that.

For a rat, every defeat brings new strength. In the kingdom, destruction is a passing thing. It is renewal which lasts.

Already citizens would be gathering in the world below. I was a hearer. I had seen the battle. They needed me.

And yet I stayed under the hedge as the sun shone down coldly. Within me, the memory of that human revelation troubled me.

—Little dancer.

I would go home. Malaika had shown me how easy it is to fall under the power of the enemy. Some humans fight with weapons and dogs. Others conquer with gentleness and words.

When the sun was high in the sky, I was ready to leave. The touch-path through the mountain was familiar to me now, and I moved swiftly, knowing I could escape danger even in the daylight.

They were there, Malaika and the boy. He sat, sharpening a stick with the knife that he carried. She slept, her body resting against the side of his leg.

My first revelation from the depths of the mountain awoke her.

She looked around for a moment, then moved towards me.

When we met, she greeted me loudly and, although I was determined to be strong, I heard my sounds of joy when we touched. What could I do? I loved her.

—Stay with us.

Malaika knew. Before I had revealed, she understood that I was going.

—I must return to the kingdom, Malaika.

—But the kingdom is destroyed.

—There is always a kingdom. While the heart beats within a single citizen, the kingdom is still alive.

—Help us, Efren.

I nudged her away from me. It was time for the truth.

—Your human is the enemy.

—No. He is different from other humans. He listens. He reveals. He cares for Caz.

—Believe me. He is the enemy. He is as bad as any of them. You must leave him.

—Must?

There was a scent in the air which surprised me. It was anger.

—I can protect you. The kingdom is where you belong.

—He saved me— Malaika looked at me with a cold eye —If it were not for that human, I would have been killed by dogs.

I thought of the battle. The massacre.

—I have seen what dogs and humans can do. All humans. You are wrong to trust them.

And she was upon me. Eyes flashing, teeth bared. I let her attack, wondering all the while at her rage and strength. She was a fragile, yet her loyalty made her strong. Her loyalty to the enemy.

After a while, I pushed her off. We faced each other, nose to nose. Malaika was breathing heavily after her attack. She revealed softly.

—Help us, Efren. Then go.

—Help? How?

—You can find Caz. You told me about being a hearer. You found your king. You found me. You can lead us to her.

I stared at Malaika. The anger on her was fading. She sensed her victory. She revealed again.

—Efren, do it, and I shall return with you to the kingdom.

Help the enemy? Use my powers for a human who had killed citizens? The thought made me feel sick to the stomach.

Malaika touched me with her nose.

I asked again.

—Why?

—Because you are Efren. Because you are strong. Because it is right.

—Returning to the kingdom is right.

—Because you love me.

72 There are a lot of Champagne Charlies...

... in this town, but none of them seems to be called Knightley. That is what I discover as I wander the streets talking to the people who truly know this town: the beggars, the muck collectors, the raggies, the dips, the street-corner girls.

'Champagne Charlie?' they say. 'That would be old Pete, or Posh Gerald, or Lawrence, the bent lawyer.'

None of them has heard of a man called Knightley. A lot of them might be interested in dancers, but collecting them? No. Their Champagne Charlie wouldn't do that.

I return to the tip that afternoon. My feet hurt, and I can still hear in my mind the voices of the day, spelling out despair. Girls disappear. A nasty piece of work. His hobby. Lots more fish in the sea.

I am sitting, thinking of what Rose and the pale-faced girl have said about Champagne Charlie, when something strange happens.

Malaika, who has been sleeping on the ground next to me, wakes up suddenly and disappears into the tangle of rubbish near to the entrance to our little room. Moments later, I hear the squeal of beasts meeting.

Her friend Efren, the rat who might have heard Caz, is still around. There is silence from the rubbish for a while, then the sound of some kind of fight.

A few minutes later, the pet rat reappears alone. I pick her up to see whether she is injured, but she is unmarked.

I am just about to put her down when I feel the tickle in my brain. The rat is revealing to me.

—We shall find Caz.

I look at Malaika and wonder again whether my imagination is playing tricks on me. Maybe I am hearing what I long to hear. Maybe I have managed to persuade myself that good news is coming from a rat. Maybe I am beginning to lose my senses.

Then the tickle is there again.

—Believe. We shall help you.

I close my eyes. The last thing I need right now is false hope. But still, I'm curious. I stare at Malaika and try to do the revealing thing again. I think my question to her.

—How?

Malaika climbs on to my leg.

—Efren is hearing her. He can follow her voice. He will take me to her. And you.

I groan. What new madness is this?

—It is not madness. Efren will talk to me. I shall tell you. He says that Caz is not too far away.

I sit up. It has been a bad day, and my mind is shattered with despair. Perhaps that is why I allow myself a moment of crazy belief.

—Now?

—When the sun goes down.

I smile at the rat. If this is madness, there is this to be said for it – it makes me feel happier. The rat reveals again.

—He is good, my Efren.

I pick her up gently, and place her within my shirt.

—I'm sure he is.

—He'll lead us to Caz tonight.

And, in spite of myself, a spark of hope lights within me.

73 As I followed the voice, I saw…

… not the face of Caz, but that of my love, my Malaika. I was doing this one last thing in the world above for her. Once it was done, we would return together to our destiny in the kingdom.

The voice took me away from the grass and the trees and the damp earth. The ground beneath my feet was hard and danger was all around, but I was good now at finding my way through the human world. I knew the secret of surviving among the enemy. It is not to hide from every sound and movement around you but to know the real dangers when they come along.

Smell them, sense them, hear them, see them.

The streets grew quieter, and yet more dangerous. Here there was human life all around. There were fewer holes and hiding places.

The voice was there in my head, calling me on. The human was following me with Malaika.

I was moving fast. Soon I would have fulfilled my promise, and I would be free.

… through the streets? It is not something an impatient person would want to do. The doctor might think that rats are the great enemy with many weapons to cause men and women to fear them, but there is one gift they do not possess, and that is speed.

I am not a casual footler, a wanderer through life. I like to get from one place to another as quickly as I can. That night, though, I dawdle like someone with all the time in the world.

Within my shirt, Malaika guides me onwards, listening for the revelations of the wild rat Efren, who is ahead of us, taking his own sweet time. Often I have to loiter while we wait for the next message to take us forward.

The spirit of Caz is calling out to Efren who tells Malaika who reveals to me. Sometimes it is all I can do not to call an end to this nonsense and return to the tip.

Yet Efren is taking a straight enough path. He may be deadly slow, but he seems to know where he is going.

It is deep into the night by the time we reach a street with grand houses on each side of it. It is quite short and leads into no other street. It is into this place of quiet money and privilege that our guide takes us.

I hang back. If I am seen here, there is no reason or excuse for me to be in the street. Although they are tall, reaching up to the night sky on each side of us, the houses are close together, with no alleyways between them. Once in the street, there will only be one way of escape – the way we came.

It is as I stand there, unsure what to do, that an unfamiliar sound reaches me.

A piano. It is playing softly from the far end of the street. I walk a few paces. On the top floor of one of the houses, a light flickers.

—Ahead.

Even before Malaika prompts me, I know where I am going. No longer afraid of being seen, I walk down the middle of the road, my eyes fixed on the light.

As I approach, I recognise the song that is playing. It is an air I hear almost every day around the music halls of the city. A man, with a thin and reedy voice, begins to sing.

> 'After the ball is over, after the break of morn,
> After the dancers' leaving, after the stars are gone...'

The rat Efren has stopped. I hear Malaika's voice within me.

—She is here. Caz. Efren is certain of it.

—I know.

What to do now? It is dead of night. I am alone but for a couple of rats. Maybe I should return when it is light, watch the house, wait for my moment.

But is Caz there? It is no time to do the sensible thing. I have to know for certain.

There is a tall sycamore tree in front of the house.

—I need to see her, Malaika. I'll leave you here for the moment.

I feel the rat quaking with fear against my skin but at that moment the feelings of a pet rat are the least of my worries.

I reach into my shirt, gently take out her warm, soft form and set her down at the foot of the tree.

She looks about her for a moment, then scurries to a nearby hedge. I hear the unmistakeable sound of two rats greeting one another. She has found her Efren.

It is going to be no small matter to climb the sycamore for the lowest branch is some ten foot above the ground. There are other trees across the street, though, and they have lower branches. If I can only snap them off and lean them against the big tree outside the house, I can reach that first branch.

I break one, the crack echoing in the dark street. Then another, and a third. Laying them against the trunk, I find that I can scramble upwards to reach the lowest bough of the sycamore.

Hauling myself on to the branch, I sit for a moment, listening as the song floats through the dark air above my head.

'After the ball is over, after the break of morn...'

I kick away the branches beneath me, then look upwards. The light is flickering through the limbs of the tree above me. I begin to climb.

The sound of the piano and the voice grow louder as I make my ascent. Now and then there is a crack as I stand on a branch made brittle by the winter cold, but I know no fear. Almost at the top of the tree, I reach a branch that stretches out to the house, over the pavement below, towards the lighted window.

I can hear the voice, singing quite clearly now.

There is a candle on the piano. It seems to flicker in time to the music. Beyond it, a white curtain is moving in the breeze.

But there is no breeze. Lying on the branch, I see that the movement is not from a curtain at all.

It is a girl, dancing in a white nightdress to the music. Dancing, dancing, back and forth, skipping, twirling.

The little dancer.

Her face is difficult to see as she moves, but there is a moment when she comes to rest, wide-eyed, her face empty, waiting for instruction from the pianist.

It is her.

I have found Caz.

75 I thought she would die...

... on our way home, my Malaika. A fragile is not made for effort. The muscles are too soft, the breathing too weak. Ask them to run, jump or swim for any distance, and you will see an old rat even in the skin of a young one.

That night, there was no choice for us. The human came down from the tree, half climbing, half falling. From my hiding place nearby, I could see that his face was wet.

Malaika called out to him, but he was in no state to hear her revelation. She turned to the house, revealing again and again to Caz, but there was no reply.

The human was soon gone, stumbling blindly down the street, quite forgetting who had brought him here.

We were alone. I found to my surprise that Malaika was trembling.

—What is it?

—I have not been in the world above without a human before.

—At night when we look for food together we are alone then.

—Humans are near then.

I could smell her fear. She looked in the direction her human had gone, as if expecting him to return. He would not, of course. A human is a human, not a citizen.

She started walking ahead of me, slowly but with determination.

It was a long night. Fragiles are not made for long journeys. Malaika was cold, and soon the pads on her soft paws were bleeding. The scent of her pain filled the air. Yet still she continued.

Daylight came, murky, grey and full of fog, but we were still far from the mountain. The shapes of humans shuffled by, walking near to us quite often, but on days like this they were less dangerous than usual. The last thing that interested them was a rat.

Dogs, of course, were another matter. Malaika would be easy prey for the smallest of them. Even a cat, the most cowardly of creatures, would not hesitate to make deadly sport with her.

We rested in a gouge beneath a log pile for much of the day. Malaika was too tired and in too much pain to eat. When light began to fade, we continued our slow progress.

—Leave me, Efren. I can find my way home.

—Never. Together we'll go to the mountain.

She hesitated, leaning against me. We carried on, slower than before.

Walk. Rest. Walk some more. Rest longer. The further we went, the weaker Malaika became.

There were times when I cursed her human for his cold and selfish ingratitude.

76 In my home, my mind reeling
from what I have seen…

… I feel a sort of incompleteness. It is only when I am back at the tip and I see the small bowl of water that I understand the reason. I have left Caz's rat behind.

There is a sharp pang of sadness within me – Caz loved her Malaika and would have wanted to see her when I have rescued her – but at this moment I can't think about those things.

When all is said and done, a rat is a rat.

I close my eyes, but can only see Caz, dancing, swaying to the music which I have come to hate. By the time a blackbird, in the big hawthorn near the tip, announces the new day, I have hardly slept at all.

Today is the day when I shall free Caz. My head aches with tiredness but, having crammed my mouth with some bread, I am soon on my way to seek help. Why not? I am not entirely alone in the world, after all. I know some powerful men.

But the doctor is not pleased to see me when he opens his front door.

'Mr Smith. What can I do for you?'

I shrug, wordlessly.

'You are here for more pennies, are you?'

I say nothing, standing in the doorway. The doctor makes no move to invite me in.

'You're all the same, you street boys – out for yourselves. Where were you yesterday? And the day before? I needed you.'

I take a deep breath. It is time to talk to the doctor. Before I can speak, though, he has turned, grumbling, into the house. Since the door has been left open, I follow.

'What's the matter with these people?' Muttering to himself, the doctor walks through the hall. To my surprise, he passes the entrance to his study and opens the door to a room I have never entered before.

'We're in the library,' he says.

We? The library?

It is a small room with books to the ceiling on every wall. There are three leather chairs before a fire that has been lit. In one of them is the MP, Mr Petheridge.

As we enter, he makes to stand up. Then, seeing that it is only me who accompanies the doctor, he slumps back into his chair.

'The boy's here,' says the doctor. 'I thought he might be able to help us.'

To my surprise, he waves in the direction of one of the armchairs. Nervously, I sit down.

The politician is staring at me, an impatient frown on his face.

'Doesn't speak, does he? How can the child help us if he is as silent as the grave?'

A cold smile flickers on the doctor's face. 'He can speak when he wants to. Can't you, boy?'

'Yes,' I say quietly. 'I can.'

I sense a flicker of curiosity from the direction of Mr Petheridge. My voice surprises him.

'We need to find the rats, boy,' he says. 'We've got the hunters, we've got the dogs. The gentlemen from the council are pleased with our work. We have had newspaper reports on our campaign.'

I nod. Then, sensing the doctor's disapproval, I mutter, 'That's good.'

'People are bringing in rats' tails but we need another concerted attack like the other night,' says the doctor. 'And we need it soon. The beasts have scattered.'

Both men look at me in silence as if I have the answer to this problem, but all I can think of at that moment is Caz, imprisoned by Champagne Charlie.

There is no choice. I blurt it out.

'My Caz. She's only little. She's my friend. She's been kidnapped by a gentleman. I don't know why.'

'What are you talking about, boy?' asks the doctor.

'He makes her dance.'

They both stare at me as if I have gone quite mad.

'It's wrong.' My voice cracks. 'If you could just come with me to visit the gentleman, tell him to release my Caz, it would be the best thing in the world. I would help you catch every rat in the town. Help me with Caz, and there is nothing I would not do for you.'

My words, more than I have ever spoken to either of them, bring silence to the room. For a moment, I can believe that they are thinking about what can be done to rescue Caz, but when the MP speaks, it is not with kindness.

'Mr Smith, it is good to know that you can talk. I hope you are as good at listening.' He takes out his timepiece and looks at it for several seconds, as if deciding whether he has time to talk to me.

'I have learned one important lesson in my life as a politician,' he says eventually, and actually smiles at me, like someone who has thought of a rather good joke. 'One dabbles in the private life of ordinary folk at one's peril. It is always a mistake.'

'Caz isn't ordinary. She's only eleven, sir. She needs rescuing.'

'A girl and a gentleman.' The politician sits back in his chair and directs his smile at the doctor. 'Tell me the old, old story.'

'Just a call from you, sir. It's not far from here.'

The MP shrugs. He looks annoyed that I have dared to persist. I turn to the doctor but, before I can speak, he holds up his hand impatiently.

'Forgive me, Mr Smith. We have urgent matters to discuss here. If there has been some untoward event involving your friend, I'm sure the constabulary will take an interest. I suggest you speak to them.'

'But, doctor—'

'We need to identify the next place of extermination.' The doctor speaks to Mr Petheridge as if I am no longer there. 'Mr Smith, are you willing or unwilling to help us in this matter?'

I have heard enough. Without a word I stand up from my chair, leave the library and that house. I will look for help elsewhere.

77 That day, as I lay with Malaika…

… I thought of what had become of my life. Of the moment I had slipped out of the Great Hollow and saw my king captured by the enemy. Of the death of Tzuriel. Of Jeniel and Swylar, and how they had won power in the kingdom. Of Malaika, and how I loved her. Of the human she called Dogboy, who had saved her life and yet left her alone in the world above.

She slept, exhausted by our long, slow journey home. What had happened after her human had forgotten she even existed had reminded me of a sad truth.

Malaika was different from the fragiles I had met in the world below. She was stronger in her spirit. But, as with all those of fragile blood, something had been lost. She was in love with the bars of her cage.

Yet, in her way, she had been braver than any warrior. It was Malaika who made me lead the human to Caz. It was Malaika who had journeyed the world above, bleeding and hungry. It was Malaika who, in spite of all that he had done, was prepared to stay with the enemy.

I had never met a doe like her. So gentle, yet so strong. I gazed at her, as she lay against me for warmth. I would never love another rat in the way that I loved Malaika, and yet I sensed that part of her was for ever beyond me. It belonged to the enemy.

I had told Malaika that she could return with me to the world below, and perhaps, one day, she would. Not now, though. I was a hearer. The kingdom needed me.

Love, and Malaika, would have to wait.

78 I walk, and my eyes are blinded by tears...

... as I think of how the MP and the doctor had looked at me when I told them about Caz.

It was as if a beast had suddenly spoken, and about beastly things. I am Dogboy, Mr Smith, the assistant. I am not supposed to have a life of my own. For me to ask for their help is as strange and extraordinary – and as embarrassing – as anything could be.

Caz. Dancing for the elegantly dressed man, Champagne Charlie, on the top floor. I see the empty look of fear and sadness in her eyes.

Without knowing it, I have entered the park. A thin plume of smoke draws me towards the house of the only other person in the world I can turn to.

Bill is seated in front of a small bonfire. When I push open the door to the compound he glances up, then quickly turns his attention back to the fire.

'Bill?'

There is a log on the far side of the fire from where he is sitting. I take my place there.

'What do you want, Dogboy?' he asks.

I decide to go for a lie for the moment. 'Just called by.'

'Sent you, did they? Your fancy friends? Ready for another cull, are they?'

'It's what I said. I just called by.'

We sit in silence for a while, Bill now and then prodding the fire. I know him well enough to see that something is on his mind, too.

'Got many rats in, have you?' I ask eventually.

Bill shakes his head. 'They're gone. Scattered. Every Tom, Dick and Harry out there's hunting beasts, for the money.'

'The war on rats.'

He laughs grimly. 'That's one war that will never be won.'

'They want another hunt.' I tell him the news casually. 'It's what they're planning.'

Bill gives a low growl. He is too poor to be able to turn down the offer of Mr Petheridge's money, but I can see that he is none too happy about it.

'Well, I got no work for you, if that's what you're looking for. There's not many rats around and all the setters are too busy catching their rewards to worry about sport.'

'It's not for work I'm here.'

There must have been something in my voice because he glances up, half surprised.

'I thought you said—'

'I've got this friend.' I dive in before he can go any further.

'That's good.' Bill tries to smile, but his face can only manage a sort of scowl. 'Friends are good in this world.'

'She's been kidnapped.'

'How d'you mean "kidnapped"? What you talkin' about, boy?'

Haltingly, as we both stare into the fire, I recount the story of Caz. The only part I fail to mention is the help I received from the rats. In the version I tell Bill, it was one of the girls who told me where he lived.

'You want to get her back?'

'Yes. Of course. How could you ask that?'

'Maybe she's better off where she is. Ever thought of that?'

'That's what everyone says.' I close my eyes and see Caz's face as she danced. 'She's not better off. I just know.'

'Well then.' Bill sniffs deeply. 'We need to start thinking about how to free her then, don't we?'

I nod, unable to speak, ashamed that there are tears in my eyes.

79 I waited until the human was with her...

… before I left my Malaika.

It was as the light faded that he returned. There was a new sharpness in his movement, which made me wary. Humans are safer when they are sad.

—Something has happened.

As Malaika revealed to me, I was reminded once more why it was time to go. To survive, a rat should only smell two things in a human: danger or fear. Once we begin to sense the enemy's happiness, sadness, hope, love, we are weaker. When I replied, there was more coldness than I intended.

—It's not for me to know how the human feels.

Malaika looked at me, surprised.

—What is it, my love? What's happening?

I turned from her. After a moment, she moved towards the human. He was eating and he gave her food, speaking to her all the while in low, crooning tones. She ate, sitting upon his leg.

Yes, now I can admit it. I was becoming jealous of a human.

It was time to go. I moved into the undergrowth of the mountain where we had lived and watched the two of them, Malaika and her Dogboy, for a while.

Maybe I should have explained to Malaika why I had to return to the world below without her. How difficult would it have been to make her see that, in the kingdom, there are different kinds of citizens? Some are made to work, to carry, to father or mother, to die in battle if needed. For a few of us, it is not enough to follow duty. We have no choice. The future, the survival of the kingdom must come before all else.

She did not look round. That helped. As I watched her with her human, I grew stronger, colder, more like a true citizen of the kingdom. It had been a strange adventure, living with the enemy, but it was over.

Without another look, or word of revelation, I turned to leave the mountain of Dogboy and Malaika.

I was eager to be away from that place and, my mind empty of the past, I made my way down the hedges and pipes and gutters which led to the river.

It was a cold, moonlit night by the time I reached the field where so many citizens had died, killed by dogs and humans.

I passed the building from where I had seen it all. Shape-reading as I went, I sensed that the place had changed since I had last been here. There was no fence around the field any more, and the ground no longer smelt of death. The earth and its creatures had drawn life from the flesh of the citizens. As I crossed the field, the whiteness of bones planted there caught the moonlight. The kingdom into which I had been born had disappeared, yet I felt as if I was coming home.

A human had filled with stones the entrance to the world below which would lead to the Great Hollow but I soon found my way through. It felt good to be working again. With a last glance at the moonlit world above the ground, I descended into the kingdom.

Something strange. Now that I was in the world below, following the familiar runs and touch-paths downwards, I heard less. The sounds within me, the faint voices calling me back, seemed to fade. I was in a world without revelation.

The kingdom had changed. As I passed the hollowed trunk of an ancient tree I heard the squeak of citizens in conflict. There were five young rats scrapping over a piece of food.

I was about to continue when I saw for the first time the food over which they were biting and squeaking. It was the body of a young rat, barely a week old.

I made my way towards the Great Hollow. Around one corner, I encountered a doe with four young. When she saw me, she seemed overcome with terror. She issued a shrill alarm call and scurried away, followed by her young.

The hollow was deserted. The Rock of State was a slab of stone. Now and then, from nearby, I heard a hurried scrabbling. Once I found myself looking into a pair of dark eyes. Then they were gone.

The kingdom, as I knew it, was no more.

I followed a touch-path to where the Tasting Court used to be. Alpa, I knew, was dead, but what of the others?

When I had been with them, the tasters had occupied a small gouge which was sometimes flooded when a nearby underground stream was full. Now it was dry, but empty, with not the slightest tell or scent on the earth or stone.

One hope remained. I took the path back towards the Great Hollow. To one side, in a chamber which had once been a burial place of a human whose bones were now turning to white dust, there had once lived the one group of citizens who would not have fled the kingdom, whatever had happened.

As I approached, the smell of death which hung faintly in the air wherever I went in the world below grew stronger. The entrance to the chamber was usually guarded by two warriors, but not tonight.

I hesitated for a moment, fearful of what might await me, then made my way into the chamber of The Twyning.

What I saw was against all nature. Citizens who were part of a twyning, whose tails had been entwined together in the nest when young, were sacred. Their round of life is the very soul of the kingdom. When one of their number dies, it is quickly removed. The health of the group, its survival until the very last death, is what matters in the world below.

Yet here the Twyning of life was now a Twyning of death. It was a tangle of rotting flesh through which worms and maggots glided. Some of the rats had died more recently, their dull eyes staring upwards, their mouths open. I glanced at the shape of one body and began to understand what had happened.

The Twyning had been abandoned by the kingdom. Its members had died from thirst and hunger.

—The kingdom is no more.

The revelation came from within me, and seemed to hang in the foul, dark air around me. I turned slowly to leave, and as I did so I was aware of the faintest tickle of revelation within me.

—No.

I waited. Was it my imagination?

—No.

The revelation was there again, stronger this time.

I moved forward, into the darkness. The stench was stronger, and the remains of The Twyning almost filled the space of the chamber.

It was on the far side of the circle of bodies that I discovered that there was life there.

A rat, bigger and stronger than the rest, lay helplessly on his back. His eyes flickered as I approached. His jaw, wide open, closed and opened. I revealed to him.

—You're alive. The Twyning lives.

The rat gazed at me. I tried to reach him again.

—Stay still. I shall release you.

There was a flicker of alarm, perhaps anger, in his eyes.

—Too late.

Tradition is part of a twyning. None of its members have a name. They are more sacred than other citizens, including those who are in the Court of Governance. Above all, it is believed that they should only be released from The Twyning when there is no longer breath in their bodies.

Now, though, was no time for tradition. The rat's tail entered the tangled centre of The Twyning about halfway down its length. I began to gnaw at it and found to my surprise that it was hard and brittle, and that the blood it contained was dark, like that of a corpse.

He remained silent while I worked, giving only the quietest squeak when his body, for the first time since he was a ratling, broke free from that of his brothers and sisters.

He scrabbled feebly until no part of him touched the dead Twyning.

—Are you all right, citizen?

The rat looked at me, his eyes conveying neither gratitude nor anger.

—I am dying.

—I shall get you food and water.

The rat twitched again. Now I saw the problem. Because he had not moved throughout his life as a rat there were no muscles in his legs. He was unable to stand, let alone walk.

—Listen, ratling.

His revelation was more urgent now. I swallowed the temptation to remind him that I was Efren, a citizen who was trying to save him.

—The kingdom...

—What of the kingdom?

—It shall live.

The revelation reached me, but I did not believe it. There was no point in contradiction: the last survivor of The Twyning had no interest in what I revealed. Breathing heavily, he continued.

—Every rat is a king.

—I shall get you water.

—No. Attend. This is important.

I backed towards the opening, sensing that, unless I could bring him water, the rat would soon fade from life.

—I shall return. You will get stronger. I hurried to the river, took a mouthful of water, and returned.

When I entered the chamber, stillness was everywhere. I leant over the rat, put my mouth to his, let the water pour.

It spilt through his teeth, on to the earth below. The light in his eyes had gone. His flesh, when I touched it with my nose, was cooling.

The last member of The Twyning was dead. At that moment I felt more alone, more lost, than ever before in my young life.

Suddenly, in the silence, I was hearing.

It was not a memory, and it was not an echo. It was the last great truth, uttered by a sacred twyning, and it would remain in my heart until the day I too would die.

Every rat is a king.

Every rat is a king.

Every rat is a king.

80 The tails are coming into the Town Hall...

... but still Mr Valentine Petheridge MP is not entirely happy. He visits the doctor a few days after the great hunt by the river. As the two men make their way through the hall, the MP asks the question which seems to have been on his mind.

'How many of the beasts do we have now?'

'Over 2,500,' the doctor replies. 'Mr Woodcock is beginning to complain of the cost. It seems that our friends in the ratting community have taken to bringing in beasts from other boroughs.'

'Bad show.' Mr Petheridge purses his thin lips. 'This is my campaign. I'm not paying good public money for the tails of rats from other MPs' constituencies.'

I follow the men into the library.

Why am I there? It is the day after I have found Caz, and I know that I must keep working for them. Without their money, and maybe without their power, I shall be truly lost. The moment when I dared ask for their help was not mentioned by the doctor when I appeared on his doorstep. As usual, the MP ignores me.

'We need to persuade the public,' he is saying. 'Convince them that if we don't act against this terrible scourge, their little ones will be eaten alive in their cots. There is to be a public meeting at the Town Hall the day after tomorrow. We'll need him' – he nods his head in my direction – 'to help out.'

'Are you available, Mr Smith?' The hint of mockery in the doctor's voice is unmistakeable.

'Yes,' I say quietly.

'Make the public afraid, and they'll soon vote for you.' The MP sits down and holds his bony hands up to the fire. 'We need to put on a show for them. The press will be there. We must have something newsworthy to give them.'

The two men sit in silence for a moment. Then the doctor glances in my direction.

'We'll need Grubstaff,' he says.

I shake my head. 'Mr Grubstaff isn't happy,' I murmur.

Mr Petheridge gazes at me. His look is not friendly.

'Mr Grubstaff lives in the park, does he not, Mr Smith?'

I nod.

'It is council land, I believe. Grubstaff has been allowed to live in his shed until now, but of course that can always change.' He smiles nastily. 'A word in the right ear and your friend will be without a home.'

'There must be a health risk, having a rat man in a public park,' says the doctor.

Both men are now staring at me. Bill, I know in my heart, will be no match for these men and their power.

'I'll tell him,' I mutter.

'Tell him we want a show.' Mr Petheridge stabs a finger in my direction. 'Something which will play well in the newspapers.'

'People need to hate the beasts.' He turns to the doctor. 'Once rats are truly the enemy, our war can begin in earnest.'

That night, after work, I visit the park to see Bill Grubstaff. Before I break the news to him that he is going to be forced to fight in the great war on rats whether he likes it or not, I have more important matters on my mind.

'When, Bill?'

He sits, shoulders hunched, gazing at the bonfire in that sad, distant way of his.

'When what?'

'When are we to rescue Caz?'

A low, complaining mumble, like that of an old bull being annoyed by a calf, comes from him.

'Need to know who's got her.'

'We know that. And where she is.'

He pokes the fire. 'Need a plan,' he says. 'Can't just go and knock on a gentleman's door like that.'

'He's not a gentleman. He captured Caz. She's his prisoner.'

He looks at me. 'Maybe, maybe not. No one's going to believe us. They don't even see us most of the time.'

In my heart, I have always believed that Bill's world begins and ends with beasts – finding them, catching them, preparing them for the pit, getting paid for them. Now I see an anger in his eyes which I have never seen before.

'We have to do it ourselves,' he says quietly. 'But maybe we're not alone.'

Between us, we work out a plan. It is desperate and risky, but it is better than nothing at all.

I leave him long after darkness has fallen. I walk quickly to the street where Knightley, Champagne Charlie, lives.

I stand on the dark street, looking up at the single light on the top floor. The piano is being played softly tonight, its sounds floating over the rooftops of the city.

'I'll be there soon,' I whisper. 'Hold on, Caz.'

81 The death of The Twyning…

… changed everything. The scuttling shadows I saw as I made my way through the world below no longer reminded me of the great massacre that had just taken place.

There were citizens. They were alive. While they breathed, the kingdom was not dead. It was in the heart of each of us.

I was no longer just Efren of the Tasting Court. Every rat is a king. I had to act.

I went to the Great Hollow and, without a moment's hesitation, I ascended to the Rock of State. The time when I would have been fearful of punishment was past. There was nothing now for me to lose.

In this war, fear itself was the enemy.

Soon after I took my place on the rock, a doe rat hurried by with three of her young.

She put her head down and headed for a nearby rest. I was aware that she was watching me from there.

I waited, exploring the corners of the Rock of State as if it were my natural home. Soon, the doe, followed by her ratlings, ventured out, as I knew she would. I revealed, quietly, in the manner of a citizen.

—Welcome, sister, which court do you belong to?

The doe humbled briefly and nervously.

—Translators.

She looked at me and revealed again, less fearful now.

—There are not many of us left after…

—After the battle, yes. I saw them. They fought well, the Translators.

—You saw the battle?

I was aware of rustles of movement at the back of the hollow. Eyes, curious and afraid, glinted in the darkness.

I continued.

—I was in the world above. I was not able to reach the fighting, but I saw what happened. It was a great victory.

—Victory?

—It was a trap. The enemy tricked us. We fought bravely. The kingdom will be stronger now.

The shapes below me moved closer. When I revealed again, it was louder and with a quiet certainty.

—Now we must prepare for the future.

There were more citizens in the darkness than I had first thought. They looked hungry and lost but the smell of fear in the air was beginning to fade. I could sense a hint of hope.

We. Prepare. The future. This was the message for which they had been waiting.

It was a young warrior on the far side of the river who asked the question that was in the minds of all the citizens there.

—What shall we do?

I allowed a silence to settle upon the Great Hollow. When I revealed, it was with a new strength that would reach all the citizens in that place.

—We shall do what we always do. We shall unite and be strong.

At first it seemed as if my revelation would not be enough. The rats and does and ratlings who were gathering in the Great Hollow had been confused by their leaders in the past.

King Tzuriel had urged peace upon the kingdom but had died in the hands of the enemy. Queen Jeniel had taken it to war and into a massacre. I revealed once more.

—We have an enemy who wishes to destroy us. We need to decide if we should fight or flee. What is best for the kingdom.

There was a new restlessness below me. Citizens were not used to being asked. They were told.

A young rat beyond the river was first to reveal.

—What is your name?

—My name is Efren.

I awaited the challenge, but it never came.

—Are you a part of the Court of Governance?

—Yes.

—What do you tell us, Efren?

—The kingdom must unite. We must build again after this great battle. And, if we must, we should fight the enemy.

There was another long silence, broken only by the ripples of the river as it rolled through the kingdom.

I looked out, knowing that there was no escape now.

I was on the Rock of State. I was not part of the court. At that moment, I *was* the court. I revealed with a confidence which in my heart I did not entirely feel.

—It is time to work. The kingdom is alive again.

82 A man with rounded shoulders and a shuffling gait...

... is walking through the streets of the town. A large leather suitcase is in his hand. Beside him is a boy of thirteen. Neither speaks.

We are on our way. Bill and I, with a few friends, are about to pay a visit to Mr Ralph Knightley, known to some people as Champagne Charlie.

It is a bright and cold winter's morning, and the frosty ground crunches beneath our feet.

We turn into the street, ignoring the wary glances of a nanny taking two young children for their morning constitutional.

As we approach the house, I think of our plan. So much can go wrong but, perhaps strangely, I have faith in Bill. He is angrier than I have ever known him to be.

As we draw nearer, he murmurs, 'Just do what I tell you, boy, and your girl will soon be safe.'

'It's there.' I point to Knightley's house, looking up at the top window in the hope of catching a glimpse of Caz. The curtains behind every window except those on the ground floor are drawn.

Without hesitation, Bill approaches the house. He opens the garden gate, walks past the giant sycamore I once climbed, and strides up the stone path as if he owns it. He lifts the knocker on the door and hammers loud, twice.

I feel braver, being with Bill.

The house is silent. Behind us, a carriage rattles along the main road at the end of the street.

After a few moments, Bill knocks again. This time I notice that he is glancing towards the basement windows. He has told me stories of his teenage days when he was part of a gang of child burglars. Since then, he once said, he has never broken the law. I have wondered to myself how true that is.

He knocks a third time, more insistently now. The sound echoes off the walls of the houses opposite.

There is a noise from within.

Latches on the front door are drawn back, and the door opens.

He is not at all how I expected, Knightley. He wears a well-tailored dark suit and has shiny black shoes. With a trimmed beard and a clear eye, he is utterly confident, every inch a gentleman.

'Yes?'

The voice is that of someone used to giving orders. I judge that he is older than he seems at first glance. There are flecks of grey in his beard and hair. He is a man on the dangerous turn of life, approaching fifty perhaps.

'Beg your pardon, sir.' Bill gives a humble little bob. 'We're from the council. If we can just inspect your water closet.'

'No.' Knightley makes to close the door but, to my surprise and his, Bill's foot keeps it open.

Knightley opens it again and puffs out his chest like a cockerel. 'My good man—'

'Public health,' Bill says firmly. 'Council says if we're refused by householders then the constabulary will become involved.'

'My housekeeper will be in later this morning. She shall show you the... facilities.'

'Constabulary says it's urgent.'

'Oh, really, does it?'

'You'll have heard of the war on rats,' Bill says.

'What on earth is that?'

Bill glances at me as if shocked by this show of ignorance.

'Great problem to health, sir. Disease and all sorts. Our job is simply to check your system. If rats appear in your water closet, it can be very unpleasant.'

'This is a very bad time.'

'Perhaps you would like to tell that to the constabulary.'

A nervous look flickers across Knightley's smooth features. I sense that he would prefer that the police are not invited to his house.

'How long will the inspection take?'

'No more than five minutes, sir.' Bill holds up his case and I am almost sure that I can hear a sound issuing from it – a muffled scrambling and squeaking – but Knightley is too keen to be rid of us as quickly as possible to hear it.

He steps back into the dark house and, with an impatient jerk of his head, leads us into the hall.

The house is very different from its owner. It has not been tended or tidied the way those whiskers have. There is a thick layer of dust on the hollow table. The air is heavy with the smell of old cigar smoke and drink. No housekeeper has been near this place for a long time.

As we follow Knightley down a narrow corridor, I notice that empty bottles are lined along the wall on the floor.

He opens the door to a small room.

'Be as quick as you can,' he mutters. 'I'm expecting guests.'

'Yes, sir.' Bill does another of his ever-so-'umble bobs of the head.

'What is the war on rats anyway?' Knightley asks.

'Very serious war, sir.' Bill is almost enjoying himself now. 'The beasts are coming up through the sewers. Biting kiddies. Are you a family man yourself, sir?'

'I'm a bachelor.'

'Ah yes, they come up the pipes, rats – big 'uns too. Into houses. Bathrooms. Water closets. Some folk have had nasty nips where they were least expecting it.'

Mr Knightley shudders. 'I'll leave you to it.'

I glance at Bill. We both know that we are too far from Caz.

'Maybe we should start with the upstairs water closet.'

'That won't be possible.' Knightley speaks sharply. 'It's out of order.'

'Rats like a water closet that's out of order,' says Bill. 'We have instructions to inspect all water closets. From the constabulary.'

Knightley licks his lips nervously. 'This is outrageous,' he mutters. 'Wait here, I shall investigate whether it is available.'

He leaves us. We hear him climbing the wooden stairs above our heads.

'Well done, boy.' Bill gives me a wide, toothless smile. 'I think you're getting the hang of this.'

'She's on the top floor, Bill. I'm sure of it.'

'Patience, boy.' Bill gives the suitcase a little shake, and winks.

We wait. Minute follows minute. The house is silent once more. What is he doing up there?

'Maybe he's hiding her,' I whisper.

'Time for us to do a little investigating.' Bill picks up the suitcase and moves quietly into the corridor.

The staircase Knightley took is at the back of the house. Narrow and steep, it is for servants to use.

Stealthily, we climb.

The first floor is, if anything, grimier and dustier than downstairs. We stand on a landing and look about us. The door to every room is closed. On a table in the passageway is a tray with dirty dishes and mugs. There is a smell of stale food in the air.

From above us, we hear a faint scraping noise. It sounds like furniture being moved.

The stairs leading to the next floor are even narrower, and gloomy. Bill looks up into the darkness.

'Mr Knightley?' he calls out. 'Shall we come up?'

Something is wrong. We both sense it. Bill passes me the suitcase.

'I'll be back in a minute, boy.'

He has his foot on the first step when we hear the sound of someone descending rapidly.

'Stay there! Don't move an inch!' Knightley stands half hidden where the stairs turn. He is in shadow but I can see he holds a heavy silver-tipped cane in his hand. He moves towards us, holding the stick in front of him, like a club.

'How did you know my name?' His voice is low and threatening. 'Who are you? What do you want?'

Bill steps back, his eyes fixed on Knightley. 'It's the war on rats, sir. The council has—'

'Liar!' With surprising speed, Knightley takes the last four steps in one bound and, flailing his walking stick, is upon us.

'Oh, no.' Bill sounds almost disappointed. He dodges to one side and grabs the arm holding the stick.

The two men fall heavily against the wall, Bill's suitcase dropping to the floor with a clatter.

An elegant, pale-skinned gentleman against Bill Grubstaff – it is a fight which can only go one way.

'Take my money!' Knightley cries in a strangled voice. 'There's no need for violence. Please!'

Without a word, Bill lifts him so sharply that his polished shoes leave the ground for a moment.

With a sound that is half a grunt and half a swearword, he pushes him against a wall, grabbing the silver-topped cane in the same movement.

His right arm moves so fast in an upward jab that it looks like a punch but, as Knightley cowers, Bill grabs the hair of his beard on his left cheek and leads him like a donkey to a small door nearby. Bill twists the ring-latch and pushes the door open. It is a small, dark dressing-room.

He holds Knightley in the entrance, then turns him, almost as if they are dancing together, towards the room. With the sole of his boot against his back, Bill pushes him sharply into the room, sending him sprawling across the ground.

'There you go then.' Bill closes the door briskly and reaches for the cane. Then he seems to have another thought.

'Give me the case, lad.'

I pass it to him. Holding it flat on his raised right knee, he lifts both latches. 'Open the door,' he says.

At the very instant that I push against the door, Bill opens the suitcase and jerks it wildly in the direction of the figure lying on the floor. Scores of rats fly through the air like a flock of birds taking wing, landing on and around Knightley. I catch a glimpse of him, turning, his eyes wild with terror and disbelief, before Bill pulls the door shut. The squeals of the beasts are drowned by his shouts of panic.

Bill picks up Knightley's walking cane and, with a quick, easy movement, thrusts it through the latch of the door, jamming it closed.

For a moment, we listen to the thumps and yells.

Bill frowns, as if he were a little embarrassed by how easy the job has been. Then he closes the case and hands it to me.

'Let's find the girl,' he says.

Taking two steps at a time, he goes up the narrow stairs. It must have been a maid's room because by the time we reach the closed door at the top, Bill is crouching beneath the slope of the roof.

He pushes the door open. From the light of a single small window, we can see a dingy little room, bare of furniture but for a narrow bed, a chair, a table and a washstand in one corner.

'Caz?' Even to me, my voice sounds despairing. 'Are you here?'

Silence.

Bill walks to the bed and pulls back the sheet.

'Someone's been here, that's for sure,' he mutters.

He checks the window. The latch is off the hook. Standing on the chair, he pokes his head through it.

'Roof's flat enough,' he says. 'Maybe your little bird has flown.'

'No.' I look under the bed. There is a pot there, unused.

I stand up and look about, a growing sense of desperation within me.

This room is different from the rest of the house – cleaner and with less clutter. And yet, in its centre and with no chairs nearby, there is a small table.

Underneath, there is a rug, of almost the same measurements of the bed. Something about the way it is arranged seems out of place.

I pull the table aside, then tug at the carpet.

A long crack in the floorboards is revealed. When I look closer, I realise that I am looking at some kind of secret hiding place.

'Bill!' I shout. 'There's a trapdoor here.'

Bill hurries over. Half the trapdoor is under the bed, so we have to heave it aside. Now we can see the door clearly. To one side of it there are two holes. Bill pokes his fingers through them and lifts.

She is dead. Those are my first thoughts as I look down into the space beneath the floor. In the same nightdress in which I had seen her dancing, she lies motionless, her arms wrapped around her knees. She is held in a sort of crate which fits perfectly between the floor joists.

I kneel down, sick with foreboding. I move the hair away from her face.

Her eyes are wide open, and she blinks rapidly.

'She's alive!' I say the words out loud.

Around her mouth, I see now, is a gag. Her wrists have been bound to her legs with silken curtain ties.

'Caz!' With trembling hands I untie the knot of the gag at the back of her head.

'Peter.' It is a weak, terrified whisper.

The ropes around her wrists and legs are tightly tied. I reach for the knife in my back pocket. But the rope is thick, and my knife blunter than I had thought. Bill, with an urgency in him I have never seen before, pushes me aside and takes the knife.

He manages to cut through Caz's bonds until her body within the crate begins to relax. Caz is looking upwards, her eyes darting around the room as if expecting Knightley to appear at any moment.

'Can you move?' Bill whispers.

Caz shakes her head. Leaning down, Bill reaches beneath her arms and lifts her out. With difficulty she straightens her limbs, looking about her like a princess in a fairy tale, awoken after a long sleep.

She looks fearfully at Bill.

'Have you got shoes?' he asks. 'A coat?'

She stares at him, saying nothing, almost as if she is unable to understand the question. We hear a thump from downstairs, and she starts.

It's no time for conversation. Bill pulls a blanket from the bed and puts it around Caz's shoulders.

'Time to go, children,' he says. 'Follow me.'

He goes down the stairs slowly, carrying Caz. When we reach the landing below, it is surprisingly still, with not a sound issuing from the room where we left Knightley in the company of a hundred or so rats.

'Had we better check he's all right?' I ask.

'Don't be soft, boy.' Bill continues his way downstairs.

I put my ear to the dressing-room door. It seems to me that I can hear a low moan. Without making a sound, I gently slide the walking stick which is holding the door firm through the ring-latch. At least, when we have gone, and when he dares, Knightley will be able to free himself from his prison.

We descend to the next floor, and Bill puts Caz down. She looks around her. Then, slowly, like someone in a dream, she walks towards a closed door. She opens it.

I see the piano, the candle, the little stage. It is the room where she danced for Champagne Charlie.

Caz's shoulders are shaking. I look at her and see the tears on her cheeks.

'Dogboy!' Bill has gone ahead of us and is downstairs. His voice is urgent. 'Let's go!'

I take Caz's hand. I shut the door to the room and we make our way downstairs.

83 In the world below there was a scent in the air…

… and a stirring in the blood, which every rat understood.

The kingdom was coming to life again.

I remained in the Great Hollow. The time for revelation was past. It was not for me to search for citizens and bring them to this place. They must come here under their own will. Each would decide in his or her heart whether to be part of the kingdom or to seek their future elsewhere.

Yet ours was a kingdom without a king. Citizens looked up at me, alone on the Rock of State, and there was often a furtive questioning in the air around them.

Who was this citizen who had revealed to them? Was he king now? There had been no fights, no ceremonies, no great gatherings of citizens. It seemed, if not wrong, then unusual.

I gazed at them with what I hope seemed like calmness. King Efren? I had no wish for that. I was a citizen, one who had seen what the enemy could do to our kingdom. I knew that the kingdom must survive and that, just possibly, I could help it to grow stronger. There was part of me that longed to be among them, just another citizen doing his duty, but I knew now that I had no choice.

Someone had to be there on that Rock of State and I knew in my heart that someone could only be me.

I too would need help. I looked down to the citizens who were gathering in the hollow. There were, I knew, leaders and fighters among them. But how was I to find them?

A ratling from the Court of Translators brought some food, a morsel of meat found in the world above, but, having laid it at my feet, he scurried away before I could thank him.

It was at the end of the night when I stepped down from the Rock of State and moved through the hollow.

As I went, citizens moved aside. Some looked at me suspiciously. They had seen enough of leaders to know that they should never be trusted.

—We need courtiers.

My revelation was quiet. It took in one group at a time. There was no reply.

—The last Court of Governance has died. No one knows where they have scattered to. Who wishes to be a courtier?

They avoided my eyes. I heard a snicker sometimes. An older rat, a historian, revealed quietly as I passed.

—And who, tell us, shall they be following?

I turned to him.

—My name is Efren. If you wish for another leader, then say so.

He skulked away, teeth chattering mutinously.

I left the hollow, climbed towards the world above. I took the trail to the network of runs below an ancient tree where the Court of Tasters used to stay. The touch-path was familiar, yet now everything was different. There was a scent of tell but it led away from the runs and paths. I listened for the woodnote, the sound of all nature which reveals danger or safety. It was quiet. Citizens everywhere were lying low, looking after themselves.

I stood in the place which I knew from my younger days. Now it was deserted. I waited there for a moment. Citizens are more at ease when surrounded by others, but my stay in the world above had changed me. I liked to be alone, and other citizens sensed that within me. It set me apart.

Everything here, I knew now, had changed. Fear was at every turn. No one was trusted. I wondered what hope there was to unite citizens again after the terrible events in the world above.

The strongest had surely been killed in the battle. Some warriors had survived – I had seen their mighty leap to freedom – but I had no idea where they were now, or whether they would have the stomach for another fight.

It was while I waited there that I sensed the presence of another rat. It shuffled slowly across the hollow. She: I smelt, while she was several lengths away from me, that it was a doe; still young, but a mother.

She approached me, with neither fear nor curiosity. When I greeted her, she looked at me for a moment, then revealed.

—Efren?

She moved closer, whiffling as she approached. A rat's instinct is to assert itself, but I let her smell me. She revealed again.

—It is Efren. We thought you were dead.

—I was trapped in the world above. I didn't fight. I saw the battle.

The doe looked at me, as if to decide whether she was in the company of a coward.

Let her decide. It was no time to tell my story. Instead, I asked her where her ratlings were.

She sniffed sharply and the sour smell of grief was in the air.

—They were taken. By other rats. They were my first. Staying with them saved my life. Now they're gone.

—It is not citizens who are to blame.

—The enemy did this?

—In a way, it did.

—We must fight.

I sensed defiance in her now. I asked her name.

—Driva.

—I remember you now, from the days when Alpa was captain.

—Poor Alpa.

—The kingdom is not finished, Driva. We can bring it back.

There was no hesitation.

—Of course we must. For my ratlings, and those of the future.

—You and me? Then we find others.

—We should start now— She nudged me with her nose, and I felt stronger, less alone —You and me, Efren.

So it was that Driva became the first member of the new Court of Governance.

84 We stay in the tip…

… even though Bill offers to look after us. I can see from Caz's eyes that she needs to be alone and safe with me and Malaika.

The next day I talk a lot. Caz sits, Malaika slumbering in her lap, her eyes empty. Maybe she is listening, probably she is not. I tell her about how Bill helped me, about the hunt by the river, about the war on rats. I decide not to ask anything about Champagne Charlie.

We have no money, and Caz seems hungrier than before. I have no choice but to go back to work, leaving her in the company of her pet rat.

The doctor is excited when I arrive. It is the day of the public meeting. Another battle in the great war is being planned. He is a man who sees his great mission in life happening before his eyes.

As we make our way by carriage to the meeting, he gazes out of the window. Then, as if the thought has just occurred to him, he says casually, 'Your job will be to take charge of the rats' tails.'

I must have looked puzzled or displeased because he speaks impatiently.

'I know, Dogboy,' he says. 'It's not a wonderful job, but it's necessary. The war on rats' – he dropped his voice, as if a rat hiding in the carriage might overhear him – 'is about to enter a new phase.'

'Dr Henry Ross-Gibbon,' he says to the clerk behind the desk when we arrive at the Town Hall. 'I am to see Mr Woodcock of the

Public Health Department. My colleague here will be collecting an item from the basement.'

The clerk smiles at the doctor. 'Of course, sir.' Without so much as a glance in my direction, he walks to a small door at the back of the hall and opens it.

'Down the stairs, following the corridor to the end. You'll see them,' he says.

I look down the dark stairs.

'I'll need a candle.'

Sighing like a man forever having to deal with unnecessary requests, the man goes to a cupboard behind his desk and takes out a lantern. He lights it and gives it to me with a hard look in his eye.

I hesitate. 'How long shall I wait there, doctor?' I ask.

The doctor is gazing out of the window across the hall. 'Someone will collect you when you are needed,' he says.

I descend the wooden stairs, the lamp before me, and reach a stone-floored corridor. Along the entire length of one wall there are piles of ledgers and boxes of papers. It is chilly, damp and mouldy down here, and a trace of something rotting and unpleasant hangs in the air. At the end of the corridor, I see a door.

I push it open and walk in. The foul smell of putrefying flesh makes me cough and gag. I am in a large cavernous basement which seems at first to be empty.

I hold up the lamp and peer into the gloom. Against the far wall is a heap of earth, and a few sacks. When I move closer, I see that there are thousands of rats' tails, only some of which have been put into sacks.

I back towards the door. There is a loathsome taste in my mouth. I lay the candle on the damp stone and cover my mouth and nose with my hand.

Time passes slowly when you are in a cellar with only rats' tails for company. I close my eyes and try to force the filth and evil – Champagne Charlie, the hunting of beasts, the stink of their tails – from my mind. In the lobby of the Town Hall there are pictures of men on horses hunting foxes. I think not of the men in the pink coats or their hounds and horses but what surrounds them. The trees, the fields, the hedges, the streams. One day I will take Caz away from the town and its cruelty into the green of the country.

I am deadly cold by the time I hear the sound of steps on the stairs. The door opens. It is the clerk.

'You're wanted in the chamber,' he says. 'Bring one of the sacks.'

'But—'

'Just do it, boy. And don't come too close to me.'

I cross the room, the lamp in my hand. I am used to filth, but the sight and smell of the heap of tails is more repellent than anything I have known. Close to them, I notice there is movement in the tangle of flesh. The white, writhing skin of maggots at work catches the light. Coughing, I reach for one of the sacks and lug it over my shoulder. I seem to feel the dampness and movement of maggots against my back.

I follow the clerk up the stairs, into the light of the entrance hall and up some wider stairs. Halfway down a corridor, there is a small door, beyond which I can hear the sounds of a meeting.

As I approach, the clerk winces with distaste.

'Wait near the door until you are called.'

Quietly he opens it, and stands back for me to enter with my sack of tails.

I am in the biggest room I have ever seen, and it is full of people, standing in silence, their eyes fixed on the stage. A few of those close to the door catch the smell of the sack and, casting reproachful looks in my direction, move away.

Mr Petheridge is making one of his speeches. It is the usual stuff – 'war', 'health', 'danger to our children', 'the great challenge of our age' – but I am too amazed by what I am seeing in that hall to pay much heed.

Everything has changed. The last time I saw the MP making

a speech, there was laughter and chat. Now it is as if he has some great secret to impart, something which will affect each of them, and which they have never heard before.

He is talking about what he calls 'the great extermination campaign' when he glances in my direction.

'This borough has shown the world that the rat can be defeated,' he declares, holding a finger in the air. 'My esteemed colleague Dr Ross-Gibbon' – he gestures to where the doctor is standing towards the back of the stage – 'has shown us how to destroy the beasts. And you, the people of this great borough, have shown that each of us can help.'

He beckons to me.

'Mr Smith,' he calls out. 'Kindly join me on the stage.'

I am about to put down the sack when he adds, 'No, bring your booty with you, my boy.'

With some difficulty, I drag the sack of tails across the hall and up the few steps which lead to the stage. There is alarm in the audience as they notice that the sack is leaving a trail of dark blood on the floor.

'Thus far' – the MP raises his voice – 'our people's campaign has resulted in over twenty thousand beasts being exterminated from our streets. And we have the proof.'

I look down on the crowded hall. No one is looking at Mr Petheridge now, nor at me. Their eyes are on the bulging, bloodstained sack that is beside me on the stage.

'Show them, Mr Smith.'

I reach for the bottom of the sack. Those nearest the stage back away hurriedly.

'No, I don't think we need to see all the contents of the sack, Mr Smith.' Mr Petheridge gives a nervous laugh. 'Just show us a sample.' He made a scooping gesture with his hand.

For a moment I stare at him in disbelief.

His look becomes more threatening.

'Show us a sample, Mr Smith, please.'

I take a deep breath, reach into the sack, grab a slimy handful of tails, and hold them aloft. One or two slip from my fingers and fall to the floor. There are screams and shouts and pandemonium from the audience.

'Calm down, everyone,' Mr Petheridge says, nodding eagerly in my direction. 'They are safely dead, and can now be returned to the sack.'

I do as I am told, then pick up the stray tails from the stage.

'There are many sacks like that, and we need more,' the MP continues. He pauses for a moment, as if a sudden thought has just occurred to him. 'We should, though, be on our guard. The enemy is now on the attack.'

At this point, the doctor moves to the front of the stage. He is carrying a newspaper.

'Ladies and gentlemen,' he says. 'I believe that I have explained in the past how my research has shown the rat to be a cunning and vicious creature. Its instinct is to fight and destroy any species which competes with it. That is, us.'

He unfolds the paper slowly until he finds what he is looking for.

'We are engaged in a war, and we now know that the war has entered a new and dangerous phase. The rat is desperate, and it is fighting back. We know already that it likes to attack babies in their cots. Now it is going further.'

He flourishes the newspaper before him. 'Some of you may have read yesterday's newspapers. They made shocking reading. The headline here says it all – MAN EATEN ALIVE BY RATS.'

He holds up the newspaper, showing everyone in the hall the headline.

'We have the first known adult victim in the war against rats, ladies and gentlemen,' the doctor continues. 'His name' – he glances at the paper – 'is Mr Ralph Knightley.'

85 It was not heroes we were looking for...

... but citizens who could lead. Driva and I knew it was not enough to believe in the kingdom. Every rat believes in the kingdom. We needed courtiers who would show citizens that, if they believed in something, they should be prepared to fight for it.

It was to be a Court of Governance unlike any other in the history of the kingdom. Those who would be part of it would not have fame or reputation or great heroic deeds to offer. They would simply have the hearts of ordinary citizens, and a determination that we should not be defeated by the enemy.

When Driva set out alone in search of leaders, she faced a harsh struggle. She was a doe, and the only member of her sex who had been a courtier was Jeniel, whose name was now never mentioned in the kingdom.

Her revelation was weak. Why, rats would ask, should we follow a doe who reveals no more clearly than an ordinary mother of ratlings?

Yet we had no choice. It was to be a court of ordinary citizens. That would be our strength.

We agreed to meet on the Rock of State at the end of the night. By then, we would know if the kingdom had a new court.

I sensed Driva's doubts as we said farewell.

—Strength is what we need, sister. Others like you.

She looked at me, communicating her feelings as only a doe can, and for the briefest of instants I thought of Malaika. It was like a sharp jab of pain within me.

Driva left, and I headed for a small wood near the river where, I knew, rats foraged for food during the night.

It was strange, emerging once more from the drain into the world above but not turning towards the home I had made with Malaika and her humans. I wondered about them for a moment. Had Malaika found her human? Were they safe? Did she ever think of me, back in the kingdom?

I moved towards the trees. I needed warriors, and I knew that some had survived the battle. But where were they? If their captain was alive, they would be together somewhere. If he had died, they would have dispersed and would be causing trouble somewhere.

I listened. From across the town, human sounds reached my ears. They meant no more to me than the rustling of the wind through dried leaves on the forest floor.

Advancing slowly, I made my way into thickets of brambles. There were rabbits here, mice and hedgehogs, but little sign of citizens of the kingdom.

It was as I crossed a clearing that I smelt that I was not alone. Something was tracking me. I froze for a moment, my senses alert.

It was a rat, and not a cunning one. It was making too much noise, not listening for danger. Only a warrior would be that clumsy.

Backing into a rabbit's burrow, I waited as he followed the touch-path. When he appeared through the undergrowth, I saw that although he was strong like all warriors, his coat was dull and matted.

Head down, in a world of his own, the warrior followed my trail until it turned towards the burrow. There was something wrong. No warrior would be that unguarded. I looked about me, suddenly aware of the scent of other rats, but it was too late.

Several heavy bodies were upon me. For a few seconds, the rats nipped and nosed me. Even as I was attacked, I knew that I should not offer or even humble. I stood my ground as their teeth cut into my flesh.

Only when they sensed that I was not fighting them did they release me and shuffle backwards, eyeing me all the while, their teeth bared.

I was surrounded by six strong, large warriors.

—My name is Efren.

My revelation sounded feebler than I intended. One of the warriors snickered.

—I mean no harm. Are there many warriors in these woods?

The first rat I had seen was about to reply when an older warrior nipped him into submission.

I moved towards him, and revealed.

—I come from the world below. The kingdom needs fighters.

—The kingdom?

The warrior seemed less guarded now.

—Yes. There is still a kingdom. Even after the battle.

—What do you know of the battle?

—I saw it.

A rat behind me bit my flank painfully.

—You watched while we were fighting and dying?

—I was not able to reach you.

—What do you want with us, now?

I waited, my eyes on the older warrior in front of me. With a warning glance at the others, he moved closer to me. I took my chance.

—I am from the Court of Governance. Are you the leader here?

—I am. My name is Growan.

—The kingdom is being rebuilt. There will be a new court.

A sharp smell of suspicion filled the air. One of the young warriors revealed.

—We've seen enough of new courts. Where was Jeniel when we needed a leader in battle?

Growan silenced him.

—Why should we trust you?

—Because trust is all we have.

We stood for several moments, one rat surrounded by six others. Then Growan seemed to reach a decision.

He turned away from me, revealing as he went.

—I'll take you to the other warriors.

86 The news that Champagne
Charlie has been eaten alive…

… by rats shakes Bill.

All his life he has been afraid of the law. Now he thinks it is only a matter of time before he will be tried for murder.

'Tell me again,' he says, as we sit together in front of his fire that night. 'What exactly does it say in the newspaper?'

'Knightley was found dead. There were rats in the room. When they opened the door, they were feasting on his body.'

'They must have been starving, them beasts,' he mutters, holding his head in his hands. 'I never should have trapped him in that room.'

'You didn't.'

He looks up at me, surprised.

'The walking stick. I left it—'

'I pulled it out. Knightley could have escaped.'

We stare at the fire, the same question forming in our minds.

'So what happened?' Bill breaks the silence. 'How did he die?'

'In the newspaper it said that the doctor thought the rats attacked him.'

Bill pokes the fire. 'Shows what he knows. Beasts aren't like that – not against a man, anyway.'

'There would have been a fight,' I say. 'Even if they did attack him. We would have heard something from that room.'

'Maybe the doctors will find something.'

'They won't.'

Bill is looking more confused than ever.

'They want the rats to have done it,' I say. 'That way the war can continue.'

A low moan comes from Bill. 'Now what are they planning?'

'Another hunt. Bigger than the last one. The hunt to end all hunts. They want you there and all.'

He stands up and wanders over to the empty well. 'Who would have thought a few rodents would be of such interest to humans,' he growls sadly.

'Maybe it's what rats can bring them. The politician gets his votes. The doctor becomes famous. The hunters get money.'

Bill sighs. 'Poor beasts,' he says.

87 The word was spreading in the world below…

… as the kingdom became one again. There was a court once more. A great battle lay ahead. We would arise again.

The Great Hollow was a place of activity and hope. Citizens now looked to me for guidance. When I revealed, they fell silent. When I passed by, they made way.

I wanted to tell them that there was nothing unusual about me. I was simply Efren of the Tasting Court. There were other hearers in the kingdom. In the Court of Spies, Translators and Tasters, there were more cunning citizens. Every warrior rat was stronger than I was.

All I had was this. I had seen the great battle, but was not part of the defeat. I knew that the kingdom could rise again if only rats dared to hope once more. I believed.

—Every rat is a king.

That was the message, the simple word from the last dying member of The Twyning, which I revealed when citizens looked to me.

At the dawning of one night, I visited the hollow where the new Court of Spies had gathered, and listened as they planned their campaign. It had been Driva who had found a young spy called Barcas who, like me, had been in the world above when the massacre had taken place. Barcas was young but had an authority about him. He was innocent when it came to politics and, in normal times, that would have mattered among the guileful spies, but not now.

They are strange citizens, spies. From an early age they have known that they are slightly different from others. They forage and gather (spies are always bucks), yet their true interest is in rumour, gossip, secret information. They are only really happy when they know more than other citizens.

Barcas moved among his fellow spies, revealing as he went.

—What do we know about the enemy? Why had we not known about the battle they planned? It must never happen again. Go up. Spread out. Listen. Smell. Tell no one except me what you hear. Enemies are at every turn.

The rats seemed to be paying no attention to him as they snuffled the ground, questing the air occasionally, but that is the way with spies. They take in information while apparently doing something else. There is only one moment when you can be certain that a spy is not listening to you, and that is when he appears to be listening to you.

Barcas stopped his revelation when he saw me.

—Efren.

Like all spies, he was careful not to give anything away, even in his greeting.

I nudged him to put him at ease.

—What are you hearing, Barcas?

—We shall know more tomorrow. The spies are going into the world above tonight.

—They need to find out if the enemy is behaving unusually. Any sign of a new attack on the kingdom must be reported immediately.

Barcas looked at me in the cold, knowing way of the spy.

—Enemies are not only in the world above.

He moved closer to me.

—Be wary, Efren.

I waited for more. Getting information from spies was never easy.

—You have enemies. They are waiting for their moment. We have heard reliable reports.

—Thank you for your concern, Barcas. Can you tell me more?

—Enemies within the kingdom. You need guards with you. Even they may not be enough.

I moved on through the hollow. At every turn, the kingdom was repairing itself. The Court of Tasters had been studying where poison air had been left by humans. The last attack, they had discovered, was less deadly than the first.

The poison had not killed any citizens, but had driven them in a state of panic to the world above and into the jaws of the dogs.

They nibbled and shifted around the passages which led to the Great Hollow, discovering where the traces of poison still lingered. If those could be blocked, the tasters reported, then in the future poison air would spread more slowly through the kingdom, allowing citizens to spread out and escape in an orderly way.

The Court of Diggers were already at work on this project.

I climbed to an area almost in the world above where the Court of Strategists was discussing the kingdom's last disastrous battle, learning lessons for the coming conflict.

And here was something surprising and pleasing. Among the strategists was several historians, including their captain Gvork. As I approached, the attention of the group turned to me.

—The battle we have experienced was unusual, Efren.

Gvork revealed in the manner of historians, as if his only audience was himself.

—Normally humans are deadly but disorganised. They see us, they try to kill us. The need to terrify is part of their natures.

I thought of the humans I had known; the boy who had rescued Malaika, the girl who had looked after her so gently.

—Not always. I have known humans to be kind.

The captain of the strategists, a rat called Joram, drew closer.

—That is how they seem, but if you truly know them…

—I have known them.

The twenty or so rats nearby looked at me with disbelief and suspicion. I revealed again.

—But it is true the battle showed that there are few who are kind. What is your advice, Joram?

The strategist hesitated.

—We are still working on the details, but we believe that the kingdom should move as soon as possible.

—Citizens are still gathering.

—True. And there is the danger that humans will attack again.

Gvork, the historian, moved forwards.

—There is no record of the enemy behaving in this way towards us. Something has changed in the world above.

—We must defend ourselves— Joram continued —Courts must only gather occasionally. We were attacked last time while we were together.

—Are you sure that there will be another battle?

—Yes. And probably greater than the last one.

It was another strategist who now revealed. His fellow rats chattered their agreement. All of them now seemed eager to express their views.

—Once humans start behaving like this, they continue. They get a taste for it.

—And they are organised like never before.

—They will be planning for the next battle.

—They want us dead.

This last revelation was from Gvork. He went on:

—That is my conclusion. For whatever reason, they have resolved to destroy us.

I waited for their advice. It was Joram who revealed what was in all their minds.

—We could always attack first.

All eyes were on me. Now was not the time for a decision, yet I sensed that I should not appear indecisive. I revealed with my best imitation of certainty.

—Prepare a plan for that. I shall return tomorrow for your views.

It was time to return to the world below. I bade farewell to Joram and his court. Gvork asked if he could accompany me.

It was a surprising move. Historians like to stay with their own kind.

As we made our way through the wood, our feet rustling the frosty dead leaves beneath our feet, a glow in the light in the east was bringing the city slowly to life. It had been a long night.

—There is something else you must know.

Gvork revealed as he followed my tracks. So this was why he had wanted to travel with me.

—A decision is needed from you.

—About the battle? Whether we should attack or move?

—Before that, Efren.

Gvork was not an old rat but, like all historians, he was unused to taking exercise. I waited for him to catch up with me.

—History teaches us one thing above all. In times of trouble, of war, the kingdom needs a strong leader.

I knew where he was heading now.

—Many citizens will die. Terrible decisions will have to be made.

—I know.

—Only you can take that role. You have shown it already. Although you are not a warrior, citizens look up to you. It seems you have the instinct of authority.

I let him continue.

—It is not enough merely to lead.

Gvork stopped walking, and turned to face me.

—You must be king— he continued —King Efren. It is what citizens expect.

The trees around us seemed to stir while he revealed. Beyond them, I thought I heard a distant woodnote, but I ignored it.

—Citizens may expect many things. I must follow my own destiny. The truth is that I have no wish—

301

I stopped, my nose suddenly sensing an alien smell. Leaves were rustling but there was no wind. The noise was of an enemy. I let out a warning squeal but, as I did so, I was knocked off my feet. I felt sharp teeth upon my neck. Somewhere nearby, Gvork screamed.

Rats. Several of them, and they were strong. They could only be warriors. Helpless, I waited for the end.

The teeth around my neck slackened, and the two warriors who were upon me slowly and warily released their grip.

I found my feet but I was surrounded. There were five powerful warriors there, all from the kingdom. One squatted upon Gvork, who seemed to have swooned in terror.

—Not much of a fighter, are you, ratling?

I knew that revelation.

Two of the rats moved aside to allow a smaller, darker, smoother citizen to sidle through until his nose touched mine. It was Swylar.

—The coward, Efren.

Swylar nipped me contemptuously on the shoulder.

—Efren, the citizen who avoided the battle. And now he is back, telling the kingdom what to do.

—Swylar. I thought you were…

—Dead? Yes, a lot of citizens assumed that. I was unfortunately too late to fight in the battle. I have remained in the world above.

—Where is Queen Jeniel?

—Queen no more. She stayed in the world below and died in the poisoned air. Hiding in a gouge, alone. It was not a glorious death.

Swylar ambled over to Gvork and bit him sharply on the ear. The historian screamed.

—Historian, you will die.

Gvork trembled, his eyes held tight shut.

—But not yet. We shall release you. Your task is simple. Tell the kingdom that Efren is no more. Swylar has returned.

The dark rat sank his teeth into Gvork again. I smelt the historian's blood as it flowed from the wound.

—Is that understood, citizen?

The warrior rat which had been holding Gvork released him slowly. The historian opened his eyes and looked about in terror. As Swylar moved closer, he cowered.

—You have questions?

Gvork seemed too terrified to reveal.

—Go then. Spread the good news through the kingdom. Swylar is back. The coward Efren is dead.

88 The Town Crier soon plays…

… his part in the war against rats. I hear him, near and far in the town, his voice echoing off the walls of houses.

'Oyez. Oyez. Be it known that in this here town Mr Ralph Knightley, gentleman, was murdered ever so tragic by rats in his very own house and home. Be it known also that he be found, nothing but the bones and the skull of him, all massacred and grievously eaten alive by rodents. So all people, men and women, who bring news of attacks by these here werry deadly rats upon the people of this town, shall be rewarded at the Town Hall. Oyez. Oyez…'

No one is making jokes about rats now. The word has spread about the thousands of rats' tails at the Town Hall. Mr Petheridge's speech is on the newspaper hoardings on the street corners. The doctor has been asked by *The Times* to write an article about his work. He plans to call it 'The Menace of Rats'.

But it is the death of Champagne Charlie, the news of it spreading around the town, becoming more horrible with every telling, that has really changed everything. We are all in danger, or so people have begun to believe. The beasts are on the attack. There is a new saying that you hear on every street corner, in every tavern.

It's them or us.

The day after the meeting at the Town Hall, I go with Bill to the Cock Inn. He has had the idea that 'the rat madness', as he calls it, will interest people in watching bouts at the pit. Or maybe he just wants to see Molly Wall again.

'We might have to go outside the borough to find beasts, but that'd be worth it,' he tells me on the way to the tavern.

'Maybe.' It is good to see Bill with a little hope in his heart, but within me I know the truth. The times have gone when rats were sport. He is longing for a past which will never return.

For the first time in my memory, Bill and I enter the Cock Inn without a crate of rats between us. At first, without our beasts, no one recognises us.

Bill walks to the bar and asks Little Timmy, the boy serving beer, whether the landlady is at home. He goes to fetch her and, as we wait, Bill looks around.

'Crowded, considering there's no sport to watch.' He sounds a bit disappointed.

'Not the same without the pit, though,' I say, more to please him than anything.

We both gaze across to the centre of the bar. The pit has been covered with polished flooring boards, and Molly has put a few cushions on it. What was once a place of death and betting is now just a big, circular seat.

'Well, if it isn't Bill and the lad.' Molly bustles out, wiping her hands with a cloth. 'What brings you here without your rats?'

Bill blushes, as he always does when Molly speaks to him.

'Thought you might be needing another pit day.'

Molly laughs. 'Every day is a pit day these days. They're all out there with their dogs, cutting off tails to get the reward. I've never known anything like it.'

'It's wrong.' I speak the words without thinking. Molly looks down at me, smiling, and I realise that she may not have heard my voice before. 'They're only animals, aren't they?'

She ruffles my hair in a way that makes me jump at first – the only time that adults touch me is to hit me. She laughs, then touches my head more gently.

'You can keep the tails, if you like,' Bill says. 'There'd be good money after a few bouts.'

'You know what, Bill?' She lays a hand on his arm. 'I'm beginning to feel sorry for those beasts of yours. Maybe it's time for us to leave them alone.'

Bill is staring at her hand, still resting on his arm, unable to think of anything else.

'Let me buy you both a drink.' Molly breaks the spell. 'On the condition that you both promise not to talk to me about rats.'

She pours Bill a pint of stout and gives me a ginger beer.

After she has gone, we sit drinking in silence by the bar.

'Not out catching beasts, Bill?' A short, heavily whiskered man, with a head as bald and round as a billiard ball, stands at the bar. I recognise him as a regular from pit days.

'Not today.' Bill gazes into his beer. 'There aren't too many rats around right now.'

The man chuckles as if he has just heard a rather bad joke. 'Course there are. They're movin' in. Everybody knows that.'

Something – maybe the disappointing news from Molly, maybe the beer – stirs Bill to reply.

'I know rats, my friend,' he says, raising his voice slightly. 'They're not moving in and they're not attacking no one. It's all a load of nonsense.'

A man and a woman sitting at a nearby table start taking an interest in the conversation.

'You tell that to the mother I've heard about,' the woman calls out. 'Her youngest boy was taken in its cot, poor little thing.'

'Dogs and all,' the man mutters. 'I've heard terrible stories of dogs being attacked in the street.'

'Great gangs of rats.' The woman sounds angry now. 'Marauding, they are. You're not going to tell me that's normal, mister.'

Bill shrugs. It's obvious he's regretting that he mentioned the subject.

'If we don't stop them now, they'll be after us.' The woman looks around her, addressing the bar as a whole. 'It's the little children I'm worrying about. They don't understand how dangerous a rat can be, poor mites.'

The whiskered baldie at the bar nods in our direction.

'Bill here knows more about rats than most of us,' he says. 'He's a rat-catcher.'

306

'Well, he should be out there, helping with that war against rats they're all talking about.'

The atmosphere in the place has changed in the last few minutes. I notice now that people are looking at us in a way that is definitely unfriendly.

'Maybe we ought to go, Bill,' I murmur.

He gazes into his beer as if the answer to all his troubles can be found there.

'All right, Grandad.' A man in his twenties who had been drinking at the other end of the bar joins the discussion. 'If you know so much about rats, tell me this. Last week, when my mates were packing up the market at the end of the day, a gang of beasts waited until the last fruit stall was being taken down, then they attacked.'

'Attacked?' Bill shakes his head. 'The only thing they attacked was the food. They were just doing what comes naturally.'

'Yes, old man, attacked.' The man at the bar moves closer. 'Are you calling me a liar? There was some down a side street, some around the gutters of the square. My mate and his friend were surrounded – surrounded by rats.'

'What did your mates do?' asks the woman who started the discussion.

'They scrammed, both of 'em – only thing they could do. I reckon my mates had a lucky escape there. A few more minutes and the rats could have had them.'

'It's true what they're saying.' The woman is staring hard at Bill. 'It's them or us.'

Bill takes a slow sip of his beer.

'I have, now and then, seen a beast attack a human,' he says quietly.

'There you are.' The young man at the bar looks around, quite pleased with himself now.

'But,' Bill wipes his mouth with his hand, 'only when the human is attacking them.' He pauses, and the whole pub is quiet. 'If you corner a group of rats, they'll go for you, all right – they're fierce little fighters – but they'd never do harm to a human for the sake of it. They're afraid of humans.'

There are raised voices of disagreement all around us.

'So what happened to Knightley, then?'

'Yeah, they attacked a grown man, ate him alive.'

'Babies, they have too. Everyone knows that.'

'Them or us, mate, them or us.'

The young man is now next to us, and squares up to Bill. His eyes, I can see, are bloodshot. He is more than halfway drunk.

'Are you saying my mates made it all up?'

Bill is uneasy now. 'I'm telling you them rats in the market place weren't hunting humans. They were just looking for food.'

'Are you on their side, or what?'

'I know rats, is all.' Bill glances in my direction. We need to be out of here and fast.

'I've heard of people like you.' The man taps Bill on the chest. 'People who say that your rat is just an animal, that everything will be fine if we just understand them, and act nicey-nicey to them.'

'While they kill our children.' It was another woman's voice from the back of the pub. Several other people shouted their agreement.

'You know what I call traitors like you?' The man is now standing so close to Bill that he has him trapped against the bar. 'I call 'em rats.'

He looks around for approval.

'He's a rat, all right,' the woman at the table calls out. 'He's got a mouse with him and all.'

They turn their attention to me, and laugh. I clench my knuckles in rage.

There is such a noise in the Cock Inn that it is only now that the drinkers notice that Molly has appeared behind the bar. Under her glowering gaze, the hubbub slowly dies down.

'What's going on?' she asks.

The young man steps back from Bill and wipes the front of his jacket as if being close to us has left him with something unpleasant on his hands.

'I'm not drinking with no traitor,' he says. 'If this man's welcome at the Cock Inn, then I'm going somewhere else.'

'Yeah, me too.'

'And me.'

'Get him out, Molly.'

Molly lays her big hands on the bar.

'What's our friend Bill done to you then?'

'He's a rat,' says the young man, and there is laughter round the room. 'If we was all like him, the rats would have won their war already.'

The presence of Molly has done nothing for Bill's confidence.

'The beasts are all right,' he says, but defeat is in his voice.

As jeers echo around the pub, Molly winks in our direction.

'I think you'd better go now, Bill,' she says quietly. 'But you're welcome back any time.'

We make towards the door, watched in silence by everyone in that pub.

'Rats,' mutters a man, sitting alone at a table. He spits into the sawdust on the floor.

We leave. As the door swings shut behind us, we hear clapping and laughter from the pub.

89 Terrified and bloody, Gvork blundered…

… away from the warriors and into the undergrowth. We listened until the sound of his progress faded into the night. Then, casually and taking his time, Swylar turned his attention to me.

He considered me as I was held, helpless, by his warriors. When he did finally reveal, he showed no anger. It was almost as if we were friends.

—Why?

I waited for him to explain the question.

—Why did a ratling from the Court of Tasters want power so much?

When I remained silent, he moved towards me. The two warriors who had been holding me backed away.

He circled me, and I faced him as he went, not wishing to be attacked from behind.

He revealed again, more sharply this time.

—Why? How many battles have you fought? Have you even killed in your short life?

—I have not. And I am not ashamed of it. I have just wanted to be a good citizen, to do what was right for the kingdom— I glanced at the warriors, including them in my revelation —Like all of us here.

A faint smell of uncertainty was in the air. Sensing that his warriors were listening to me rather than him, Swylar darted forward and nipped me.

I waited. I was not going to be drawn into an attack.

I turned to face him.

—And you, Swylar? Battles? Killing? Have you done those things?

The dark rat was still, but he could sense, I knew, that the loyalty of his followers was weakening. He revealed now with a quieter menace.

—You are right, ratling. I have had citizens killed. Quite a few traitors and weaklings, rats like you, have died because of me. But I have not had the pleasure of doing the job myself. Until now.

A sound from the depth of the wood could now be heard. Rats were approaching.

Swylar squealed a command.

—Prepare to fight.

In the gloom of the wood I saw the eyes. Something strange had happened. Gvork must have told the strategists and historians that I was facing death but, instead of spreading the news throughout the kingdom as Swylar had expected, they were here.

Swylar snickered.

—Historians and strategists facing warriors! I've seen everything now.

The five warrior rats, their bodies tensed for battle, faced the advancing group. Swylar stood behind them. He now revealed with a sharp urgency.

—My warriors, look at them. They are feeble strategists, dusty old historians. Rattle their bones for them!

—Do not fight.

The revelation came from me. If it was the last thing I could do as a citizen facing death, I would speak against citizens fighting one another within the kingdom.

—Save your blood for battles against the enemy. Now is the time for us to be strong together.

The strategists and historians continued to advance. Although they outnumbered the warriors, they were weak, and they were hopeless fighters. They were walking towards their deaths.

When they were a few lengths from the warriors, they slowed. Swylar hissed his orders out loud.

—Attack! Now!

The warriors remained motionless.

—Warriors! That is an order!

—No.

I was surprised by the strength of my own revelation.

—No citizen will attack another citizen. Too much blood has been spilt.

Swylar looked at me, his teeth bared. I turned to face him.

—This is a matter between Swylar and me.

A strange, sweet scent was in the air, and it came from both the warriors and the raggedy band which stood beyond. It was relief. No citizen in that wood, not even warriors who would fight their own shadows given the chance, was eager for battle right now.

—So. Be. It.

There was a different tone in the dark rat's revelation now. It was silky, reasonable.

—We should resolve matters between us, you and I, Efren. You are right. Now is no time for fighting amongst ourselves.

He actually yawned, and settled back on his haunches.

—Maybe I have been too gentle.

He revealed so quietly that I had to move towards him to understand what he was saying.

—Because I'm not a warrior, I have been on the side of peace. That's why I supported you at court, Efren. I thought that you and I could change things.

—Why did your warriors attack me?

Swylar half closed his eyes.

—Because I thought you were harming the kingdom. Now, from the way you've been tonight, I have seen you are a leader. Together, you and me, Efren, what could we not achieve?

He crouched low, humbling before me, his eyes gazing up at me. The citizens who watched us were restless, embarrassed.

Those in the Court of Governance never made this gesture of submission in public.

For a moment, I looked at him there. By putting himself at my mercy, he had taken the fight out of me.

Perhaps the dark rat was right. It was, at last, a time for reconciliation. He had put his trust in me. He had shown the courage to lay himself low before me in the presence of citizens. I, too, would show that, for the sake of the kingdom, we could work together.

—Citizen Swylar.

I revealed softly as I looked down at him.

—Arise. We shall work together.

Swylar closed his eyes. His whiskers twitched, a gesture of ease and friendship.

—Let us humble before one another, and then stand together.

Awkwardly, I stood over him. Humble? Together? What was this?

Swylar opened his eyes. I noticed a glint of threat in them and was about to move back.

Too late. With the speed of a striking snake, he lunged at me, his teeth closing around my throat.

I reared backwards in pain, carrying him with me. Together we fell, writhing on the forest floor, only now it was he who pinned me down. I felt a burning agony in my neck. Swylar may not have been a warrior, but someone had taught him how to kill. His grip stopped my breath.

—Swylar.

In desperation, I revealed. I felt the strength of my revelation, so close to him, shake his body.

—This is wrong. We could work together. For the kingdom.

—Die, ratling. You are as foolish and innocent in death as you were in life.

My body was becoming weaker, as the life ebbed from it.

I closed my eyes and there before me, in that instant, was a vision from the past. It was Fang while he was being attacked by a cat. I saw him through the mist of pain. He gathered his hind legs upwards in a slow bundling movement.

I gathered my legs.

Almost in a ball, like a hibernating mouse of the fields, Fang had brought his feet to rest against the throat of the cat.

I brought my feet to rest against the throat of Swylar.

He had slackened his body.

I slackened my body.

Then he had tensed and kicked, as if making the greatest leap of his life, hurtling the cat.

Hurtling Swylar backwards, I was aware of a roaring in my ears, a rage I had never known, as I found my feet and pounced with all my weight on him. He wriggled away from me but my teeth in a quick double-bite caught and then tore the flesh of his cheek.

Screaming, he backed away from me, but I held him. The strength was returning to me now and, even in the thick of the fight, I could smell Swylar's fear.

For a moment, we were locked together. Then, quite soon, I felt his muscles slacken. Remembering how I had been tricked last time, I shook him by the head.

He went limp. With my weight on top of him, I changed my bite until my teeth were upon his throat. It would take the smallest twitch of my jaws to end the life of Swylar.

The sound in my ears had changed. I heard a chattering of teeth from the citizens watching me. No one, it seemed, liked Swylar. They were glad to see him facing death.

I slackened my grip. Carefully, my eyes fixed on him, I moved away, and waited.

My teeth had left a deep wound in the side of his face. When, slowly, he took to his feet, I saw that one eye was wounded beyond repair.

I began to relax. There was no fight left in Swylar.

—Torture, will it be? A slow death?

His revelation was weak.

—No.

—Giving the citizens a bit of a show, are we? Let them see that the mighty Efren can fight?

He shook his head, and his damaged eye was loose in its socket as he revealed.

—You can fight, all right. Strong and cunning. Quite a surprise, ratling.

I was not to be provoked. The strategists, historians and warriors looked on, expecting, hoping for, the traditional end to a fight of this kind.

Power or death. That was the way it had always been in the kingdom.

And now I would change that. My revelation was not only for Swylar but also for the citizens who were watching us and who would tell other citizens.

—You were right, Swylar.

He gave a shudder of impatience, eager for it all to be over. I ignored his reaction.

—You were right about the kingdom. Now is no time for its leaders to be fighting. Enough blood has been shed.

Swylar looked at me warily.

—It's not a trick, Swylar. You can go, but on one condition, which you must agree to before these citizens.

—And if I do not?

—If you do not, you can return to the court from where you came. You shall serve the kingdom in your own way.

Although Swylar crouched before me, the way he stood told me he no longer expected to die. His one good eye watched me as he began to lick at his wounds.

I revealed firmly.

—Swylar, I shall tell you where I think your duty lies. You should remain part of the Court of Governance. We need your brains and your cunning.

There was a smell of suspicion in the air. None of the rats watching us liked what they were hearing. It was a widely held belief in the kingdom that citizens, once they have grown, do not change the way they are. I was embracing danger.

Swylar continued his licking. He had recovered some of his old coolness. When he revealed, there was something different about him, something which gave me hope.

—Thank you, Efren. I agree to what you propose.

90 For days after her return from the house of Knightley...

... Caz says nothing to me. Sometimes I wake at night and look across at her. Her eyes are open, staring at who knows what visions in her mind.

I shall not ask her what happened at the house. To this day, she will not talk about it.

It is Malaika who pulls her through. The pet rat offers company and love in a way no human can. There are no questions within the animal, beyond perhaps a gentle enquiry for food and water.

They communicate in that strange mind language of rats, revelations, which seems to have slipped away from me again. Sometimes, lying in the tip, I am aware of a faint tickling in the brain, and I know that Caz and Malaika are in conversation. As to what they are saying to one another, I have no idea.

I talk to her, though. I bring her the news of the doctor, Mr Petheridge and the great war on rats.

'They are heroes now, Caz – or so folk believe,' I tell her the morning after Bill and I all but found ourselves in a fight at the Cock Inn. She listens to me carefully, silently, stroking Malaika who is on her lap.

'Heroes to the people. They are recognised on the street. The doctor tells me that he is asked questions in the newspapers. There are rumours that Mr Petheridge may become something high-up in the government. All because of rats.'

Caz lifts the chin of her own rat, and smiles into its dark eyes.

'There is to be a big meeting tomorrow. The doctor says they are planning a great hunt – "the big push", he calls it. He thinks that, in a matter of days, there will be no more rats in the borough. Extermination – that's what he calls it. Extermination.'

Caz looks at Malaika, then at me.

I think I know what is in her mind.

'We'll look after Malaika,' I say. 'She'll be safe with us.'

Just as I look at them, a troubling thought occurs to me. If it were not for the other rat, the wild one who stayed with us a while in the tip, everything now would be different. We would never have tracked down Champagne Charlie. Caz would be there now. It is because of that rat that she has been saved.

Caz looks at me, with that weird, calm, unblinking gaze, and whispers the first words she has spoken since she was rescued.

'We must save Efren.'

91 The Court of Governance gathered...

... in the gouge behind the Rock of State next night. There were no elders to tell us the way of doing things. We hardly knew one other. We had no idea who was strong and who was weak, who was to be trusted and who might be traitor.

We were there because there were no other citizens to do what we were doing.

As I moved among my courtiers, I wondered at the strange course of events which had brought me to this place.

I can admit it now. I was lonely, and full of doubt.

I felt like someone pretending to be a leader in some strange game. At any moment, I thought, a citizen might recognise me for what I was, and reveal in surprise.

—Efren? What are you doing on the Rock of State?

And yet, courtiers still looked to me, and expected me to make decisions, issue orders. That night, I revealed to them.

—We have reached the moment when we must decide the way forward. Each of you will speak. We shall then summon the kingdom to order what is to be done.

I looked around at my new court. There was Growan the warrior, Driva the doe, Barcas the spy, Joram the strategist, the historian Gvork. Swylar stood near the back of the group, the wound on the face giving it a look of permanent, wide-eyed horror.

—Who wishes to reveal first?

Barcas raised his head. In the manner of spies, he revealed so quietly that we had to move more closely to him.

—There are reports that the enemy is preparing for a great new battle.

He looked around him, as if expecting to be contradicted. We waited for more.

—There are dogs everywhere. Attacks are more frequent. They want to destroy the kingdom.

—They always want to destroy the kingdom.

It was Gvork, the historian who revealed. Barcas reacted with surprising certainty.

This is different. There is a new mood in the world above.

—How do we know this? I asked.

Barcas seemed to close in on himself. His reply was the spy's favourite revelation.

—Information received.

—Is there any understanding of why the bodies of citizens are being abused?

This was Driva.

—Tails are being removed. We believe it is a simple act of cruelty on the part of humans.

—What happens to dead citizens is not our concern— I revealed firmly —It is the living who matter now.

Joram, the sleek young rat from the Court of Strategy, pushed to the front.

—Barcas is right. The evidence is clear from the world above. What needs to be decided is what the kingdom should do. There is a choice of three ways forward. We move. We prepare to defend. Or we attack.

—Attack!

Growan reacted like all warriors. For them, fighting and killing was the answer to all the big questions.

—History...

Gvork began to reveal with the irritating reasonableness of his court.

—History teaches us that the kingdom is strongest when it moves. When humans move, we follow. In the fields, we move together. Movement is strength. It is part of our nature.

For a moment, the Court of Governance seemed convinced. Then, to the surprise of us all, Swylar revealed.

—As always, the historian speaks with logic.

There was a contemptuous snicker from Growan, but Swylar silenced him with an angry glance from his one eye.

—It is no joke. We learn from the past.

He turned to me, then continued.

—I have learned from the past.

I raised my nose in acknowledgement, and Swylar looked away quickly, as if suddenly remembering our battle. He continued:

—But if we move, what then? The enemy will believe it has won the battle. It will want to win the war. Other kingdoms will be attacked. Maybe ours. What do we do then? Keep moving? Retreat for ever?

—Never!

Growan's revelation was so impassioned that he actually allowed a squeak of anger to escape him.

I waited for Swylar to continue, but he sat back on his haunches. All eyes were on me.

—We shall ask the kingdom.

I sensed a faint scent of disappointment. Driva revealed next.

—If I were a citizen in that Great Hollow, I would be waiting to be told, not asked. We are meant to be leaders, not followers.

—Attack!

Growan moved to the front of the court, daring any courtier to contradict him.

—Enough.

I revealed strongly.

—The way of the past, of ordering citizens what to do, has failed. I shall explain the decisions which face the kingdom. Many will die. They have a right to be heard.

I moved towards the entrance.

—Wait.

Once again, it was Gvork, the historian, who surprised me by revealing.

—Who are we?— He moved to the entrance barring my way —We are a group of citizens. We have but one true warrior among us. Only Swylar has been in the Court of Governance. How can we be leaders if there has been no ceremony to make us so?

—It is too late for ceremonies, Gvork.

I revealed with quiet firmness and moved forward, but he barred my way.

—History shows us that to be strong a kingdom needs a king.

There was a chattering of agreement among the courtiers.

Swylar sidled his way to the front.

—The historian is right. A short ceremony is all that is needed. King Efren.

The others revealed, every one of them.

—King Efren!

—King Efren!

—King Efren!

—Hail to King Efren!

I faced them, suddenly more convinced than I had ever been before.

—No. I shall lead, but I shall not be king.

I turned and, for the briefest moment, Gvork stood in my way. Then he moved aside, allowing me to make my way towards the Rock of State.

92 Caz has had the kind of lunatic idea…

… which has me wondering whether she will ever recover from what happened in the house of Champagne Charlie.

'You want us to find this rat—'

'Efren. He has a name.'

'—and warn him of what the doctor has planned.'

'He saved me. Now I'm going to save him.'

'But we have no idea where to find him?'

'How did you find me?'

'The beast led me there.'

'No. He led Malaika there.' She strokes her pet rat. 'Efren heard me. He followed the sound in his head. I know it's a mystery, Peter. No one in the world would believe that we can hear a rat's thoughts and that he could hear me from so far away. But we know it's true, don't we?'

I think about it for a moment. I have to admit that, even though I still think Caz may be becoming a lunatic, I am beginning to see how her plan might just work.

'So if he could hear you then, you think we could reach him now. With our thoughts?'

'We have to try to warn them.'

'Like, spies?'

'Yes, spies for rats.'

93 Noses twitched for the smell of poison…

… and eyes darted towards the shadowy entrance where the river entered the Great Hollow.

It was the first time since the massacre that citizens of the kingdom had assembled here. Twice we had been caught there by the enemy. Twice there had been death, terror and defeat. Now there was an atmosphere of quiet, but it was the quiet of fear.

When the courtiers filed out, one after another, on to the Rock of State, there was no acclamation beyond a rustle of interest. I moved to the tip of the rock with the Court of Governance behind me.

The sour smell of distrust became more difficult to ignore. Behind me, Gvork revealed quietly to me.

—I told you. They need a king. It's not too late. They must have a king.

But no. I knew it was not that. Citizens had looked to the Court of Governance for guidance, for strength and honesty. For those things, they would follow and fight and die. Instead, they had seen that there had been fighting and rivalry in the Court of Governance. They had lost faith in their leaders.

They looked up and saw not a court but a group of rats much like themselves, only luckier and more driven by greed and ambition. As I waited for the attention of the kingdom, I sensed something like anger amongst those on the far bank of the river; the tasters, translators, the spies, the strategists, the warriors.

They had seen Swylar among us. No rat, not even Queen Jeniel, reminded them more powerfully of the ugliness of power than the dark rat.

—My name is Efren.

The revelation was as strong as that of any king or courtier, but it was not enough to break through. The restlessness grew as I continued.

—I have seen a king die at the hands of the enemy. I have seen a terrible battle in which many of our friends have died. I was born into the Court of Tasters.

There was a snickering from the back of the hollow.

—And I am proud of that. It is time for a rat who is not a warrior to lead the kingdom.

A revelation from the minds of hundreds of rats hung in the air. It said:

—Jeniel. That was what Jeniel once told us.

—The past is past. You have a new court. Growan, a great warrior. Barcas from the Court of Spies. Driva is here, and she will lead our does, and even older ratlings, into battle if there is a need for them.

The smell of hostility grew stronger. More death, more betrayal. That was what citizens were hearing.

—We have the strategist, Joram, to help us plan for the struggle ahead. And a historian, Gvork.

There was open chattering in the hollow now. The idea of a historian in the Court of Governance was not only new to citizens, but slightly ridiculous.

I revealed with all the strength within me.

—For the battle ahead, we must have the wisdom of the past. That is also why I have asked Swylar to return to the court.

A low hissing could be heard from my audience.

—Ceremony!— It was Gvork again —Give them a king! That will silence them!

I paused, looking around the Great Hollow.

—It is good that citizens are showing what they believe.

A few citizens were listening more carefully now, but not many.

—It is a moment of change. The times when citizens were told what to do by the mighty warriors of the Court of Governance are past. They are what led us to the terrible battle in the world above. We need, each of us, together, to decide how to defend ourselves against the enemy. The threat is greater than ever. Another battle will soon be upon us. We must fight in a new way.

I sensed that even the courtiers behind me were becoming restless, but there was no going back now.

—I shall lead you, but I shall not be king. It is not my wish and I believe that it is not your wish either.

There was a sharp revelation from a doe who was among the translators.

—We must have a king. There is no kingdom without a king.

A few of the younger warriors revealed too. Soon the place was riven with one great shared thought.

—King! We need a king!

A warrior near the front of the crowd stood tall on his hind legs. Looking around him, he squealed angrily, revealing as he did so.

—If you will not be king, Efren, give us one who will.

There was a movement behind me. At first I thought Gvork had stepped forward to have his say. But it was worse than that.

—You know me, I believe.

Standing beside me was Swylar.

—I have changed a little— He turned his head, revealing the gashed, eyeless side of his face —I have fought with a great warrior, brave and fierce. It was this citizen.

He faced me and, before the kingdom, he humbled, like a subject.

—Efren. You are a great leader. The kingdom needs you. It needs you more than it needs any king.

The gathering was still now. The eyes of every citizen was

upon me as I stood over Swylar. Some great revelation was needed now, but there were no thoughts within me.

Silence filled the Great Hollow, moment after moment, and it was in that void that a new sound could now be heard. It was the chattering of teeth, together, pulsing in time.

There was a disturbance among the citizens who were nearby.

I was about to bring the gathering to order when I heard a single note, pure and strong.

Then another note.

And another.

We knew that sound. Every buck and doe in the kingdom understood what it was and what it meant.

It was a plaining.

The chattering of teeth from the back of the Great Hollow grew louder. Citizens were acclaiming what they were seeing. The heady scent of hope and joy spread through the multitude, entering every heart.

I looked over the backs of the multitude. It was as if a dense crowd of citizens was moving slowly forward, edging its way through the throng.

It reached the centre of the Great Hollow. As those around it fell back, I saw it at last.

The Twyning.

It was being carried slowly forward by a team of young warriors, as if that great wheel of bodies had itself grown legs.

I understood in that instant why the kingdom had felt incomplete and uneasy. Its old twyning, the repository of its wisdom, its soul, had died. Only a new twyning could take us forward, bringing with it all that was good in the kingdom of rats.

Courage, resolution, kindness.

The Twyning reached the far bank of the river and, to a deafening acclamation, was laid gently down. There was a writhing tangle of rats, bound together by their tails. They looked young and strong as they gazed at the citizens who surrounded them.

One of the warriors slipped into the river and began swimming towards the Rock of State. There was something familiar about him.

He reached the bank below me, shook the water from his coat, and then ascended to the Rock of State where he stood before me. My heart beat loudly, filled with relief and gratitude. He revealed briefly.

—Hail Efren, leader of the kingdom.

He crouched before me as the acclamation in the Great Hollow seemed to shake the earth around us. Above the noise, I revealed.

—Welcome home, my old friend Floke.

94 It is different this time…

… when the townspeople gather to plan the great hunt, organised for the following day in the field next to the river. There are only a few women and no children. Dogs of all sizes are there. Someone has brought along a cage full of ferrets.

As I approach, walking with Bill a few paces behind the doctor and the politician, I notice that the men are dressed differently today. They are in the greens and browns of hunting clothes. They talk quietly among themselves, laughing only now and then.

The death of Champagne Charlie – murdered, it is believed, by rats – has changed everything. Hunting beasts is no longer just a sport. It is survival. These men have honestly come to believe that we have to get them before they get us.

As the MP and the doctor reach the bridge, the men gather around, their faces as solemn as I have seen them. When Mr Petheridge speaks, he hardly has to raise his voice in order to be heard.

'Our task tomorrow will be to eradicate our enemy. The rat has shown how cunning and cowardly it can be. It is for us, the men of this borough, to show that we cannot be terrorised. When we are hurt, we fight back with all the weapons at our command!'

There is a murmur of defiant agreement.

'It's for the kiddies – they'll be coming for the kiddies next,' someone says, and there is applause.

The doctor moves forward to speak.

'In the opinion of our Mr Grubstaff here' – he waves an arm towards Bill, who stares stolidly at the ground – 'the rat does not make the same mistake twice. He learns.'

'Vicious devils,' someone mutters near the front of the crowd. 'They're Satan's creatures, that's the truth of it.'

As the hubbub of voices grows louder, the doctor raises a hand.

'Our aim tomorrow will be to trap the remaining beasts in an enclosure around this field. They will be unwilling to use the drain that brought them to death last time, but we shall block it just to make sure.'

He points downstream with his cane.

'There is another issue from the sewage network some hundred yards in that direction. Bill and the boy, Mr Smith' – he nods towards me – 'will block all exits from the sewerage lines except for that one. The rats will be driven by gas towards that one exit. Once they emerge, the dogs will do their work. But we must be organised.'

For the next few minutes, the men discuss where each of them will be standing. There is no rivalry now between the setters. The dogs, picking up the sombre mood, are less playful and excited than usual.

'It's as if it really was a bloomin' war.' Watching them as they earnestly make their plans, Bill shakes his head. 'They're only a few beasts.'

'Will they kill them all?' I ask.

Bill chuckles, as if I've made a really good joke. 'They'll think they can, but somewhere a couple of beasts will survive. In no time, there will be more of them than ever. Rats is rats. That's what happens when they're under attack. Nature tells them to have more young.'

'Gentlemen.' Mr Petheridge has stepped forward. 'We shall meet tomorrow at dusk. Gather at this point at four p.m. Please leave your womenfolk and your little ones at home. This will be no occasion for them. Bring only the bravest, strongest dogs. Rats have a nose for the weak. They destroy them. And bring gloves, clubs, sticks. We shall need them!'

With that, he walks over to us.

'You shall have three council workers at your disposal, Mr Grubstaff. We want all escapes from the sewerage lines blocked today.' He lowers his voice. 'It will be a good pay day for you both.'

He turns out to be right, but it is a hard day of digging and lugging and blocking too.

I return home well after nightfall. Caz has found some vegetables at the market and, on our little fire, there is a stew of swedes and carrots that smells better than anything should in a rubbish tip. We eat together, the three of us, Caz, Malaika and me.

'So?' Caz asks eventually. 'Did you find out the plans for tomorrow?'

'I did,' I say. 'I know the plans.'

95 The many heads of The Twyning looked up...

... to the Rock of State where I sat alone with Floke. They had said nothing, done nothing, when they had been carried into the Great Hollow by Floke and his warriors, a tangle of young rat bodies, bound together for all their living days.

Their lives would be empty of fighting, fathering or mothering. They would never belong to a court, or even have a name. Yet The Twyning changed everything. Its sacred presence calmed the kingdom. With it, with them, we all had hope. There was a future.

—Thank you, Floke.

I was alone with my old friend in a passageway behind the Great Hollow. It was his return, more even than the appearance of The Twyning, which had given me strength.

—A kingdom must have a twyning. I was doing my duty. I had no idea that the leader of the kingdom was none other than little Efren.

I nudged him, rather as I used to when we were ratlings, and Fang was still with us. He was a huge, powerful rat now, and bore the scars of a fighter. There was a sadness in his eyes which had not been there before. I nosed him again.

—Tell me about your brother.

—Fang? He fought in the battle. He did better than most warriors with four legs would do. Together we faced a dog and tore its face so that it ran away, yelping. But there were too many. They were everywhere. We went for the wire. Normally, Fang could flyte as well as any warrior but, with a single back leg, there was nothing he could do.

—I saw his body.

Floke looked at me suspiciously.

—You were there? And not fighting?

—I was living in the world above. I saw the battle, but from the far side of the fence. There was nothing I could do.

We sat in silence for a while. After the arrival of The Twyning in the Great Hollow, each court, under the leadership of a member of the Court of Governance, had gone to prepare for the battle which, if the spies were right, would be coming soon. We were to meet the next day, to make the greatest decision in the history of the kingdom. Whether to attack or to wait until the enemy attacked us. There had been no more talk of ceremonies, of the need for a king.

—What should we do now, Floke?

He rested his chin on his front paws, a pose I remember from when he was young. It meant Floke was thinking.

—It must never happen again. A massacre like that.

His revelation, when it came, was uncertain.

—You think we must act first?

—That is what I should think as a warrior. Attack. Always attack. But there is something about humans now which is different. It is as if it is not enough to kill us. They are working together as never before.

—Perhaps it is time for the kingdom to move to another place.

—The enemy will follow us. It is everywhere.

—Yet we could live in peace.

Floke sat up, shocked for the first time by what I had said.

—The enemy will never be peaceful. Destruction is all it knows. Humans and rats. They are never far apart. We need each other.

And it was at that moment that something beyond me, outside what I was seeing and hearing in the Great Hollow, seemed to shake my body.

—Efren? Are you all right?

I was aware that he was looking at me oddly. I could sense that he was revealing, and yet nothing reached me.

Then, suddenly, I knew what was happening. I was hearing. Someone, something was trying to reach me.

My body shook, full of a desperate yearning which I had all but forgotten. A rat must never become caught up in the past, yet now I was travelling back to the world above, to a place of kindness.

Floke was standing over me now. I was on my side, twitching, wide eyed, but I could do nothing about it.

Before me, within me, I saw a mountain, moving shapes, the enemy. Then, as clearly as if she were there on the Rock of State, the love of my life.

—Malaika!

—Efren, it is me.

I closed my eyes, and I heard her reveal again.

—You must listen to me. I have news.

96 Malaika sits on the palm of Caz's hand...

... looking into the darkness by the river. The grey and white hair on her small body stands on end, her eyes are wide and she trembles like a bird about to take its first flight.

'She has found him,' Caz whispers.

It is a moonless night of grey mizzle, and we are seated on a tree stump by the riverbank as the rats talk to one another in their brains.

Life, truly, cannot be any stranger than this.

Caz raises a finger. Her face and hair are dripping but she has thoughts only for the rats.

'Can you hear her call?'

I smile, not wishing to confess that I hear nothing but the sound of raindrops on the water.

'She's calling Efren. She's telling him she has news.'

So it continues for a while, the rat chat. Staring into the darkness. A whispered translation. Silence. Cold. Boredom.

I have been worrying about my Caz recently. She has never been the same since she was held captive by Champagne Charlie. She is more awake at night than she is during the daytime. When I touch her arm, it is as chill as a corpse's, and yet, such is her trance tonight, that she seems not to notice the cold at all.

Suddenly she starts.

'There!'

'Caz? Are you all right?'

She turns to me, and a strange smile is on her face.

'There he is. Surely you can hear?'

'Who is, Caz? What's happening?'

She actually giggles now. It's the first time I have heard that sound for a long time.

'Efren,' she says. 'He's revealing to Malaika.' She points to the dark tunnel leading into the earth. 'He is there.'

'The rat? You've found it?'

Caz is gazing silently at her Malaika. Once more we are waiting on that winter's night.

At some point, Malaika turns on Caz's hand so that she is facing away from us and towards the tunnel. It is then that I notice a movement in the water.

The heads of two rats, as they swim together through the water, are moving closer to us. They turn and make for the bank, a matter of yards from where we are sitting.

'She's shaking.' Caz smooths the fur on Malaika's back.

The beasts, still in the water, are close to land when they see us. After a moment's hesitation the first of them, one of the biggest rats I have ever seen, moves towards us, heaves himself out of the water, and shakes himself like a dog.

'That's not Efren,' Caz whispers.

The second rat is on land now. He moves past the larger beast and stands, boldly staring at us.

'But that is,' says Caz.

With a strange little squeak, Malaika makes a bolt for it. She slips down from Caz's dress, and scuttles towards the river. When she reaches the smaller of the two rats, they welcome each other noisily. He pokes at her eagerly with his nose. In response, she lies on her side, looking at him.

'That's your rat all right.' I smile at Caz.

'Efren's saying that the other rat is called' – Caz frowned – 'Foke or Floke, I think.'

'Whatever he's called, he's quite a beast,' I say.

Efren, followed by Malaika and then Floke, walk almost casually to another tree stump nearby and climb up on it.

They turn to face us, the giant, the pet rat and Efren. They are now close enough for me to see, even in the dark, the movement of their whiskers.

'Tell me what you know, Peter.' Caz speaks in a low voice, her eyes fixed on the two rats. 'Then I'll reveal to them.'

What to say? That they were to be destroyed tomorrow? That every man with a dog that could kill rats will be doing his best to wipe them from the face of the earth?

'Just tell me what is planned,' Caz whispers.

'There will be another attack,' I tell her. 'It will be when the sun goes down tomorrow.'

Caz takes a deep breath as if reaching the rats through the power of her thoughts requires an effort of her body.

The rats remain still as they listen, only their whiskers twitching.

Caz looks at me again.

'They are to poison the sewage channels with gas,' I tell her. 'They plan to force all the rats out of all the sewerage runs by the river. All escapes have been blocked.'

I decide not to mention that I was one of those who had done this work.

There is more silent, glassy-eyed communication between Caz and the rats.

'Efren needs to know where the battle will be.'

'Tell him that the battle will be here once more. The rats are to be trapped inside the wire.'

Caz passes on the message.

'There will be more dogs, more men. The gas released in the sewers will be stronger. It will be a bigger hunt.'

After Caz has revealed to them, the rats remain immobile for what seems like several minutes. I watch Efren, and I swear I can see when he is revealing. There is a tension in the body, his eyes become blank. I could almost swear that, at that moment, I can feel a tickling in my brain. His question reaches me.

—Why?

I close my eyes and reply, not through Caz but directly to the rat.

—They are afraid of you.

—Afraid?

Caz stares down at the ground. I sense that she shares my sense of shame.

—There are humans who want to destroy you and all other rats.

Hearing this, Efren seems to make himself bigger, his fur standing up on his back. The big rat places his body between us and Efren.

'We are here to help the rats.' I speak softly to Caz. 'Tell them that not all humans are bad. He will understand it if you tell him.'

Caz revealed, opening her palms as she did. When she has finished, Malaika moves closer to Efren.

Beside me, Caz murmurs, 'She's telling them we are good.'

'Trust,' I said. 'They must trust us.'

The rats remain tense, on guard.

'They must get away from this place before it is too late.'

Slowly, the smaller rat, Efren, begins to relax. The big beast, though, still has the look of one who might attack us.

Then, without warning, Efren turns to make a slow, sorrowful progress towards the water. The other rat, Floke, follows, leaving Malaika alone on the stump. As Efren reaches the bank of the river, she scurries after him.

Efren turns sharply and nips her. She squeals in surprise.

'He wants her to stay with us here,' Caz says. 'She wants to follow him.'

'Let her decide.'

Malaika looks up at us. Caz kneels on the wet ground, her hand held out.

'Malaika.' She says the name out loud. 'Come, Malaika.'

The pet rat makes her way slowly up the bank. Without a backward glance, she climbs on to Caz's hand.

Caz stands, holding her rat close to her.

From the riverside, Efren is watching us. Then, within my head, I heard him reveal more clearly and strongly than I have ever experienced before.

—We shall stay. If we retreat now, we shall always retreat. We have a right to our world.

'Not all humans are your enemies.' I spoke loudly, but the rats were not startled or afraid.

—The future will hold the truth.

With that, Efren slips into the water, followed by Floke. They swim slowly into the dark cavern, and soon are gone.

97 Our fur was still wet from the river when...

... Floke set off to find all the members of the Court of Governance. It was time to prepare for the battle ahead.

Now I was alone in the Great Hollow, except for The Twyning, which writhed and undulated with its own strange form of life on the far side of the river.

—What is the right thing to do?

My revelation was to myself, but also to the many-headed Twyning. At that moment we felt as one, alone and uncertain.

I had never fought for the kingdom. While others were dying, I had watched. At the very moment when the enemy had been preparing to attack the kingdom, I had been among them. Citizens looked to me for decisions which would cost the lives not only of them but perhaps of the entire kingdom.

How did I, Efren of the Court of Tasting, come to be in this position? What right had I to decide anything beyond what I should do? If I crept away right now, to move quietly among the rank of citizens, what harm would that do? I had never wanted power. There were times when I thought that all I wished for was a life with Malaika.

—Efren, listen.

It was one of the heads of The Twyning that was revealing to me, or maybe it was all of them. I was unable to tell.

—It is your moment. We all have a duty to other citizens. This is yours. Do this, then you can live your life.

—If I still have a life.

—Somewhere, whatever happens, a citizen will live. You, Efren, will be part of that citizen and its future generations. The kingdom is each of us, and all of us.

—Every rat is a king?

I gazed at The Twyning, and what I heard in my revelation was not the voice of a leader but a citizen, much like all the others.

The Twyning replied.

—Every rat is a king, and this is your time, Efren. You should be proud to have been given this moment, and brave.

—What if it is the end of the kingdom? It will have been my decisions which helped cause it.

The tangle of intertwined rats seemed to swell before my eyes. I understood for a moment why the enemy was so fearful when it encountered a twyning.

—The kingdom will not die. It is for ever. It is beyond all of us.

I felt the power returning to my body.

—Thank you.

—Have faith in the kingdom and in yourself, Efren. Be strong. It is your fate.

There was a stirring at the back of the Great Hollow. Floke entered, followed by Growan, Barcas and Gvork.

—The others will be with us soon. Shall we meet on the Rock of State?

I turned from The Twyning to face them.

—No. For this meeting, we must be in the world above.

98 That night, I am wide-eyed and sleepless for thinking of the rats…

… and the way they looked at us down by the river. There is a heavy feeling in the pit of my stomach which feels very like betrayal.

I see the dark, unblinking eyes of Efren as Caz explained what was soon to happen. At that moment, he saw me, and perhaps even her, as all the same. We were killers. We destroyed as naturally as we breathed. The rat did not understand why we wished evil upon our fellow creatures. He simply knew that we did, we do, and we always will. While we remain in this world, no other living creature is safe.

The rat, of course, is right.

In the darkness, I creep out of the tip, leaving Caz asleep with Malaika dozing close to her hand.

The rain has gone, and it is a clear night with the smell of damp in the air.

What good have we done tonight? We have told the rats that they are about to die. Efren must have seen at that moment that there is nothing a mere animal can do against the might of men and their dogs. Maybe he had even suspected that I, Dogboy, would be there in that hunt to the death.

I walk down the lane which leads from the tip towards the town, and stand on the road gazing towards the river.

I will not hunt. I will stay away. Caz and I may be hungry without the pennies I earn from the doctor, but I will not be part of his accursed war on rats.

In the distance, I hear the sounds of the town stirring. Horses' hooves on cobbles, the occasional voice – a dog barking, its voice cutting through the darkness.

Slowly I make my way back to the tip, and dip my way into the passage leading to our home.

The embers of our little fire are still warm. I put a couple of small branches upon it and hold out my hands before the flames.

It is the smell of burning which wakes Caz. She sits up, blinking.

'Peter, are you all right?'

'I think it's time to move from this place.'

'Where will we go?'

'We'll find somewhere, you and me. We know how to survive in this town.'

'But we'll stay together.'

I hear fear in her voice, and see, as if I have slipped into a terrible dream, a window, the light flickering from within, a girl dancing, a man watching her. Dance, little dancer, dance.

'Of course, we'll stay together,' I say. 'Stick with Dogboy and you'll be all right.'

She looks solemn. 'What about the rats?' It is a despairing whisper.

'We're only children, Caz. What can we do?'

'You saved me. You and Efren and Malaika.'

'And Bill.'

She looks at me and I notice something which I have not seen for a long time: a grim set to her jaw, and hardness in her narrowed eyes. Sometimes I forget how tough my Caz can be.

She sits up and pushes some more wood on to the fire with the heel of her bare foot.

'And he can do his bit again. We'll go and see him when it's light.'

'And tell him what?'

Caz sniffed decisively. 'Tell him that we're going to save the rats.'

She looks at me and sees the doubt in my eyes.

'You're not running from this, Peter. If you do, you'll be as bad as the hunters. If you want to leave, you will be by yourself.'

I gaze at her for a moment. I knew, we both knew, that we were going nowhere.

99 The cockerels were calling...

... by the time the members of the Court of Governance emerged, one after another, into the world above. I was to be at the front of our group – or, rather, Floke was, just in front of me. Since his return to the kingdom, he seemed to have decided that he was my protector.

We gathered on the riverside, then climbed the bank. A touch-path led me to the stump where I had faced the two young warriors earlier that night, and I took up position, facing the courtiers.

—The battle will be here.

I looked across to the field, enclosed by a wire fence.

—The enemy plan to trap us in that enclosed place. We shall be driven from the world below by poison. Other escapes will be blocked. There will be a line of humans along the road to prevent us escaping into the river.

Some of the court were looking at the battleground, but Barcas, the spy, sniffed dismissively.

—We had much of this information already, of course, but we did not trust its source. May I ask, Efren, how you, on your own without help from spies, know so much about what the enemy plans?

I gave him the hard eye.

—Information received, Barcas.

The spy seemed keen to question me more, but there was no time for that. I turned to Joram, the strategist.

—We need to prepare, to have a plan of battle.

Joram crossed the road, nosed the wire and stood on his hind legs, sniffing. I suspected that he was playing for time.

—We must surprise them.

He revealed from where he stood, gazing across the field.

—The enemy sees us in a certain way. When they are strong and have their dogs, we flee. It is what humans expect in their arrogance and pride.

—So we attack?

Growan, the warrior, was usually the first to argue for the boldest, bloodiest approach, but even he seemed concerned about Joram's suggestion.

—That is certain death, Joram.

The strategist hesitated. He was no fighter himself.

I revealed, trying not to betray my own uncertainty.

—Growan is right. But so is Joram when he says that surprise is our greatest weapon. We know what the enemy is going to do.

I looked around, anticipating a challenge, but none came.

Driva pushed to the front of the group.

—We need to bring the kingdom into the world above, and as soon as we can.

Gvork nipped her with an aggression surprising in a historian.

—It is dangerous in the world above when the sun is in the sky. We shall be divided. No battle in history has ever been won—

—You are wrong, Gvork.

I interrupted his speech. Historians like nothing better than to bring bad news from the past, and now was no time for weakness.

—It is dangerous in the world above, but not as dangerous as being poisoned in the kingdom, and then driven into the jaws of dogs.

Gvork looked away moodily.

—Driva, organise the does and ratlings to escape from the world below, if possible before it is light. The rest of you will lead your courts up here to prepare for battle.

To my surprise, Swylar stepped forward.

—Of course, Efren is right. The kingdom must be made safe

from poison. But if the humans find no rats in the world below, what will happen? They will go away and attack us again, when we are not prepared.

We waited to hear what the dark rat proposed.

—Some rats must stay below. Strong citizens – warriors probably. When the poison arrives, they will flee upwards, as expected by the enemy, out of the hollow and into the field.

—Death.

It was Joram who revealed what each of us was thinking.

—Yes, death— The single eye of Swylar glittered —Those who enter the field will have little chance, although we have to prepare an escape route so that a few may get away. But these warriors will attract the attention of the enemy so that citizens in the world above can attack.

What he revealed, of course, was true. We all understood that. The question was, who would lead the rats on this mission of death? Understanding the direction of our thoughts, Swylar revealed more quietly.

—I would be proud to take the task.

The scent of suspicion was in the air. It was always possible that Swylar was following his own plan to win back the kingdom. If the rats left in the world below escaped before the poison was released, they would be the only citizens to avoid the battle.

Did I trust Swylar? To my surprise, I found I did.

—You are a noble warrior, Swylar. Find your troop of citizens today.

I glanced across the river. The light was glowing softly beyond the horizon.

—And now we must prepare. The enemy has strength, sticks, the sharp teeth and deadly speed of dogs.

The court looked at me. I thought of The Twyning. The kingdom is in each of us, all of us. I felt a new strength within me, a pride that we were about to fight for future generations of citizens.

—And what has the kingdom got?— I looked around and revealed softly —It has knowledge. It has surprise. It has the means to inspire terror and confusion. It has the right of all breathing creatures to fight for their survival.

Beside me, Floke stirred, and nudged me gently with his nose.

—And, of course, it has the greater intelligence.

We dispersed to set about preparing for battle.

100 Through the afternoon, we
work along the riverbank…

… blocking the holes and runs which rats like to use. There are three men from the council with us, and they know their beasts. Now and then I attempt to leave an escape hole from the sewerage runs, but it is no use. One of the council men always notices, and shouts roughly at me.

'Just do your job, lad.' Beside me, Bill wears the closed, unhappy expression I have come to know so well. 'Keep yourself out of trouble, and do your job.'

I am glad now that Caz has remained at the tip with Malaika. She had wanted to be there for the hunt, to help in any way that she could, but even she, the strongest-willed girl in the world, could see that she could do little when the killing started. She has helped Efren prepare. Now she and Malaika must stay at home, safe.

The light is beginning to fade by the time we reach the Locks Inn, a public house by one of the canals which lead into the river. There is little sign of beast activity around the lock, but Bill seems unusually interested in it.

'When do they open the gates?' he asks one of the council men.

'Not often,' the man replied. 'In summer, when it's dry and the sewers need to be sluiced out.'

'So they won't be doing it now?'

'In winter?' The man laughs. 'Only if you want to flood part of the town. There's too much water in there to be safe when it's this wet. A wave will go down the river, breaking its banks.'

Without a word, Bill nods and returns to work.

My arms are aching by the time we first hear the dogs. As we reach the bend in the river, we can see the men lining the bank, standing on the bridge. Beyond the barking, there is a hum of excited conversation.

'Ah yes, they're all here,' Bill mutters to himself. 'And they'll have brought some friends along, too. It is a good day for hunters.'

'I wouldn't want to be a rat today,' says the oldest of the council men, and laughs.

'You got a choice, ratty boy,' another of the men, standing over a bolt hole, calls down. 'Poisoned in the sewers down there or torn apart by dogs up here.'

I see the face of Efren, staring at us as he learned the truth of what was to happen today. 'Why?' he asked. I still have no idea as to the answer to that question.

As we approach the bridge, I see that the doctor is already there, moving among the hunters like the important man he believes himself to be.

There is no sign of Mr Petheridge, the MP. He is not a man who likes to be around when work is to be done, I have discovered. He prefers to appear, fresh-faced and full of words, take the credit, and then leave. I judge that his carriage will appear in about an hour's time.

The doctor, surrounded by hunters, sees the five of us on the road. He beckons Bill and me over to join them.

'Ah, Mr Grubstaff and Mr Smith.' His tone has the fake joviality which he likes to assume when among working men. 'Everything will be fine now. The ratting experts have arrived.'

The hunters look at us without particular interest. One tugs at a skinny Manchester he has on a lead and mutters a command. I sense that he and the other men are as impatient as their dogs. They are here to hunt rats. With every moment, the light is failing.

The doctor glances at his timepiece. 'We have four parties of men, with gas masks, down the sewerage runs,' he says. 'They will be releasing enough gas to drive the rats to the junction where the main pipe meets the river. In approximately five minutes, the beasts will issue from the drain.' He points to the runs near the bank. 'They will be driven away from the river into the enclosed field. There the dogs will do their work.'

He waves a hand above his head. 'All take your positions, please.'

Some of the men with dogs line the bank. Others move beyond the wire of the field so that the hunting ground is surrounded. The dogs will merely have to be lifted into the arena to do their work.

'Are we all right, Bill?' The doctor lowers his voice as, with the hunt approaching, the men stop their chatter and silence their dogs.

'You never know with beasts,' Bill murmurs. 'It's rare they do what you expect.'

The doctors frowns irritably. 'I'm trusting you two to make sure they find no escape.' He gives me a light, jokey punch on the arm. 'You are my lieutenants in this great battle, Mr Smith!'

I look around me. There must be a hundred men with dogs. Ponies and traps line the road. There are lights on the bridge and on the far side of the river.

What chance will the rats have against this mighty army of humans and their killing dogs?

'Good luck, Efren,' I murmur.

The doctor, standing nearby, mishears me.

'Yes, good luck to them all, Dogboy,' he says.

Below us, there is a sound. Some of the dogs whine with excitement. The noise from the earth grows louder. It is the squealing of beasts.

And suddenly, there they are.

The hunt has begun.

101 I looked down and saw the warriors screaming...

... as they went into battle.

The dogs were being held back by the enemy until our brave fighters entered the field.

Then with a baying and barking and howling that made my whole body tremble, the dogs were released.

I saw Swylar in the front troop leading the dogs away from the river.

A second group cut away towards the fence where, that day, the Courts of Tasting and Translation had worked on the wire so that there was an escape from the field.

—They are on to Swylar.

Beside me, Floke revealed.

The dogs, stupid animals, had all followed the first troop. As they reached them, the warriors turned and, for a moment, faced them in a ring of defiance.

In that moment of hesitation, Swylar made his move. He darted away from the group. The dogs, fooled by the movement, went after him, allowing more warriors to escape.

Swylar could only escape for a few lengths but, just as the dogs caught up with him, he turned and, in the same movement, hurled himself at the throat of the one nearest to him. It yelped with surprise and fear and, for a moment, it seemed as if the dogs had turned upon themselves in one snarling, biting frenzy.

When they parted, all that was left of the dark rat were stains of blood around the fangs and snouts of those that had killed him. It was a hero's death.

The second group of warriors was nearing the wire. Too late, the humans called their dogs, running and pointing.

The first warrior to reach the wire scrambled through the hole that had been gnawed the previous night. The enemy, seeing now that there was an escape from the field, moved to stop them as they came through, but a human against a rat is an uneven contest.

The enemy stamped and thrashed the ground with sticks. The warriors, in their strength and bravery, ran through their ranks.

Over half of the troop was through before, within the field, the dogs reached them. There was a terrible massacre but, at the end, humans were still shouting with rage, urging the dogs which were now trapped inside the wire and unable to reach the citizens who had escaped.

—Yes. It worked.

Floke looked at me, his eyes shining.

—We shall win this battle, Efren.

—We can and we will.

—When can I fight?

—Our moment will come. The humans are reaching the wood. Watch.

102 The hunters urge their dogs...

... after the prey, heading towards a small wood beside the river, past the path where Bill and I are standing. In the trees, someone gives a long cry.

'Waaaaay! Waaaaay!'

'That's a hunting holler,' says Bill. 'It means "Gone away". Some rats must be over there.'

Then we saw them – twenty or thirty rats, big, strong beasts – are running down the path from the field. They are so close together that they look like a single animal.

'How did they get out of the field?' Bill mutters.

'There was a hole in the wire,' I say. 'And they knew where it was.'

I can see Bill puzzling over this when we are interrupted by a group of hunters with their dogs, running down the path towards the wood. Behind them, sweat pouring down his face, is the doctor. I doubt if he has had this much exercise for years.

'Come on, Mr Grubstaff and Mr Smith. We'll have them in the wood. They'll be trapped there.'

Shrugging, Bill follows him with me, but at a slower pace.

To tell the truth, it is hardly a wood – more of a scrubby cluster of ash and oak – but the evening gloom is drawing in, and the path surrounded by trees is now quite dark.

So, when the screaming starts, it is difficult to know exactly what is happening.

'Look out! Look out!'

The doctor is shouting, undisguised fear in his voice. 'They're attacking from above.'

On the path in front of him, hunters have fallen to their knees. Some are beating their head and shoulders. Others blunder, panic-stricken, into the wood. The air is thick with curses and shouts.

'I don't believe it.' Beside me, Bill actually laughs at what he is seeing.

As we draw closer, I notice something fall from a tree, like snow melting from the branches. Then another, and another – on to the heads and shoulders of men.

It is raining rats.

'They're in the trees!' someone shouts.

One of the hunters, lying on the ground, his face bleeding, curses and blows a whistle for his dog, but it is too far ahead in pursuit of the rats which led them into the wood.

Now sounds can be heard from the direction of the river. At first it is as if stones are being thrown in the water, but soon the splashes grow faster. The rats are making their escape.

Dogs, confused by what is happening and by the noise of human shouts, are dashing through the trees here and there.

'The water! The beasts are in the water!' one of the hunters cries, and there is general movement towards the river.

I hear the doctor's voice, shrill and excited above the uproar.

'Get the dogs into the water. The rats can't escape.'

'They'll be finished now. Eh, Bill?'

But Bill is no longer there. I am standing on the woodland path alone. I look around, then back up the river. There, in the middle distance, is the figure of a man, running.

103 There are good trees and bad trees...

... and those we had chosen by the river were of the friendly kind. By nature, citizens are wary of climbing trees, a fear which historians claim dates back to the great war on the black rat, but when bark and branch wish us no harm, caution quickly disappears.

So it was now. Floke and I heard the screams of the enemy as they were caught in the ambush we had prepared. Falling from trees was easy work when the prey was human. Surprise worked better than teeth and strength. Fall, hang on, scream, attack. Citizens from the Courts of Translation and Spying, under the leadership of Growan and a few of his senior warriors, did their work to perfection.

For the first time during the battle, the smell of human terror was in the air.

—I must fight, Efren.

Beside me, Floke trembled, his warrior blood coursing hot through his veins. I nudged him.

—Patience. The battle has just begun. We shall all fight.

I turned to look at my troops. Together we waited in the human dwelling from where I had seen the first battle. There were hundreds of citizens, holding close to one another. We were an impressive sight. The time for running was over. We would draw the enemy to this place and show them that the kingdom will not be destroyed.

It would be a battle for peace.

The comfort of darkness had fallen and the room where we were waiting was filled with the various citizens. Large, small, rats, ratlings, does. Every type of citizen was there, waiting for this great moment of destiny. I revealed to them all.

—It is not long now, citizens. Soon we shall fight.

Yet even as I addressed them, I felt an unmistakeable tremor within me.

I was hearing. From afar, a message was reaching me.

—The river will rise.

I turned towards the field. The lights of the enemy were on each side of the river. I heard the thrashing of water as the killer dogs dived from the bank.

I turned to Floke.

—What can that mean? The river will rise.

Before he could reply, I heard once more.

—The river will rise. Escape from the waters!

With all the strength at my command, I revealed to the brave citizens who had plunged into the river.

—Make for the land, now!

—What's happening, Efren?

Floke was looking at me in alarm.

For the first time that evening, I had to reveal the unhappy truth.

—I have no idea.

104 A distant roar can be heard...

... and, in that moment, I understand what is about to happen.

The hunters are too caught up in urging on their dogs to hear the sound of approaching danger. It seems to come from the earth itself.

'You beauty, Bill,' I whisper.

There is the faintest tremble on the surface of the river. Then, with a mighty crash, a wall of water hurtles downstream like something out of a nightmare, appearing from the tunnel where the river emerges into the open from underground.

In an instant, what was a gently running course of water is a boiling confusion. The dogs which are in the river are hit by the torrent and some of the men on the banks are swept by the rushing wave into the water.

The doctor is staring at the river, wild-eyed.

'What's happening?' he asks. 'Where's Grubstaff gone?'

Before I can answer, one of the men from the council runs past us on the path. He is heading upriver.

'Someone's opened the lock,' he yells.

'Lock?' The doctor calls out. 'What lock? What's he talking about?'

I shrug. 'There's a lock from the canal into the river.'

'Who would want to open it now? The rats are getting away, Dogboy.'

Moments later, he has his answer.

On the road, I see a familiar figure walking towards us between two other men, one of whom holds him by the arm.

Bill.

The river is calming now, although it is still dangerously swollen. Some of the hunters head downstream in search of their dogs. Others are walking back to the path.

The doctor walks slowly up the path, meeting the men holding Bill near the bridge.

'What the hell's going on?' he asks. 'What's Grubstaff doing here?'

'Found him at the lock,' one of the council workers, a short, grey-haired man I had never seen before growled. 'Red-handed, he was.'

'Said something about rats.' The younger of the two men spoke up. 'Thought he must be something to do with the hunt.'

'He is.' For a moment, the doctor seems lost for words. 'What's going on, Grubstaff?'

Bill says nothing.

'He's a loony, that one.' A young hunter, broad with light red hair, laughs. 'I've always said he's a bit simple.'

Jem Dashwood pushes his way to the front of the crowd. 'If he's harmed any of our dogs, he better watch out for himself late at night.'

There are murmurs of agreement.

The doctor, looking weary now, approaches Bill and stands before him.

'I don't understand,' he says. 'What were you doing?'

Bill lowers his head and stares miserably at the ground.

'I know what he was doing.' I mumble the words softly. All eyes turn towards me. 'Bill said he was going to drown the rats.'

There is a disbelieving silence.

'It was his plan,' I say, as convincingly as I can manage. 'He wanted to help in the war against rats.'

'Drown the rats?' Dashwood moves towards Bill, as if to strike him. 'Drown the dogs, more like.'

'I told you.' The red-haired man speaks again. 'He should be locked up in the loony bin, that one. He's not all there.'

Away from the river, on the outside of the fence, a terrier

begins to bark, as if the hunt is not yet over. Heads turn in its direction. The noise it is making is that of a dog who has picked up a scent.

A young boy, no older than me, is standing in the field nearby. Suddenly he points to a path near where the dog is giving tongue.

'Rats,' he yells. 'Loads of 'em.'

105 The warriors brought the enemy to us…

… and we were waiting.

Floke and I watched as the humans gathered by the river. For a moment, I had worried that the dogs were so scattered that the last group of warriors would not be able to lead them to us.

But there is always one dog which can be fooled.

The warriors had left a trail around the field. As the dog neared the house, the warriors broke cover.

I saw the pale faces of the humans as they heard the dog's barking. I heard their shouts as they set out in pursuit. One dog and the enemy were advancing towards us.

The door below us was half open. I heard our warriors scramble through, their bodies thudding against the timber. Moments later, the dog crashed in.

Its eager barking turned to yelps of terror. In the darkness, the warriors turned on it.

We watched the fight from the top of a flight of stairs where we waited for our moment.

Small dogs fight well, and this was a brave one. With warriors attached to it, their teeth embedded into the flesh of its face, neck, back and flanks, it still attacked those in front of it, staggering in the darkness under its deadly burden until it collapsed.

Beside me, Floke stood with four other warriors and our weapon of terror, ready as the humans approached.

I revealed to the warriors below.

—Do not kill the dog. It has fought well. Take up your positions!

At that moment, the door of the house is filled with the enemy, their dazzling lights and their shouts.

—Now!

106 The hunters' blood is up by the time...

... they reach the abandoned house. They are angry too. They have had rats falling from trees on to their heads. They have watched as beasts escaped when they were meant to be trapped. They have seen their dogs swept away by a torrent. All they want now, all they need, is to kill rats – a lot of them, if possible.

By the time I arrive at the house, they are gathered in a hallway around the bleeding, panting body of the terrier which had brought them here.

'The beasts are in here,' one of the men shouts. 'The house is boarded up.'

There is a noise from the top of a wide staircase ahead of us leading to darkness upstairs.

The men hold up their lanterns. Looking down at us, unmoving but for the glittering of their eyes in the light, are hundreds of beasts. They seem strangely unafraid. I feel a faint prickling of fear.

The doctor speaks with an unsteady voice from the back of the room.

'Just hold hard, everyone. Let's keep them here until we get the dogs to deal with them.'

'We've got weapons, haven't we?' A gnarled old hunter, his bald head bleeding, bangs a walking stick against the floor.

For several moments, no one moves. We look up at the rats. They gaze back. Then, as we watch, the beasts begin to make a sound. At first it is like the patter of rain on a roof. Then the

363

noise seems to take a shape. It surges back and forth in a rhythm of its own.

'What's 'at?' one of the men calls out.

'It's their teeth,' another answers. 'They're afraid of us.'

But the noise grows louder, and it is not the sound of fear. One of the rats begins to make a long squealing sound. It is almost like a horrible song.

'Where are them dogs?' a man near the front calls out, a tremor in his voice.

Another rat is making a different note, and others follow. Soon there is a heart-chilling chorus of noise from the beasts as they stand looking down at us.

The men nearest the stairs start to back away.

The rats are on the move. As the squeals grow louder, the dark mass of brown bodies begins to part. Out of the gloom beyond them, something appears, moving slowly towards the top of the stairs. Even as it enters the light, it is difficult to see exactly what it is.

'It's a monster!' one man screams. 'It's a monster rat!'

At that moment, as if the hundreds of beasts at the top of the stairs were but one animal, the mass twitches, expelling from its heart, rolling and writhing down the stairs, step after step, a truly terrifying sight.

It is a large ball of hissing and snarling rats, all tugging at their tails, which are merged together. It is like one grotesque beast with glittering eyes looking every direction and countless deadly teeth.

There is a roar of fear from the front of the group – 'Get out! Get out!'

– and panic is upon us. Bellowing like stampeding cattle, the hunters scramble for the door.

'It's only a rat king!' I hear the doctor calling out. 'There is a scientific explanation for it.'

He sounds terrified, too.

I am near the back of the group. As I pass the wounded terrier,

I grab it. I am last out of the door before it is slammed shut behind us. The bodies of the leading rats thud angrily against the timber.

Nearby, hunters who have found their dogs downriver are running in our direction.

The doctor addresses the men, but he is unable to disguise the fear in his voice.

'That was what we scientists call a "rat king" – it's completely harmless,' he says breathlessly.

'Didn't look harmless to me,' someone shouted.

'The rats are trapped in the house,' said the doctor. 'Once we have enough dogs here, we shall send them in to finish the job.'

It is while we are waiting for the dogs that the strangest event of this strange evening occurs.

I feel a tickle, a sort of tug in the brain.

No, it can't be. Not now.

I shake my head but the feeling grows stronger.

Without wanting to, I hear it in my head. A revelation.

—Save us.

The revelation is so loud within me that I glance at the doctor who is standing beside me, fearing he might have heard something too.

—Save us now.

It is Efren, reaching me from within the house.

As the men talk among themselves, I slip away and into the darkness.

The windows on the ground floor of the house have been nailed shut with boarding, but those on the first floor are covered only by shutters inside the house.

I look up, and know at that moment what I have to do.

There is a thick growth of ivy against the wall of the house. The night is now too dark to see if it is strong enough to take my weight, but I am a good climber.

It is time to take a chance.

Stealthily, I make my way upwards. One or two of the branches snap beneath my feet but the main stem of ivy holds. When I reach a window, I push against the shutters within. They are held tightly closed by a latch on the inside.

I reach into my back pocket for my knife. Silently, I slip the blade between the shutters and lift it. I lay a hand against the shutter and push.

The room is full of rats, each one looking up at me. I close my eyes and concentrate with all the brain strength I can manage.

—Escape, Efren— I manage to reveal —This way. Through the window.

There is a stirring in the darkness before me. I feel a tug within my brain but it is nothing I can understand.

A rat runs over my hand, then another, and another.

'That's it, beasts,' I whisper.

Soon the ivy around me is alive with rats making their escape to the ground.

It is time for me to move, too. As quickly as I dare, I climb down the foliage.

Even as my foot finds the safety of solid ground, I know that, if I return to the men, my deed will quickly be discovered.

I steal away into the darkness, looking back to the house only once. It is as if a living waterfall of rats is gushing down the ivy below the window.

Some hundred or so yards away, I remember, there is a ruined shed in which Bill and I have hunted for rats. There are no more than a couple of walls to it, but within those walls there are steps leading to what used to be a cellar.

I walk briskly towards it, until the sound of the men's voices is little more than a distant murmur.

I hear the barking of dogs. Some of the animals which were swept down the river are now returning to the hunt.

Through the darkness, there is a crack of breaking timber as the door of the house is kicked open. The dogs – it sounded like four or five of them – bark in excitement from within the building.

A pause. Then raised voices. Anger.

'They got away!'

'The window's open.'

The dogs pick up the scent of some of the escaping rats but there is confusion and defeat in their barking as their hunt leads them in different directions.

I wait in the gloom and damp.

A few of the hunters continue their work but most seem to have drifted back to the river, on to the road and away.

It is time for me to go home, too. I am about to move from my hiding place when I become aware that someone is walking across the waste-ground towards where I am.

I strain my eyes. Against the lights of the town, I see the outline of a man, hunched, trudging, something large dangling from his hand.

Even before I hear the voice mumbling to itself, I know it is Bill.

I give a low whistle. Almost as if he is expecting it, Bill turns towards my hiding place.

As he approaches, I scramble out of the cellar and stand before him. I see now that whatever he is carrying is alive. He holds it up.

'Rat king.' He smiles. 'I've not seen one of these for years.'

His big hand holds a ball of rats' tails which have grown into one another. There are twenty or so beasts hanging down. Their eyes are glassy with shock but they are still alive.

'Found it in the house.' He looks at the writhing creatures with something like affection. 'Under the stairs.'

'What will you do with it, Bill?'

He looks around, and notices the stone steps behind me.

'I'll leave them in the cellar there, I reckon,' he said. 'It's bad luck to harm a rat king.'

'So this could be your lucky day,' I say.

'It's certainly theirs.' He gives a little chuckle, then walks to the cellar, down the steps and into the darkness below.

When he comes back without the rat king, he does something unusual. He lays his big right hand on my shoulder.

'Someone opened a window,' he says.

'Did they? Fancy that.' I manage to laugh.

'Are you all right, boy?'

'I am, thanks, Bill.'

'Not much of a hunt, eh?'

I shake my head.

'I've said it before and I'll say it again.' He sniffs, like a man used to being proved right. 'You should never take liberties with a rat.'

'They got a bit of help down at the river. Are you in trouble?'

'They believed what you told them. They thought that was the kind of stupidity which Bill Grubstaff would do. Sometimes it's useful when folks think you're a fool.' He looks away, then adds quietly, 'It's you we should be worried about.'

'I'll be all right.'

'They know who opened the window. Someone saw you climbing down.'

I think for a moment. 'There'll be no more work from the doctor then.'

Bill frowns.

'It's not your job you should be worrying about,' he says. 'Turns out one of the setters knew where you live. They're on their way to the tip to find you. They're saying they're going to set light to it and burn you out.'

It takes a moment for the full horror of what Bill is saying to become clear to me.

'Lucky you're not there, eh, boy?'

'Caz.' I whisper the name.

'What's that, boy?'

I hear his words behind me.

I am already running.

107 When a dog loses heart, you can hear it...

... in the bark. It is no longer making noise to strike fear in the prey, to summon other dogs. It is merely telling its owner that it is doing its best.

When a rat hears that sorrowful note, it knows that today it will survive.

After the escape from the house, there were battles as citizens escaped in every direction. Now and then the unmistakeable sound of death could be heard in the darkness, causing those of us who had found hiding places to crouch down, motionless.

Soon, though, the dogs were making the sound of defeat. They were tired. Their owners were angry.

What would I have done without Floke? It was he who led the citizens in the house into battle after The Twyning had done its heroic work. In the moments after we left the house, I discovered that I was no warrior. Beside Floke, I was slow, weak. When he leapt over obstacles, I scrambled and fell, short of breath, as panicky as a ratling.

I may have been the leader of the kingdom but, when it came to facing the enemy, I was a taster, no more and no less. With a dog before me, I was as helpless as any citizen. I could reveal as loudly as I liked. I could be a hearer and hear great truths. These gifts counted for nothing when deadly white teeth were flashing, blood was flowing, and bones were being crushed in mighty jaws.

Floke knew that. His only revelation, repeated with every stride and gasp, was:

—Survive! Survive! Survive!

And I did. When the dogs were heading away from the river, we moved with speed ahead of them. Then, as others moved onwards, we doubled back and into a clod-cave which, through that strange instinct only warriors have, Floke knew would be there.

As still and silent as two stones, we heard the men and the dogs as they passed, their barking and their shouts fading.

We waited there, until the last sounds of battle had died away and the air no longer smelt of fear and rage and blood, but was simply night-time in the world above.

Floke climbed out of the hollow we had found.

—All is safe now, Efren. The battle is over.

I climbed out and looked around me. There were no lights, no human voices. The enemy had gone.

—Floke, I...

For once, I had difficulty revealing. My friend looked at me.

—You were a leader, Efren. You did what you had to do. You owe me nothing.

—I didn't really fight.

—In your way you did.

There was nothing more to be revealed. It was time to gather the kingdom, to start again.

There was a stump nearby. I climbed up on to it, composed myself, and prepared to reveal.

—Growan?

Silence.

—Growan, are you alive?

Nothing.

—Driva?

—I am here, Efren. Some of the does and ratlings died but many are with me.

—Stay where you are, Driva. Do not return to the world below until I give the order. Barcas?

—Here, Efren. On the far side of the river.

—Gvork?

There was no reply, and I felt a twitch of sadness. Gvork had been a brave historian.

One after the other, I called my leaders. Most, I discovered, had survived. The kingdom may have been scattered about the world above but it was still there.

—Victory.

The word was Floke's.

—There is no victory when citizens have died but, yes, there is still a kingdom.

Yet Floke seemed restless, and I knew why.

—Stay here, Efren. There is something I must do.

Before I could reveal, he was gone.

I waited, thinking of all that had happened on that terrible, glorious night. The flight of the warriors, the ambush from the trees, the mysterious rising of the river which had changed the course of the battle, The Twyning advancing towards the enemy, plaining as it went, the courage of citizens, led by Floke, within the house, the escape. The Court of Historians would have much to record.

It was growing cold by the time I heard from Floke again, and the safety of darkness was fading.

—Efren?

—Floke.

—I have found it. The Twyning lives.

108 The men are angry as they walk…

… through the town, silent, their lamps swinging beside them.

But when Bill and I catch up with them on the road which leads to the tip, they are on the narrow road leading to the lane. There is no easy way to overtake them without being noticed.

We follow them, unseen, a few paces behind.

When they reach the tip, I will find my way in to warn Caz. Nobody knows that rubbish tip better than I do.

As we grow closer, a sound beyond the fall of men's boots on the road reaches us. Voices – many voices. At first, I think some sort of revelry is taking place in one of the houses near the tip. But then there is no laughter, no music. This is no party.

Ahead of us, the men turn into the lane, and at that moment a terrible fear grips my heart.

'Wait,' Bill mutters beside me. 'Just wait, Dogboy.'

A crowd has gathered at the end of the lane – men, women, children, even babies in their mother's arms, their faces flickering in the pale light of the lanterns.

They are staring at the tip, as if waiting for a command of some kind.

At the back of the crowd I can see the doctor standing in silence. Beside him is the person I have not seen all night – Mr Valentine Petheridge MP.

The hunters we have been following push their way through the waiting throng. One of them, a powerfully built man with a dark beard and angry eyes, turns to face the crowd.

'Is he in there, the brat?' he asks loudly.

'Rat, more like,' a woman shouts.

A man near the front of the crowd. 'There's two of them in there,' he says. 'Someone's seen them – a boy and a girl. Living with the rats.'

'They are rats and all,' the bearded man says. 'And we've seen what the rats can do in this town. Once they used to eat our food. Now they're attacking us and eating us alive!'

'They drowned some of our dogs,' another hunter shouts. 'They're attacking from the trees, tearing people's throats out.'

A woman screams. A small child standing nearby starts to cry.

'It's them or us.' The bearded man clenches an angry fist as he speaks. 'Plain and simple – them or us. And, if someone helps them, they should be treated like rats, too.'

All the while, I am looking for a way to reach Caz. The crowd is so thick that it surrounds the tip on every side. It is impossible to see how I can get through.

'We had 'em tonight,' the hunter's leader is saying. 'Thanks to the skill of the doctor and the bravery of our dogs, we trapped them in a boarded-up house. You know what happened?'

There is silence around the tip.

'A nasty little tyke from the streets let them escape.'

'We saw him!' the other hunter calls out.

'Mark this, my friends. If any of our children die, it will be those little devils in there' – he points to the tip – 'who's to blame.'

The crowd are shouting now. They are like dogs, baying for their prey.

I shout as loud as I can.

'It was me! It was me!'

No one so much as looks at me. My voice is lost in the uproar.

A chant starts up – 'Rats! Rats! Rats! Rats!' – as the hunters move around the tip. One of them lights a flare.

I scream, but Bill holds me fast.

'Wait,' he said. 'I'll go. Where's the entrance?'

But now flames are licking upwards on the far side of the tip. Fanned by a gentle wind, the fire crackles into life. The chant is deafening now.

'Rats! Rats! Rats! Rats! Rats!'

Bill squeezes my shoulder. 'Stay here, boy. I'll get her.'

He pushes through the crowd, barging men and women aside, but when he reaches the front, he stops.

Something is emerging from the tip. At first it seems like a whiff of smoke caused by the fire. Then in the lights, it changes.

A small figure crawls slowly on its hands and knees out of the tip. Once out, it slowly takes to its feet. Then stands motionless.

'Look!' someone shouts. 'It's a little girl.'

Caz stands there in her nightdress, looking around her in wonderment. The flames behind her are taking hold and must be hot on her back, but she ignores them.

She bends her right leg in the way I know so well, the toe barely touching the ground. She spreads her arms as if they are wings and she is about to take flight.

Then she begins to dance. She skips, turns, jumps, whirls in front of the blazing furnace, a restless shadow who seems as it moves to be part of the fire itself. The crowd is silent now but Caz is singing as she dances. Men, women, children watch in astonishment. The only sounds in the lane are the crackling of burning wood, the roar of the flames and, through it all, a small voice singing.

The fire makes quick work of our home but, for every moment that it burns, Caz dances and dances and dances.

Slowly, she moves towards us.

The fire is so dazzling behind her that she is but a darting shape until she reaches the crowd. Then she half turns, and at last the face of my Caz, smeared with soot and dirt, her eyes wide and sparkling with tears, can be seen. Those at the front move back from her, as if she is some kind of spirit.

She is smiling, but with a peculiar kind of rage that I have never seen in her, or anyone else, before or since.

The crowd watch her, bewitched, as she dances, still singing a ghostly wordless melody all of her own.

Then, as if noticing the fire for the first time, she stops dancing and singing and gazes at the flames as they begin to die down.

She turns, stares at the crowd, a sort of madness in her eyes. Then she reaches into her nightdress and takes something out.

She holds it close to her face for a moment. Then, in a sudden movement, she darts, arms outstretched, towards the crowd. There is a panicky retreat.

She offers what she is holding to the crowd.

There is a scream.

There, in Caz's small hand, looking around in fear, is Malaika.

'Yes.' Caz's voice, when at last she speaks, is surprisingly strong and confident. 'It's a rat, ladies and gentlemen.'

Staring at them, she laughs, and there is contempt in the sound. Out of the corner of my eye I notice Mr Petheridge lean towards the doctor and say something under his breath. When I look again, the two men have disappeared.

Caz shows Malaika to those on the front row. She lowers her hands so that a small boy could see what she is holding. He smiles, and then hides his face in his mother's skirt.

'Is this your enemy?' Caz asks, looking around her. 'What is it about this animal that is so bad and terrifying to you? She's clean, she's intelligent, she's gentle – she's never bitten anyone.'

'That's 'cos she's a pet rat,' shouts a voice from within the crowd.

'Yeah, you wouldn't be holding a wild beast in your hand,' says the mother of the little boy.

Caz smiles as if someone has told her a familiar joke. She looks over her shoulder to the smouldering remains of the fire.

'That was my home,' she says.

'Poor little thing,' someone mutters.

'I didn't mind. I was happy there. Every night we were kept

375

company by rats. They never harmed us. We left them alone, and they left us alone. They helped us in ways you will never understand.'

She narrows her eyes, and I can see the sight of the tip, our home, reduced to a few burning pieces of wood has truly angered her.

'You know the truth? The only time a rat will attack is when it's afraid, when it's defending itself. You've all been fooled. Rats don't want anything from us. They're not the enemy. They're just…' She shrugs and smiles. 'They're just animals who want to survive in peace.'

'Where's the boy?' The bearded hunter speaks up. 'You said "we". Where's the other kid?'

I wriggle free of Bill's grasp and push my way through the crowd until I stand beside Caz.

'I'm here,' I say.

I tense myself for strong hands to grab me but at that moment something strange happens. The people around me seem to lose interest. As I look into their faces, I sense a sort of embarrassment about them. It is almost as if they suddenly feel ashamed by what they have been shouting and saying.

There is a disturbance at the back of the crowd.

'Out of the way!'

It is a woman's voice, and one that I recognise.

'Make way for Molly,' someone says.

She reaches us, short of breath, red-faced and very angry.

Molly Wall.

She stands beside me and places a heavy arm around my shoulders.

'What are you all doing?' she asks the crowd. 'When my husband told me they were looking for a kid because he had done something in the war on rats, I thought the world had gone mad. Now I see it with my own eyes, I still can't believe it. I know some of you. What are you doing?'

There is silence for a moment. Then a man near the front mutters. 'It's them or us, Molly. Them rats are taking over.'

'You *what*?'

It is a screech from Molly, and it makes some of the people laugh. It is as if, in that moment, the full craziness of the doctor's campaign, the great rat terror, has become clear.

'It's stupid,' says Molly. 'And you should be ashamed of frightening children who've got nothing in the world. What's happened to them isn't any fault of theirs, is it? Would you like your kids to be living in a rubbish tip?'

Heads turn towards the burning embers of what was once where we lived. One or two people at the back of the crowd are drifting off into the night.

'What's going to become of them now?' asks a woman standing near us. 'They've got no home.'

Molly looks at us both.

'Yes, they have. We've got loads of rooms at the tavern.'

There is a murmur of relief from what is left of the crowd.

I whisper something to Molly. She looks into the crowd.

'Bill? Are you there? Sounds like you've earned yourself a pint, too.'

Without waiting for a reply, she puts her arms around each of us and walks determinedly towards the lane. The crowd parts before us. As we walk to the town, I look over my shoulder.

Bill, smiling, is just behind us.

109 It was Floke who descended to the world below...

... as light faded the next day.

Scattered after the battle, citizens had been preparing for our return, gathering, making contact with one another.

The leaders who had survived were ordering their courts, helping ratlings who had lost their mothers, finding safe shelter in the bright and dangerous world above.

Where a court had no leader, I sent another citizen to take charge. There were complaints, mutterings, but I had no time to consider them.

—Do it.

My orders were sharp, impatient. Now was no time for discussion. I was becoming so used to giving commands that I might almost have been a warrior.

Where did I get my strength? It was not entirely from victory. I was strong because at every moment Floke was beside me. When I was uncertain over a decision, it was Floke who revealed the obvious, simple answer. It was not that he thought more than me, but the very opposite.

He was a warrior. He did things. Action explained itself.

Battle had changed Floke. He had fought, and led, and the kingdom had survived. His revelation was stronger than it had been, his eye harder. One of his ears had been badly torn, giving him the scarred look of a great warrior.

—I shall go before you to the world below, Efren.

There was no doubt, no question in his revelation that afternoon as darkness began to descend.

I hesitated. A true leader would show citizens the way back to the kingdom. Sensing my uncertainty, he added.

—You must remain safe. You have decisions to make. Stay.

And he was gone, into the dark passage which led downwards to the Great Hollow.

I looked around me to the battleground of yesterday. Stay. Floke's revelation had sounded like an order, even though I was the leader of the kingdom and Floke my deputy.

The truth is, I didn't care. My thoughts were not in the world below at all.

At some moment after the battle, while I was reaching out to citizens and revealing as a good leader should, I heard deep within me a cry for help.

I told myself it was another citizen, perhaps trapped by the enemy or lost in the world above, having made an escape, but later, with daylight, I knew the truth.

I had been hearing. The message was not a revelation from a citizen but a voice reaching to me from across the town.

Malaika. She was in trouble.

For the rest of the day, the cry was within me. She had called me, the only rat I had loved, and I was too busy with the kingdom to go to her.

Even when Floke returned, the faintest smell of poison on his fur, my thoughts were still of Malaika.

Could Floke sense my doubt? Almost certainly not. He was brave and decisive, but part of his strength came from not concerning himself too much with what other citizens were feeling.

—All is safe.

Floke stood before me. Beside us, the river, now back to its normal flow, rolled quietly. He continued:

—There is still a smell of danger, but it is not harmful. Citizens will be safer in the world below than up here. Dogs may return at any time.

I walked to the stump and revealed to the kingdom.

—It is time to return to the world below, citizens. We shall meet in the Great Hollow.

Then, walking behind Floke, I entered the ground. Together, we followed the familiar touch-path, past the hollow where once I had lived with the Court of Tasters, down the long dark passages, until it opened out.

Slowly, feeling more weary than triumphant, I climbed the Rock of State.

And soon, as Floke and I waited upon the rock, the kingdom came to life. Rats appeared from every entrance. There were noisy reunions, gatherings of the courts. The air was heavy with a scent of relief and sadness for those who were lost in battle.

A moment of acclamation greeted the arrival in the Great Hollow of a group of young warriors, moving slowly and carefully. On their backs, its many faces looking about in wonder, was The Twyning.

On the rock, those from the Court of Governance who had survived the battle. No Growan, no Gvork or Swylar, but Driva was there and Barcas, and the new captains of the courts.

Some humbled briefly when they saw me.

I moved to the front of the rock, with Floke, as usual, at my shoulder. Citizens were moving towards us, standing on the far side of the river. Floke revealed with quiet pride.

—We won, Efren.

I turned to him and, in that moment as we faced each other, nose to nose, I knew what I would do.

So did he.

The citizens were growing silent. It seemed to me, as I looked down at them, that their eyes were not on me but were to my right where Floke stood.

At great occasions like this, the leader of the kingdom is announced by a senior courtier but, as Floke moved forward, I turned and nipped him lightly.

He tensed and, for the briefest moment, became a warrior facing a foe. Then, understanding, he moved back.

It started at that moment. First, the sound of The Twyning, chattering first, then singing, then plaining. Soon citizens, one after another, joined in the acclamation. The mighty noise of victory rose until it became a great single cry of triumph.

I raised my head, and slowly silence descended upon the Great Hollow.

I waited. The kingdom was expecting a great speech from its leader. The battle. The lessons we have learned. The brave dead. The future.

The smell of hope, shared by all citizens, was in the air.

I continued to wait. There was the beginning of restlessness in the Great Hollow.

—Every rat is a king.

Citizens chattered their teeth politely. I looked down to the many wise, innocent eyes of The Twyning, staring up at me.

—Every rat is a king.

Again, they acclaimed, but some of them sensed that something unusual was happening.

My revelation was quieter than it once was. I was no longer revealing like a leader, or even a member of the Court of Governance.

I was beginning to sound like each of them, like a mere rat.

—Every rat is a king.

Beside me, Floke moved closer, a friend to the last.

I revealed as strongly as I could.

—But this rat is now your king, to take you all forward, every court and every citizen, to a new age of power and peace.

I turned to my friend. He moved forward as with all my strength I pronounced his name.

—Floke! King Floke!

The kingdom can always sense where its safety lies. The acclamation for Floke was as loud as any I have ever heard. The air filled with love and loyalty.

Floke began to reveal. A new Court of Governance was needed. Plans should be made for the future, a meeting of the Courts of Strategy and Spies.

All eyes, all thoughts were on Floke, the new king. I backed towards the shadows to the side of the Rock of State, then slipped downwards.

The river was cold when I entered it and, it seemed to me, that the acclamation of the kingdom was growing louder.

I swam slowly downstream, as King Tzuriel once had, already smelling the world above which awaited me.

110 There is a rumble beneath my feet, and the smell of smoke...

... rises through the floorboards. It is evening time at the Cock Inn, and the customers are gathering in the bar downstairs. In my room, it is sometimes too noisy to sleep, and the stale tobacco smell is on the sheets and curtains, but those things only make it feel more like home.

Room. Sheets. Curtains. Home.

Yes, I can say those words today and not feel a state of longing within me. Sometimes, alone in my little room at the Cock Inn, I touch the walls just to remind myself that I am no longer on the streets.

Sometimes I help Molly in the bar.

She shouts up the stairs, 'Peter, can you give me a hand?'

I am Peter again. It was Molly who refused to call me Dogboy. Even when I told her that I quite liked my name, that I was proud of being good with dogs, she held firm. She was not having anyone called Dogboy sitting at her kitchen table, serving her customers beer in the bar.

So I took the name I had once left with my past.

Peter Simeon is back.

Now and then, when we're away from the adults and talking about the past, Caz will call me Dogboy and somehow, the way she says the word, it causes a little leap of happiness within my heart, a reminder, just between us two, of the past we share.

It's our name now. I am Caz's secret Dogboy.

I never returned to the doctor. One of the setters who comes to the tavern has told me that the town's rat men asked him if there would be another hunt. He had shrugged as if, in his mind, rats were no different from any other pest.

There is a rumour that fleas are his new area of research.

The politician has taken fright. That's what they say in the bar. The blaze at the tip, Caz's fire dance, set stories going around that the war on rats was more about winning votes than saving lives. The council lost interest. Mr Petheridge found other campaigns to support.

Sometimes grown-ups prefer to behave as if unpleasant things never really happened.

It can be a good thing. Caz and I have learned that when we are with Molly and Jack in our new home, the past is not mentioned. For them, we have become the children they never had.

They feed us. They talk to us. They take us to school. When a stranger talks to Molly of 'your son' or 'your little girl', she no longer corrects them.

Even when Bill Grubstaff sits in the bar, there is no talk of the strange events which brought us all together, although now and then, when no one's looking, Bill will wink at me and say, 'All right there, Dogboy?'

That night changed his life, too. He says he is too old to be out hunting for rats that can be sold for sport. Places like this very tavern have given up the sport of setting dogs on rats, in a pit. He has taken to breeding pet rats for sale to the gentry. No one mentions the moment that he opened the lock and caused the river to flood, although I notice one or two of the setters move away when Bill takes his stool by the bar.

The suspicion that, for his own strange reasons, Bill actually helped the rats that night will always hang in the air when setters and hunters meet at the Cock Inn.

Not long after Caz and I settle into our new home, her pet rat Malaika begins to act strangely one evening.

We are in Caz's room, talking after supper, when the rat begins to tremble. After a few moments, she slips off Caz's bed where she has been, and scurries across the floor. She looks up at the small window which leads to a flat roof over the kitchen.

'He's here,' Caz whispers.

I look around the room, bewildered.

'Efren,' she says. 'I can hear him.'

She walks to the window and opens it. The night is crisp and clear but, despite the cold, Malaika is scuttling backwards and forwards, her eyes on the open window.

Caz leans out.

—Efren? Is it you?

She smiles then, and reaches down to pick up Malaika and sets her down on the window ledge. Without hesitating, the rat disappears into the darkness.

Caz turns to me, her eyes sparkling. She holds up a finger in anticipation.

From outside there come the unmistakeable squeals of rats meeting joyfully.

Caz laughs. She's different now we live at the tavern – more open and at ease. She is still shy, and rarely goes in the bar, but she no longer has the pale sleepwalker look which I remember from those last days when we lived in the tip.

Because Molly and Jack prefer not to talk of the past, and I know that the memories are too hurtful to Caz, I never mention her stay with Champagne Charlie to anyone.

Stories, though, need to be told.

The day after Efren's first visit, Caz asks Jack if she can have one of the notebooks where he keeps a record of what has been bought from the market for the tavern.

That night, she sits at the table in her room. She opens the book, looks at me and, almost like a teacher, says, 'Let us start at the beginning.'

According to Caz, what has happened to us is too important to drift away into forgetfulness. So every night, before we sleep, I

385

tell her more of my story. Together we travel back to the past and into the war on rats.

As we work, Malaika will go on to the roof to see Efren.

Then one night, something changes. Caz moves her table to the window. She opens it and stares into the darkness for a while.

'What are you doing, Caz?' I ask.

'I think we need to tell the whole story,' she says. 'Your story and Efren's.'

I am about to speak again, when she holds a finger to her lips. She is listening.

Perhaps you might think we are a strange little group of breathing creatures here at the Cock Inn, if you were to see us tonight. Downstairs there is Molly and Jack and the drinkers in the bar. Bill will be there for sure at his usual table, watching Molly as she works.

Upstairs, I am with Caz beside an open window. On the ledge, Malaika waits, already growing larger with the sons and daughters of Efren which she is now carrying.

We are all listening for sounds from the chilly outside world where we used to live.

There is a rustle of leaves, a brief chattering of teeth, and Malaika has gone. Frowning with concentration, Caz picks up her pencil and opens her notebook to a new page. She waits for the revelations of Efren, then begins to write.

There was a smell of hope in the Great Hollow that night...

It is time for the story to be told.

Glossary of terms used in the kingdom

Acclamation, an
A loud noise made by a great gathering of rats. It is a combination of keening with a chattering of teeth.

Carry, to
Also known as **fathering**, carrying refers to the act of mating. For rats, sex is an everyday necessity, a basic duty conducted by all citizens except **hearers** or members of **The Twyning**. A male rat can carry with up to twenty does in a period of six hours. A doe becomes fertile again soon after giving birth and can produce twelve litters of twenty rats in a year. As Dr Ross-Gibbon says, a single pair of rats have the potential to produce fifteen thousand descendants in twelve months.

Clod-cave, a
A small hole in the ground, made by rats to be a hiding place in times of danger. See also **gouge** and **rest.**

Corrector, a
A member of the Court of Correction, trained in torture and death.

Express, to
When expressing contempt for another citizen, a rat will express – that is, defecate – in front of it.

Father, to
See **Carry, to**

387

Flyte, to
It has been noted by those who observe rats that, when cornered or pursued, they have a startling ability to jump so high that it seems as if they have almost taken wing. In the kingdom, this is known as flyting, and is practised in its most impressive form by members of the Court of Warriors. The gift of flyting is partly physical, a combination of muscular strength and loose skin, but is also mental. A skilled warrior will be able think himself into an extraordinary ability to flyte from danger.

Fragile, a
A rat which has been bred and domesticated by humans, normally with white, brown and grey markings, and which has returned to the kingdom.

Gouge, a
A resting place below the ground which has been hollowed out and is used by rats as a home. See also **rest, a**.

Glow, a
Before there is any great movement of the earth – a volcano, earthquake or tsunami – certain animals are sensitive to what rats call 'the glow'. Changes in the earth's crust release certain scents in the air, water and in the taste of plants which alert some creatures that a cataclysm is on its way. The glow usually takes place two or three days in advance of the event itself. In 2011, scientists discovered that toads show this awareness. It is less well known that rats can also feel the glow.

Hearer, a
A few rats are born, like Efren, with the ability to hear what is happening in other places, in other times and even in other minds. They have no control over what they hear and, once adult, will lose the gift of hearing if they **carry** like other rats.

Humble, to
A rat which is humbling is adopting a low crouch of submission. In the kingdom, it is a basic form of politeness and is not regarded as shameful. See also **Offer, to.**

Length, a
The rat's measure of distance, a length is simply the length of a large adult rat, for example a warrior, from head to toe – that is around twenty centimetres.

Offer, to
Offering is a more extreme form of **humbling** and involves a rat rolling on its back, often with its eyes closed, in an act of total submission. Fights which do not end in death will invariably be brought to a close by one of the rats offering to the other.

Plaining, a
A chorus set up by a twyning at times of importance for the kingdom. It is a single note, but sustained by the many voices of the rats who are part of The Twyning. Plaining only occurs at moments of great solemnity in the kingdom.

Pulse, the
Unlike almost any other animals, rats are unselfish. Scientists have proved that their most powerful instinct, even when offered a reward, is to help another rat in trouble. This sense of comradeship is known in the kingdom as the pulse. Rats who need help are described as pulsing.

Rest, a
A small hollow, slightly larger than a **clod-cave** but smaller than a **gouge**, in which rats can shelter and hide.

Reveal, to
Rats communicate through thought. The stronger a citizen's talent for revealing, as it is known, the greater his or her power.

The revelations of members of the Court of Governance will be able to reach all members of the kingdom when gathered in one place.

Shape-reading
Rats know where they are by shape-reading. Any difference in the skyline, or a **touch-path** is sensed.

Still, to
At times of danger, a rat will become stone-like. Even its whiskers are immobile. Scent is reduced to a minimum. Stilling is an art learned by rats in infancy.

Tell, to
Male rats have the ability to leave a thin trail of urine in their path, a practice known as telling. Most often, a tell is left when rats wish to show other citizens the way through danger, particularly when they are outside a **touch-path**, but it is also used to show rats from other kingdoms that they have strayed into another territory. Warrior rats most often tell. Members of the Court of Spies are trained not to tell from an early age.

Touch-path, a
All animals prefer to follow paths for reason of safety, but rats are more sophisticated. They can sense the trails that have been established by the touch of their whiskers and the hair of their fur. Not depending on sight allows citizens to use touch-paths as escape routes quickly and instinctively in moments of danger.

Trem, a
A sound felt through the ground when something is approaching. Obviously, the trem of a mouse, stoat or another rat can be felt from a distance of around ten **lengths**. A human's trem will reach a rat from up to fifty lengths.

Twyning, a
Known by human scientists as a 'rat king', a twyning is a group of as many as twenty or thirty rats whose tails have become entwined in the nest and who have grown together. The Twyning has profound religious significance in the kingdom.

Whiffle, to
Rats are able to sense the mood of other citizens – aggressive, wary, affectionate – by the smell of their breath. This action is known as whiffling.

Woodnote, a
Rats are alerted to danger by the sound of all other animals, except humans, the alarm calls of birds being particularly important. In the kingdom, these warnings go under the general name of woodnotes.

Acknowledgements

Several books were particularly helpful when I was researching this book: Hans Zinsser's *Rats, Lice and History* (1935), Robert Hendrickson's *More Cunning Than Man* (1983), Charles Golding's *Rats: The New Plague* (1990), S. Anthony Barnett's *The Story of Rats* (2001), Robert Sullivan's *Rats* (2004), Stephen Smith's *Underground London* (2004) and Liza Pickard's *Victorian London* (2005).

Phil Drabble's chapter 'Stafford and baiting sports' in *The Book of the Dog* (1948), edited by Brian Vesey-Fitzgerald, was useful for the sections in the Cock Inn.

From the days when it was but a ratling of an idea to its publication, this book has been lucky to have had great and encouraging champions. I am profoundly grateful to Caroline Sheldon, Xan Blacker, Georgina Capel, Anthony Cheetham and my first and bravest reader, Angela Sykes.

Being part of the launch of a great new publishing house, Head of Zeus, has been a genuinely exciting experience. I would like to thank the entire Head of Zeus team, and the line editor who worked on the manuscript, Helen Gray. Above all, thanks are due to my brilliant, firm but fair editor, Mathilda Imlah.

Terence Blacker